EXPIRY DATE

ALEX WALTERS

ALSO BY ALEX WALTERS

DI Alec Mckay Series

Candle & Roses (Book 1)
Death Parts Us (Book 2)
Their Final Act – (Book 3)

Winterman

Print ISBN 978-1-912986-74-3

It was still only early afternoon, but the sun was already low in the sky, throwing unexpectedly long shadows from the ranks of gravestones.

Donaldson stopped and looked around him, rising to his feet, suddenly feeling self-conscious and slightly nervous. He was born and brought up here, but had never quite grown accustomed to these deep-midwinter days. It wasn't so much the shortness of the days themselves. It was more the way that, even on a bright, clear day like today, the sun barely scraped above the horizon, rising and setting in the southern sky. It was dark almost before you knew it.

It was cold, too. One of the coldest winters he'd experienced in recent years. He'd wrapped himself in layers of clothing, topped with a heavy waterproof jacket, in preparation for his visit. But he could still feel the chill, the icy wind coming off the firth.

He crouched down again, and continued arranging the flowers. He always felt uncomfortable with this task, aware of his own ineptitude. All fingers and thumbs. That was what she used to say, as she watched him carrying out some task requiring the delicacy she'd had in abundance. He could imagine how she'd have responded to this clumsy offering.

It was the best he could do. He moved the stems backwards and forwards in the jar, trying to capture the balance that would have come so naturally to her. Somehow it never looked quite right. Uneven, unkempt. Nothing quite where it should be. The story of his life after she went.

Eventually, he abandoned his attempts to improve the arrangement and rose stiffly to his feet, resisting the urge to seek support from the gravestone as he did so. That would have seemed just a little too symbolic.

The tribute was less elegant than he'd intended, but it would have to do. If he worked at it all afternoon, it would never match the display he'd envisaged. But that was always the way. He'd leave here, as he always did, feeling that somehow he'd failed her, that he hadn't lived up to her expectations. Even though he knew full well that, in most respects, her expectations of him had never been high.

It was one reason he didn't come here more often, though that made him feel guilty, too. At first, after it had happened, he'd visited frequently. Probably too frequently for his own sanity, he realised later. He hadn't come here with any real purpose, although he'd made a point of refreshing the flowers every week or so. It was as if he was simply seeking proximity to someone he knew was no longer there. He'd neglected everything else. Even his daughter. Especially his daughter. Not that he'd cared much about that.

Eventually, he'd had to force himself to stay away, trying to busy himself with other tasks, other interests. And then, of course, they'd caught up with him and he hadn't been able to come here at all. Years had passed. The sense of need had lessened. His daughter was no longer there as a reminder of what he'd lost. It wasn't exactly that he'd moved on. But he'd recognised that, whatever it was he needed, he wasn't going to find it here.

Now, he came over only a few times each year. Her birthday. Their anniversary. Usually at Christmas, though this year he'd been too tied up trying to sort out whatever the hell was happening with the business. It was more of a gesture now. Something he did because he felt it was the right thing to do, without knowing quite why it mattered.

The breeze was increasing from off the Cromarty Firth, and he found himself shivering slightly from the cold. Sunset was at least a couple of hours away, but already the shadows were thickening. He'd always enjoyed coming up here, and it had been a place they'd visited often in their early days. But at this time of year, it had an eerie, almost threatening air. He felt now as if someone might have been watching him as he'd worked, gazing at his hunched back crouched by the gravestone.

He looked around, peering into the shadows of the undergrowth, the dark recesses of the half-ruined Gaelic Chapel. There was nothing but the movement of the leaves and grasses in the rising wind. He rarely encountered anyone up here. In the height of summer, when there were likely to be more visitors, he tried to come later in the day. He didn't particularly mind if he did run into someone, but he preferred to have the place to himself.

Time to leave. He had a meeting to get to. He screwed up the paper wrapping from the flowers and stuffed it into his coat pocket. As he turned to leave, he took one final glance down at the gravestone.

He'd struggled for a long time with the wording. The stonemason had come up with the usual selection of anodyne suggestions, but he'd wanted something more personal. Something that captured the nature of their relationship.

He'd spent days searching through books of poetry, books of quotations, hoping that some author or poet had succeeded in expressing the feelings that he was striving to articulate. But he'd found nothing that felt quite right.

In the end, he'd settled for something much simpler and more straightforward. Other than her name and the dates of her birth and death, there was only a single word on the stone.

The mason had tried to talk him out of it, arguing that he should choose something more poetic, or perhaps simply something more conventional. But he'd stood his ground. It had been the only way he could think to describe her, to say quite what she'd meant to him. Just a single word etched in the very centre of the stone.

'Irreplaceable'.

'Oh, for Christ's sake,' McKay said. 'Look at the bloody numpties.'

Fiona glanced at him sharply, her expression suggesting disapproval. Chrissie had already warned him to moderate his language in Fiona's presence, but he'd spoken without thinking. In fairness, his exclamation had been pretty mild by his usual standards.

By now, the others had followed his gaze and seen what had prompted his outburst. 'Ah,' Chrissie said. 'I see what you mean. Goodness.' McKay sometimes wished he shared her talent for understatement.

At first, he'd assumed they were kids. Youngsters buggering about on the fort ramparts. Now, looking more closely, he realised they were older than that. In their late teens or twenties, as far as he could judge at this distance. A young man and woman.

When he'd first glanced in their direction, they'd just been messing around on the top of the ramparts. Stupid enough, in McKay's opinion, but it wasn't the first time he'd seen someone up there. Then they'd gone further and ventured out onto the grassed slope below the ramparts. The slope, which had presumably been part of the original defensive design, was relatively steep and ended in a sheer drop to the moated area below. There was no fencing.

'If they slip...' Fiona said. There was no need for her to complete the sentence. It was obvious to all of them what would happen if either lost their footing.

'Don't you think you should do something, Alec?'

'Me being a police officer and all? What should I do? Arrest them for being empty-headed bampots?'

'I don't know, but–'

She was interrupted by an irate bellow from behind them. 'Oi, you two! Get down! You'll fall to your bloody deaths!'

McKay turned to see that the speaker was the man from the ticket office by the entrance. Presumably part of his duties included ensuring that, if at all possible, visitors managed not to kill themselves while on site. Whether yelling at them unexpectedly was the soundest way of achieving that goal, McKay wasn't sure.

In fact, the shouting had the desired effect. The two looked down, apparently surprised at the intervention, then made their way back up the slope to the ramparts, jumping down into the interior of the fort.

'Bloody idiots,' the man said to no one in particular. 'Wouldn't be sorry to see one of them actually fall.'

'Aye,' McKay said. 'But think of the paperwork.'

The man nodded, as if McKay had made a serious contribution to the discussion. 'Anyway, enjoy your visit, folks. Just don't let me catch you doing anything like that.'

'You'd be waiting a long time.' McKay turned back to the rest of the group. 'We'd best get inside. We don't have all that long.'

He wasn't even quite sure why they'd come here. Historic buildings weren't really McKay's thing. Fiona's lugubrious husband, Kevin, had suggested it, and Chrissie and Fiona had

seconded the idea with apparent enthusiasm. Kevin was supposedly keen on history, though McKay couldn't recall the man
showing much interest in anything during his infrequent visits
up here. Certainly, his expression at the moment wasn't that of a
man filled with excited anticipation.

At least they had decent weather for it. It was cold enough,
colder even than usual for early January. But it was a bright, clear
day, the low sun hanging in a largely cloudless sky. The only
other time McKay had visited this place, it had been pouring with
rain, and they'd spent their time scurrying from one exhibit to
another.

He followed the others across the footbridge into the fort
itself. Chrissie and Fiona were chatting animatedly. Kevin hung
behind them, seemingly lost in his own thoughts. McKay
supposed he ought to initiate some conversation, but the
prospect seemed too daunting. He'd long ago learnt that he and
Kevin had virtually nothing in common. He wished now they'd
accepted the offer of the commentary headphones available in
the ticket office. That would at least have given him an excuse to
match Kevin's silence.

Once they'd passed through the main gateway, the full interior of the fort was visible. It was impressive enough, McKay
acknowledged. He knew little of the history, except that it had
been built after Culloden with the aim of keeping the rebellious
Scots firmly under control. Remarkably, although now open to
visitors, for the present it still operated as a working garrison.
Probably just in case the Scots ever needed suppressing again.

McKay recalled from his previous visit that the visitor areas
were well laid out and informative. Despite the limits of his own
interest, he'd found himself engaged with the exhibitions, fascinated by the continuity of military life in this confined fortifica-
tion. Today, he was content to follow the others around the place,
enjoying a rare escape from the pressures of his working life.

They'd had a hectic few months, still dealing with the complicated fallout from their last major case up here. Trying to make sure, in particular, that the prosecution case was as watertight as possible. That was mostly behind them now, and they were as confident as they could be. But McKay had long ago learned not to take anything for granted, and his recent experiences had made him more wary than ever.

On top of that, they'd had the usual heavy caseload, especially in the period leading up to Christmas. Everything always seemed to get more insane in December, when every pisshead in the city tried to cause as much trouble as possible. Most of it was trivial stuff that came nowhere near McKay's desk. But there were always one or two more serious incidents. Domestics. Bar fights that went too far. Fatal road traffic collisions. More than enough to keep them occupied.

At least things were back on track with Chrissie. It wasn't exactly that they'd resolved all the issues they'd been wrestling with. But at least it didn't feel as if they were bottling them up anymore. McKay had been persuaded to have another shot at joint counselling, and this time they'd found someone who actually knew what he was doing. McKay had forced himself to relax into the process, and it finally felt as if they were making some progress.

So that was all good. But it had left him feeling exhausted and, at least at work, even more jaded than usual. Christmas had come and gone in a low-key way, as it always had in the McKay household except when Lizzie had been small. Hogmanay had been more lively. They'd had Chrissie's other sister, Ellie, round with her husband and a few other friends and neighbours, and everyone had drunk and eaten too much to the point where they all, even McKay, seemed more or less happy. But now they were into January, season of short days, long nights, bloody endless cold, and nothing much else to look forward to.

'Penny for them, Alec,' Fiona called back to him. 'You're looking very pensive.'

'Ach, my thoughts aren't even worth a penny. Just contemplating the futility of existence. You know how it is.'

'Alec always brings a ray of sunshine into our lives,' Chrissie observed. 'It's one of his few skills.'

Fiona laughed. 'Alongside being the great detective, I assume.'

'Aye, that too.' McKay had decided, after some initial hesitation, that he rather liked Fiona. She was Chrissie's elder sister but they saw little of her. She and Kevin had long ago moved, for reasons best known to themselves, to some godforsaken part of Southern England. They usually tried to visit over Christmas or New Year, but this year their arrival had been delayed by some work commitment of Kevin's. McKay wasn't even clear what sort of work Kevin was involved in, except that it was something incomprehensible in IT. He'd only once made the mistake of asking.

But Fiona was likeable enough. Like Chrissie, she was strongwilled and opinionated, and, with the obvious exception of Kevin, not one to suffer fools gladly. All qualities that McKay admired, and one of the reasons why he'd been attracted to Chrissie in the first place. So he was quite happy to have them up here for a few days. It seemed to cheer Chrissie up too, which was never a bad thing.

'So what's worth looking at here?' Fiona had stopped and was gazing around the clusters of stone buildings inside the fort.

'It's years since we've been here,' McKay said. 'There's the Highlanders' Museum. Highland regimental stuff, if that's your thing. But the whole place is worth a look. Recreating post-Culloden military life. Makes you grateful you didn't have to be part of it. Oh, and there's a café.'

They made their way slowly around the perimeter of the fort, occasionally pausing to enter one of the exhibition rooms. Kevin, predictably enough, made a point of stopping to read each display, apparently several times, while the others waited patiently by the door. Initially, McKay had expected that Kevin might offer some opinion or insight at the end of this extended perusal, but instead he remained his usual taciturn self, providing them with little more than a grunt, apparently indicating satisfaction.

This was fine by McKay. He had no great desire to make conversation and, as they strolled in the winter sunshine, he found himself relaxing for what felt like the first time in weeks. That was surprising in itself, he thought. Not that he was relaxing, but that he felt the need to. He'd always thought of himself as someone who thrived on the job – the intensity, the adrenaline. Maybe it was just because he'd been through so much over the last couple of years, domestically and personally. Or maybe, as Chrissie kept half-jokingly telling him, he was finally showing his age.

They stopped briefly for a cup of tea in the small café, and then continued their walk up onto the battlements at the far end of the fort. As they made their way up the sloped pathway to the upper level, it occurred to McKay that, although they'd seen a few other visitors in the course of the afternoon, they hadn't run into the couple who'd been messing about on the parapets earlier.

This side of the fort overlooked the Moray Firth, the pale blue water sparkling below them. Over the other side, McKay could see the villages of Fortrose and Rosemarkie, the curved spit of Chanonry Point stretching out between them. It was still an hour or so from sunset, but the sun was already low over the Black Isle, throwing the far side of the firth into a mauve shadow. The wind from the sea was bitterly cold.

'Brass monkey weather,' Kevin offered.

McKay had almost forgotten that Kevin was standing beside him. It was the first time he'd uttered anything approaching a coherent sentence since their arrival here. 'Too right. I'm going to head down in a sec.' He saw that Chrissie and Fiona had already had the same idea and were making their way towards the path to the lower level.

Kevin had already wandered across to the edge of the battlements and was peering out. 'I might stay here for a bit. It's a nice view. I'll catch you up.'

Twenty or more years of policing had taught McKay not to be surprised by people, but he'd never envisaged Kevin as a devotee of landscapes. Perhaps he just wanted time to himself, even though he'd never seemed a man troubled by the niceties of social interaction. 'Aye,' McKay said. 'We'll go and have a look at the chapel and then the old barracks. Give one of us a ring if you have any trouble finding us.'

He left Kevin staring out over the waters, and hurried after Chrissie and Fiona. Fiona turned as he caught up with them. 'Where's Kev?'

'Fancied a few minutes enjoying the view. Said he'll catch us up.'

'Is he okay?'

'Seemed to be. Why?'

'Not sure. He's been a bit quiet for the last few days, that's all. Since we got up here.'

McKay couldn't say that he'd noticed any major differences in Kevin's demeanour from his usual self. 'You want me to stay with him?'

'Don't be daft. No, I just wonder if he's worrying about something.'

They continued their exploration of the fort, paying a brief visit to the chapel before proceeding to the old barracks. On their previous visit, that rainy weekend, McKay had found the barracks both fascinating and oddly disturbing. They had been set up to recreate the lifestyles of the fort's original inhabitants, with the aim of giving a sense of what that past military life must have been like.

'Grim' had been McKay's one-word summary of the living conditions. Dozens living side by side with only the most basic of facilities. Freezing in winter and probably stifling in summer.

And always subject to the most rigorous, not to say brutal, military discipline.

On that previous rain-soaked afternoon, his primary sense had been one of misery. Today, the place struck him differently. The sun had already disappeared behind the walls of the fort, and the gloom was thickening. The barracks felt eerie, the sense of history almost palpable in the stones. As they made their way down the corridor in the barrack building, he heard a sudden gasp and stifled expletive from Fiona at the front of the group.

He'd have warned her if he'd remembered. He recalled now his own momentary shock at peering into that room and seeing a figure, dressed in military garb, crouched at the table. It had taken him only a second to realise the figure was nothing but a mannequin, positioned as part of the recreation of the original layout. But the initial surprise had been real enough, and Fiona had clearly had the same experience.

Fiona was already laughing at her own foolishness. 'I can't believe I fell for that. It's obviously a model.'

'You just don't expect it,' Chrissie said. 'We did the same when we first looked in here. Like a ghost.'

Like a ghost. That's it, McKay thought. The whole place felt teeming with ghosts, so it didn't seem surprising that one might have been made manifest. You expected to find the dead in here.

'It's well done, though,' Fiona conceded. 'The whole set-up, I mean. Gives you a real feel for it.'

McKay moved to stand behind the two women, peering past them into the room. 'Bit too much of a feel, if you ask me. Place gives me the creeps.'

'Developing an imagination in your old age, Alec?' Chrissie asked. 'First time for everything.'

'Aye, well. This reminds me why I never wanted to develop one in the first place. In my job, reality's more than enough.' The narrow corridor, with its close whitewashed walls, suddenly felt oppressive. He turned and took a couple of steps towards the entrance, wanting to get back into the open air. Then he heard another stifled cry from behind him.

He looked back, a half-formed quip dying on his lips as he saw the expression on Chrissie's face. 'What is it?'

Chrissie's mouth opened and closed, as if she couldn't work out what words to articulate. Finally, she said, 'I think you'd better come and look at this, Alec.'

Fiona was immediately behind her, her face equally ashen. They were both outside the door of another of the rooms, which McKay recalled was set up as a recreation of a barrack room, complete with the original metal bedframes.

As he approached, they moved aside to allow him to look. It was as he remembered. A closely-packed line of narrow beds, each topped with a thin, rough-textured blanket. The most basic of sleeping facilities, crammed side-by-side into a space smaller than their living room at home.

On one of the nearer beds, there was a figure wrapped loosely in one of the blankets.

'I thought it was another model,' Chrissie said from behind him. 'But it looked wrong somehow. Out of place.'

He could see what she meant. The mannequin in the adjacent room had been positioned as part of the exhibition. A figure seated at a desk, dressed in uniform. This just seemed random.

Visitors weren't supposed to enter the rooms, but it took McKay only a moment to unclip the barrier and step inside. His professional instincts were already coming into play and he approached the bed cautiously, taking care not to disturb anything more than necessary. He reached out and, taking hold of the top end of the blanket, pulled it back.

He'd known already, he supposed. The sixth sense that comes from years of experience. Spotting the signs without even knowing what you were seeing. He looked back at the two women, still clustered in the doorway. 'You'd better get outside. Don't touch anything. And stop anyone else coming in here.'

3

Once the two women had left, McKay turned his attention back to the figure on the bed, carefully dislodging the tangled blanket so he could see more clearly what lay underneath. The pale white face of a young male. Probably early twenties, he guessed. He pressed his fingers to the man's neck, searching for a pulse. He already had little doubt that this was a corpse. It hadn't been here very long and there was still some warmth to the body. But McKay was as sure as he could be that life had departed.

His first priority was to call it in and get a team out here to protect the scene. Given that this was a military location, there were probably protocols about potential army involvement, but McKay had never been one to allow such niceties to distract him.

It took him a few minutes to explain the situation and his own involvement to the call-handlers, but he finally got the promise of an ambulance and a response team. How long it would take them to get here was another question. This should be high on their priority list on a quiet Sunday afternoon in January, but he knew it didn't always work out that way.

Any unexplained death was treated as suspicious until the

circumstances became clear. Even so, this was more suspicious than most. An odd place for a body to turn up in broad daylight. Maybe some junkie who'd finally had one hit too many, but from his superficial examination it hadn't felt like that to McKay.

He found Chrissie and Fiona waiting outside in the twilight. 'Don't tell me,' Chrissie said. 'I can't take you anywhere.'

McKay shrugged. 'What can I say? It's a gift. Trouble wherever I go.'

'So what now?'

'I have to wait. You two can get off if you want to. I can always sweet-talk one of the uniforms into giving me a lift home.' He looked around them. 'No sign of Kevin yet?'

Fiona shook her head. 'I was beginning to get concerned, to be honest.'

'If he went into the chapel we might not see him for days,' McKay said. 'No shortage of stuff to read in there.'

'Aye, you're right,' Fiona said. 'He does like the detail.'

'If you two are going to stay here to wait for him,' McKay said, 'I'll head out to the ticket office. I need to make sure chummy out there doesn't let anyone else in and warn him we've got police and ambulances coming. I'm hoping he'll know how to get in contact with whoever's in charge here. Probably quicker than trying to track down anyone myself.' They'd seen the occasional official-looking figure as they'd strolled round, but on a winter's Sunday afternoon even the military buildings seemed largely deserted.

The ticket-office man was standing by the entrance as McKay approached, seeing off the last of the visitors before locking up. He looked up quizzically at McKay's hurried arrival. 'Something wrong?' It was clear that, seeing McKay, his mind had gone back to the earlier incident on the battlements.

'Aye, you might say that.' McKay brandished his warrant card. 'Bit of an issue inside. I've had to call out an ambulance and a response team.'

'What, an accident?'

'Not for me to speculate, son. Let's just say we've found someone not in the best of health.' McKay knew better than to give any member of the public too much information. On the other hand, he wanted to inspire the man with some sense of urgency.

'Anything I can do?' The question was asked in a manner that unquestionably sought a negative response.

'You got a contact for whoever's in charge in there?' McKay said. 'Commanding officer or whatever. I need to make them aware.'

The man looked flustered. 'I'm not sure. I've got some contact numbers...' He led McKay back into the ticket office and began searching behind the counter. Finally, he pulled out a sheet of paper and slid it over the desk to McKay. 'This is what I've got.'

Most of the numbers on the sheet related to activities such as deliveries and catering but there were a couple for general enquiries. McKay dialled one at random and found himself connected to a switchboard operator who sounded as if she might be based at the other end of the country. He was eventually transferred to a Captain McGuire. McKay held his patience through several minutes of military-sounding hold music before finally a very English-sounding voice said, 'Angus McGuire. Can I help you?'

'Aye, son, I'm really hoping so. We have a bit of a problem. I assume the good lady I spoke to has explained?'

There was a moment's silence at the other end of the line. 'I understand you're a police officer?'

'DI Alec McKay. I understand you're in charge here?' McKay successfully managed to inject a note of scepticism into the question.

'I'm the senior officer currently on site, yes. Look, I'm sorry, but how do I know this isn't some kind of hoax?'

'You don't,' McKay acknowledged. 'At least not until we meet face-to-face. Do you get many hoaxes of this nature?'

'I–' McGuire had clearly run out of responses. 'Where are you?'

'I'm in the ticket office,' McKay said. 'But I'll head back in and meet you. The body's in the exhibition in the old barracks.'

'You're sure it's dead?' McGuire sounded as if he was looking for some kind of reassurance.

'I'm pretty sure he's gone to meet his maker, aye,' McKay said, placing a gentle emphasis on the personal pronouns. 'I'll see you over there.' He ended the call before McGuire could offer a response.

He turned to the ticket-office man. 'Military. Even worse than the fucking police. Thanks, son. You did good. Now just make sure no other visitors come in. Oh, and leave me your contact details. We may need to be in touch depending on how this pans out. Then, if I were in your shoes, I'd very swiftly bugger off home.'

As he crossed the open ground towards the old barracks building, McKay saw a tall figure in military uniform already standing by Chrissie and Fiona, clearly awaiting McKay's arrival. McKay wondered whether McGuire had somehow managed to don the uniform in the few minutes since they'd spoken, or whether he spent his Sundays dressed like that. Either was impressive in its way, McKay supposed.

'Captain McGuire?' McKay was holding out his warrant card to pre-empt the next question.

McGuire gazed at the card for longer than McKay thought strictly necessary. 'Lucky you were the one to stumble across this, I suppose.' His tone made it sound as if McKay had somehow been responsible.

'Not very lucky for the poor bugger in there.'

'I suppose not. Look, McKay, I'm not even sure whether this falls within your jurisdiction.'

17

McKay wasn't entirely sure either, though he generally took the attitude that most things fell within his jurisdiction if he chose. Particularly when his authority was being questioned by someone who addressed him only by his surname. 'We can sort the niceties out later, son. For the moment, I think we're better concentrating on our dead body, don't you?'

'Of course. Can I see the body? Just in case I can identify him.'

McKay's preference would have been to leave the scene untouched, but he knew a positive ID at this stage might save them a lot of time. 'As long as you don't touch anything.'

'I'll be careful.'

McKay glanced over at Chrissie and Fiona. Fiona was listening to her mobile, a mildly anxious expression on her face. There was still no sign of Kevin. McKay raised a quizzical eyebrow to Chrissie, who gave an almost imperceptible shrug in return. The sun had long disappeared behind the fortified walls, and it was beginning to grow dark.

McGuire stepped back to allow McKay to lead them back into the building. McKay had never thought of himself as imaginative, but he felt now as if he could almost taste the history in here. He shivered slightly and not, he thought, only from the cold. 'In here.'

McGuire peered past him. 'Dear God. As you say, poor bugger.'

'The face is uncovered,' McKay said, 'so you won't need to disturb anything.'

McGuire took a couple of steps into the room and peered more closely. 'The dead look different somehow, don't they?'

McKay wondered how many dead bodies McGuire had seen. Possibly not a question to ask a serving soldier. 'Aye. Somehow.'

'I'm pretty sure he's not one of ours. Not a soldier, anyway. I know most of them by sight at least, and his face doesn't ring any bells. He might be one of the civilian staff, I suppose. I don't see all of those.'

'Or he might be just a visitor.'

'You haven't checked if there's any ID?'

McKay shook his head. 'I've disturbed the scene more than enough already. Much as I enjoy pissing off the examining team, that's probably a step too far. We'll find out soon enough.'

Taking his cue, McGuire followed McKay out of the building. After the white-walled glare of the barrack rooms, the darkness outside seemed almost complete, although it was still only late afternoon. Chrissie was still waiting, but Fiona was no longer with her.

'I've let the chaps on the gate know to expect your people,' McGuire was saying. 'How long are they likely to be?'

'No way of telling. This will be a priority. But there are always a lot of priorities.' He glanced at Chrissie. 'Can you excuse me for a moment?'

McGuire nodded. He was staring pensively at the door of the barrack room building as if he half-expected the corpse to follow them out.

Chrissie looked up as McKay joined her. 'Still no sign of Kevin. He's not answering his mobile. Just going straight to voicemail.'

'Trust bloody Kevin to go AWOL at a time like this.'

'She's really worried, Alec.'

McKay was about to offer some quip in response, then read her expression. 'Does she have any reason to be?'

Chrissie was silent for a moment. 'She told me not to tell anyone. But Kevin does have a history of depression. He's been okay for years, but when he was younger, there were a couple of incidents.'

'Does she have a reason to be concerned now? If he's been okay for years, I mean.'

'It never goes away, does it? She just says he's been behaving oddly recently. Quieter than usual.' She allowed him a faint smile. 'Aye, *even* quieter, before you say it.'

'He'll just have got himself engrossed in something. If he managed to get into the Regimental Museum before it closed we won't see him till the summer.'

'I hope you're right. How's it going with your mate over there?'

'Ach, he's a ray of sunshine right enough. But seems smart enough.'

'He's not getting in your way, you mean?'

'Something like that.' He glanced over her shoulder. 'Looks like the cavalry's arrived.'

The pulse of a blue light was visible through what McKay presumed was one of the vehicular access gates. A moment later, he saw a uniformed soldier waving a police car into the interior of the fort. The car drew up beside them and two uniformed police officers climbed out. McKay walked forward to greet them. The driver was a middle-aged male, his partner a younger female officer. McKay knew both and liked them, which wasn't universally true of his colleagues.

'Jesus, Alec. You got here quickly,' the man said.

'You know me, Drew. Always one step ahead.' He nodded to the female officer. 'Afternoon, Morag. All well with you?'

'Other than the prospect of nursemaiding a dead body, you mean? Aye, all grand, Alec.'

'Who's yon lanky bugger?' Drew MacClean gestured towards McGuire standing awkwardly some yards away. McKay hoped he was out of earshot.

'Bit of respect, Drew. That's Captain Angus McGuire. Top dog round here. Or at least the top dog on site. Don't antagonise him. We'll need his co-operation if there's anything to be investigated.'

'If I need lessons in how not to antagonise people, Alec, I'm not sure I'll be coming to you. But, aye. I take your point.'

McKay grinned and led them over to McGuire. 'May I introduce you to my two colleagues, PCs Drew MacClean and Morag

Roberts. They'll take care of the site till the forensics team and others arrive.'

McGuire nodded. 'I assume this could all take some time?'

'I'm afraid so, sir.' McKay had decided that, in the presence of other officers, it was better to cease the verbal sparring with McGuire. 'I assume we won't be disrupting anything?'

'Not at all. Can I leave you to get on with it?'

'No problem. But it would be useful to be able to contact you if we run into any issues.'

'Of course.' McGuire reached into his pocket and, slightly to McKay's surprise, pulled out a business card. McKay wasn't sure why an army officer would need a business card, but it seemed as if everyone carried them these days. Even police officers. 'It has my mobile number on there. Just call me if you need anything. And let me know when you're done.'

So you can check we've done no damage, McKay added silently. 'Of course, sir. We're very grateful for your assistance.'

McKay glanced back towards Chrissie, who had walked some way back along the pathway, looking out for Fiona. He'd been trying to decide whether to leave now the uniforms had arrived. This might or might not end up back on his desk, depending on what the cause of death proved to be, but for the moment he was content to let others deal with it. He was supposed to be off-duty, after all.

He walked over to Chrissie. 'Any news?'

'Fiona just called me. She's walked all the way back to the far end of the fort but there's no sign. He wasn't in the chapel. She tried the museum but they were locking up and reckoned all their visitors had left. She said she'd walk round the other side in case he's over there, but everything's closing up.'

McKay wasn't inclined to take Kevin's supposed disappearance seriously. From everything McKay knew of the man, it was most likely he'd just got caught up in reading some display. It was even possible he'd managed to get himself locked in somewhere. 'Has she tried the phone again?'

'Still just voicemail. She reckons that's not like him either. He normally always leaves it on.'

The ambulance and another police car had arrived behind them. The last thing he needed at the moment was to have to worry about Kevin's whereabouts. 'Okay,' he sighed. 'Just give me a minute to deal with this lot, then we'll see what we can do.'

He made his way back over to Grant and Roberts, who were already isolating the area around the old barracks building. 'I'm going to leave you good people to it. Assuming you're up to the task.'

'Bugger off, Alec,' Grant said amiably. 'Leave it to the real coppers. Reckon we can cope without a pen-pusher like you.'

'Glad to hear it. We probably need the paramedics to confirm death, but don't let them bugger up the scene, will you? Or you'll have Jock Henderson to answer to.' Jock was one of the senior crime scene examiners. McKay had some semi-serious needle with him for reasons that were long forgotten by both.

'Like I say, Alec, leave it to the professionals. You get home to your roaring fire and a wee dram.'

'I might just be tempted to do exactly that,' McKay said, glancing over to where he could see Chrissie walking anxiously back and forth. 'That is, assuming I can manage to prise my bloody elusive brother-in-law away from this place.'

4

'She just called again,' Chrissie said, as he approached. 'Still no sign.'

'Where the bloody hell can he be?'

'She's getting really worried. I keep telling her he'll just be squirrelled away somewhere.'

'Where is she now?'

'She's heading back over here. Probably best if we just wait till she finds us. I don't want us all getting lost.'

'Me neither,' McKay said with feeling. 'You don't think he could have just forgotten about us and headed back out to the car? I wouldn't put it past him.'

'Who knows? Doesn't explain why he's not answering his phone, though. What do you think we should do?'

McKay had no ready answers. He assumed that the main visitor entrance would be closed and locked by now. They'd probably have to make their way out through the vehicle entrance he'd watched the police car come through earlier. There was no quick way to check whether Kevin was out there. 'Let's just hope the daft bugger turns up before we all freeze to death.'

He was about to add some further choice expletives when

Chrissie's phone rang again. 'Let's hope she's found him.' She thumbed the call button. 'Fiona?'

There was a long silence as she listened to what Fiona was telling her. McKay watched impatiently, waiting for the punch-line that might finally allow them all to go home. The last thing he wanted was still to be here when the crime scene examiners arrived. With McKay's luck, Jock Henderson would be on duty to provide the perfect ending to the day.

Finally, he heard Chrissie say, 'We'll come round.' She ended the call and looked up at McKay. 'She hasn't found him. But there's some commotion at the far end of the fort.'

'What sort of commotion?'

'She wasn't being very coherent. They seem to have found something but she didn't dare go close enough to see what it was.'

'Oh, Christ,' McKay said. 'Let's go and find her.'

They made their way between the buildings, emerging at the far side of the fort. It then took a few more moments to track down Fiona standing near to the chapel. As they approached, she pointed towards the battlements. 'Over there. I heard shouting so I came to see what was going on, just in case...' It was obvious what she was thinking.

The interior of the fort was generally well-lit, but the corner under the battlements was in the shadow of the stonework above. McKay could see a small group of young men – soldiers, presumably, though they were all in casual dress – gathered around something or someone on the ground. From this distance, it was impossible to make out anything more.

'Wait here,' McKay said. 'I'll see what's happening.'

As he drew closer, he saw that the object on the ground was definitely a human body, face down on the earth. One of the men glanced back quizzically at McKay as he approached.

McKay held out his warrant card. 'DI Alec McKay. Scottish Police. Is there some problem here?'

The man blinked. 'Police?'

'Aye. You've no doubt heard about us. What's going on?'

The man clearly wanted to ask what the hell a police detective was doing in the middle of a military establishment. It seemed word of the incident in the old barrack rooms hadn't yet hit the grapevine. Finally, he said, 'We found this guy. Here on the ground. Don't know who he is or what's happened to him.'

Other members of the group had now registered McKay's arrival. Behind the puzzlement, McKay detected relief at the prospect of someone else taking responsibility. Another of the men said, 'I found him. I nearly tripped right over him. I called over the others to see if we could do anything. But we don't know if he's injured or unconscious or...'

McKay assumed soldiers would be trained in first aid, not to mention how to deal with a crisis. Maybe all that was still to come for this bunch. 'Let me have a look.'

He took a step forward but he already knew what he was seeing. He recognised the coat, the shoes. There was something about the positioning of the body that made him catch his breath. He crouched down and touched the exposed neck. The skin was warm to his touch, but there was no sign of a pulse. He took a breath and tried again, but still there was nothing.

The face was twisted away from him. He moved round to the opposite side of the body, still hoping desperately that he was wrong.

But there was no doubt. McKay looked over to where Chrissie and Fiona were waiting.

'Fuck,' he whispered. 'This is turning into a really fucking bad day.'

5

F*uck,* Helena Grant thought, *this is turning into a really fucking bad night.*

The keys had to be somewhere. She'd had them just moments before when she'd locked the car doors. They couldn't have disappeared in the thirty seconds between then and now.

But she couldn't find them. She plunged her hands into her coat pockets, hoping she might have dropped them in there, but there was nothing. She reopened her handbag and peered inside, rummaging through the contents one more time in the hope the keys might magically reappear.

She'd forgotten to leave a light on when she'd left, and the only illumination was the pale glow of a streetlight some distance away, so she was relying largely on touch. But it was an electronic car fob with a couple of house keys attached, so it shouldn't have been difficult to identify.

She peered into the darkness. Why the hell hadn't she just kept the keys in her hand? She'd been distracted, still thinking through the events of the evening. Still well and truly pissed off. She hadn't been concentrating. She couldn't recall what she'd done after locking the car. At that point, the keys had been in her hand. Now they weren't. What the hell had happened to them in the interim?

This really was the last thing she needed tonight. All she wanted to do was get inside, climb out of this bloody smart suit, and knock back a very stiff drink. Was that too much to ask?

She wearily retraced her steps to the car, peering intently at the ground. If the keys weren't in her handbag or pockets, she reasoned, she must have dropped them between the house and the car.

But there was no sign of the keys. How could that be? If she'd dropped them, they'd just be lying there. They couldn't have rolled away. It wasn't possible.

She straightened up and leaned against the car. Then she swore again, this time loudly enough to disturb the neighbours.

The keys were there. Sitting mockingly on the car roof. Why in God's name had she put them there? She had no recollection of having done so. This really was the ageing process in action.

She strode back towards the house, this time clutching the keys firmly in her fist. It took her a moment's fumbling to open the door, and then finally she was inside. *Jesus, what a night.*

Ten minutes later, she was in the kitchen, smart suit well and truly ditched, in her dressing gown with a bottle of Glen Ord Singleton Malt in front of her. The bottle was only a quarter full and she was tempted to finish it, but there was still work in the morning. A glass would have to do.

She poured a dram and headed back into the sitting room. The woodstove was still alight, so she threw in a couple more logs and slumped back onto the sofa.

What a bloody night.

This was the worst so far, and none of them had been exactly brilliant. Each time she went with hope that this might be the one, that they'd both know as soon as they started talking. They'd click and everything would flow smoothly from there.

Each time she came away with a gnawing sense of despair.

Despair at her own inadequacies or unsuitability. Despair at the apparently universal awfulness of the opposite sex. Despair at the general unfairness and randomness of the universe and its workings.

So, no, it hadn't been a great success so far.

Tonight's had been the worst, though. Some arse called Martin Delaney. He'd arranged for them to meet in a smart restaurant in Inverness, down by the riverside. She'd been mildly pissed off by that to start with, given that he was based in Inverness and she was all the way up here. But, in fairness, there was no sensible midpoint to meet and the choice and quality of restaurants in the city were better than round here. But it would have been nice at least to have been asked.

She'd arrived a little early, as she tended to, and had sat at the table sipping at her sparkling water. That was another problem about having to come into the city. She couldn't even boost her confidence with a G&T or a glass of wine.

Delaney, inevitably, had been fifteen minutes late. He'd had her mobile number, but obviously hadn't thought it worth calling. She'd sat there calculating how long she should wait before deciding she'd been stood up. After that she'd been thinking about whether, if so, she should just bugger off home or stay and treat herself to a decent solo supper.

She was still thinking through all that when he'd finally turned up, breathless but with no apology. He'd dumped himself down in the seat opposite and said, 'Got a bit held up. Hope you've not been here long.'

Only since the time we agreed, she'd said to herself. Out loud, she said, 'Just a few minutes. No worries.' *No fucking worries.* She'd actually said that.

The photographs he'd used on the site were not recent, and the age he'd given had been a generous underestimate. He was significantly older than she was, and significantly balder and fatter than the pictures had indicated.

Not that any of that troubled her unduly. Her late husband had been ten years older than she was, and not exactly Mr Universe. She was less concerned about Delaney's appearance than his dishonesty. And there was something else about him already making her feel uneasy. Something she couldn't immediately pin down.

It hadn't taken long for that initial instinctive dislike to be justified. 'Right, then, let's get the menus,' he'd said. After that he'd actually fucking snapped his fingers at a passing waitress. 'Menus, please, lass. Chop-chop.'

She couldn't quite believe it even now. But those had been his exact words. *Chop fucking chop.* She knew he was English – he'd included that in his profile, apparently as some mark of distinction – but even that wasn't an excuse for such mind-boggling boorishness.

So the evening had started badly, and then quickly careered even further downhill. Delaney had read through the menu with enthusiasm, advising her confidently on what to order. Naturally, she'd made a point of ignoring his advice, earning her a disapproving shake of the head. 'You'll be sorry you didn't order the venison. Mark my words.'

'I'm not that keen on venison, I'm afraid.' She loved venison. 'I'd rather stick with the sea bass. A bit lighter.' *And why the hell am I justifying my decisions to this pompous oaf,* she'd asked herself.

So it had gone on. He'd ordered wine without bothering to consult her. She didn't care because she wasn't intending to drink anyway, but again it would have been good to have been asked. Over the starters – he'd recommended the terrine, she'd opted for the beetroot and feta salad – he'd described his job in mind-numbing detail. He was apparently the finance director of some local hotel chain, and he'd offered her a wealth of instantly forgettable insights into the hospitality industry.

Finally, just as they were about to start the main course, he'd asked her, 'So what about you?' He was already beginning to shovel down the food. She suspected he'd only asked her the question to give himself time to eat.

'Me?'

'Yes, what do you do? Work, I mean.'

'I work for the police.' She'd long ago decided there was no point in prevaricating about her occupation.

He'd looked up, clearly surprised. 'The police? What, some sort of admin role?'

She'd smiled sweetly. 'No. A police officer. A detective, actually.'

He'd put down his knife and fork, his expression suggesting he was finding her words too baffling to compute. 'A detective? Like a detective constable?'

'Sort of. Except I'm a chief inspector.'

Delaney's jaw hadn't literally dropped, but it might as well have done. She'd been able to read exactly what he was thinking. The major upside was that, from that point, he'd largely lapsed into silence, clearly having no idea how to interact further with her. She'd at least been able to enjoy her sea bass in relative peace.

After that she'd cut her losses as quickly as she could, turning down dessert and coffee. He'd seemed only too happy to bring the evening to an end. She'd insisted on splitting the bill as she always did, even paying for half of the wine she hadn't tasted.

But that hadn't quite been the end of it.

She'd been keen to get away as quickly as she could, but still felt obliged to say a polite goodbye to him on the street outside. She was trying to find something to say that wouldn't sound sarcastic, when he'd suddenly lunged at her. She hadn't been sure whether he was aiming for a simple peck on the cheek or something more amorous. Either way, it suggested he'd either fundamentally misread the evening or, more likely, didn't care.

She pulled back involuntarily, her face no doubt revealing her disgust. He'd stared at her, his expression moving from bafflement to anger. 'Like that, is it?'

She'd had no real idea what he was talking about. Before she could respond, he'd turned and strode away down the riverside. She'd heard him say, 'Bloody typical', as he'd disappeared into the darkness.

She'd stared after him, feeling oddly wrong-footed, as if she'd somehow been the one behaving badly. Maybe that had been his intention. To leave her with a sense the whole crappy evening had been her fault, even though he'd been an obnoxious entitled buffoon.

Yes, that had definitely been the worst one so far. The previous ones had been stressful, occasionally hard work and never exactly fun. But at least the dates had been mostly half-decent human beings, even if they hadn't been right for her. Tonight's had been something else again. It hadn't just been his obnoxious behaviour. She realised now that her first instinctive discomfort in his presence had developed into something more substantial as the evening progressed.

She took a sip of the whisky, enjoying the warm burn in her throat. She could just stop the experiment now, she supposed. She'd only embarked on this to see what would happen, egged on by a couple of her friends.

She'd made the decision a month or two back, deciding it was finally time for her to try to move on. She felt as if she'd been in stasis in the years since Rory's death. It had been so unexpected, so shocking, that it had almost left her without the will to continue. In the end, she managed to carry on largely by focussing on work, the day-to-day routine. There'd been more than enough of that to keep her busy.

Eventually, she'd decided to sell their house and move up here. At the time, that had felt like a decisive moment, the start of a new life. In some ways, it had worked. But she knew that, at heart, it had changed nothing. It just meant she was now living alone in a smaller house.

When Alec McKay had temporarily separated from Chrissie,

she'd vaguely wondered whether the answer might lie there. There'd always been something between her and Alec. Nothing serious. Nothing that Chrissie had ever needed to worry about. But a spark. Something that might have caught fire if the circumstances had ever been right.

But they never had been. McKay was now back with Chrissie, apparently happily enough, and that was almost certainly for the best. But it had left Grant wondering what to do with herself, with her life.

She'd been talking about this – not about McKay but about her need to change things – one semi-drunken night with a couple of friends, and one of them had suggested internet dating.

It hadn't even been a serious suggestion. But somehow it had stayed with her. It wasn't as if she had many other options. She might meet someone at work, but it seemed increasingly unlikely. In any case, she'd recognised, in her half-serious fantasies about McKay, that any work-based relationship was likely to be fraught with problems.

Outside work, she wasn't involved in any activities likely to bring her into contact with potential soulmates. She supposed she could take up some hobby or pastime to put her in contact with others, but she'd never been the clubbable type. Beyond that, she couldn't think of any other obvious ways to get out and meet people.

So she'd decided to give it a try. She'd signed up to a couple of what she understood to be the more respectable websites, and then had plunged right in.

So far, it hadn't been a conspicuous success. Maybe her standards were too high. But it wasn't really that. It was just that, so far, she'd had almost nothing in common with any of the men she'd met. The evenings had been hard work. You had to give it long enough to get beyond the initial nerves, to see whether the stilted awkwardness would eventually transform into something more relaxed. Sometimes it had, but so far that had just exposed the lack of anything substantive to talk about. Then you had the problem of extricating yourself without appearing rude. Although some of the men hadn't had many qualms about that.

Should she just give it up? She'd asked herself this at the end of each one of these evenings, and every time she'd decided to try just one more time. It was easy to be suckered in by a promising-looking profile. Tonight was a perfect example. It wasn't so much that he'd used out-of-date photographs of himself. She'd found that more amusing than anything else, and perhaps indicative of insecurity rather than vanity. It was more that his profile had made him sound a different person – more interesting, more sensitive – than the pompous boor who'd sat opposite her.

She sighed and took another sip of the whisky. Probably best to sleep on it. See how she felt tomorrow, faced with the prospect of another working week. That was what she was looking for. Something additional to that daily grind. She loved her job, but it could be all-consuming. She needed something more than just that and lonely evenings at home.

She swallowed the last of the whisky, started to clear up, ready to head up to bed. As she rose, her mobile buzzed on the table beside her. She picked it up and looked at the screen. A text.

There were only three words. 'Bitch. Watch out.'

The sender's number had been withheld. Was this Delaney continuing his unique form of charm offensive? It was possible. He had her mobile number, and he'd certainly struck her as unpleasant enough to do something like this. She just wouldn't have imagined he'd have the bottle to send a threatening message, however untraceable it might prove to be, to a serving police officer.

There were other potential explanations, of course. In a job like hers, you inevitably made plenty of enemies. It wasn't the first time she'd received a threat like this, and no doubt it wouldn't be the last. Usually, it was no more than empty posturing from some impotent scrote she'd put inside. Her number wasn't exactly in the public domain, but it wasn't that difficult to track down if you could be bothered. Maybe she'd look into it in the morning, but it didn't really trouble her too much.

Then the phone buzzed again. A second text. Three more words.

'Find your keys?'

This time she really did feel a clutch of fear in her stomach. Still holding the phone tightly, she turned off the lights, crossed over to the window and pulled back the edge of the curtain. The front of her house looked out over Beauly Firth, and she could see the lights on the far shore glimmering on the still water.

The road outside was silent and deserted. There was rarely any traffic down here at this time in the evening, unless one of her neighbours was returning late. Someone could be out there hiding in the shadows, but there was no sign of any movement in the pale glare of the streetlights.

She was by no means a cowardly woman, but the second text had left her shaken. Someone had been out there watching her earlier. Close enough to have worked out what she was doing. Someone who had just sent her a threatening text.

She had decent security here but couldn't fool herself the place was impregnable if someone was determined to get in. At this time of the year, she was leaving and returning in darkness, and there was no way of avoiding that walk, short as it was, to where her car was parked. If there really was a threat – and the fact that this person had taken the trouble to come here meant she had to take it seriously – she knew she was vulnerable.

Something else to think about tomorrow. She was too tired and overwrought to think about it rationally. Nothing was going to happen tonight, she was sure. The texts had been intended to unsettle her, unnerve her. The person who sent them was toying with her, and, even if they really did intend to act on the threats, they'd continue the taunting for a while yet.

Even so, she double-checked the front and back doors were securely locked and bolted, and made a further check of all the downstairs windows. The passageway along the side of the house was gated and locked so there was no easy way to access the rear of the building.

She was as safe here as she could be. Still clutching the phone, she made her way upstairs for what she knew would be, at best, a very disturbed night's sleep.

6

'My God,' Grant said. 'I thought I had a lousy weekend. Are you sure you should be in today?'

McKay shrugged. 'It was a shock, but I'm not the one most affected. I hardly knew him, if I'm honest. Anyway, what would I do at home? I'd just be under their feet.'

'I suppose.' If it had been anyone else sitting in front of her, Grant might have challenged this, but Chrissie might have been only too glad to get McKay out of the house that morning. It wasn't that he was insensitive – on occasions Grant had been surprised by his ability to negotiate delicate issues. It was more that enforced idleness never brought out McKay's best side. It was probably better he'd left Chrissie to support Fiona through her grieving. 'Do you know who's looking after it from our side?'

'I've not heard yet.'

As with any sudden or unexplained death, there would need to be a report to the procurator fiscal, who would determine whether further investigation was needed. Grant assumed that, as there were presumably no suspicious circumstances, the process would be relatively swift and straightforward. 'I'm assuming it was an accident?'

'I imagine that's where we'll end up,' McKay said. 'It was either an accident or, well…'

She looked up, momentarily surprised by his unwonted squeamishness. Then she reminded herself that McKay's own daughter, Lizzie, had died in what might have been an accident or might have been self-inflicted. 'Are there grounds for thinking it was anything else?'

'Who knows? According to Fiona, he'd suffered from depression before and there'd been one or two "incidents", as she described them. But that was years ago. She said he hadn't been himself recently. Even quieter than usual. Not that he was ever exactly the talkative type.'

'Doesn't sound a lot.'

'Doesn't, does it? And the other part of the equation is that it was getting dark, it was bloody windy up there, and there are no barriers. Kevin was always prone to be lost in thought. It's entirely possible he just got too near the edge and somehow tumbled over.'

'I imagine that'll be the conclusion unless there are strong reasons to think otherwise.'

'There's no point in making it any more painful for Fiona than it needs to be. She's in pieces already.'

'Must have been a hell of a shock. I mean, you go for a Sunday afternoon out, and then that happens.'

'Aye, tell me about it.'

'I didn't mean–'

'Ach, I know you didn't. There's no point in thinking that way, anyway. Doesn't help anyone. Obviously, my destined role this weekend was to expose my sister-in-law to death in all its forms.' He laughed mirthlessly.

Grant knew there was no mileage in pursuing that line. 'So what about this other death? That's already landed on my desk.'

'Really? I wasn't really in a state of mind to take in what was going on. I was too busy focussing on Fiona and Chrissie. You can imagine the bloody chaos.'

'At the moment, I'm treating it as unexplained and potentially suspicious. Cause of death not clear. There was no obvious sign of any trauma to the body, so could be natural causes. We won't know more till we get the pathology report. Identity as yet unknown. No ID on the body. Fingerprints and DNA don't match anything on the database.'

'If it was a natural death, how would the body have ended up in there, though? And why would there be no ID? Most people carry something. Bank cards, driving licence and the like.'

'I can see you're a trained detective. Aye, there's the rub. So I think for the moment we have to treat it as potentially suspicious.' She paused. 'You're not going to like it, but I think I ought to excuse you from this one, Alec.'

She'd half-expected some sort of explosion in response. Experience had taught her that McKay was happy only when he was really in the thick of things. Not that he wasn't busy enough – as always, they had numerous major investigations at various stages. But she knew that what he really wanted was to get his teeth into a new enquiry.

His response surprised her. 'Aye, you're probably right. Probably a bit too close to it.'

She felt mildly wrong-footed. On another occasion, she might have thought that was McKay's tactic. He was quite capable of finding unexpected ways to disconcert her. But now he just looked weary. He hadn't even begun his usual restless prowling round her office. 'You okay, Alec?'

'I'm grand. But, you know, got plenty on my plate already, workwise, I mean. And I was the one who found the body.'

She hesitated. 'And there's the question of your brother-in-law's death.'

'Kevin? You're not suggesting there's any connection?'

'Alec, we currently have two unexplained deaths in the same

location apparently within approximately the same timescale. Almost certainly that's just a very tragic coincidence. But we can't assume anything.'

'You didn't know Kevin. He was the most inoffensive man I've ever met. Almost offensively so. I can't imagine anyone wanting to harm him. More to the point, what connection could there be between him and the other body? Nobody could have known we were going to be there yesterday. We didn't know ourselves until about half an hour before.'

'Like I say, it's almost certainly coincidence. But we can't be seen to take anything for granted, especially when it's one of our own involved. The position might be different once we've got a decision on your brother-in-law's cause of death.'

'It's your call. I've plenty to keep me busy.'

'It may well be something and nothing anyway. It's an odd set-up, right enough, but we've had odder. I'm not going to push it too hard until we've got a cause of death. First priority is to try to find out who our mystery man actually is.'

'No car left in the car park, presumably?'

'I had that checked this morning. There were no vehicles left overnight that couldn't be accounted for. So either he arrived there by public transport – which is possible – or someone was with him. We need to check the CCTV footage and anything else that might give us a clue how he got there.'

'I'm not too sorry to be leaving all that to you,' McKay said. 'Tell you what. Bring me back in when it starts to get interesting.'

She laughed. 'Seriously, Alec, are you really okay? It's not like you to accept being excluded from a murder enquiry without a fight.'

'Ach, I'm just a bit tired, you know? It's been nose to the grindstone stuff for the last couple of months. That, and trying to sort out things with Chrissie.'

'How's that going?'

'It's going. Going well, I think, even if it sometimes feels like two steps forward and at least one step back. But at least it feels like we're on the same side now. But it's been hard work for both of us.'

'And now you've got to deal with what happened yesterday?'

'It knocked me sideways a bit when I saw Kevin's face, aye. It's not really our tragedy, but it'll put more pressure on Chrissie. And, well...'

She nodded, knowing what he couldn't bring himself to say. About the memories that would be stirred up for both of them. Perhaps just at the point when they were finally beginning to consign those memories to the past. 'If you need some time off, just take it. I need you on top form.'

'Thanks for the offer. I'm not really one for taking time off, though.'

'You'll presumably need to take leave for the funeral. Assume that'll be down south?'

'Actually, we're not sure about that. Chrissie thinks Fiona wants him buried up here. It's where he comes from originally, and all his family are up here. I don't know, though. Fiona wasn't exactly in a state to make any decisions last night, so she might change her mind when she's time to reflect on it.'

'Okay. But if you need time off, for whatever reason, don't hesitate.'

'Message received and understood. How are things with you, anyway? Found Mr Right yet?'

She sighed inwardly. She wasn't entirely sure why she'd told McKay about her adventures in online dating. It was partly because she wanted to let him know she was trying to move on. But it was mainly because, if he'd subsequently found out from any other source, the piss-taking would have been even more relentless.

'Actually,' she said, 'I was going to talk to you about that.'

'I'm all ears.'

She told him about the events of the previous evening, ending with the threatening texts.

'It sounds worth taking seriously,' McKay said. 'You're sure he could have only known about the keys if he was actually watching you?'

'How else? It's not like I posted an account of me being a numpty on social media. No one could have known about it unless they actually saw me.'

'What about a neighbour?'

She hadn't considered that possibility. Her house was part of a row of adjoining cottages. It was conceivable that someone could have been watching her through a window. 'I can't see it,' she said, finally. 'There's an elderly couple on one side, and a young woman on the other. I don't see a lot of any of them, but they don't strike me as the sort to send threatening texts. In fact, I'm not sure the couple would even know how to send a text. There's no bad blood between any of us. At least, not that I'm aware of.'

'Neighbours can be weird, though. Sometimes they bear grudges for the oddest of reasons.'

Grant wondered whether this observation was based on experience, but decided it was better not to enquire. 'Still can't see it. I don't really know the neighbours further down the road. I suppose I might have been visible to one of them.'

'It's a line of enquiry, anyway,' McKay said. 'As is the arsehole you had dinner with. You really think it might have been him?'

'Who knows? He was enough of an arsehole, but I wouldn't have thought he'd have the balls.'

'Could he have got there before you?'

'It's possible. He stalked off and left me standing there. Then it took me a few minutes to walk to the car, so if he had a car nearby he could have beaten me to it. He'd drunk a bottle of wine, so if he was prepared to drive in that condition, he probably wouldn't have been too bothered about the speed limits.'

'I assume you're going to report this?'

'I don't think I've any choice. Apart from anything else, if I've received a credible threat, I need to make it official so there's no risk of appearing compromised if it's connected with some current or past case.'

'I think it's credible enough,' McKay said. 'I mean, it'll almost certainly turn out to be some wee gobshite who's just trying to put the fear of God into you. But if that gobshite really did take the trouble to come and spy on you, that does take it to another level.'

'Tell me about it. I've faced plenty in this job, but this one left me unnerved.'

'It's always worst when it comes home,' McKay said. 'It's the one place you can escape everything here.'

'But, like you say, it'll just be some deadbeat who wants to scare me. Takes more than a couple of texts, though. But last night it was the perfect end to a perfect evening.'

'You going to continue with this dating lark, then?'

She thought McKay sounded vaguely disapproving, though she wasn't sure whether he was concerned about her safety or her romantic life. 'I don't know. It's bloody hard work. Much easier to stay home and hit the wine. But, you know...'

'I know.' She could already detect the mischievous grin he was trying to suppress. 'You know,' he went on, 'I could always do some matchmaking for you. I know some lovely people. Just your type.'

'Oh, bugger off, Alec McKay,' she said. 'Just bugger right off.'

7

'Just yourself, is it?' the man said. 'That'll be nine pounds, then, unless you're a member?'

She shook her head. 'I'm not a visitor.' She held out her ID card. 'Mr Lewis? Detective Sergeant Horton. You should have been told I was coming?'

'They did tell me. I just wasn't...'

Expecting a woman, Horton thought. As always. 'That's fine. I'm sorry I wasn't able to give an exact time. It's been a hectic morning.' She looked around at the ticket office and souvenir shop. 'Are we okay to talk in here or would you prefer somewhere quieter?'

'I can't really leave the desk. There's only me on this morning. But we shouldn't be disturbed too much. Monday morning in early January isn't exactly our peak time.' He gestured behind the desk. 'You can sit here. Can I get you a coffee or something?'

'I'm fine,' she said. 'I don't want to take up any more of your time than I need to.'

'I don't really know if I can help you. It's a terrible business, right enough. Did I hear that there were two bodies?'

The police hadn't yet released any information, but she wasn't entirely surprised that the grapevine had already been at work. 'I'm not in a position to say too much at this stage. But, yes, we're dealing with two deaths. It's really too early to say any more.' That, basically, was the gist of a press release she knew the communications team would be issuing later that morning.

'But you think they're suspicious?' Lewis pressed. 'I mean, that's why you're here?'

It was the usual story, she thought. People wanted to be part of something exciting, something outside of their usual mundane lives. The problem was that it sometimes made them over-eager witnesses. They told you what they thought you wanted to hear, rather than what they actually knew. She said, 'We investigate all sudden or unexplained deaths until we're sure of the circumstances. We have to report to the procurator fiscal, who then decides whether a further investigation is merited. At this stage, I'm just trying to gather as much background information as possible.'

'Of course. Understood.'

Lewis had an air of authority about him, Horton thought. He was probably in his late sixties, with a full head of grey, swept-back hair. He looked trim and fit, as if he kept himself in shape. He sounded English, though she thought she could detect a trace of a Scottish lilt. She imagined he was some sort of retired senior manager or civil servant, keeping himself occupied with this part-time work. 'At this stage, we're primarily interested in seeking to identify one of the two deceased.' She left Lewis to infer what that might reveal about their knowledge of the second body. 'He was a young man, white, probably in his early to mid-twenties. He was wearing a dark blue waterproof jacket over a black jumper, jeans and a pair of unbranded trainers. Do you recall seeing anyone of that description yesterday?'

Lewis frowned. 'We didn't have a huge number of people through. Maybe twenty or so in total across the day. Most of them were couples, usually middle-aged or elderly. That includes the police officer who came to tell me about what had happened.'

Horton kept her face expressionless. Presumably, the grapevine had not yet caught up with the link between McKay and the second death. 'You don't recall seeing any younger males?'

'I'm just trying to recall. We had a small party of foreign students through over the weekend. Dutch, I think, though they all seemed to speak good English.' He paused. 'But I'm pretty sure that was on Saturday.'

She nodded, her momentary hopes of a useful breakthrough dashed. 'You're certain?'

'When you get to my age, it's difficult to be sure of anything. But, yes, now I think of it, I'm sure it was Saturday. They sheltered in here for a while after buying their tickets because it had started to rain. It was Saturday we had rain, wasn't it?'

She nodded, thinking back to her own weekend. She lived relatively close to this spot, and she'd been caught in rain showers during her morning run. Sunday, by contrast, had been bright and cold, with unclouded skies. 'You can't think of anyone on Sunday who might have fitted that description?'

'Not that I can recall.' He hesitated. 'Except…'

'Yes?'

'It was actually just after I'd sold tickets to that policeman chap and his family. I followed them out to get a breath of air, and there were a couple of idiots messing around on the battlements just by the main entrance. A man and a woman. I was too far away to see their faces properly, but they looked about that sort of age. Just from the way they moved, if you see what I mean.'

'What were they actually doing?'

'I'm not sure exactly. It looked like some kind of play-fight.'

'What happened to them?'

'Nothing much, luckily. I shouted at them to stop and they did. I don't recall seeing anything more of them after that.'

Horton nodded. McKay hadn't mentioned any of this during their brief conversation about the weekend's events, but he'd no doubt had plenty of other matters on his mind. She wouldn't be the one to take a formal witness statement from him, but she'd make sure this was checked out in case McKay had anything to add. 'And you don't think you'd sold this person a ticket?'

'I couldn't be absolutely certain. The old memory's not always what it was. But I'm pretty sure. I usually notice when we get younger people coming in, partly because they have a tendency to get up to those sort of tricks.'

'So how would he have got in?'

'To be honest, at this time of year it wouldn't be too difficult. We don't get many visitors, and yesterday there was only me on duty. I try to keep an eye on what's happening outside when I can, but if I was serving someone or doing something with the shop, people can slip past without buying a ticket. Wouldn't even necessarily be deliberately dishonest. Some people don't bother to read the signs and assume they can just walk in.'

'What about CCTV?'

'There's plenty of that. For security more than commercial reasons, as it's a working garrison. But that's the army's responsibility, as far as I know. You'd have to contact them for the footage.'

'Of course.' One of her colleagues had already been tasked with this, but it was another point to double-check when returned. The footage was unlikely to help determine the deceased's identity, but it might at least tell them whether or not he'd arrived alone. There might also be revealing footage from the car park or the interior of the site.

There would also be the possibility of getting hold of the bank card details of the visitors who'd passed through here on Sunday, but that would be a lengthier procedure and might be a waste of time if Lewis was correct.

Those were all next steps, though. For the moment, she'd extracted all she was likely to from Lewis. Not that she'd expected much more. The priority at this stage was simply to ascertain the dead man's identity, and the only way to do that was to follow up any reasonable lines of enquiry in the hope some lead would emerge. They were working through recent missing persons reports in the hope that one would match the man's description. If that failed, they'd be making an appeal to the local media in the hope that someone would know who this man was. One way or another, they should eventually discover the answer. The next question, depending on the cause of death, would be whether there was anything further to investigate.

'Thanks for your time, Mr Lewis,' she said. 'That's been very helpful.'

'I'm sorry I couldn't help you more. Awful situation.' He paused. 'You didn't ask me anything about the second body?' He sounded vaguely disappointed.

'We've identified the second body. Again, at this stage, the investigation is just routine until we know the full circumstances.' Like all police officers involved in major enquiries, she'd developed a knack for generating empty verbiage. She slid a business card across the desk to him. 'My details are on there, Mr Lewis. If anything else occurs to you, don't hesitate to give me a call.'

She finished thanking him and stepped back out into the afternoon sunshine. It was another fine but chilly day, a sharp wind whipping from the firth. Horton always found midwinter frustrating, her opportunities to go running constrained by the shortness of the days. She used a headtorch to enable her to run before heading into work, but, given her past experiences, she was wary of spending too much time running alone in the darkness.

47

She didn't allow it to stop her, but she was more cautious, more attentive to the environment around her. That made it harder for her to enter the distinctive mental state that, for her, was one of the joys of running. When it was going well, when she hit the rhythm, there usually came a point when she could switch off conscious thought and allow her mind to run free. That was often the state in which unbidden insights and ideas came to her that would open up new ways of thinking about work or domestic issues.

She promised herself she'd undertake another run along the shoreline after work even though, yet again, she'd be running in the dark. It wasn't ideal, and she knew her partner Isla also worried about her, but she couldn't allow herself to stop.

Still thinking, she stepped over to the bridge that led to the main entrance to the fort, looking up at the spot on the battlements where, presumably, Lewis had seen the young man and woman.

Horton had never had a problem with heights but the sight made her momentarily catch her breath. The sloped grass-covered area below the battlements was relatively narrow, ending in an unfenced drop to the ground some distance below. Her guess was that the distance would be sufficient to render any fall potentially fatal. It was a ridiculous place to be playing around. In her police career, Horton had seen more than enough evidence of people's capacity for stupid, self-destructive behaviour. Even so, she wondered whether the interaction between the couple might have been more than it had appeared. Had they really just been messing around, or had one of them actively been trying to harm the other? At this distance, it would be difficult to distinguish a mock fight from a real one.

If the struggle had been real, one of the two had been trying to push the other down the slope. If so, they'd have two similar deaths within a short period, and, even knowing the identity of the second body, they would inevitably be considering a possible link.

She knew she was speculating far ahead of any information they currently had, and everything would depend on the pathologist's decision about the cause and nature of the death. Even so, it was a train of thought she couldn't entirely disregard.

It was not, she thought, a train of thought likely to please Alec McKay.

8

Jana pulled her thin coat more tightly around her body and made her way cautiously down towards the water.

She had known cold before, of course, and worse than this. Cold that she had faced without real shelter, with no warmth or protection. Cold she'd had to endure day after day, night after night, as they made their slow way towards the border.

Compared with that, her life now was comfortable. But it wasn't what she'd expected. None of it was what she'd expected. She knew she was one of the lucky ones. She had a place to sleep. She had enough to eat, more or less. Her duties here were onerous, but not yet degrading or humiliating. She was not treated well, but so far she had been treated much better than many others.

She was trapped here, but at least they allowed her the illusion of freedom. If she came out here into the garden during her very short breaks, as tonight, no one stopped her. They didn't need to. There was nowhere she could go. She had no money, no resources. She knew no one. If she tried to go to the authorities, she would be arrested, imprisoned and, in due course, sent back.

She was smart enough to understand that, and they knew that all too well.

In any case, they'd made it very clear what they would do to her if she were caught trying to leave. So far, she had avoided any physical violence, any kind of assault, but she had no doubt what they were capable of. She had seen what had happened to some of the other women – she refused to think of them as girls – when they had somehow crossed the wrong person. She was aware, too, of the women who had simply vanished. There were countless rumours about what might have happened to them, but no one believed it was anything good.

She made her way down the stone path to the edge of the water. An icy wind was blowing in from the firth, the scent of snow in the air. The sky was clear, heavy with stars, the pale smear of the Milky Way visible through the bare branches of the trees.

At the bottom of the path, a narrow wooden jetty stretched out into the water. She assumed it had once been functional, but she had never seen any boats down here, and she had no idea how deep the water was. The jetty was long unused, the wooden boards slimy and quite probably rotten.

That was characteristic of the whole place. She turned and looked up at the square mass of the building behind her. She imagined that it had once been a decent hotel, perhaps a destination in its own right. Those days were long past. The paintwork was cracked and peeling, the carpets and curtains faded and worn, the furniture chipped and scarred by years of use.

She couldn't imagine how the place kept going, even with a largely unpaid and exploited workforce. At present, it was empty, other than the rooms that were rented by companies on a long-term basis for contractors working in the area. They'd had a few others staying over Christmas and New Year, but most of those had just stopped here to break their journeys further north or west. She'd heard them complaining about the decor and the food, but she knew they chose this place mainly because it was cheap.

She assumed the place would become busier in the summer, but she couldn't imagine how it would ever attract the clientele it needed to be commercially viable. Her late husband had been an accountant, once upon a time in a different life, so she had some understanding of the economics of a place like this, and none of it made any sense to her.

The wind was growing stronger, and she could see a bank of clouds building on the horizon. Across the firth, the lights of a town were visible, doubled fuzzily in the choppy waters. She had the same view, more or less, from the dormitory. Occasionally she stared out there, wondering who lived in that town, what sort of place it might be.

She had seen almost nothing of this country in her brief time here. Nothing but the inside of vans, bleak rooms lit by bare bulbs, and the shabby interior of the building behind her. That was why she came out here in her breaks – to get a taste of the fresh air, a brief sight of the trees, the sky, the water. To remind herself there was a world outside her current life.

Perhaps she might return to that world one day, take her place again in a society where people had nothing to fear, where they could live freely and happily, where they could think and act as they pleased. She couldn't imagine how it might happen. She was unlikely ever to return to the place she still thought of as home, even assuming it still existed. She was excluded from any meaningful form of life here, and it was difficult to see how that would ever change, except perhaps for the worse.

She always tried hard to prevent herself from thinking like this, knowing nothing but despair could result. But sometimes, as now, the reality of her situation crept back into her mind, a darkness she couldn't entirely manage to dispel. She felt as if it were happening more frequently lately, even though she tried to lose herself in the mindless repetition of her work here.

Taking a final deep breath of the cold pure air, she turned to return indoors. There was a figure standing further up the path, between her and the rear entrance to the hotel.

The fat man, she thought. It was always the fat man.

She tried to tell herself he didn't scare her, but that wasn't true. She thought she could probably handle him, if it should ever come to that. But he scared her. Not because of what he might do or try to do, but simply because of what he *was*. There was something about him that caused her stomach to tighten in fear. It was nothing about his physical appearance, unprepossessing as that was. It wasn't even the unpleasant way he behaved.

It was something else. Something that hung around his corpulent body like a miasma. A scent of wrongness.

Now he was standing on the path, blocking her way back into the building. She wasn't surprised. He pestered the women continually, though she'd avoided the worst of his attentions, finding an excuse to absent herself the moment he appeared. But she'd given him an opportunity by coming out here alone.

'Jana?' he said. 'That's your name, isn't it?'

She wanted more than anything not to offer him the confirmation. It felt as if, by acknowledging her name, she was yielding some power, some authority to him.

'I need to get back inside.'

'Your English is very good. Better than most of the others.'

She shook her head, feigning incomprehension but fearing it was already too late. He knew she could speak English. She didn't know why that mattered, but she felt as if it did.

She moved onto the damp grass, intending to step past him, but he held out an arm. 'You don't need to go in yet. If you're late, you can blame me.'

That was nonsense. If she were late, the fault would be entirely hers. There was no point in trying to shift the blame onto anyone else, certainly not onto the fat man.

'You're a fine-looking woman, Jana. You know that?'

She mumbled some unintelligible response, still looking to move past him.

'You're not as young as some. But I like that.' He leaned towards her. His face seemed unnaturally smooth, and she caught a strong scent of aftershave. She found herself flinching, but he seemed not to notice. 'I could help you, Jana. I could get you away from here. Keep you safe. Look after you.'

Despite everything, she was almost tempted. But the fat man wasn't interested in helping her. He was interested only in helping himself.

'I need to get back inside,' she repeated, as if this was the only English phrase she knew.

'I have no intention of preventing you, dear lady.' The fat man took a step back, and gestured for her to walk past. 'I merely wanted to introduce myself.'

She was conscious of how little she wanted even to walk past him. She stepped forward, noting how he leaned forward as she passed, as if preparing to whisper something in her ear.

She didn't release her breath until he was behind her, and she was hurrying towards the rear door of the hotel.

Behind her, she heard him say, 'Don't forget my offer, Jana. I can help you. I can look after you and keep you safe.'

She pushed open the door into the hotel, trying to resist looking back. He had uttered the words, she thought, as if they were some kind of threat.

9

'Alec.'

'Charlie.'

'Good of you to pop along, Alec.'

'Don't think I had much of a choice, did I?'

DCI Charlie Farrow laughed as if McKay had made some sort of joke. That was par for the course with Farrow. All chummy bonhomie until he suddenly turned nasty. 'Shouldn't take us long, Alec. Just the formalities, you know.'

As no invitation had so far been forthcoming, McKay took the initiative and seated himself opposite Farrow. 'I know. Any word from the pathologist yet?'

Farrow looked as if he might be about to suggest that wasn't any of McKay's business, but finally said, 'Not yet. Won't be high on their list, I imagine.'

McKay nodded, trying to work out whether Farrow was dropping him a hint about the likely outcome of this initial enquiry. But he knew Farrow too well. Farrow was the kind of copper who did you a favour only if there was a better than evens chance of him getting something in return. He was also the kind of copper who wouldn't commit to anything unless his backside was well and truly covered.

'So what do you want from me?'

'You know the drill, Alec. We have to investigate the circumstances surrounding the death of…' He consulted the paperwork in front of him. 'Kevin William Andrews. We'll need your account of what happened on the day. Any relevant background. Just so we can get the paperwork off to the Fiscal.'

'You'll be wanting to talk to Fiona – that's Kevin's widow – and Chrissie, no doubt.'

'I'll send someone out to talk to them, aye. You reckon the widow's up to it?'

The widow. McKay knew Farrow wouldn't be asking out of any concern for Fiona's welfare, but because he wanted to ensure everything was done by the book. This sort of case, especially when involving a colleague, was always sensitive. 'As much as she'll ever be.'

'Terrible business.' Farrow had opened his notebook. A copper of the old school. McKay almost expected him to lick the tip of a pencil before proceeding to take notes. 'Let's get started, then. Just talk me through events on Sunday from your perspective.'

McKay ran through his recollections of events as fully as he could, beginning with their decision to visit the fort – Kevin's suggestion, ironically enough – up to the moment when he'd identified Kevin's body.

'Were you expecting it to be him?'

Farrow had remained silent during McKay's account, and the direct question was unexpected. McKay hesitated for a moment, trying to recapture his thoughts and emotions in those few seconds before he'd seen Kevin's face. 'I was desperately hoping it wouldn't be. I mean, not that it wouldn't have been just as bad whoever the poor bastard had been, but you know…'

'You'd just rather it was someone else's poor bastard. Aye, of course.'

'But I guess I knew. As soon as I saw the body lying there.'

'How did you know?'

McKay wasn't sure if he was misplaying this, unnecessarily feeding Farrow's suspicions about Kevin's state of mind. But, whatever else he might be, Farrow was no fool. It was better to be honest. 'You know how it is. Somehow you just feel it's going to turn out shite, and there's no way of avoiding it. That's how it felt.'

'Was it the case that Mr Andrews had been in low spirits for some days?'

McKay wondered how Farrow had extracted that particular piece of information, given he hadn't yet spoken formally to either Fiona or Chrissie. 'I couldn't really say, to be honest. Fiona seemed to think he'd been a bit down, but he'd been pretty much his usual self to me. He was never exactly the chatty type.'

'Did she say why he might have been down?'

'I don't think she knew. He'd apparently suffered a little from depression in his earlier life, but nothing recently. She just thought he wasn't himself.'

'That was why she was worried when he went missing?'

'Seems so. I thought at first it was all a fuss about nothing. He'd not been gone that long. Kevin was exactly the sort to get himself locked in after closing time, you know.'

'But she thought something might have happened to him?'

'I don't know if she seriously thought that at first, or if she was just a bit concerned. She was in a bit of a state of shock by then, anyway.'

Farrow looked down at the paperwork again, though it was unclear whether he was really reading anything or just engaging in the usual interviewer's mind games. McKay had seen it all before, usually from the other side of the table. 'Quite the afternoon for you, wasn't it?'

'You might say that.'

'How did Mrs Andrews seem? After you found the first body, I mean.' Farrow made it sound as if McKay made a habit of stumbling across corpses.

'She seemed okay. It was a shock, obviously. But I thought she'd pretty much taken it in her stride.'

'Even so, finding something like that must have intensified her concerns about her husband?'

'You'd have to ask her that. But I imagine it wouldn't have helped.'

'You were the last to speak to Mr Andrews before his death?' It was an abrupt change of tack.

More mind games, McKay thought, though he wasn't sure to what end. 'As far as I know.' McKay paused. 'Unless you discover differently.' *After all,* he added silently to himself, *that is your job here, old son.*

Farrow nodded. 'Quite so.'

'You'll have spoken to the men who found the body? I assume they were soldiers. I asked them to wait while the scene was protected.'

Farrow clearly recognised he'd been unexpectedly forced onto the back foot. 'They're on the list, yes. I don't imagine they'll have much useful to tell us.'

'There might be witnesses who saw Kevin after I left him,' McKay added. 'It was beginning to get dark and there weren't many people around. But someone might have been passing–'

'You don't need to tell me how to do my job, Alec.'

Satisfied he'd managed to goad Farrow into a response, McKay sat back in his chair and smiled. 'Of course not, Charlie. Just trying to help.'

'Always grateful for your input, Alec.' Farrow hesitated. 'Is there anything else you think I should know about Mr Andrews?'

'Not that I'm aware of. To be honest, I wouldn't claim to know him well myself. We never had much in common. He was just family. Married Fiona – I don't know, must have been the best part of twenty years ago. It was only a year or two after Chrissie and I married. Kevin was a local lad, I think, but the first time I met him was at the wedding in Inverness. We saw a fair bit of them at first, because Chrissie and Fiona were close. But then Kevin's work took them down south, and after that we only saw them on high days and holidays. They usually came up over Christmas and Hogmanay to see the family.'

'But not this year?'

'Kevin had been tied up with some work stuff before Christmas, I think, so they came up a bit later. They'd been staying with Chrissie's other sister, and they came over for a couple of days with us.'

'Do you know what sort of work he did?'

'Something in IT, I think. Something too smart for me to understand, anyway. You'll have to ask Fiona.'

Farrow nodded absently and jotted something in his notebook. McKay was generally skilled at reading upside down, but Farrow's scrawl defeated him. 'As far as you know, is there any reason we should suspect foul play in Andrews' death?'

The question was unexpectedly blunt, but McKay supposed Farrow had to ask. 'I'd have imagined Kevin to be the archetypal man without enemies. To be frank, he didn't have the personality to antagonise anyone.'

'People aren't always what they seem.'

'No, and it's possible Kevin was secretly a criminal mastermind, co-ordinating a network of crime across the globe. But I'd be surprised.'

'Alternatively, even the mildest of people can be topped by some passing nutter, if they're in the wrong place at the wrong time.'

'Again, it's possible. If Kevin had been standing near the edge, it wouldn't have taken much to send him over. Though, to be honest, I can more easily imagine Kevin absent-mindedly taking himself over the edge. But like you say, Charlie, I'm not here to teach you your job.'

Farrow flicked back through his notes, apparently at random. 'Just one small thing. We understand that, when your group first arrived at the fort, there were a couple of people messing around on the parapets by the entrance. You didn't mention that?'

McKay looked up, meeting Farrow's gaze. 'I'd forgotten about it. It seemed something and nothing.'

'You don't think there might be a connection with your brother-in-law's death?'

'Anything's possible. It just looked like a couple of numpties playing silly buggers.'

'Maybe they decided to play silly buggers with Mr Andrews, too?'

McKay's mood was growing darker. Was Farrow really going to try to pursue this line? As far as McKay was concerned, Kevin's death had been tragic but almost certainly straightforward. Most likely, the poor bastard had just been his usual preoccupied self and had strayed too close to the edge, maybe slipping or stumbling on uneven ground. There was a small possibility that, for some unfathomable reason, he might have taken his own life. Or some combination of the two – that an encroaching depression had made him less careful than usual for his own well-being.

Given the latter conclusion was unlikely to be provable, McKay had assumed the simple and generous outcome of Farrow's enquiry would be that the death was most likely accidental. It had never occurred to him there might be any reason, however tenuous, to suspect foul play. 'Like I say, Charlie, anything's possible. But it seems rather a stretch. Unless you've other evidence or witnesses to shed more light on what those two were up to?'

Farrow's expression was inscrutable. 'It's early days, Alec.

We're still identifying potential witnesses. But you know how it is. We're keeping an open mind. Keeping everything on the table.'

McKay nodded, wearily. He shouldn't have been surprised. Farrow was exactly the sort to make a meal out of a relatively cut and dried case. Maybe hunting for a little glory, or maybe just wanting to be a pain in the arse, particularly given McKay's involvement. Either way, it looked as if this might be more drawn-out and painful – not just for himself but also for Fiona and Chrissie – than he'd hoped. 'I know, Charlie. Just doing your job.'

'Just doing my job, Alec. You know better than most what's involved in this kind of case.'

McKay's hands tightened on the arms of his chair and he took a deep breath, biting back a response. *You bastard,* he thought. *You absolute state-of-the-art fucking bastard.* He had no doubt Farrow was alluding to the death of McKay's own daughter, Lizzie, a similar potential suicide ultimately recorded as an accidental death. He had no doubt, too, that Farrow was entirely aware of how McKay still felt about Lizzie's death.

After a moment, McKay released his breath, finally able to speak. 'I do, Charlie. I know all too well. So you just make sure you do your job properly, eh? I'll be watching.'

Without waiting for a response, McKay rose and left the room, taking care not to slam the door behind him.

10

'I was beginning to think you'd stood me up too. I must be getting paranoid.'

'Oh, God. Am I late? It was the kids–'

Helena Grant laughed. 'I'm only joking. It's not seven yet. I only got here a couple of minutes ago.'

Jacquie Green dumped herself down on the seat opposite Grant, finally stopping to look at her watch. 'That's something, then. Jeez, what a day I've had. Then the kids started playing up just as I was leaving. Fighting over some bloody computer game. I left the babysitter to sort that one out. She's much better at dealing with them than I am.'

Grant doubted that. From what she'd seen, Green was more than capable of dealing with anyone. Even Alec McKay on occasions. 'You sound like you need a drink.'

'Gin. Ideally by the bucketload. With maybe a small drop of tonic.'

'I'll see what I can do.'

Grant made her way to the bar and ordered large gin and tonics for each of them. It was midweek and the place – a relatively upmarket bar tucked away off the main drag – was quiet with only a handful of after-work drinkers occupying the other tables. It occurred to her that this was the most relaxed she'd felt on an evening out in weeks.

She returned to the table with the drinks, sliding one of the chilled glasses over to Green. 'Shall we eat here or go on somewhere else?'

Green took a mouthful of the gin. 'We could just sit here and drink. Bugger the food.'

'You're supposed to be a doctor.'

'There's no "supposed" about it. I am a doctor. That's why I need the booze. You ask any hard-working quack.'

'Tough day?'

'No more than usual. So, yes.'

Grant shook her head. 'Everyone seems utterly jaded at the moment. Even Alec reckons he's fed up with the job.'

Jacquie Green laughed. 'Alec McKay? He'll be up to his oxters in the job until they nail him in his coffin. Even then, I wouldn't put it past the bugger to claw his way out and back into the office.' She took another large mouthful of gin. 'No, I'm grand really. It's just the time of year, isn't it? Short days, long nights. Christmas and Hogmanay behind us. Back to the old grind. And it's our peak period. Everybody pops their clogs in winter.' Green was the senior pathologist who carried out many of the post-mortems for the police. She was generally known in the force as 'Doc' Green. Helena Grant suspected that many of the younger officers weren't even aware that this was originally supposed to be a joke.

'Is that right?'

'Sort of. The pattern of death differs across the year. But people often just seem to slip away when the year's at its coldest and darkest. Usually in the wee small hours.'

'That's what I love about coming out with you, Jacq. You always know how to raise a laugh.'

'I do my best. Actually, do you want to talk shop, just briefly? I did the PM on your young chap today.'

'My young chap?'

'The one who was found in Fort George. Look, sorry, we don't have to do it now. You'll have the report tomorrow anyway.'

Grant looked around her. She was always nervous about discussing cases in public environments, in case some sharp-eared eavesdropper decided to share something sensitive with the local media. But there was no one close enough to overhear. 'No, that's fine. Anything interesting?'

'Looks like it. Death was caused by asphyxiation. Something pressed onto the face. A pillow. Cushion. Something like that. There are a few fibres in the mouth, so forensics should be able to match those with anything around.'

Grant thought back to the crime scene report. There had been a thin pillow – part of the display – lying by the body. 'You think it happened there? In that room?'

'There was no sign of the body being moved after death. So it looks like it.'

'Which means we're talking murder.'

'That's your job. But, yes, unlawful killing. I suppose it's possible to conceive of circumstances where it might have been manslaughter. But it wasn't an accident or self-inflicted.'

'So it looks like we've got a fully-fledged investigation on our hands,' Grant said. 'Alec will be livid.'

'I thought Alec loved that kind of thing.'

'Oh, he does. It's what he lives for. But he's compromised on this one until we know differently.'

'Compromised?' Green frowned. 'Oh, the other body. Some relative of Alec's, wasn't it?'

'By marriage. Brother-in-law. But close enough that we have to keep Alec's size nines out of this until we're sure the cases aren't connected.' She hadn't bothered to ask Green whether she'd also carried out the PM on Kevin Andrews. If she had, she'd be reporting the findings directly to DCI Farrow. Grant had no desire to cause her friend discomfort by trying to extract inside information.

Green's expression suggested she'd read Helena Grant's thoughts. 'Haven't got to that one yet,' she said. 'It's a treat in store. Especially as lovely Charlie Farrow's looking after it. But I'll give it priority, if that helps you.'

'Depends on what you find, I suppose. But, yes, thanks. It's not as if we're awash with detectives of Alec's calibre.'

'It's not like we're awash with staff of any kind.' Green gestured towards Grant's nearly empty glass. 'Another?'

'Just a single or I'll be under the table. Then we'd better think about food.'

In the end, they decided to treat themselves to dinner in one of the restaurants down by the river. On a weeknight in January, they were able to get a table easily enough, and Grant felt comfortably anonymous at a table tucked into a discreet corner at the far end of the room. 'This is the most relaxed night out I've had in ages,' she said, once they were settled with an opened bottle of Shiraz between them.

'Ah. How's that going?'

'Not brilliantly.' She recounted a short selection of the more grisly anecdotes from her recent dates, ending with her recent encounter with the self-obsessed Martin Delaney.

'You really think he might have sent you that text?'

Grant held up her hands. 'It's possible. But I've made more than my share of enemies over the years, so who knows? Anyway, I reported it and it's being investigated, supposedly, but I don't imagine it'll be high on the list unless there are further developments.'

'You've had nothing since?'

'Not a word. Whoever it was, I'm hoping it was just a one-off.'

'Disturbing, though.'

'Tell me about it.' The previous evening, the night after it had occurred, Grant had found even the short walk from her car to the front door unexpectedly nerve-wracking. She'd realised she was repeatedly glancing behind her, peering down the street into the darkness, her eyes searching for any movement. She'd made sure the house was as secure as possible, but even so she'd slept uneasily, troubled by anxiety dreams that left her fearful she was not alone in the house. 'Just glad I won't have to head back there late tonight.'

'I wouldn't want you to. Glad of the company myself, to be honest. Makes a change from just having the kids there.'

They'd developed a routine, on these too infrequent nights out, that Helena Grant would leave her car at the office and stay over in Jacquie Green's spare room. It made sense. This way, they could have a few drinks without Grant having to incur the cost of a taxi back over to the Black Isle and deal with the further challenge of getting into work in the morning. When Jacquie Green's husband Craig had been around, Grant had occasionally worried that he resented her presence, though she hadn't usually seen much of him.

The question was academic now, anyway. Craig had unexpectedly walked out on Green some months before, having apparently been engaged in a long-term affair with some much younger colleague from work. Green had been shocked by the suddenness – not least, the fact that she'd been left as the sole carer for the three children – but had seemed far from devastated by her husband's departure. 'I knew fine well what he was up to,' she'd said to Grant at the time. 'If he hadn't gone, I would have done. She's welcome to him. Not that she'll want him for long.'

The last comment had proved prescient. The relationship had come to an end within weeks of Craig moving in with his new partner, and he'd turned up one evening on Jacquie Green's doorstep begging for another chance. She'd made it clear that any future contact would be through their lawyers.

'You've not thought about trying online dating?' Helena Grant said now.

'Good God, no,' Green said. 'It's bad enough coping with three kids. I don't want to be taking on a fourth. Not for a good while, anyway.' She was silent for a few minutes while the waiter delivered their starters. 'But I can understand you giving it a try. Your circumstances are a bit different.'

'I'm heading for a lonely old age, you mean?'

Green laughed. 'No, I don't mean that. I mean the opposite. That you're young enough to get back in the game. Assuming that's what you want.'

'I don't know what I want,' Grant said. 'That's the trouble. I just feel as if I'm in a rut. I need something new.'

'That's bloody January again, though, isn't it? The month when they start advertising the summer holidays and people put their houses on the market. Anyway, do you reckon you'll keep trying? Despite the charmers you've met to date.'

'I don't know. You keep thinking the next one will be the right one, but there's been no sign of it so far.'

'I suppose it's bound to take a while– What is it?'

Grant had been gazing blankly across the room as they talked, chewing absently on her calamari. Suddenly her expression had changed. 'That's him,' she said. 'That's the bastard. Delaney.'

'This is where you tell me not to turn round, isn't it?' Green said. 'Hang on.' She moved her hand abruptly, knocking her butter knife onto the floor of the restaurant. One of the waiters hurried over, anxious to replace the piece of cutlery. Green twisted in her chair, apparently to speak to the approaching waiter, but allowing her plenty of time to follow Helena Grant's gaze. 'I'm so sorry. I'm just clumsy tonight,' she said to the waiter. 'Don't worry. I've finished with it anyway.'

Grant said, 'You've done that before, haven't you?'

'When you've had an errant husband, there aren't many tricks you haven't tried. You're sure that's him? Your arsehole from the other night, I mean.'

'That's him all right. No question. I don't know if he's spotted me.'

'Seemed too intent on impressing his new lady friend, if you ask me.'

'Boring her to death, more like. She looks young enough to be his daughter. If not his granddaughter.'

'You're just jealous. Maybe it is his daughter.'

'If that's the way he looks at his daughter, someone should call the authorities.' Grant gave an instinctive shudder. 'He's a creep.'

'You reckon he's spotted you?'

Grant was conscious that, thankfully, their table was in relative shadow, and that the man's attention was fully focussed on the young woman sitting opposite him. 'Not yet, thank God. It's a pain, though. Just when I was beginning to relax.'

'Ignore him. Even if he sees you, so what? If he comes over here, we can both have the pleasure of telling him to bugger off.'

'True enough. And, if that woman's anything like me, she'll already be planning how to cut her losses and leave.'

Almost as if she'd overheard Grant's words, the young woman suddenly rose from the table, apparently pausing to offer the man some explanation. At first, Grant thought the woman was coming in their direction, but then realised she was heading towards the lavatories behind them.

'That's her,' Grant whispered after the woman had hurried past. 'Christ, she looked tense.'

'She certainly moved as if someone was coming after her,' Green said. 'You reckon she's going to climb out the window of the ladies?'

'If she is, she's left her coat on the back of her chair. Mind you, taking your coat to the lavvy would probably be too obvious a signal.' She paused, playing idly with her fork. 'She really did look anxious. You think I should go and see if she's all right?'

'I don't know. What's our friend doing now?'

'He's still sitting there. Doesn't look best pleased. Looks bloody livid, in fact.' Grant hesitated for a moment, then bent down to pick up her handbag. 'I'm going to check she's okay. Can you move over this side and keep an eye on chummy over there? If he does anything, just text me.'

Green nodded. 'I'm not sure what he's likely to do, though.'

'Me neither. I just have a bad feeling about him.'

Keeping her back to the room, Grant made her way across to the women's lavatory. She'd half-expected that the young woman would be in one of the cubicles, but instead she was standing in front of the washbasins, her mobile phone in hand. She still looked tense, her face ashen in the bright glare of the tiled room.

Grant moved as if to wash her hands, then said, 'Look, by all means just tell me to bugger off, but is everything okay?'

The young woman looked up, startled. 'Sorry?'

'It's just that when you came past our table out there, I thought you were looking – well, distressed. But, like I say, tell me to bugger off if it's none of my business.' Before the young woman could respond, she reached into her handbag and drew out her warrant card. 'DCI Helena Grant, for what it's worth. But I'm not on duty. Just wanted to check you were all right.'

'I–' The woman stopped and looked at the door behind her. 'No, I'm not okay, actually. I…' She tailed off again. 'Are you really a police officer?'

'I'm afraid so. But I'm here to help. If you need it.'

The woman hesitated, clearly thinking. 'Yes. If there's anything you can do.'

'Try me.'

'It was supposed to be a date. Well, something like that.'

'You and the man out there?'

'Yes, except it wasn't supposed to be him.' The woman shook her head. 'Sorry, I'm talking rubbish. Let me start again.'

'Take your time.'

'We got in contact through one of those dating app things. I've tried a few times and they were always disastrous. But this guy seemed more what I was looking for.'

'Seemed?'

'That's the thing. We hadn't met till tonight. We'd talked on the phone a few times, and spent a lot of time messaging each other. He said he lived up here, but worked in Edinburgh in the week and hadn't had a chance to come back up here for a few weeks.'

Grant raised her eyebrows. 'That was what he told you?'

'Yes. Then he called me a day or two back to say he was taking a few days off and was keen to meet me. He invited me for dinner at his house.' She finally gave a weak smile. 'I'm not always the brightest star in the sky, but I'm not that daft. Told him I'd meet him somewhere more public the first time. I was expecting just a bar, you know, but he suggested this place. Told me he was happy to pay.'

I bet he did, Grant thought. 'But he's not what you expected?'

'I knew he sounded too good to be true. He'd sent me a few photos which were supposed to be him. I was expecting him to be maybe a bit older, not quite all he claimed to be. I'd tried to be realistic.'

'But?'

'Well, Jesus, did you see him? He wasn't the guy in the photographs at all. He's old enough to be my granddad. Actually, I reckon he's older than my granddad. And I think everything he'd told me was bollocks.'

'Maybe you should have just walked out straightaway?'

'Yeah, looking back I should have done. But you know how it is. You don't want to make a scene in public. Then he started being all apologetic. Saying he knew he'd exaggerated a few things–' For the first time, she laughed. '*Exaggerated!* Lied through his bloody teeth. Which are probably false. Told me he knew I wouldn't have been interested if he'd just told the truth. Said all he was looking for was a bit of company. An evening out. In the end I just thought I'd go along with it. Enjoy a nice meal. Make it bloody clear to him that he wasn't getting anything else. I thought if he starts anything, I can always just pay my share and leave.'

Grant could imagine the conversation. With her, Delaney had been boorish and pompous, eager to demonstrate his social superiority. But she could imagine that, with someone much younger and more vulnerable, he could turn on the charm, coax her into believing and doing what he wanted. It was a form of grooming, and sexual predators tended to be skilled at it. 'So what happened?'

'At first, it was just boring. Him going on and on about his job. Some bloody finance thing. And how he knew all about the hospitality industry, and why this restaurant was doing it all wrong. All that bollocks. I didn't mind too much because I didn't have to make much of an effort. I just nodded politely and tuned most of it out.' She swallowed. She was clearly calmer now, but Grant could still read the anxiety in her eyes. 'But then it sort of changed. He started to ask about me. What I did, where I worked. Where I lived. Whether I lived on my own. I thought he was just being polite, and at least it made a change from listening to him talk about himself. Then I realised he was pumping me for information. Working out that I was going home on foot and that I lived on my own. He started to get pushier, said he wanted to walk me home, make sure I was okay. Maybe come in for a coffee.'

'Maybe he's just a gentleman.'

The young woman snorted. 'That's the thing. He was already giving me the creeps. But it started to feel really nasty. There was just something about him. I began to think that, even if I just got up and walked out, he'd follow me and then I wouldn't be able to get rid of him and – well, he scared me.'

Grant thought back to her own encounter with Delaney, and to the threatening texts. 'You're sure you weren't overreacting?'

'Don't you believe me?' The woman suddenly sounded even younger than she looked.

'I do believe you. I've come across Delaney before.'

'Delaney? Who's Delaney?'

'What name did he give you?'

The woman blinked. 'Gary Ellis. Isn't that his name?'

'I don't know,' Grant said. 'I've come across him as Martin Delaney.'

'But–'

'You already knew he was a lying scumbag. This just shows he was even more of a lying scumbag than you thought. Sounds like you were right to be worried. What were you planning to do?'

'I hadn't really thought it through when I came in here. I just wanted to get away from him. Then I thought I'd start phoning round my mates and see if I could get someone to come and meet me. I'd tried a couple of people when you came in, but no luck.'

Grant was about to respond when her phone buzzed in her bag. She picked it up and glanced at the screen. A text from Jacquie Green. 'He's buggered off.'

She showed the text to the young woman, then texted back. 'Safe to come out?'

There was a pause before the response came. 'Looks like it. All hell breaking loose.'

'Looks like we'd better get out there. What's your name, by the way? It might be helpful if we appear to know each other already.'

'Maggie. Maggie Clennan.'

'Okay, Maggie Clennan. Let's go and find out what's going on out there.'

Grant led the way back into the restaurant, to be greeted by the sight of an anxious-looking waitress hurrying in their direction. As she saw Clennan emerging from the lavatories, she stopped, her expression changing to one of mild relief.

Grant led Maggie Clennan back to the table where Jacquie Green was watching in some amusement. The waitress arrived a moment later, clearly now unsure how to handle the matter.

Grant gave the waitress her best official smile. 'Can we get another place set for our friend here? She's decided to join us.'

The waitress opened and then closed her mouth. 'I– We thought you'd done a runner.'

'Obviously, our friend here has done no such thing. I can't speak for her companion.'

The waitress looked back towards the bar, clearly wanting the manager to come and bail her out. 'He just put his coat on and left without paying.' She looked at Clennan. 'Then we realised that you'd gone too, so we thought–'

'My coat's still there,' Clennan pointed out.

'That's one of the tricks they use. Cheap coat from a charity shop. Leave it on the back of the chair while they go out for a smoke or whatever. So we don't realise till it's too late. We've had all of them.'

'I'm sure. But, as you can see, that's not the case here,' Grant said. 'Although I'm afraid that the gentleman may well have been – well, let's say less than chivalrous. We'll cover the cost of his meal.' She glanced back at Jacquie Green. 'And in the meantime, I think we'd be grateful for another bottle of wine and the dessert menu.'

11

'Are you a police officer too?' Maggie Clennan was still looking bewildered at the company she had found herself in.

Jacquie Green shook her head. 'I'm a forensic pathologist.'

'A–?'

'I cut up dead bodies. Yes, I know. Someone's got to do it.'

'Jacquie works with me sometimes,' Helena Grant explained. 'Does post-mortems on unexplained deaths, that kind of thing.'

Clennan looked as if she had entered some kind of alternative universe. 'Bloody hell.'

'Exactly. So what do you do, Maggie?'

'I work in a call centre.' She laughed. 'God, I feel embarrassed even saying that.'

Grant shrugged. 'You're young. At your age, I was stuck in some dead-end admin job. There's plenty of time.' She turned back to Green. 'So what happened with our friend over there?'

'Just what the waitress said.' She paused. 'I've a feeling he might have clocked you when you went into the ladies. He was too far away for me to see clearly, but there was some kind of reaction. I think he recognised you. He was up straightaway, grabbed his coat and was out of the door. I could see the waiting staff had noticed and were debating what to do. That poor waitress got the job of going to check whether Maggie had somehow done a runner through the rear door.'

'If I'd known there was a rear door, I would have done.' Clennan looked at Helena Grant and reddened. 'To get away from him, I mean, not to avoid paying.'

'We know what you mean.' Grant waited while the waitress delivered the requested wine and menus. 'Interesting that that was his reaction, though. If he did recognise me. Suggests he might really have something to hide.' She turned to Clennan. 'If it makes you feel better, you're not the only one he's tried it on with. The reason I recognised him was that I'd been on a date with him too.'

Clennan opened her mouth to give some response, then clearly thought better of it.

Grant laughed. 'Don't say it. I'm guessing you and I didn't use the same kind of website, so he's obviously spreading his attentions very widely. Which again makes me wonder what his game is. Not just looking for companionship.'

'Whatever his game is, he's a lying bastard,' Green said.

'I'm beginning to think he's more than that,' Grant said. 'I'm wondering now why he clammed up so completely when he discovered I was a police officer. At the time, I thought it was just the usual misogyny. But maybe there was more to it.'

'Maybe he's a scam artist,' Green said. 'Otherwise, why use false names? You wouldn't need to do that if you were just trying to lure some unsuspecting women into bed.'

'You might, if you didn't want them to be able to track you down afterwards,' Grant said. 'Maggie, did he make any efforts to extract money from you? Anything like that.'

'Other than doing a runner from here, you mean?' Clennan seemed to have perked up considerably. 'No, he didn't try anything.'

'Doesn't mean he wouldn't have,' Green pointed out. 'If he'd managed to worm his way into either of your affections. Not everyone's as fussy or smart as you two.'

Grant nodded. 'I reckon I might get someone to do a bit of digging, assuming we can identify who he really is. Maggie, can you send me any info you might have on him? Any emails, user details on the site you used, anything like that.' She slid one of her business cards across the table to the younger woman. 'Just email me anything you've got. It may well be that the dating sites are just dead ends if he's used false details, but worth a shot. Did he tell you anything else about his work or where he claimed to be living?'

'Not really,' Clennan said. 'Reckoned he had a house in Inverness somewhere. Implied it was somewhere fairly central, but he never gave me the address or told me where it was. Said he rented a flat in Edinburgh during the week but again never gave me the address. I've an email address and a mobile number for him, but that's all.'

'Same for me,' Grant said. 'Be interesting to see if they match. But I'm willing to bet they won't get us very far, anyway. What about work?'

'Like I said, some finance job in what he called the hospitality industry. Assume that's a fancy way of saying restaurants.'

'Restaurants, café, hotels, all that stuff. He told me he was finance director of a hotel chain, so that's not too far away from what he told you. Maybe that bit is true, or at least a version of the truth. Might be a line to follow up.' Grant took a mouthful of wine. 'He never mentioned Edinburgh to me, though. Gave me the impression he lived and worked up here somewhere.'

'He's sounding like a tricky man to pin down,' Green said.

'He is, isn't he? I'm not sure I can justify a serious investigation, given what little we have on him. He may be a nasty piece of work, but we've no evidence of any actual wrongdoing. Not criminal wrongdoing, anyway. But he feels like the kind of character who's likely to prey on the vulnerable, whether it's for sex or for money. I'd say it merits taking further.'

'You should put Alec onto it,' Green said. 'He's got a nose for unpleasant bastards.'

'I might just do that,' Grant said. 'He could do with a treat.' She picked up the dessert menu. 'Speaking of which, let's at least end the evening on a high. Even if it's only a sugar one.'

'How is she?' McKay was in the kitchen, going systematically through his morning routine. This largely consisted of emptying the dishwasher while the kettle was boiling for his black coffee.

Chrissie had been upstairs to check on Fiona. 'Sound asleep still, fortunately. Those pills she got from the doctor seem to do the trick up to a point, but I heard her prowling around in the night again. She's still all wound up. She still can't believe it. Doesn't know how to come to terms with it. You know.'

'I know.' McKay also knew they were both thinking the same thoughts. About the way they'd both reacted to the news of Lizzie's death. The same sense of confusion, disbelief. 'How were the police yesterday? Didn't want to ask too much last night while Fiona was around. Hope they behaved better than Charlie Farrow.'

'You ever thought about trying not to get up people's noses, Alec?'

'It's a thought. I'll give it a try sometime.'

'You do that. No, they were fine. Just a couple of PCs. A bit wet behind the ears but they handled Fiona with kid gloves so I was grateful for that. The woman did most of the questioning and it was very gentle.'

'Did they ask about Kevin's state of mind?'

'A bit. I don't think there was much Fiona could tell them, to be honest. She just thinks he hadn't been himself for the last few weeks. A bit down and anxious. Nothing more than that, really.'

'Farrow'll make a meal of it, like he always does. But I can't see them concluding anything but that it was an accident. There's no substantive evidence to support any other decision.'

'I hope you're right. I don't want to see Fiona suffer any more than she has to. As it is, she'll be blaming herself.'

McKay finished making his coffee and walked over to the kitchen window. 'I hate this time of the year. Dark when I leave for work. Dark when I get back. Bloody miserable even at the best of times. Even without all this.'

'I know.' She had moved to stand behind him. Then, unexpectedly, she wrapped her arms around his body, pressing herself against him. He couldn't recall the last time she'd displayed that kind of spontaneous affection. 'We're going to be all right now, Alec, aren't we? You and me, I mean.'

He turned to face her, moving in her arms. 'Of course we are. Whatever shite the world might throw at us.'

'You old romantic, Alec McKay. You'd better be getting off to work.'

'Before you drag me upstairs, you mean?'

She released her grip and allowed him to retrieve his mug of coffee. 'In your dreams, Alec McKay. I need you out there earning.'

'Story of my life.' But they were both smiling, and it was the most light-hearted conversation he could recall since they'd got back together. It might be the arse-end of the year, he reminded himself, but things were moving in the right direction.

HELENA GRANT ROLLED over in the single bed and reached out for her mobile on the bedside table.

She'd somehow managed to sleep through the alarm she'd set. Only by a few minutes, thankfully. The loud buzzing had clearly been sufficient to penetrate her sleep without fully dragging her into consciousness. She sat up, rubbing her eyes.

She'd slept well enough, but she still felt mildly knackered. The outcome of the previous evening had been that they'd finished the second bottle of wine in the restaurant, then moved on, with Maggie Clennan still in tow, to a bar in Church Street where they'd had at least one more glass each. Thinking back, Grant couldn't be absolutely certain it wasn't more than that.

Too much for a weeknight, anyway. It had partly just been an attempt to give Maggie Clennan some reassurance, to remind her there were better people in the world than Delaney or whatever the hell his name really was. Clennan had clearly been disturbed by her encounter, and she didn't strike Grant as the kind who would normally be too fazed by some standard-issue lecherous old creep. Grant herself had dealt with some fully-fledged scumbags in her working life, but Delaney had still made her feel uncomfortable. Somewhere below that lying, pompous, self-obsessed exterior, there was something even more disturbing.

She pulled on her dressing gown and stepped out onto the landing. The bathroom was free, and she could hear the sound of a radio and chattering children downstairs. There was a scent of burnt toast. It all felt reassuringly normal.

Maggie Clennan lived in a rented flat just outside the city centre. It had been in the opposite direction from Jacquie Green's place – not that they'd told Clennan that – but the two older women had insisted on accompanying Clennan back there. 'That old bastard will have buggered off with his tail between his legs hours ago,' Grant had said. 'But it's not that far and we just want to see you home safe. We can get a taxi to do the round trip.' She'd wondered about putting Clennan in a taxi on her own, but she knew she'd feel much happier if she'd seen the young woman right to her front door.

They'd asked the taxi driver to wait until Clennan was safely inside, and Grant had felt more relaxed when she saw the lights coming on inside the house as the taxi pulled away.

'You really are a bit spooked, aren't you?' Jacquie Green had said.

'Is it that obvious? Aye, I am a bit. When I got back last night, I felt like someone was watching me. I didn't want Maggie to have to go through that.'

She'd told herself she'd just been understandably disturbed by the texts. But she wondered now whether, at least subconsciously, it had had more to do with Delaney himself. She'd initially downplayed the discomfort she'd felt in his presence, but she was genuinely disturbed now that he might have been watching her outside her home. After last night, it felt both possible and horrifying.

She showered and dressed, then, having packed her overnight bag and grabbed her phone and charger from the bedside table, hurried downstairs. Green and the children were gathered in the kitchen. She was standing by the sink sipping a mug of coffee. The children were at the table, managing to eat cereals noisily. Radio 3 was playing gently in the background, Green's usual ineffectual attempt to calm the morning atmosphere.

'I see you've had a lie-in.' Green smiled. 'I was just thinking I might have to come and wake you.'

'Sorry. Managed to sleep through the alarm. Only just, but not like me.'

'Stressful night. Coffee?'

'Can you serve it intravenously?'

'Help yourself to cereal and toast, if you want.'

'Coffee's fine. I'm not really awake yet.'

She sat at the table and chatted with Chloe, the eldest of Jacquie Green's three children. The other two were largely still absorbed in their own worlds, but Chloe was reaching the age where she had some interest in what a grown-up might have to say. It didn't take a lot to get her talking animatedly about what she was doing at school, or whatever the latest craze was among girls of her age. Grant thought she'd been similar at that age, full of unshaped enthusiasm she was eager to share. The enthusiasm had undoubtedly waned over the subsequent decades but she hoped it hadn't disappeared completely.

Jacquie Green sat down next to them and slid a mug of hot coffee over to Grant. 'There you go, the cup that cheers. Right, you lot, time to finish getting dressed. Hurry up!'

After the children had disappeared upstairs in their usual flurry of noise and energy, the kitchen felt unexpectedly calm. 'Morning meltdown phase one completed,' Green said. 'Now a brief respite before phase two.'

'I don't know how you do it.'

'Neither do I, sometimes. But I'm used to it. Even when Craig was around, he made sure he buggered off to work early so I was left with the kids. So it's not as if it's any harder now.'

'Sorry last night was a bit more fraught than expected.'

'No worries. It wasn't your fault. Anyway, Maggie seemed a decent enough kid. Hope she wasn't too traumatised.'

'By Delaney or us?' Grant smiled. 'She seemed pretty resilient to me. I imagine she'll pull through.'

As she spoke, her phone buzzed in the top of her handbag. She picked up the phone and glanced at the screen. The second of two texts received in the last twenty minutes. Presumably the first had arrived while she'd been in the shower.

A number that wasn't in her address book and which she didn't recognise. The first said simply, 'Bitch.' The second, sent some ten minutes later, added, 'I'm watching you.'

She held up the screen so that Green could read what had been sent.

'Is that the same number as before?'

'I don't think so.' Grant scrolled back through her texts. 'No, different.'

'Doesn't mean it's a different person, though.'

'Given we know Delaney's using multiple names, it wouldn't be a surprise if he made a point of changing his phone number too.'

'You think it's him?'

'Who knows? But it's a coincidence, isn't it? A second text, the morning after I run into him again.'

'You can't ignore it now. And last night gave you a reason to start delving into the mysterious Mr Delaney.'

'I can't just go off on a frolic of my own. If there is anything in this, I need to play it as much by the book as I can. Like I said, I've reported it, but don't imagine it's going to be high on anyone's agenda. I need to find a way to expedite it.'

Green took a sip of her coffee, then gazed quizzically at Grant. 'You sound like a woman with a plan.'

'Not really. But in a matter like this, I've got one big asset I can draw on.'

'Which is.'

'The pain in the arse's pain in the arse. Alec McKay.'

13

M cKay was on the prowl, making his way systematically around her office, peering into books and papers as if conducting some form of inspection. This was his familiar way of displaying restlessness, with the usual undertone of mild disapproval, as if his state of mind was somehow Grant's responsibility.

Finally, he stopped and looked back at her. 'So definitely unlawful killing?'

'That's what Jacquie said. We should have the formal report later today.'

'Asphyxiation.' He spoke the word with relish, as if perhaps it was the title of a poem he was about to declaim. 'Suffocation.'

'That's what she said. We'll have to have another look at the scene and see what the examiners' view is, but looks like the pillow on the bed is the likely tool of choice.'

'She reckoned it had happened there? That the body hadn't been dragged from somewhere else?'

'We didn't go into a lot of detail. This was over dinner, you understand. But that was my understanding.'

'Funny old place to murder someone,' McKay said. 'I mean, it's very public. Even on a January Sunday afternoon, there's a fairly high risk of someone walking in. It can't have happened long before we got there.'

'Presumably not. Which suggests it probably wasn't premeditated.'

'I'm guessing not. But still hard to envisage how it might have happened.'

'May be easier once we know a bit more. Jacquie didn't say if there were any traces of drugs or alcohol in the body, so that might be one explanation. People aren't always in the best condition to be aware of their surroundings.'

'I rarely am.' McKay at last condescended to lower himself onto the chair opposite her. 'You still think I shouldn't be involved in the enquiry?'

'Not till we've got a decision on your brother-in-law, no. Thought you were happy with that.'

'I am. In principle. I mean, you're obviously right. It's just I know Charlie bloody Farrow's going to drag his heels and keep me in limbo as long as possible.'

'You're not telling me you've managed to get up Farrow's nose as well, Alec?'

'Ach, I've been firmly wedged up Farrow's nose for most of our respective careers. We've never exactly been soulmates, if you get my drift.'

'The thing is,' Grant said, 'I had a thought about that. Though I'm not sure you're going to like it.'

'It makes me nervous when you say things like that,' McKay said. 'That's supposed to be my role in our professional relationship.'

'Farrow's been whingeing for months about being short of resources. I was just wondering whether to offer him a temporary attachment from my team.'

McKay's eyes widened. 'Me? Jesus, Helena, I never thought

you hated me, despite everything I've put you through over the years.'

'I've come close a few times. But, look, you want to keep an eye on Farrow and stop him buggering you about with regard to your brother-in-law. And, as it happens, Farrow's also in charge of an investigation that's dear to my own heart.'

'Which investigation?' McKay stopped. 'Your threatening texts?'

'Exactly. I reported it to standards, just to make sure my own backside was covered. But the investigation into the texts themselves has landed on Farrow's desk. Not that I'm expecting him to give it any priority.'

'Farrow just chases glory. The impossible task of trying to track down an anonymous texter won't be high on his to-do list.'

'I don't entirely blame him for that,' Grant said. 'But there have been some further developments.' She told McKay about the events of the previous night and that morning. 'Trouble is, apart from getting a second text, there's nothing really substantive there. I'll update standards and Farrow, but I don't think it'll increase Farrow's eagerness to progress it.'

'Except now, there is at least a circumstantial reason to link this Delaney to the texts.'

'Maybe. But we both know Farrow. That won't count for much.'

'So what are you suggesting?'

'That I offer you to Farrow on a short attachment on condition he allocates my case to you. That means I can ensure that something gets done sometime this century, and you're able to keep an eye on what Farrow's up to. You wouldn't be involved in the enquiry into your brother-in-law's death, so there'd been no risk of compromise.'

'Why would Farrow take me? Like I say, we disbanded our mutual admiration society a good few years ago.'

'He's been complaining about being short staffed for so long and so loudly, he'll look pretty bloody stupid if he turns the offer down.'

'It wouldn't be the first time for that. Him looking pretty bloody stupid, I mean.'

'That's not the point. The point is that if he spurns my generous offer, he'll get short shrift if he tries to cadge extra resources from anywhere else. Even Farrow's not that dim.'

'If you say so. Okay, what about the question of using me to investigate your case? Doesn't that risk compromise?'

'I don't see why. We're not related. Our relationship is purely professional. You'd be reporting to Farrow, not me.'

McKay nodded slowly, clearly trying to think of some good reason why Grant's idea wouldn't work. 'If Farrow's got me as a free resource because you can't currently use me on this major enquiry, what's his incentive to complete the investigation into Kevin's death quickly? He'll be only too delighted to keep me hanging on while he gets his pound of free flesh.'

'You reckon so, do you, Alec? You don't reckon that, after a few days of working alongside you, he'll be desperate to offload you as quickly as he possibly can?'

'Aye, I'm told I can sometimes have that effect on people. Especially if I put my mind to it.'

'Trust me, Alec, you can. You don't even have to try that hard.' She could tell he'd reached the limits of his potential excuses. 'So what do you say?'

He shook his head. 'You're a smooth-talking bastard, Grant. It's against all my better judgement, but I'm not sure you've left me with any option but to say yes. Just remember you owe me one.'

14

It was the young one. The one who seemed to have too many teeth crammed into his mean-looking mouth. The one whose face was ravaged by the after-effects of severe acne. The one who was always chewing gum.

'Are you happy with us, Jana? Are you happy to be here?'

Why are you asking this, she thought. *You know the answer only too well.* But his tone had been mocking, and she wondered whether he realised how well she understood English. Quite possibly, he taunted all the women like this, knowing full well that they could understand only a fraction, if anything, of what he was saying.

'I happy.' She tried hard not to reveal how well she under-stood and spoke their language. She wasn't fluent, but she could hold a conversation and she could understand most of what they were saying. She had decided early on that it would be to her advantage if they weren't aware of that. She had occasionally been able to pick up snippets of useful information from over-hearing their conversations, even if they tended to be relatively discreet in the women's presence.

She had nearly slipped up when the fat man had addressed

her the previous evening. This one would probably have noticed, registered the significance of her being able to understand and respond to his question. The fat man had been too self-obsessed to register more than a moment's unease.

'You're one of the lucky ones,' the young man continued. 'Wonder if you even realise that? We're the good guys. Well, better than some, anyway.'

She had her back to him, scrubbing away at the wash basin in the room's en-suite bathroom. She turned to him, her face blank, her expression feigning incomprehension. 'Sir?'

He was leaning against the bathroom door, watching her as she worked. 'You don't understand at all, Jana? You haven't a clue what I'm talking about.'

'Sir?'

'You just clean, Jana. Clean.' He pointed to the basin and mimed her scrubbing actions. 'Ignore me.'

She blinked, trying to look confused, then turned back to her work. She was conscious the young one was still standing close behind her. She wanted to show him she did a good job, that she cleaned the rooms thoroughly, though she wasn't sure if he cared.

'You're not a bad looking woman, you know that, Jana? Pretty fit for your age, I'd say. Bit old for me, though you never know your luck.' He laughed in a manner than seemed devoid of any humour.

They were all like this. Their individual motives were different, of course. The fat one, and maybe a couple of the others, were genuinely lustful, even for an older woman like Jana. The others just wanted to demonstrate that the women were their property. Mostly, they did nothing bad, but they wanted you to know that, if they wished, they could do anything.

And sometimes, she thought, they did do bad things.

She had no real evidence of that. But there were stories the women whispered to each other, recounted in the languages the men couldn't follow. Stories about the women, sometimes little more than girls, who had gone missing. The ones who, one morning, had simply not been there. The ones who were never mentioned.

She had witnessed one instance of this herself, a month or two previously. A woman, much younger than herself, who had already been here when Jana arrived. She and the woman had had no language in common, and had done little more than acknowledge each other's presence. Jana had thought the young woman pretty, and had been distressed to see how the hard work and conditions here were gradually wearing away at that youthful bloom. She had wanted to find some way to talk to her, find out how she had come here, what life she had been fleeing.

But it had never happened. One day, Jana had noticed the young woman was no longer around. At first, Jana had optimistically thought the young woman might have somehow succeeded in getting away from this place. Perhaps she had somehow managed to make her escape, found her way back into the world out there.

But then Jana had realised that, if the woman had absconded, the men would have made more fuss. Even if they had not wanted the other women to realise what had happened, they would have panicked among themselves. There would have been blame, recriminations. She had seen enough of the men's behaviour to know that, whenever anything went wrong, however trivial, there was always an argument.

But that time there was nothing. No sense anything was amiss.

Jana had tried asking one or two of the other women what might have happened, but no one had wanted to talk about it. Some had mentioned bad luck and turned away from her. Others had simply ignored her questions. Whatever had happened to the young woman, Jana knew that it was nothing good.

'I wonder what's going to happen to you, Jana?' the young one said from behind her, almost voicing the thought in her own head. 'You're a fine woman but you're getting on a bit, aren't you? You can't stay here for ever.'

She could sense he had moved even closer to her, crowding the tiny bathroom. She had finished cleaning the basin, so she turned to face him. He was standing only a few centimetres from her, and she could smell his sour breath.

'Do shower,' she said, gesturing with the damp cloth in her hand.

He took a step back. 'You're doing a good job, Jana. You're a hard worker. Not that any of us really gives a fuck.' He gave another mirthless laugh. 'I wonder what will happen to you, Jana. When you're no longer any use to us.'

She had wondered that herself sometimes. She had never slept well here, uncomfortable on the hard mattress, struggling to keep warm under the thin blankets, the only heat coming from the presence of the other women in the room. Often, she found herself lying awake for hours in the thick darkness, unable to move for fear of disturbing her roommates. This was the kind of thought that crowded into her brain. *What will happen next? What comes after this?*

She tried to envisage life somehow becoming better, but she couldn't conceive how that might happen. She could only imagine it getting worse in some ill-defined and unknown way.

She told herself that, really, she was still young. Older than many of the women here, but not the oldest. She had plenty of work left in her. Plenty more years of doing this.

But eventually that would come to an end. Either because she was incapable of doing it or, much more likely and much sooner, because the men no longer needed or wanted her here. That could happen at any time, and what would follow that?

As if responding to her thoughts, the young one said, 'We'll find some way of dealing with you, Jana. When that moment comes. We'll take care of you.'

Take care. She knew that phrase in English. She knew what it meant, and she knew it was ambiguous. *We'll take care of you. We'll look after you.* She was on her knees, scrubbing at the shower, and didn't look up at him. He was just talking at her, she assured herself. Just amusing himself by pretending to chat with her, even though he thought she wouldn't understand what he was saying. Or, more likely, she thought, he assumed she would recognise the gently threatening tone, without even knowing what she was being threatened with.

The truth was that she didn't. Even though she could understand most of the words, she had no idea about their implications. She didn't understand this place. She couldn't fathom how it really worked or what they really wanted from her and the other women.

They worked them hard, of course. And they gave them nothing but the most basic subsistence. Jana had been threatened with violence or worse by the men, although for her, so far, there had been nothing more than threats. She knew it could be worse. No one ever spoke of it, but she knew that some of the women had been assaulted here, physically, sexually or often both. She didn't know which of the men were responsible, but she imagined they were all capable of it. Perhaps, despite her age, her turn would come.

She glanced up uneasily, trying not to catch the young one's eye. He had retreated from the bathroom, and was wandering round the bedroom, peering into the wardrobe and dressing table drawers, as if hoping that last night's guests might have left something of value.

'You get on with your work, Jana,' he called. 'Do a good thorough job. You'll get your reward in heaven.' That same humourless laugh.

I know I won't get it here, she thought. *But I don't know what I will get. It just feels like a holding pen. A battery farm where they work you every waking hour and give you just enough to survive. While they wait to move you on.*

Like cattle to slaughter.

The thought had entered her mind unbidden, and she had no idea where it had come from. It was an image she had never thought of before, but suddenly it seemed right.

Cattle to slaughter.

She dipped her head down into the shower, not looking back at the young one, and continued to scrub, scrub, scrub.

15

'How are we doing on IDing the body?' Helena Grant asked.

'Not brilliantly,' Ginny Horton said. 'Or, more accurately, not at all.'

'You wouldn't believe it was possible for someone to remain anonymous in this day and age, would you?' Grant shook her head. 'I know we'll get there eventually, but aren't we all supposed to be tracked and trailed wherever we go these days?'

'Never quite seems to work like that for us,' Horton agreed. 'Not when it really matters, anyway. He had no ID on him. No mobile phone. His clothes are either mass-produced chain store stuff or charity shop purchases. He's got no tattoos or other identifying characteristics. There's no trace of his fingerprints or DNA on our records–'

'I get the picture. What about the cameras?'

'We've checked the CCTV from the fort. No sign of him on the Sunday afternoon. There're a fair number of cameras, so either we've just been unlucky or he was deliberately avoiding them.'

'And had the knowledge and skills to do so? I suppose it's possible,' Grant said, doubtfully.

'Anything's possible till we know who he is. We've checked the car park CCTV, but no sign of him arriving by car and no sign of him arriving at the entrance on foot either.'

'He must have got there somehow.'

'You'd think. We've been looking at the reg numbers captured by the ANPR cameras on the A96, but even on a Sunday afternoon in January there was a hell of a lot of traffic. And the positioning of the camera doesn't help us in terms of who might have turned off to the fort.'

'Great.'

'We've got the numbers of all the cars the CCTV caught on Sunday,' Horton said, 'and we're working through those. We're also checking the buses. There is a bus service up there on Sunday, though there aren't many buses, so we may get something from CCTV or even the driver's memory.'

'Not that the driver's memory will tell us much, other than maybe where he got on.'

'I'm trying to be optimistic. Every little helps.'

Grant smiled. 'Aye, I know. It's just frustrating not even to be at first base.' She slid a set of stapled papers across the desk. 'At least we've got Jacquie Green's report. It's on the system but I've printed off a hard copy for you.'

'Anything useful?'

'Only if every little helps,' Grant said. 'Confirms the likelihood of an unlawful killing. Confirms cause of death as asphyxiation, most likely caused by something being pressed across the victim's face. No evidence of alcohol or drugs in the bloodstream at the time of death. Looks like the victim had eaten breakfast that morning, but I'm guessing you don't want the details of that just now.'

'Not really. So, in summary, not much?'

'Not that you'd notice, no. If the victim wasn't under the influence, it does raise the question of how he was killed. Examiners reckon there was no obvious sign of any struggle, so must have been taken by surprise.'

'Not easy to suffocate someone by surprise, I'd have thought.'

'Would require some distraction, I imagine. And maybe some strength. Though our victim wasn't exactly the muscular type.'

Horton was consulting her notes. 'We're trying to interview everyone who was on site on Sunday afternoon. Just on the off-chance someone might have seen our victim at some point. That's a fair number – soldiers, some civilian staff and so on – so it'll take a while. No idea if it'll tell us anything useful.'

'Only if they spotted our man with someone else, I'm guessing,' Grant said. 'Which is always possible. It's not as if the place was heaving with visitors on Sunday.'

'We've been trawling through the mispers too, but there's no one local who matches the description. Of course, he may not have been missed yet, or at least not sufficiently for anyone to report it to us. Beyond that, I'm not sure what else we can do.'

'I'm talking to comms. If we don't have any luck with the identity by tomorrow, we'll organise an appeal for anyone who knows him. We've given basic details in the media reports so far, but if we go out with something more detailed we might strike lucky.'

'Like you say, we'll pin him down eventually, one way or another. It's just that, with every day that passes, we risk losing intelligence.'

'What about a mobile?' Grant said. 'It's unusual not to carry one these days. Any chance it was dropped somewhere?'

Horton shrugged. 'My guess is it was removed by the killer, along with whatever ID he might have had. In which case, it could be anywhere. Or nowhere. We've searched the vicinity of the building, and we'll look to widening the search but I'm not hopeful.'

'I know. I'm clutching at straws. Let's hope something turns up, eh?'

'It usually does. Mostly when you least expect it.' Horton shuffled together her notes, preparing to end the meeting. 'I hear we're to be deprived of Alec's company for a while?'

'Only briefly, I'm hoping. Just till we have a view on his brother-in-law's death.'

'If he's working with Charlie Farrow, I can't imagine it's going to last long. One of the many people that Alec's never quite managed to rub along with.'

'Not exactly an exclusive club.'

'Most people aren't as tolerant as we are. I wouldn't mind being a fly on the wall in their meetings, though.'

Grant nodded, a mildly weary expression on her face. 'Oh, aye. I'd pay good money to sit in on any of those, right enough.'

16

'You planning on joining us any time soon, Alec, or is this some kind of hiking holiday?'

McKay had been prowling aimlessly round the room in his usual style, and had now stopped to peer earnestly at Charlie Farrow's bookshelf. 'You got any Barbara Cartland, Charlie? I hear she's very good.'

Farrow had clearly already made a decision to ignore any of McKay's jibes. 'We don't have all day, Alec. Some of us have work to be getting on with.'

McKay nodded. 'Need to fit something in before you go golfing,' he said. 'I understand.' He crossed the room and lowered himself onto one of the chairs opposite Farrow's desk. Farrow had a reputation, at least in summer, for slipping away early on Wednesday afternoons to fit in a round of golf. McKay assumed that wasn't the case at this time of year, but he'd never been one to let the facts stand in the way of a half-decent riposte.

'So, gentlemen,' Farrow said patiently, 'first of all, let's welcome our good friend Alec McKay, who's apparently here for a week or two to help us out.' The last three words were spoken as if in quotation marks. 'That right, Alec?'

'Just an additional pair of hands,' McKay said, 'and a brain.' McKay managed to make it sound as if the latter hadn't previously been available in Farrow's team. To his right, one of Farrow's team, DS Johnny Dolan, uttered something that sounded like a cross between a cough and a snigger. McKay knew that even Farrow's own team didn't have the greatest of respect for their boss. From what he knew of them, they were a decent enough bunch – all male, because that was invariably the way with Farrow's teams – but capable enough. It had already occurred to McKay that, if he played his cards carefully, he could recruit one or two allies during his time here.

Dolan was a burly man, probably in his mid-forties. He wasn't someone you'd look to for an unexpected insight or a brilliant analysis, but, from what McKay had seen, he was sound enough. The sort of copper who'd do what he was told and not much more, but who could be relied on to do it pretty well.

The second officer present was DS Benny Edwards. He was younger than Dolan, probably only late twenties. He seemed bright and enthusiastic, a youngish graduate keen to make a name for himself. He probably wouldn't put a foot out of line, but would come up with some good ideas when you needed them.

McKay didn't have a lot of time for Farrow's management abilities, but he knew Farrow was adept at recruiting officers who could make him look good. These two, along with the other team members McKay had met, had very different qualities, but would both do a decent job when needed. Farrow could just sit back and wait for them to do it.

'So, Alec, I just thought we'd have a little informal briefing. Just bring you up to speed with what we're up to, and see where we can most effectively deploy your talents. I should say it was good of Helena to spare you. Man of your undoubted talents ought to be in high demand.'

McKay assumed Farrow was implying, for the benefit of the others, that Grant had been trying to offload him. 'Just thought you might benefit from my experience, Charlie. She gives to charity as well.'

Farrow gazed at him for a moment with an expression most other men would have found intimidating. 'Let's move on, shall we?'

'I'm all ears.'

Having spoken those words, McKay largely tuned out for the rest of the discussion, paying attention only when something caught his interest or Farrow inadvertently offered some titbit McKay thought might provide useful ammunition later.

'The main thing, Alec,' Farrow said, in a tone that suggested he might finally be drawing the meeting towards a conclusion, 'is we need to ensure we have a proper Chinese wall between you and the investigation into your brother-in-law's death.'

McKay nodded. 'Of course. But you'll be done with that pretty soon?'

There was an unexpectedly long pause before Farrow responded. 'I wouldn't necessarily assume that.'

'We're just taking a bit of a look at his background,' Dolan added.

It was immediately clear Dolan had spoken out of turn. Farrow shot him a sharp look and said, 'Chinese wall, Johnny. Don't want to put Alec in an awkward position.'

Dolan nodded but offered no other response. McKay wondered whether to pursue the issue, but decided he was unlikely to extract much more from Farrow. 'That's fine. I can't imagine there'll be anything in Kevin's background to detain you for long. But who knows?'

'People are full of surprises, Alec.' Farrow shuffled his papers. 'So, plenty for you to be getting on with, I hope.' As McKay had expected, Farrow had pushed plenty of administration in his direction, along with allowing him to take charge of the enquiry into Helena Grant's threatening texts. McKay's own intended strategy was to take that enquiry as far as he could – which in truth might not be very far, given the limited resources available to him – and carry out as little of the administration as he could get away with. It was going to be a lively few weeks. 'Aye, you seem to have got me nicely loaded with work.'

'Idle hands and all that, Alec.'

The meeting broke up and McKay returned to his desk, leaving Farrow and Dolan deep in conversation. Dolan was no doubt getting a bollocking for what he'd said about Kevin.

McKay was still mulling that over. He knew little about Kevin's background, other than that he was originally from over on the Black Isle. He'd been born and brought up in Cromarty, as far as McKay knew, though by the time he'd married Fiona he was living and working in Inverness. Other than that, and the fact that he was some kind of IT specialist, McKay had really known little about him and had always imagined there was unlikely to be much else worth knowing.

Now, for the first time, it occurred to him to wonder if it was strange that he knew so little about Kevin's past or even his present. Kevin had never been the most talkative of individuals, and McKay hadn't been sufficiently interested to encourage him to reveal more. But it felt odd to have almost no knowledge of a man who, after all, was a close family member.

But families were like that, he thought. They were just there. Sometimes you were close, but often you weren't. McKay himself had a brother still living in Dundee. They thought of themselves as fairly close and got on well whenever they met up, usually over a few pints. But they hadn't seen each other now for over a year, and their only communications had been a card at Christmas and the odd text or email about some bit of family news. That was how families worked.

Across the room, Farrow and Dolan were still talking away, Farrow casting the occasional glance in McKay's direction. Whatever they were discussing, it was clearly something that Farrow at least was taking very seriously. McKay looked quizzically across at Benny Edwards who shrugged and went back to tapping at his keyboard. *Fair enough,* McKay thought. He didn't expect Edwards to rock any boats.

McKay had already kicked off the investigation into Grant's texter, having noted that Farrow had so far done nothing on the matter. He'd requested a check on the provenance of the two mobile numbers, although he expected that both would turn out to be pay-as-you-go burners. He supposed it might be possible to ascertain at least the approximate location of the phones at the time the texts were sent. That might be significant if the first had been sent from somewhere near North Kessock – it would at least confirm whether Grant's house really had been under observation – but it wouldn't reveal the identity of the sender. Still, it would be better than nothing.

For the moment, he was more interested in Martin Delaney or Gary Ellis, or whoever the hell the guy really was. He'd already taken a statement from Helena Grant to obtain a formal account of her evening with Delaney, and he'd obtained from her Delaney's details on the dating site. It might be worth interviewing the young woman, Maggie Clennan, about her meeting with the man who was then calling himself Gary Ellis, though it wasn't clear whether she'd be able to add much.

McKay knew little to nothing about online dating etiquette. Was it usual to employ different pseudonyms on different sites? He supposed there might be good reasons for someone to keep their identity secret, at least initially. But there might also be less good reasons.

Idly, he did an internet search on Martin Delaney, looking for any suitable candidates in or around Inverness. There didn't seem to be any candidates who fitted the man that Grant had described to him or the photographs she'd provided.

He carried out a similar search on Gary Ellis, with a similar lack of success. That didn't prove much in itself – not everyone lived their life online – but he was beginning to suspect that the man's real name was something else again. It would be worth checking whether either name was registered on the PNC as well as checking the electoral roll, but he didn't have high expectations of getting a result.

In the meantime, he continued idly searching on the internet, looking at variants on 'finance director', 'leisure sector' and 'hotels'. Inverness was a relatively small city, and there could be only a limited number of suitable candidates in the area, if the man was telling anything approaching the truth. Which, McKay acknowledged to himself, was a large 'if'.

Slightly to his surprise, he had some success almost immediately. One of the first news items he'd stumbled across had been a brief piece from the business section of the *Press and Journal* about the appointment of a new finance director to a local chain of hotels. The man's name was Gerry Elliott, which had been sufficiently close to Gary Ellis to attract McKay's attention.

He found the hotel chain's website, which had an 'About Us' section in the menu. That in turn carried a link to the 'Our Management Team'. There, under the name Gerry Elliott, was a copy of one of the photographs Grant had sent him earlier. The man she'd had dinner with, albeit in younger and slimmer days.

Christ, McKay thought, *if only all detective work was that easy.* It was often the case that one stroke of luck could give you the answer you were looking for, but it didn't normally happen that quickly.

He hesitated for a moment, and then picked up the phone and dialled. The call was answered almost immediately by a young-sounding woman who carefully enunciated the name of the hotel chain in a manner that suggested she hadn't previously spoken the words out loud.

'Can I speak to Mr Elliott please? Your FD.'

The receptionist sounded flummoxed for a second. 'You mean Gerry Elliott?'

'That'll be him,' McKay agreed. 'He's your finance director?'

There was a short hesitation. 'I think so.'

The whole set-up was sounding much less professional than the website had suggested. But then Elliott was apparently fatter and balder than the website suggested too. 'Is it possible to speak to him?'

'Oh, aye. Hang on a wee sec, will you?'

There was a pause, which thankfully wasn't filled by incidental music, and then a voice said, 'Elliott here. How can I help you?'

'Good morning, Mr Elliott. This is DI Alec McKay, Scottish Police. I wonder if it would be possible for me to pop in to see you today?'

There was a long silence before Elliott responded. 'Can I ask what this is in connection with?'

'I'm just hoping you might be able to help us with an enquiry. It's something perhaps better discussed face-to-face.'

There was another pause before Elliott responded. 'I don't see what information I'm likely to have that would be pertinent to any police enquiry.'

'Nevertheless, Mr Elliott, if you're just able to spare me a few minutes of your time, I'm sure everything will be resolved satisfactorily.' This time, McKay allowed a note of unspecified threat to creep into his tone.

'Resolved?' Elliott was sounded worried now, which was interesting in itself. In McKay's experience, men who blustered like Elliott were generally easy to intimidate, often because they felt they had plenty to hide.

'Absolutely. It'll just take a few minutes, and I'm sure we can iron everything out.'

'I– Well, yes, of course. If you really think I can help.'

McKay glanced at his watch. Ten thirty. 'Could we say eleven? If that's convenient for you.'

There was a rustling of paper, which McKay guessed was

Elliott pretending to check his crowded diary. 'Yes, it looks as if I can fit you in then.'

Fit me in, McKay thought. *You bet you bloody can.* 'Eleven it is, then. I'll come to your office.'

'My–' Elliott stopped and for a moment McKay thought he was going to suggest an alternative rendezvous. 'Yes, that'll be fine. Eleven.'

I should have said eleven thirty, McKay thought after they'd ended the call. *Given him more time to stew.* He was definitely a man with something to hide. The only question was whether that something was likely to be pertinent to McKay's enquiry.

He looked up to see that Farrow's desk was empty. There were papers strewn all over the surface, so McKay assumed Farrow had either gone to a meeting elsewhere in the building or maybe just out for a smoke. He rose and strolled across to Dolan's desk. 'Morning again, Johnny. Long chat you were having with Mr Farrow there.'

Dolan looked up and grinned. 'No offence, Alec. But it's none of your bloody business. Don't go too far out onto the thin ice, eh?'

'You know me, Johnny.'

'Only too well.'

'So what was the stuff about looking into Kevin's background?'

'You don't give up, do you?' He glanced at the door, then over at Edwards, who was studiously pretending not to be listening in to their conversation. 'I'm all in favour of your winding up old Charlie. Never does any harm for him to brought down a peg or two. But tread carefully. He's not a nice man when he's crossed.'

'Charlie? You surprise me. One of life's gentlemen.'

'Thing is, Alec. He's got a bee in his bonnet about your brother-in-law. When he first started on it he was just looking to mildly screw you over. Delay things long enough to piss you off.'

'Like I say, one of life's gentlemen.'

'But then he stumbled across something that made him a bit more interested.'

McKay frowned. 'What kind of something?'

'That's the thing. He's playing it very close to his chest. Obviously doesn't trust us either.' He paused and the grin returned. 'Can't think why. Anyway, he thinks he's got something and he's asked me and Benny to do some more digging into your brother-in-law's personal life – his background, work, finances. You name it.'

'Kevin? He was the world's most boring man.'

'It could well all be bollocks. I mean, you know Farrow. Quite capable of adding two and two and ending up with whatever number he wants. And I'm sure he's still taking a delight in making life difficult for you. But he seems to think he's got something worth pursuing.'

'This is going to drag on forever, isn't it?' McKay said, wearily.

'One way or another, it looks like it's heading that way, yes.' Dolan hesitated. 'Look, I've told you none of this. But that's one of the things we were talking about this morning. Farrow's already having second thoughts about having you in here.'

'That's quick even by my standards,' McKay said. 'People usually take a day or two to want rid of me.'

'It's because you try too hard to ingratiate yourself. No, Farrow felt obliged to accept Helena Grant's offer because he's complained so much about being short-handed. And because he thought it might be amusing to have you under his thumb for a wee while.'

'Aye, well, good luck with that one.'

'So I'd noticed. Now he's taking the enquiry more seriously, he's wondering whether it's quite such a good idea to have you hanging around.'

'In case we have conversations like this one, you mean?'

'What conversation?'

'My lips are sealed, Johnny. About this, anyway.'

Behind him, McKay heard the door opening and, almost imperceptibly, he took a discreet couple of steps away from Dolan's desk. By the time Farrow entered, McKay was already heading towards the door. 'Won't be long,' he called back to Dolan.

'Off somewhere, Alec?' Farrow regarded him with undisguised suspicion.

'Just briefly.' McKay grabbed his coat from the rack by the door. 'Off to see a man about a threatening text.'

17

Mckay could see why Elliott might have preferred for them to have met elsewhere. The offices of the Muir Hotel Corporation were less imposing that the company name might have suggested.

In fact, 'offices' was almost an overstatement. As far as McKay could judge, there were no more than a couple of rooms in a serviced office suite above a row of shops in the centre of Inverness. The woman who had answered the phone was clearly the receptionist for the whole suite, which perhaps explained why she'd seemed unsure about the name of the company.

The receptionist herself was a remarkable character. Her hair was dyed bright crimson and styled in an indescribably asymmetrical cut that McKay assumed must be highly fashionable. He could certainly see no other excuse for it. Her clothes and make-up largely matched the colour of her hair, and she was adorned with an array of jewellery and body piercings that McKay suspected doubled her bodyweight. She seemed enthusiastic and pleasant, but possibly not the candidate you'd have chosen to exude business gravitas. She wore a badge carrying the words

'Ruby Jewell' which McKay took to be her name, or at least an adopted name, rather than simply a description.

She directed McKay to take a seat in the narrow waiting area. There was a sign above the reception desk listing the companies based in the building, though from the size of the place McKay guessed not all of them had a physical presence. He noted with interest that the name Muir appeared several times, though the other names gave no clue as to what the nature of the company business might be.

After a few moments, Elliott appeared from a door beside the reception, just about recognisable from the photograph on the website. He was a short, squat man, probably in his mid-forties. 'DI McKay?'

McKay followed Elliott down a corridor into his office. There was a door at the opposite end of the small room which presumably led into a further office but it was unclear whether the headquarters of the Muir Hotel Corporation extended any further than that.

Elliott gestured for McKay to take a seat. 'I know what you're thinking. Small place to run the whole hotel chain from.'

'I was a little surprised,' McKay admitted.

'Most of the managerial staff are based in the hotels themselves. We take a hands-on approach to management. Quality control and all that.'

'But you're here,' McKay pointed out, as if Elliott might not have noticed for himself.

'There was some talk of basing me in one of the hotels. But in the end we decided it was better to keep the finances separate. So I'm based here with the MD who has an office next door.' Elliott gestured towards the adjoining door. 'He spends a lot of his time out and about in the hotels. But when he's here, it means we can discuss things discreetly when we need to.'

McKay was no kind of a businessman, but he could read

between these lines easily enough. This was a company where the MD had no desire that anyone else should have any insight into the finances, other than a presumably bought-off FD. He wondered vaguely whether it might be worth bringing this operation to the attention of HMRC, but that was a question for another day.

He'd already decided he disliked Elliott intensely. He knew he was influenced in part by Helena Grant's description of her evening and subsequent encounter with him, but it was more than that. There was something about this large corpulent man with his slicked-back thinning hair and stench of aftershave that gave him the creeps. It occurred to McKay it might be worth his checking the sex offenders' register when he returned to the office.

'Now, how can I help you?'

'Do the names Martin Delaney or Gary Ellis mean anything to you, Mr Elliott.'

Elliott's momentary change of expression was sufficient answer to McKay's question, though Elliott had done his best to conceal it. 'I'm not sure. Should they?'

'I'm asking you, Mr Elliott. They appear to have been used as online pseudonyms.'

There was a momentary pause, and McKay could almost hear Elliott's brain working. 'I see you've discovered my guilty secret.'

'Guilty secret?' McKay placed a slight but discernible emphasis on the first word.

'I'm afraid so. I'm a widower, you understand.'

'Is that so, sir? I'm sorry.'

Elliott shrugged. 'My wife passed away a good few years ago. I just wanted to explain my circumstances. In the last year or two, I've been seeking a little – well, company, I suppose. It's difficult to meet anyone in a job like this, so I thought I might give online dating a try.'

McKay nodded. 'Of course.'

'The names you mentioned, they were just online pseudonyms I used. I was a little embarrassed, and I didn't want to risk anyone I knew coming across my profile unexpectedly.' He looked up anxiously. 'It's not illegal, is it?'

'Not in itself, no. I'm sure many people do it for the reasons you say. As long as you're not doing it for fraudulent purposes.'

'Good Lord, no. I mean, I had every intention of letting the other person know if the relationship should come to anything more serious.'

'But not when you first met them?'

Elliott shrugged awkwardly. 'It's a bit difficult, isn't it? I mean, to suddenly break the news that you've lied about your name.'

McKay imagined that few people would be too surprised given that, by that point, they would already know that Elliott had lied about his age and appearance. But perhaps that wasn't how online etiquette worked these days. 'You'd have to do it at some point,' he said. 'So why not straightaway?'

'I don't know. I just thought it would feel easier if it looked as if things might become more serious.' It was evident from his tone that, to date, none of Elliott's liaisons had reached that point.

'I'm sure you're right,' McKay agreed. 'Are those the only pseudonyms you've used?'

Elliott was silent for a moment then, in a more combative voice, he said, 'I'm not sure where this is going. You've already confirmed that there's nothing illegal in what I've done. I don't understand why you're here.'

'Do you recall a date you had with a lady named Helena Grant?'

'Helena–? Oh my God, is that what this is all about? She was the policewoman, wasn't she?'

'Ms Grant is a police officer, yes. I'm not sure I understand what you mean, though, sir.'

'She's made some complaint about me, hasn't she? What's she saying? That I assaulted her or something worse?'

'Did you assault her?'

Elliott stopped, clearly realising he'd already said too much. 'Of course I bloody didn't. We just had a bit of a misunderstanding at the end of the evening, that's all.'

'A misunderstanding?'

'Look, it hadn't gone all that well, truth be told. We just hadn't got on. It happens. It was nothing personal…'

Trust me, McKay thought, *as far as Helena Grant was concerned it was deeply personal.* 'Of course. But the misunderstanding?'

'We were standing outside. Just saying goodbye. We both knew it hadn't gone well but I was trying to be polite, a gentleman.' He paused, and McKay could tell he was thinking how to present himself in the least damaging light. 'And, well, if I'm honest, I thought it was perhaps worth giving it one last go, just to see if she was maybe a little more interested than I'd thought. So I leaned forward just to give her a peck on the cheek, perhaps a hug. You know?'

McKay offered no response. He knew Elliott's type well enough. The sort who tended not to take no for an answer.

'Anyway, she took it completely the wrong way. Reacted as if I'd tried to paw her or something. I must admit, for a moment I was furious. I felt a bit humiliated. So I said a few things I later regretted and stormed off. That was all there was to it. Look, I don't know what she's said to you–'

'For what it's worth,' McKay said, 'she described the incident just as you've presented it.'

'There you are then.'

'You said that was all there was to it. Was that all there was to it?'

'What do you mean?'

'What did you do after you'd, to use your words, "stormed off"'?

'Nothing. I went home.' He paused. 'And before you ask, no, there's no one who can vouch for that. I live alone. That's why I'm dating people on the internet.'

McKay could see that the man was already rattled and decided to press home his advantage. 'Can I ask where you live, sir?'

Elliott hesitated and then gave an address on the outskirts of the city. Not walking distance.

'How did you get home? It seems a little far for you to have walked.'

'I—' There was another hesitation. 'I had my car. I drove home.'

McKay nodded. 'Ms Grant mentioned that you'd drunk a bottle of wine that evening. Were you safe to drive?'

'I don't recall drinking that much. I'm sure we didn't finish the bottle, and I can't recall whether she drank any.'

'She says she didn't. These days, police officers tend to be careful about that, as you can imagine.'

'I don't know. I'm sure I was fine to drive or I wouldn't have done it.'

'Of course not, sir. Did you drive straight home?'

There was a further hesitation. McKay suspected Elliott was wondering what other information McKay might have up his sleeve. 'Of course. Where else would I have gone?'

'You didn't, for example, decide to follow Ms Grant home?'

'Why the hell would I do that?'

'I don't know, sir. Perhaps to give it, in your own words, another "last go"? You'd had a few drinks. Perhaps you weren't thinking straight?'

There was a long silence. There often was, McKay thought, when people were trying to recalibrate their stories.

'You're right. I wasn't thinking straight. Not because I'd been drinking. But just because – well, like I say, I was a bit annoyed at the way she'd responded to what I'd done.'

McKay noted that "furious" had been downgraded to "a bit annoyed". 'And?'

'I just wanted a chance to explain, really. I thought about going back straightaway but decided I'd probably miss her. She'd mentioned at some point that she lived in North Kessock. So I thought if I hurried up there and waited somewhere off the A9, I'd probably see her pass as she came into the village. It's not a big place and I thought there wouldn't be much traffic at that time of night.' He offered McKay an awkward smile. 'A bit hare-brained, I know, but I hadn't really got my head in gear.'

To McKay's ears, the events sounded not so much hare-brained as downright implausible. Grant would have been too smart to give any clue to her address until she was ready to, and that wouldn't have been during her disastrous dinner with this man. Which meant Elliott had already known where she lived. 'Go on.'

'I got up there, came off the A9, found somewhere to park up and waited. A short while after, a car came by I thought must be hers, so I waited a moment or two, then pulled out and followed it. I kept a fair way behind so she wouldn't notice me. But it wasn't difficult to see where she pulled in so I parked further down the road.'

'But after all that you didn't approach her?'

'My head had cleared a bit by then and I realised I was being stupid. I thought if I just approached her without warning, I'd just make things worse. So in the end I waited till she'd got into the house, and then I turned round and drove home.'

'Nothing else?'

'I don't– What do you mean?'

'You have a mobile phone, Mr Elliott?'

'Yes, of course. But what–?'

'Would you be willing to give me the number?'

'What's this all about?'

'I can't compel you to give me the number, Mr Elliott. Not today, at least. But it will make things easier if you co-operate.'

'I don't understand. But if it matters, I'm happy to give you the number.' He recited the number, which McKay dutifully jotted down in his notebook. As he'd expected, it didn't match either of the numbers from which the texts had been sent.

'Do you have just the one mobile, Mr Elliott?'

Elliott blinked, his expression that of a schoolboy caught out in an ill-conceived prank. 'I– Yes, of course.'

'You don't have separate business and personal phones, for example?'

'No. Perhaps I should. But I just use that one.'

'I see.' McKay was silent for a moment, watching Elliott squirm. 'And you didn't send Ms Grant a text that evening?'

Elliott blinked. 'A text?'

'A text, Mr Elliott. From your phone.'

'Why would I have sent her a text? I don't know if I even had her number.'

'She gave you her personal mobile number before you met. You asked for it in case you were delayed.'

'I– Look, I really don't understand.'

McKay had little doubt that Elliott was lying. But he wasn't sure he was going to gain much by pursuing the matter. Elliott was unlikely to hand over any second phone voluntarily, and would no doubt now dispose of the phone as soon as possible, if he hadn't already.

In truth, there probably wasn't much more that McKay could do. He could see whether Elliott's car registration had been picked up heading north on the A9 that night, but that would prove nothing beyond what Elliott had already admitted.

But McKay had achieved most of what he'd set out to. He'd confirmed, at least to his own satisfaction, that Elliott had been the sender of the texts. He'd given Elliott a pretty clear message that they were onto him, and McKay couldn't imagine the man in front of him would have the nerve to repeat what he'd done, knowing he was already on the police's radar. All in all, it was probably best just to leave him spinning gently in the wind.

'You sent no texts that evening, Mr Elliott? From that or any other phone? That's what you're telling me?'

'I–I mean, I can't remember exactly. But I don't think so, no.'

McKay made a play of writing this down very laboriously in his notebook, his manner suggesting he would somehow be able to check the veracity of this statement. 'If you say so, sir.' He closed the notebook with an air of finality. 'Thank you for your assistance in this matter. You've been most helpful.'

Elliott had been staring at his desk, his head lowered as if expecting the blade of the guillotine to descend at any moment. 'Is that it?'

'Sir?'

'I mean, are we finished? Is there anything else you need from me?'

McKay frowned, as if considering this question. 'I don't think so, sir. At least, not for the moment.'

'Not for the moment?'

'We'll be in touch if we need to speak to you again.' McKay paused for a theatrical beat. 'Or if we decide to progress matters.'

Elliott opened his mouth and then closed it, having clearly decided that silence was the safer option. McKay sat for a minute watching him, allowing Elliott's discomfort to build, before finally rising to his feet. 'Thank you for your time and co-operation, Mr Elliott. Much appreciated.'

Outside the office, McKay paused in the reception and took another look around. He turned to Ruby Jewell, who had been watching him quizzically. 'I assume these are serviced offices?'

She nodded. 'There's a brochure there if you'd like one. You can rent an office or just telephone services and suchlike.'

McKay gestured towards the list of companies above the desk. 'These are a mix of the two, I assume? Some based here, some using you to handle calls?'

'Yes. That's a bit out-of-date. Some of those aren't with us anymore, and we've got some other clients. I need to get round to updating it.'

'Quite a few companies with Muir in the name?'

'They're all connected.'

'What do they do? What sort of business, I mean.'

Jewell looked slightly uneasy. 'To be honest, I'm not entirely clear. Clients are supposed to provide us with a short summary of their business so we can answer questions that might come up when we're taking calls. But Mr Donaldson hasn't really done that.'

'Mr Donaldson?'

'He's the MD of most of the Muir companies. There seem to be a few people involved, but Mr Donaldson's the only one I ever see here. Along with Mr Elliott.'

'Is Mr Elliott involved with the other Muir companies?'

She frowned. McKay suspected she had just remembered that he was a police officer. She was probably wondering why he was asking her all these questions. 'Most of them, I think. He looks after the accounts.'

'But you don't know what type of business they're in?'

'Not really. Some of it seems to be import-export work, but that's only what I've gleaned from occasional comments from callers.'

'Interesting,' McKay said, in a tone that suggested it was anything but. 'All a bit of a mystery to me, business and finance and all that. I prefer a nice straightforward murder enquiry.'

Jewell blinked, clearly unsure if he was joking. 'It must be exciting. Police work.'

'You'd think, wouldn't you?' McKay smiled. 'Anyway, I mustn't take up any more of your time. You've been very helpful. Thank you.'

He made his way down the stairs, knowing she'd still be wondering quite what help she'd given him. The truth was he didn't know himself. But he felt that somehow, in that brief conversation, he'd learned something of potential value.

18

MCKay pressed the bell again, holding it down for longer this time. He wasn't optimistic he'd get a response, but now he was here he thought he might as well make sure. He withdrew his finger and stepped back, looking up at the blank windows of the house.

It was an Edwardian villa in a relatively salubrious part of the city. Most of the houses exuded prosperity, with neatly managed gardens and new cars parked in the driveways. This one was a little different, in that it had been divided into flats and most of the garden had been transformed into parking for the tenants. It didn't exactly lower the tone – it was tidy and well maintained – but it did look slightly out of place.

McKay pressed the bell one more time for luck. He'd only come here on the off-chance as his journey back to the office took him relatively close. Helena Grant had given him the address, so he'd thought he might as well try.

He wasn't really sure he even needed to talk to Maggie Clennan. He'd just thought a short chat with her might enable him to tie everything up neatly. In particular, he was interested to know whether she'd subsequently received any texts that might have been sent by Gerry Elliott.

Although he'd been satisfied with the outcome, something about the meeting with Elliott had left McKay feeling disturbed. Partly, it had simply been that the man had given him the creeps. It wasn't just the way he'd behaved on the night he'd met Helena Grant, though that was concerning enough. It was something about him as a person. There was something about him that felt wrong. McKay couldn't pin it down any more precisely than that.

McKay didn't have much time for intuition. In his view, the famous 'copper's gut' was nothing more than another word for experience. You spotted things – behaviours, character traits, body language – that most people didn't, and you had a good idea what they were telling you. Sometimes you did it without realising or without fully understanding what you were seeing. It became second nature.

In this case, his gut was telling him something his brain hadn't yet grasped. But there was something about Elliott that made him more than just a pathetic lech with an anger management problem.

That was part of the reason he'd wanted to speak to Maggie Clennan. He wanted to know whether Elliott's behaviour towards Grant had been a one-off, or whether there was a pattern of similar actions. It was that train of thought that had brought him here, in the hope he might be able to catch her in.

He assumed she was at work. She'd told Grant she worked in a call centre in town, but she'd also mentioned, in the course of the wine-fuelled chat, that she worked a shift pattern, rotating days, earlies and lates. She'd been working days when she'd met Grant and presumably hadn't changed over yet, but McKay had thought it worth a shot.

He was about to turn away when the door unexpectedly opened. It was a young woman, clearly on her way out somewhere. She peered at him quizzically. 'Can I help you?'

'I was looking for Maggie Clennan.'

'I don't think she's in,' the woman said. 'I live in the flat below her and I hear her moving around if she's up there.'

'I imagine she's at work,' McKay said. 'I only called round on the off-chance as I was passing.'

'I can pass on a message if you like. Actually, I don't think she's been around for a day or so. I didn't hear her last night. She might be away.' She looked past McKay. 'Her car's not there. But I didn't notice if it was there yesterday.'

'No worries,' McKay said. 'I'll give her a call. I only popped by for a chat, really.' It had only been a few days since Helena Grant's evening with Clennan. He wondered vaguely how long Clennan had been away, a slight unease stirring within him. 'You don't know when you last saw her?'

'Can't remember, to be honest. We don't see a lot of each other. Only if we happen to pass in the hall.' She looked pointedly at her watch. 'Sorry, I'd better be going.'

'Yes, of course.' McKay stepped back as the woman carefully locked the door behind her. 'Thanks for your help.'

He made his way back to his car, which he'd left parked in the street outside. He imagined if he waited here much longer the local neighbourhood watch representative would be taking a note of his registration number. The area had that feel to it.

Deciding he was prepared to take that risk, he pulled out his mobile and dialled Helena Grant's number.

'Alec? Missing me already?'

'Oh, aye. Every minute.'

'In that case, I might have some news for you. I take it you're not in the office?'

'I've just been out talking to Gerry Elliott.'

'Gerry who?'

'Gerry Elliott. AKA Martin Delaney. AKA Gary Ellis. Among others, I imagine.'

'Ah. That's his real name, is it? Well done for tracking him down.'

'Child's play for one of my talents.'

'I don't doubt it. How'd it go?'

'I don't think you'll have any more trouble, let's put it that way. Not entirely satisfactory. But it should do the trick.' He talked her briefly through his meeting with Elliott.

'You're sure he sent the texts?' Grant asked.

'Pretty sure. I don't see how we're likely to get any hard evidence, but he was lying through his teeth about it. If I'd pushed him harder, it's possible he might have admitted it, but he'd talked himself into a corner so I think he'd probably just have clammed up. But he knew that I knew, so I don't think he'll try anything more.'

'What did you make of him?'

'Nasty piece of work, isn't he? I mean, admitting to having followed you home was disturbing enough, even if he didn't actually do anything illegal. Just makes me wonder what he might be capable of.'

'That was my feeling.'

'I'll get him thoroughly checked out. There's apparently nothing on the PNC about him, though.'

'Assuming Gerry Elliott is his real name, or the name he's been known by in the past.'

'Quite. Anyway, you said you had some news.'

'Yup. I think you've broken your record.'

'I have a feeling I know what's coming.'

'You've managed to make yourself unwelcome with Charlie Farrow even more quickly than with anyone else you've ever worked with. Which, to be frank, is really saying something.'

'I'll take that as a compliment. So what's Farrow said?'

'It's about your brother-in-law. He reckons it's turning into a more substantial investigation than he'd envisaged, and in the circumstances he doesn't think it's appropriate for you to be working alongside his team.'

'Aye, I picked up some of that this morning. It must be bollocks, surely?'

'Normally I'd think it was just a polite way of saying he couldn't tolerate you for a moment longer. But Farrow doesn't normally do polite. By the way, he did also say you'd been a little abrasive this morning.'

'Abrasive? That wasn't abrasive.'

'Probably not by your standards. But, no, it does sound like Farrow thinks he's got something. He may well be using it to make your life difficult, but he can't just be fabricating the whole thing.'

'I wouldn't put it past him. I just can't believe there'd be anything worth investigating in Kevin's life. Other than the enduring mystery of what Fiona saw in him.'

'Even so, it looks as if I'm going to have to welcome you back into my fold even sooner than I'd expected. At least you got Elliott sorted, so thanks for that. I just hope that really is the end of it.'

'I can't see him troubling you anymore, anyway,' McKay said. 'In fact, I'm sort of surprised he sent the second lot of texts. He knew what you do. I'd have thought once the red mist dissipated, he'd have realised that trying to intimidate a senior police officer wasn't the smartest of moves.'

'Maybe the red mist descended again when he saw me the second time. If he thought I was trying to help Maggie Clennan.'

'Maybe. I'd have expected him to direct his anger at Clennan, though.' He paused. 'That's where I am, by the way. Maggie Clennan's place. I was planning to have a chat with her, just in case he'd done something similar to her. But it looks like she's not here.'

'Probably at work.'

'Not sure. Just spoken to a neighbour who lives below her,

and she reckoned Clennan hadn't been around for a day or so. Thought she might have gone away.'

'She didn't say anything about going away when we were chatting. But I suppose there's no particular reason why she should.'

'Oh, well, sounds like it won't be my case for much longer, anyway. I'll just write up a report on my meeting with Elliott and then I'll leave them to it. It won't go anywhere, but that shouldn't matter now.'

'Fingers crossed. You heading back now?'

'Sounds like I just need to go and say my fond farewells to Charlie Farrow and his merry crew, and then it'll be time to get the old band back together.'

'I'm looking forward to nothing more.'

19

J ana could tell they were worried. She was too far away to hear what they were saying, but she could see from the body language that something was wrong. She'd seen them earlier in the bar, the four of them huddled in a corner, talking earnestly. The young one, the fat one, and the other two – the one she'd privately called Mr Big and the one who looked as if he was on some kind of medication. She called him Jitters to start with, because he seemed to be permanently jittery. Now, he worried her because he looked even less predictable than the other three.

She wondered what they were talking about. Some business or financial issue? Somehow, she hadn't gained that impression. From the odd phrase she'd been able to discern while they'd been in the bar, it sounded somehow more personal. As if they were worried about some person, rather than about anything to do with the business.

Her first thought had been that one of the women had gone missing or had done something bad to herself. The men wouldn't worry about the woman, but they'd be concerned if someone had absconded. But as far as she could tell all the women here were accounted for.

At some point, they'd noticed her cleaning in the next room. It was what she was supposed to be doing and where she was supposed to be, but that hadn't stopped them being angry with her.

'Has she been listening?' Mr Big had said.

'She can't understand anything anyway,' the young one had responded. 'They're all thick as mince.'

She had tried her hardest to look baffled and scared, as if she had no idea what was going on or what was being said. She'd scuttled away, muttering 'Sorry, sorry...' repeatedly, and nobody had bothered to follow her.

Shortly after that, they'd repaired into the old drawing room that they sometimes let to local businesses for meetings, closing the door firmly behind them.

Jana had asked some of the other women if they knew what was happening, but it was clear that no one knew any more than she did. They all seemed scared, though, shuffling away without responding to her questions. They all knew that if there was some problem, whatever its nature and cause might be, they would suffer as a result. If the men were worried and angry they'd offload their feelings onto someone more vulnerable. That was how it worked.

There is no point in speculating, Jana thought. The chances were that she would never know what had happened. Either it would blow over and everything would return to normal, or it wouldn't and that might mean anything.

They had no guests staying tonight, but the routine continued as it always did. At times like this, it felt as if they kept the women working just to make them suffer. It made no real sense to her, but it continued, day after day, week after week.

And she had no idea what, if anything, might make it stop.

20

'Anyone ever told you you've got perfect timing?'

'Not that I can recall. Not even Chrissie. How'd you mean?' McKay lowered himself back behind his desk. He'd never admit it to anyone, but he actually felt relieved to be here.

The last session with Farrow and his team had gone as he'd expected. He'd arrived back at the office to find his desk there already cleared of the files that Farrow had delegated to him.

McKay had decided he might as well play dumb. 'Someone trying to tell me something?'

'If you'd been here, I'd have told you directly,' Farrow had said. 'But you were out gallivanting somewhere.'

'I was out making some progress on Helena Grant's complaint,' McKay had said, pointedly. 'I think we can treat that one as resolved. Amazing how quickly things can be done when you put your mind to it. So what do you want to tell me?'

'I'm afraid, Alec, that we're going to have to dispense with your services.'

'We were getting along so well too. I really felt I'd fitted in.' He could see Johnny Dolan behind Farrow, grinning and shaking his head.

'Well, there you go, Alec. But I'm afraid our enquiry into your brother-in-law's death is turning into something rather bigger than we'd envisaged. As it stands, I don't think it's appropriate for you to be part of the team.'

'It's always difficult to maintain those Chinese walls, isn't it?' McKay had managed to catch Dolan's eye. Dolan had put a finger to his lips in mock warning.

'That's my fear, Alec. So I'm afraid I'm going to have to ship you back to Helena with immediate effect. I'm sure she'll be pleased to have you back.'

'I imagine you've made her day. I'll write up my report on her complaint to you. That'll be one less loose end for you.'

That had pretty much been it. Fifteen minutes later, with a detour to buy himself a fancy coffee in the staff canteen, he was back at his usual desk, Helena Grant standing in the doorway. 'So why perfect timing?'

'We've just had a body called in,' Grant said. 'Looks potentially suspicious. Thought you'd like first dibs. You need something to keep you busy.'

'Too right I do. What's the story?'

'Body found on the edge of the Cromarty Firth, just outside Dingwall. Don't know too much more but it looks like the individual had suffered some kind of head wound. Uniforms are up there. Scene's all sealed off and the examiners are on their way, if not there already.'

'So we can all sleep easy in our beds.'

'I imagine so. Anyway, it's all yours.'

McKay realised he was feeling better already. Over the course of the winter, he'd begun to think he was finally genuinely tiring of the job. It had begun to feel like little more than a grind, and he'd preferred to devote his energies to rebuilding his relationship with Chrissie.

But now, suddenly, he felt the surge of adrenaline that he'd come to associate with the start of a potentially major enquiry.

This one might well come to not much or nothing, depending on the circumstances of the death, but at least it showed the old impulse wasn't entirely gone.

'You're looking cheerier already, Alec.'

'Just like to keep busy, you know.'

'You'd better get onto it, then. You want to take Ginny with you?'

'Can you spare her? Thought she was up to her ears on your other enquiry.'

'She is, really. But we've hit a bit of an impasse till we can identify the victim. We're following up every possible avenue, but at the moment, we're just hitting dead ends. Might do Ginny good to get a couple of hours break from it.'

McKay sat back in his chair. 'And?'

'And?'

'You sound like you might have some other motive.'

She nodded. 'Look, I can't involve you in this investigation formally, not till we get the all-clear from Farrow and the Fiscal's office–'

'Which might be some time in coming.'

'But I'm more than happy to have the benefits of your experience. I don't want you to feel any more excluded that you need to be. We're a team, Alec.'

'You sound like you're about to send me on one of those executive programmes where you have to build a raft out of paper napkins and string,' McKay said. 'But, aye, much appreciated. It's good to be back.'

'You were only away for half a day.'

'I know. But, trust me, half a day with Charlie Farrow felt like a life sentence.'

McKay's appreciation of being back in the fold didn't extend as far as offering to drive, so Horton was at the wheel as they headed up the A9 over the Black Isle.

'The old firm back in business, eh?' she said.

'Holmes and Watson. Batman and Robin. Laurel and Hardy.'

'Don't push it. Anyway, you're looking chipper. Funny how the prospect of a decaying corpse can cheer you up.'

'You have to take your pleasures where you can find them,' McKay said. He'd worked with Horton for a few years now, and he always felt relaxed in her company. In many ways, they were polar opposites. Horton was organised, thoughtful, cautious in her words and judgements, but with an acuity of thinking that often led her to insights others missed. McKay shared some of the last quality – though his approach tended to be more instinctive – but none of the others. Horton seemed quintessentially English in her looks and accent, but McKay had been deeply gratified to discover that, behind all that, she was as Scottish as he was. She'd just spent too much time conducting missionary work in the Home Counties.

'Hope you have more success with this one than we're having with the other case. Helena's talking to comms about doing some sort of TV appeal.'

'Worth a try,' McKay agreed. 'Mind you, when a body's that difficult to identify, I begin to suspect there's a reason for it. Either the killer really didn't want us to know who he is, or the victim had deliberately gone off-grid for some reason.'

'Or it's someone who's just slipped under the radar accidentally. Some vagrant or loner with no friends or contacts. The perfect victim for a random killer.'

'In my darker moments, I sometimes think there are more of those than we ever discover,' McKay said.

'All we can do's keep plugging away. Hope something turns up. I don't like the idea of it just drifting away, becoming one of those ever-open cases that we just can't continue resourcing.'

McKay shrugged. 'We've had a few of those over the years.'

It was still only early afternoon, and another fine, bright winter's day, but the sun was already low in the south-western sky. Another couple of hours and it would be growing dark. They crossed the Tore roundabout, still heading north. After a few minutes, they could see the snow-covered bulk of Ben Wyvis and the pale sheen of the Cromarty Firth ahead of them. Moments later, they were heading downhill towards the ribbon-like strip of the Cromarty Bridge.

'So where do I go?' Horton said.

'Left towards Dingwall apparently. The body was found on the mudflats in the firth at low tide. They've accessed it via a patch of waste ground next to the road. I was told we couldn't miss it.'

'They always say that.'

She turned left at the Ardullie roundabout, and followed the A862 towards Dingwall. The road ran close to the edge of the firth, but here and there houses and gardens had been squeezed into the land between the highway and the water. It was one of these householders who had spotted the body earlier that morning, apparently left on the mudflats by the receding tide.

As it turned out, there was no risk of Horton missing the location. To the left of the road, just before it twisted right under the railway line, there was a cluster of marked cars, blue lights pulsing. One lane of the road had been closed to accommodate the parked vehicles, and traffic was being directed around the blockage by a couple of uniforms. Horton waited patiently behind a couple of other cars until they were beckoned through, then pulled up next to the uniform. Behind them, another driver sounded his horn. McKay lowered the passenger window and stuck out his head. 'Afternoon, Andy. The real cops have finally arrived.'

PC Andy Anderson, a middle-aged officer who knew McKay well, glanced at the car waiting behind Horton's. The driver sounded his horn again. 'Aye, and causing your usual chaos, I see.'

He gestured to a space further up the line of parked cars. 'You'd better pull in there. The council's supposedly on their way with a set of temporary traffic lights but Christ knows how long they'll take to get here.'

Horton pulled into the space indicated, and Anderson waved the traffic on. 'Not the most convenient crime scene,' Horton commented.

'They never think about that when they're killing people, do they?' McKay said. 'Bloody inconsiderate.'

They climbed out of the car and surveyed the scene. The examiners were clearly already here, their tent set up towards the edge of the firth. A couple of uniforms were keeping watch over the perimeters of the area, which had been taped off. They were unlikely to face many intruders in this spot, though it was often surprising how quickly the word could spread.

The waters of the firth were spread out before them. This was the end of the firth itself, where it formed a wide, shallow bowl bounded by the surrounding hills and the town of Dingwall. The tide was coming in now, but when it receded it left wide stretches of mudflats. It was a beautiful spot in the height of summer. On a darkening winter's afternoon, it had a more sinister air.

They were greeted at the edge of the protected area by an enthusiastic young PC. 'Hi, Billy,' Horton said. 'Not the best place to be on a chilly afternoon.'

'Least I'm getting a breath of air.'

Horton had come across PC Billy McCann a few times, not least in dealing with some issues of her own a year or so previously. She'd always found him a likeable and conscientious officer, the sort who would be on his way to promotion before long, assuming that was what he wanted. 'You know DI McKay?'

McCann nodded warily, clearly recalling his previous dealings with McKay. 'Afternoon, sir.'

McKay glanced at Horton. 'Good to see some young people

showing due respect. Afternoon, son. I see our chums in the white coats are already here.'

McCann nodded. 'Arrived about fifteen minutes ago.'

'Okay, let's go and see what anyone has to tell us.'

They tramped their way across to the examiners' tent, which was set up close to the water's edge. McKay nodded to the crime scene manager, a slightly morose DS called Willy Ingram, who seemed adept at organising resources but otherwise devoid of social skills. He was more than a safe pair of hands, and McKay was generally just happy to let him get on with the job. The unmistakeable figure of Jock Henderson was standing by the tent, peering thoughtfully out at the water. As they drew closer, McKay realised that Henderson was vaping.

'Jesus Christ, Jock, don't tell me you're finally trying to give up?'

Henderson turned, caught by surprise. 'Bloody hell, Alec. Don't creep up on me like that. Could have given me a bloody heart attack.'

'Aye. Shape your heart's in, it wouldn't take much.' McKay gestured to the e-cigarette. 'Too little, too late.' McKay had given up smoking himself some years before. He didn't tend to be evangelical about it except when it gave him the opportunity to take the piss out of Jock Henderson.

'Thought I'd give it a try. Christ knows whether it's any better for me. But I've tried everything else.'

'Will power, that's all you need. Just a bit of will power.'

'If you say so. Anyway, it's always a joy to see your smiling face at a murder scene.'

'Is that what we've got, then?'

Henderson shrugged. 'I'd say so. On the basis of what we've got so far.'

'Which is?'

'Victim's a young male. Maybe mid-twenties. White.'

'Cause of death?'

'That's for the doc to determine. But there's a bloody great dent in the back of his skull. Looks like it was hit with something big and hard.'

'You think that was the cause of death?'

'Like I say, that's for the doc to determine. But it wouldn't have improved his health. My guess would be that either he was killed outright by the blow, or he was knocked unconscious and died subsequently from that, drowning or hypothermia, or some combination of the three.'

'Not an accident, then?'

Henderson peered at McKay, as if to assess whether or not this was a serious question. 'I guess anything's possible. But it's a deep and large wound. You could do it accidentally, maybe, if you fell from a height or were hit by something moving at speed. But I don't really see how that would have happened round here.'

McKay glanced up at the elevated stretch of railway line that passed by on the far side of the road. 'Train?'

'It looked too localised a wound to me. If he'd been hit by a train, I'd have thought there'd be other traumas, but there was nothing evident. But, like I say–'

'That's for the doc to determine. You need a new catchphrase, Jock.' He paused, ruminating. 'You're thinking it did happen round here? The body wasn't dumped here from somewhere else.'

'That's–' Henderson caught himself and stopped. 'It's possible. But there's not much bloodstaining on the clothes, so I reckon the injury happened not long before he went into the water.'

'And we think he went into the water somewhere near here?'

'Again, it seems likely to me. The water's pretty shallow at this point. There's tidal movement but I'm not sure there'd be enough of a current to bring the body up here from anywhere else. Looks to me like it was probably dumped into the water somewhere nearby, then left stranded on the mud when the tide went out.'

'If you wanted a body not to be found,' Horton observed, 'this isn't where you'd dump it. You only have to go a mile or two down the firth for the water to be much deeper.'

'Which suggests either that the attack happened here and the body was just dumped immediately, or that, if it happened elsewhere, the body was deliberately dumped where it would be found very quickly.' He shrugged. 'It's possible. If the killing was intended as a warning, for example.'

'On that point,' Henderson intervened, 'there's something else you need to be aware of.'

'You're excelling yourself today, Jock. Must be the vaping.'

Henderson ignored McKay, as he was prone to do. 'Our friend in there is a former druggie.'

'Former?'

'Maybe current. Who knows? There are track marks on the body that suggest heroin use, but none of them looks recent.'

McKay nodded. 'But an ex-user might have made enemies or have debts. Which might be a motive for bumping him off fairly visibly. What about ID?'

'We're still photographing the scene and the body, so not really had a chance to check properly yet. He's only wearing a thin anorak on top of a jumper and jeans, and there didn't seem to be any sign of a wallet or anything of that kind.' Henderson gestured behind them. 'If he's been rolled about in the water for a while, it might have slipped out of his pocket.'

'Oh great,' McKay said. 'I can see us trying to dredge the firth to find a wallet.'

'Not to mention a murder weapon,' Horton added.

'Yup. Any thoughts on what that might have been?' McKay asked Henderson.

'Not really. There's nothing around the body itself, but then we don't know precisely where it went in the water. It was lying on the mudflats, just a bit upstream, but we had to get it brought onto the land before the tide came in. Something fairly big and heavy anyway. Maybe a large rock or something of that kind.'

'Even better,' McKay said. 'We'll be dredging the firth for a large rock.' The words sounded morose, but the tone was vibrant. McKay felt back in his element. 'Okay, Jock, we'll leave you to it for a bit.' He gestured towards the tent. 'I see you're practising the fine art of delegation again.'

'It's the only way they learn.' Henderson dropped the e-cigarette back in his pocket.

'So I keep telling Ginny here,' McKay said. 'But will she listen?'

The doorbell rang and then continued to ring, the sound of someone holding their finger down on the bell. There was a momentary pause, and then it rang again, maintained for even longer this time.

Chrissie McKay cursed. She'd been in the middle of some paperwork for the surgery, and she knew it would take her a while to regain her focus after this interruption.

It was one of the changes they'd made since she and Alec had got back together. She was an intelligent woman, but she had realised that, over time, she'd drifted into the role of housewife, because that was just what you did. She knew female friends who had careers, glittering or otherwise, but somehow, she'd found herself occupying the same place that her mother had done.

It hadn't really been what she wanted, and it wasn't what Alec had wanted. It had just turned out that way. After their temporary split, they'd both wanted to change some things, drag themselves out of the rut, and she'd suggested that she should get a job. To her slight surprise, Alec had been enthusiastic in supporting her.

She'd decided it was better to take small steps. She'd done

various kinds of administrative and managerial work before Lizzie had been born, so she'd applied for a part-time clerical role in one of the local GP surgeries. It was a large practice, attached to the local medical centre, with a relatively substantial staff and she'd been happy to fit anonymously into her own niche. But even in these first few months her skills and experience had been recognised, and she found she was taking on more and more demanding work, with the promise of promotion and a full-time job if she wanted it. For the moment, she wasn't sure she did, but she was enjoying the new challenge.

Alec had warned her of the dangers of bringing work home – 'I've done it all my bloody career, and look where it's got me' – but her employers had been flexible in helping her cope with Fiona's loss, so she was more than happy to make up the time at home. If anyone would give her a moment's peace.

The doorbell sounded again, even more insistent this time. Whoever was there had no intention of going away.

When you're the wife of a copper, there's always the fear that the ring of the doorbell might be bringing bad news. That fear had receded as Alec had moved into CID and then into more senior roles, supposedly further from the front line. Even so, as the last couple of years had amply demonstrated, the risk never entirely vanished, and she felt that familiar tremor of anxiety as she made her way to the front door.

She opened it on the chain. Being the wife of a copper also tended to make you cautious. 'Yes?'

'Fiona Andrews?'

Chrissie peered out at the figure at the door. He was a broad man, probably in his early thirties, with close-cropped hair and a slightly cocky demeanour. *Not someone to tangle with,* she thought. There was another man behind him, of similar build but a little older and running to fat. 'Who's asking?'

'I asked if you were Mrs Fiona Andrews.'

'Aye. I heard. And I asked who was asking. I'm still waiting.'

The man sighed and thrust a piece of paper towards the gap in the door. 'Bartles Recovery Agency. Bailiffs.' He gestured towards Kevin and Fiona's car, which was parked in the driveway, unused since Kevin's death. 'This yours?'

She ignored him. 'What's this all about?'

'Like I say, bailiffs. Debt collectors. Here to collect.'

'Which?' Chrissie said.

The man looked baffled. 'What?'

'Bailiffs or debt collectors. Which are you?'

'I–' The man obviously decided there was no point in trying to argue. 'It doesn't matter. We're here to collect.'

'It does matter. Do you have any ID?'

'Look, are you Fiona Andrews?'

'ID.'

There was a pause, and then the man reached into his pocket and produced a business card. 'Kieran Yardly – Debt Collector.'

'So not a bailiff,' she said. Before he could respond, she had closed the door firmly, this time double-locking it. The doorbell rang again, even shriller than before. Chrissie ignored it, and walked back through the house checking all the downstairs windows as she went. She double-locked the back door and checked that the rear patio doors were fastened. *That's another thing about being married to a copper,* she thought. *You make sure you have decent security.*

The doorbell was still ringing repeatedly. Fiona had been sleeping upstairs. Now she came down, a dressing gown wrapped around her, rubbing her eyes. 'What's going on?'

'You tell me,' Chrissie said. 'If you can.'

'Why would he want to see me?' Fiona said, after Chrissie had explained the situation. The man had finally given up on ringing the doorbell, but a glance through the front window had shown them that he and his colleague were still standing on the opposite side of the street watching the house. 'Do you want me to go and talk to them?'

'Christ, no. They're not bailiffs. They're just debt collectors, which means they have no legal rights. Even if they were bailiffs, they can't enter the house without our permission, and I've no intention of giving that till we've got some idea what this is about. If they don't bugger off in a minute, I'm going to call Alec.'

'But I don't understand,' Fiona said, her face bewildered. 'Why would they come here?'

'I've no idea. They asked for you. I'm guessing some helpful friend told them you were staying up here.'

'But who'd do that?'

'Probably one of your mates or neighbours acting in all innocence,' Chrissie said. 'They're devious buggers. They get the information out of you without you even realising you've given it.'

'But why? And why would they come all the way up here?'

'I don't imagine they have. That guy had a local accent. They'll have subcontracted it to some local shysters.'

'But subcontracted what?'

Chrissie looked at her sister. 'That's the question, isn't it, Fi? You got some problems you've not told me about?'

McKay took the call as they were crossing the Kessock Bridge. He'd left the scene in the good hands of Willy Ingram, who'd seemed to have everything under control. They'd arranged a more formal debrief the following morning, but the scene examination was likely to go on into the night and beyond, and McKay hadn't seen there was much he could contribute, other than further provocation of Jock Henderson.

He ended the call and turned to Horton. 'You mind if we make a short detour via my place?'

'Problem?'

'Seems like it. Not exactly sure what kind, though.'

McKay's house was on an estate to the south of the city. Not the poshest bit, he usually said, but not too shabby either. Horton had visited a few times and found her way through the network of streets with only the occasional prompt.

The two men were still there, their car parked up on the kerb, their eyes fixed on McKay's house. Horton glanced quizzically across at McKay.

'Can you pull in just behind them?' McKay said.

Horton nodded and did as instructed. McKay climbed out and strolled across to the two men. The sun had set now and it was growing dark, the first streetlights just coming on.

'Can I help you two lads?'

The younger of the two, whom McKay took to be Yardly, said, 'Who the hell are you?'

'I might ask you the same question. You're rather cluttering up the neighbourhood here.'

'Any of your business?' Yardly straightened his shoulders, with the air of a peacock beginning to display.

McKay shrugged. 'Maybe. I live here. And I've a professional interest in people who seem to be hanging around for no obvious reason.' He reached into his pocket and produced his warrant card. 'My colleague in the car, DS Horton. Can I ask what your business is here?'

'Fuck. Don't tell me there's been a complaint. Fucking neighbourhood watch.'

Oh, aye, McKay thought, *and they always send out a DI and a DS to deal with over-muscled numpties like you.* 'Your business?'

'We're debt collectors. You'd better ask your neighbours there.'

'Debt collectors,' McKay said, enunciating the words carefully. 'So not bailiffs, I'm assuming.'

'I–' Yardly looked as if he might be about to bluff it out, but then clearly decided that, in the circumstances, this wouldn't be the wisest move. 'Not officially, no.'

'Not officially. Which means you have no legal powers.'

'Not strictly speaking, no.'

'Not strictly speaking,' McKay repeated. He gestured towards his house. 'Or any other way of speaking. I take it you've not been invited in?'

'Well, no—'

'In that case, sonny, I suggest you get on your way sharpish. Before I start to consider this harassment.'

Yardly exchanged a glance with his colleague. 'Okay, but—'

'Please don't say you'll be back. You'll get exactly the same response. And then it really will start to look like harassment.'

Yardly made no response, but gestured to his colleague to get into the car. 'We're just doing our jobs.'

'Must be very fulfilling.'

McKay watched as they drove away, and then turned to Horton, who had emerged from the car and was leaning on the bonnet, watching him with amusement. 'What was all that about?'

'I'm really not sure. Look, do you need to get back to the office or can you come in a minute while I find out?' He'd initially hesitated about whether he wanted Horton present if some family dirty washing was about to be exposed. Then it had occurred to him that if this really was about Kevin, he needed to ensure his own position was completely transparent.

'Sure. If you don't mind me being there.'

'I don't know what's going on,' McKay said. 'But I'm beginning to think it might be better that we both find out together.'

22

Something had changed. Jana could tell that, though she struggled to identify quite what was different.

The men were less calm, she thought. Less relaxed. There was a new tension in the air. They were arguing with each other in a way they hadn't before. Back-biting, sniping. She didn't always understand what it was they were arguing about – sometimes because they talked too fast, or used words she didn't understand, but often because they seemed to be conducting these disputes almost under their breath, as if they didn't want to risk anyone overhearing them.

It had started ever since the meeting a day or two before. The meeting where they'd locked themselves away, and she'd known that there was some problem, some issue that they hadn't known how to deal with. From then on, everything had felt different.

She hadn't seen the fat one since that day. He wasn't here all the time, unlike the young one and Jitters, but he usually turned up every couple of days. But there'd been no sign of him since.

She hadn't seen much of Mr Big either. He wasn't here all the time, but she'd had the sense that this was his base, that he was the planet around which all the others were just satellites. She'd caught sight of him the previous day, but he'd just been striding out towards his large car, clearly heading off somewhere.

The young one and Jitters had been hanging about as usual, but had seemed much more subdued in their attitudes and behaviour. She'd encountered the young one in one of the corridors upstairs and had braced herself for the usual mix of banter and innuendo. But he'd just walked past her, head down, apparently oblivious to the fact she was even there. Jitters seemed to spend most of his time curled on one of the lounge sofas downstairs, playing some game endlessly on his phone.

She'd tried talking to the other women, to see if any of them had any idea what might have happened. But, as always, none of them wanted to discuss it. Some of them denied having noticed any change. Some of them just ignored her questions, turning away as if Jana was invoking bad fortune even by raising such topics.

It was, perhaps inevitably, the young one who'd finally given her at least an inkling of what might be happening. She'd been in one of the en-suite bedrooms, rubbing away pointlessly at the already clean bath in line with her designated schedule, when he'd appeared at the bedroom doorway. 'I'm sorry I ignored you earlier, Jana. I mean, I know you don't understand what I'm saying, but I don't want you to think I'm rude.'

Though she understood the words, he was right in that, as so often, she had no real idea of what he meant. She was being held here, in what amounted to slavery under subsistence conditions, compelled to carry out meaningless hard manual labour, and he was concerned that he might have appeared rude.

'I'm sorry, anyway. I was just a bit distracted. I was worrying. There's a lot to worry about, Jana.'

She continued scrubbing, on her knees by the bath, her back to him. It suddenly occurred to her that, at times, between the jokes and the mockery, he talked to her in the way he might talk to his mother. *Perhaps that's it,* she thought. She had no idea of his circumstances, but perhaps he had seized on her as a maternal figure. She had noticed that he talked to her, despite believing she didn't understand what he was saying, much more than he spoke to any of the other women, even the youngest ones. Perhaps he wanted to talk to her as he might have spoken with his mother, if she were here, but feeling safe in the knowledge that she wouldn't be able to follow what he was saying.

'We don't know what's going on, that's the trouble,' he went on. 'We don't know who's doing it, or what they want. It looks as if they're trying to scare us, get us out of the business. But we don't know if that's really what they want, or if there's some other motive. There's no message, no words, nothing that gives us any clue. It might all even just be coincidence. We don't know. But it feels as if there's someone out there, waiting for us. And we don't know where they're going to go or what they're going to do next.'

She glanced back at him, her face blank. 'Sir?'

'This must be how you feel, Jana. Is that right? As if everything's out of your control, and that you're just being played with. You don't know what's going to happen next, and there's nothing you can do about it. You know what that feels like.'

She'd kept her back to him, not wanting to catch his eye, not wanting to give him any clue how much she had understood. Now, though, she couldn't prevent herself from glancing back momentarily. He had his head down, staring at the worn bedroom carpet.

'You know what that feels like,' he said again.

Cal didn't know why he'd even come out here. He hadn't been thinking straight, and suddenly it seemed the most insane idea in the world. He'd just wanted to clear his head, get away from all the crap, try to think straight.

The thing was, he knew he'd never been the smart one. He'd never been a leader or had wanted to be. He just did what he was told, and sometimes he didn't even do that.

Archie was the leader. That was the point. They all looked up to Archie. He was the one with brains. He was the one who told them what to do. He knew what he was about. They could rely on Archie.

Except now, it seemed, they maybe couldn't. Unexpectedly, the Archie they'd come to rely on appeared to be almost as lost as they were. He tried to hide it at first. He'd maintained the same tough-guy act, ordering them about, telling them it was all under control.

But it hadn't felt the same. It hadn't been convincing. Somehow it had been obvious that, beneath that thin shell of bravado, there'd been nothing. Cal hadn't expressed it to himself like that, of course. But he'd exchanged a look with young Franny, and it had been clear that they were both thinking the same. *He doesn't know what to do. He hasn't a scooby.*

Cal hadn't wanted to believe that. He wanted to think that Archie had anticipated all this. That he had some plan up his sleeve to do with whatever was going on.

But the more he listened, the more Cal knew Archie was simply out of his depth. There was lots of bland reassurance, lots of insistence that it was all 'in hand', that it might all be coincidence, that it was no more than had been expected anyway. In other words, a lot of bollocks that didn't really make any sense. Every word Archie spoke had just confirmed to Cal that he was as confused as the rest of them.

He wondered if it was the same at the other sites. He imagined it was probably worse. After all, it was their people who'd gone missing. They'd be in even more of a panic, and they'd probably have realised straightaway that Archie didn't know what was going on.

Cal had always been a worrier. He'd always been one to expect the worst, and usually his expectations had been fulfilled. Even at the best of times he was prone to find himself pacing up and down, contemplating how soon it would be before the next bad thing happened. Not long, usually.

Over the last few days, since the meeting, he'd been in a state little short of panic. He'd even found himself gasping for breath, feeling as if he'd been struck hard in the stomach, unable even to contemplate what might happen next.

The trouble was that they were out on a limb here anyway. He knew that. He'd spent most of his adult life on the edge of things, making a living where and how he could, usually doing stuff that was at best semi-legal. This was the biggest thing he'd ever been involved in. He was doing okay out of it, better than he'd ever done before. But he'd known all the time that if it went tits up, it was likely to take him and everyone else down with it. He wouldn't be able just to slip away, quietly disappear, like he had so often before. This time, there were just too many people with a finger in the pie.

That was what really worried him about all this. He had no idea how tangled all this really was, who might be involved. He was a tiny, tiny cog in a wheel that was beyond his imagining. He'd assumed that Archie was much closer to the centre, had the ear of whoever it was that really mattered. But the last few days had shown him that Archie was almost certainly a small fry too. A rung or two above Cal, but no more. Whatever limited power he might have had was clearly slipping rapidly away from him.

Back at the hotel, he'd found himself succumbing to another of the panic attacks, as these same thoughts came running and rerunning through his brain. He'd been curled on one of the lounge sofas, clutching his stomach as if he were about to vomit. Franny had poked his head round the door once and stared at him with what he'd taken as a mixture of pity and contempt.

After that, Cal had just wanted to get out of the place. If he was going to be sick, he wanted to do it somewhere in the open air, somewhere away from everyone, where there was no risk of anyone seeing or hearing him. Mostly, though, he just wanted to breathe in the fresh air, escape from that stale miasma of damp and furniture polish.

Archie had told them not to leave the building. It had been the usual mishmash of contradictory nonsense. There's no danger, nothing to be worried about. But don't go outside if you can avoid it, well, just because.

Anyway, fuck Archie. He wasn't going to help them.

He'd slammed the front door behind him and stormed off down the path, then turned left towards the woodland that led down to the firth. This was where he'd come before when he'd wanted to get away. When he'd had enough of Franny's jibes or the oppressive atmosphere of the building. He thought of it as his own place, since he'd never seen anyone else down here.

There were no other buildings around until you reached the edge of the village half a mile or so away. On a winter's afternoon, the place was silent apart from the occasional chirrup of birdsong. Cal pushed his way through the trees, stomping through the damp undergrowth, until he caught a glimpse of the water ahead of him.

At first, he felt a little better, soothed by the silence and the chilled, clear air. It was only when he reached the edge of the woodland and was looking out over the water that he realised quite how late it was. He still hadn't quite come to grips with the winter up here. He couldn't believe that the sun set in what felt like the middle of the afternoon.

Now, it was very low behind him, the trees casting long dark shadows out across the firth. The tide was in and there was something eerie about the deep mauve of the water under the clear, darkening sky. He shivered, and he knew immediately that the cause was more than simply the sharp breeze cutting in from the sea.

He turned, peering into the gloom, suddenly conscious of how dark the woods had grown even in the last few minutes. It felt as if the last few dregs of light were being sucked from the air.

Somewhere to his right, he thought he heard movement. A bird, or some small woodland animal.

Nothing to be concerned about, he told himself.

Archie had warned them. Not to leave the building. Not to go out on their own. Not to take any risks.

Archie knew fuck all. That was clear now.

But maybe Archie had at least been right about this.

Cal could sense the panic rising again. He could feel someone breathing on his neck, and he swung round, realising immediately that he was being an idiot. There were only a few metres between him and the water's edge, and there was no one there.

Shit. He was losing it.

It was time to get back, he thought. He'd walk slowly through the woods. He wouldn't panic, but would force himself to stay calm. He would take one step, and then another, then another, until he was back at the hotel. It was no more than a few hundred metres. Nothing could happen.

He took the first steps into the trees, his ears straining for any sound of movement other than the crunch of his own footsteps. After a few more steps, he stopped, still listening, sure that he had heard something. He looked around him, but there was no sign of any movement beyond the faint stirring of the leaves in the breeze.

The sun had gone now, and the twilight was already thickening. Somewhere ahead, he could see a distant glimmering of lights. The hotel. No distance at all.

Behind him a twig cracked.

The panic hit him without warning, almost like someone thrusting a hand hard against his back. Suddenly he was running, his feet stumbling through the thick grass, branches and leaves whipping his face.

Something, someone, was behind him, he was sure. Keeping pace with him, almost within reach of him. Not daring to look back, he pounded towards the edge of the woods, his eyes fixed on the welcoming lights, which somehow seemed further away than before.

He could hear the footsteps crunching behind him, almost as if they were echoes of his own. He tried to increase his pace, desperately wanting to lose whatever was tailing him. Now, he was only a few metres from the edge of the wood.

Then he tripped, his foot catching on the uneven ground, his weight and exhaustion pulling him forward. He landed face down, the breath knocked from his body, and he felt as if he had no strength to rise and continue.

He closed his eyes, his face pressed to the wet ground, waiting for whatever it was to catch up with him and do whatever it wanted to do.

Then he realised there was only silence.

He lay, not daring to open his eyes. The only sound he could hear was the rasping of his own breath.

Then a soft voice, somewhere ahead of him, said, 'Hello.'

'I don't understand it.' Fiona was staring, bewildered, at the computer screen. 'It doesn't make sense.'

'I'm afraid it does, love.' Chrissie had an arm around her sister's shoulders. 'I just don't know how it's possible.'

'But it's a company car. There can't be anything owing.'

Chrissie exchanged a glance with McKay. Ginny Horton was standing behind them, looking uncomfortable about what she was witnessing. 'It wasn't a company car. Is that what Kev told you?'

Fiona looked up with tear-stained eyes. 'Why would he have lied about that?'

'I don't know. Perhaps you misunderstood–'

'I didn't misunderstand. I'm not an idiot. That's what he told me. He was really proud when they gave it to him. It came with the promotion.'

It hadn't taken long for McKay to come up with some answers, though now he was wondering whether it had been a good idea. But this had been on the point of blowing up anyway. At least now they had some of the facts. The only question – the real question – was how much more was still to emerge.

He'd started by calling Bartles Recovery Agency. 'It's almost certainly a cock-up,' he said. 'These people are unscrupulous bastards. They just get given a list of names and they work through it. They don't care where the names come from or whether they're right or not. Fiona's name will just have got on there in error.'

The agency had initially been unhelpful, but became more co-operative when McKay had indicated that this was a police enquiry and that, if he didn't obtain the information he needed, he'd be visiting in person with the aim of taking a much closer look at the company and its operations. After that, they'd given him the number of a car leasing company in London, with reference details relating to the supposed debt.

He'd dialled the number and found himself on hold, waiting for an operator, the strains of John Denver playing softly in his ear. He had asked Fiona, 'Was it a leased car?'

She shook her head. 'It was a company one.'

'Maybe it's the company's fault. Perhaps they're in arrears for some reason, and Kevin's name got referenced in error,' Chrissie had suggested.

But the operator who finally responded to McKay's call had been insistent that the car had indeed been leased in the name of Kevin Andrews. Payments were more than six months in arrears, and the company had been pursuing Mr Andrews for payment or return of the vehicle for some time. She explained that it was standard practice, if the issue had not been resolved within a defined timescale, to instruct a debt recovery company to take every possible step to recover the vehicle.

McKay had taken the phone into the hall before continuing, not wanting to distress Fiona any more than he needed to. 'I'm afraid Mr Andrews is dead.'

There had been a long silence at the end of the phone. 'Dead?'

McKay had explained the circumstance, adding, 'It's a little unfortunate that the collection agency should have come here harassing his widow.'

'I do appreciate that, sir, and I can only offer our sincere apologies. But I'm afraid they weren't to know. We have been trying to contact Mr Andrews by letter and telephone for some months. This is action we only take as a last resort.'

By this point, the alarm bells were beginning to sound for McKay. He was happy to take on any bunch of faceless bureaucrats pursuing a vulnerable widow, but there was clearly more to this story than any of them had realised.

'So what happens now?' he'd asked.

'In the circumstances, I'll ask the agency to cease pursuing the debt until we've resolved matters. I'll have to hand the case over to our legal team to determine the next steps. The repayment of the debt will be an issue for probate, but I'm afraid, given the extent of the non-payment, we'll still need to repossess the car as soon as possible.'

McKay had no idea whether or not this was an accurate statement of the legal position, but that would be a question for Kevin's solicitor. He'd asked if the leasing company could provide some evidence of the debt and, after some resistance, the operator had finally agreed to email the documentation to Fiona. It had arrived within minutes.

'I'm sorry,' McKay said. 'I know it's a shock.'

'It's more than a shock,' Fiona said. 'I feel like everything's been turned upside down. How can this even be possible?'

'Did you have any inkling there was a problem?' Chrissie asked.

'Nothing. I mean, like I've said, Kevin didn't seem himself for the last few weeks but otherwise everything seemed fine.'

'I've no idea what's been going on here,' McKay said. 'But it's been happening for more than a few weeks. The debt goes back more than six months. And they must have been chasing him for it. Were there no letters?'

'Not that I ever saw. But I never opened anything of Kevin's without checking with him first.' She paused, frowning. 'To be honest, Kev never seemed to get much stuff addressed to him. Most of our stuff was joint – the mortgage, bank account, all that – but he never seemed to get much stuff just addressed to him. Not even junk mail. He reckoned it was because he was IT savvy, and knew how to keep himself off the mailing lists.'

McKay wondered whether somehow Kevin had managed to have any mail addressed solely to him redirected. He wasn't sure how the mail redirection service worked, but he imagined it might be possible. 'When did he get the car?'

'About a year ago. He was delighted with it. They'd given him some sort of promotion into a middle management role, and it apparently took him into the pay band where he became eligible.'

McKay's mental alarm bells were becoming increasingly shrill. He tried to think of a delicate way of asking the next question, but he couldn't come up with one. 'Did Kevin have his salary paid directly into your joint account?'

Fiona was clearly puzzled by the question. 'No. It was typical Kevin. He had some convoluted arrangement using a high-interest savings account. His salary was paid into that, and then he transferred a sum every month to cover our living expenses, mortgage and so on. The idea was to save up what was left for holidays and the like. He was good with money was Kevin.'

McKay wondered at the level of self-delusion that would allow a woman to utter these words only minutes after discovering her late husband had a substantial unpaid debt. He glanced at Chrissie. 'Can I just have a word?'

Chrissie looked reluctant to leave Fiona but nodded and rose to follow McKay into the hallway. Ginny Horton hesitated a moment, then followed. 'Look,' she said to McKay once they were outside, 'I think I'd better go. I feel a bit intrusive here.'

McKay nodded. 'I'm sorry. I just wanted you to be there. I was afraid that it might be something like this. This must be what

Charlie Farrow's got wind of. I just wanted to make it clear that I've nothing to hide. Farrow's going to make a meal of this, given half a chance.'

Horton nodded. 'That makes sense. I imagine you'd be wise to report it to standards, just to keep everything transparent. I'll happily endorse that. I'll leave you to it, but if there's anything I can do, just let me know. Assume you're not planning to come back to the shop tonight?'

'Probably not, given what's happened. Can you update Helena? I'll be in bright and early to get things moving on the Dingwall body.'

He waited until the door had closed behind Horton, then said to Chrissie, 'Do you know the name of the company Kevin worked for?'

'Why–?' She stopped. 'Shit. You don't think…?'

'I think it's possible. It's beginning to look like our Kevin was a man with serious hidden depths. Why would he pretend that was a company car? Why would he default on the repayments after a few months?'

'Christ, I hope you're wrong.'

'So do I.'

Once Chrissie had given him the name, it took McKay only a few moments to track down the number. His call was answered by a cheery-sounding receptionist.

'Hi. Can you put me through to Kevin Andrews, please? I don't have a direct line number for him.'

'Kevin…? Hang on.' There was a moment's pause while the receptionist checked her directory. 'You did say Andrews? We don't seem to have anyone of that name.'

'He works in IT. Only I need to speak to him because we've a query about a contract you have with us. I've got to get it resolved asap, or the delivery will end up being delayed, and I was told it was needed urgently.' *Top quality bullshit, Alec,* he told himself. *It almost sounds as if you know what it's like to do a real job.*

'I'm sorry. I can't find him in the list. I can put you through to Bob Chalmers' office. He's the head of IT. His secretary should be able to point you in the right direction.'

'Thanks. That's great.' He waited while the receptionist transferred his call. Another bright-sounding voice said, 'Bob Chalmers' office. How can I help you?'

'Oh, hi. I was actually trying to track down Kevin Andrews in IT but your receptionist couldn't find him in the directory.'

There was a pause. 'Kevin Andrews? I'm sorry, I'm afraid he's no longer with the company.'

Shit. Suddenly, McKay felt like an idiot. Of course, Fiona would have advised Kevin's employer about his death. His suspicions had been unfounded. If there'd been any issue about Kevin's employment, it would have been revealed already.

'May I ask, were you a friend of Mr Andrews?' the secretary went on. McKay noticed the past tense.

McKay had already decided to extract himself from this exchange as delicately as he could. 'Just a business contact. We hadn't spoken in a while and I was just looking to get in touch. Nothing very important.'

'Oh, I see. It's just that apparently Mr Andrews passed away a few days ago.'

'Goodness, I'm sorry to hear that. He must have been very young.' *Don't hold your breath waiting for the Oscar nomination, Alec,* he told himself.

'I don't know the circumstances, but it must have been quite sudden. Funnily enough, when I took your call I was just in the middle of sorting out a condolence card. It was good of his widow to let us know. Especially after what happened. I wish I could have spoken to her directly but I was off that day so it was a temp who took the message.'

McKay held his breath, the mental alarm bells sounding again. *It was good of his widow to let us know.* That was an odd way to talk about news of an employee. Kevin should have been back at work by now. Surely Fiona had had no option but to inform his employer. And what was it that had happened?

He wasn't sure how to frame the question he really wanted to ask. 'He must have been with you for a good few years?'

'Oh, he was. Joined long before my time. That's why it was such a shock.'

'Death's always a shock,' McKay said blandly, still trying to think of a discreet way of probing further.

'Yes, of course, but I wasn't really thinking about his death...' She stopped, as if she'd suddenly realised what she was saying. 'I'm sorry, I'm talking out of turn. Yes, Mr Andrews was with us for a long time, he only left last year.'

'Oh, I see. I hadn't realised he'd left the company.'

'I should have said. He left us about a year ago. It was rather... sudden. Is there anyone else in the department you'd like to speak to?'

McKay, unusually for him, was struggling to know what to say next. 'No, that's fine. Like I say, it was nothing particularly important. Just, you know, touching base. I'm sorry to hear the news.'

He ended the call and stood in the hallway, his phone in his hands, dreading the conversation that was going to come next.

The bastard had stood her up, she was sure of it.

She looked at her watch. He was already nearly twenty minutes late, and he hadn't bothered to call, even though she'd given him her mobile number. She'd give him the full thirty minutes and then, if he hadn't turned up, she'd bugger off.

It had been his decision to meet in a posh place like this, too. Not exactly her scene, but she was happy enough to be treated. If he did turn up, she'd make sure he paid through the nose for the privilege of her company. He'd made some noises on the phone about going Dutch, but fuck that. If he tried it, she'd walk out and leave him with the bill. As it was, if he didn't turn up, she'd have to cough up for the cost of the two large glasses of red she'd downed while waiting, and even that wouldn't be cheap in a place like this.

She was on the point of giving up and leaving when she saw him striding across the floor towards her table. At least she assumed it was him. He didn't look much like the photographs he'd sent her, but she'd never really expected he would. They never did. But he did look pretty much like she'd expected from their telephone conversation – short, fat and pompous.

'Good evening,' he said, and slumped his corpulent body down in the chair opposite her.

'I'm sorry,' she said.

He frowned. 'For what?'

'No, that's your line. I'm sorry for being nearly half an hour late. Go on, give it a try.'

He was looking mildly nonplussed. Then he glanced at his watch. 'Is it really that late? Goodness, you're right. I hadn't realised.'

'I still haven't heard it. The apology. That's all you need to do, and then we can start the whole thing again.'

For a moment, she thought he was going to get angry. *Just let him try,* she thought.

Finally, though, he smiled weakly and said, 'Yes, of course, I do apologise. I just got a little caught in traffic.'

At this time? Like hell you did, she thought. 'There. That wasn't so difficult. Now we can start with a clean slate.' She held out her hand. 'Sheila O'Rourke. Good to meet you.'

To her mild horror, he took her hand to his lips and kissed it. It took all her willpower not to snatch it back in disgust. 'Dennis Allsopp, at your service.'

She was already beginning to form an opinion of Dennis Allsopp, but she didn't care too much. Her main motive for coming out on these dates was just to entertain herself with a bit of company. If she happened to meet Mr Right and they settled down happily ever after, well, that would be a bonus, but she wasn't expecting it. She'd generally found the evenings enjoyable enough, even when she'd spent them with utter arseholes. She could talk enough for both of them, and was generally tolerant of whatever shite they might spout at her. And half-decent food was always welcome. From what she knew of this place, it was likely to be more than half-decent.

'Good to meet you, Dennis. Nice place you've chosen here.'

Allsopp looked around them, as if he'd not previously noticed where they were sitting. 'Well, it's important to do these things properly, don't you think? They do a decent venison here.'

'That right?' she said. 'I bet it's dead dear.'

The joke appeared to pass directly over his head, and he frowned disapprovingly. 'I always think you get what you pay for.'

'Oh, aye,' she said. 'Speaking of which, are you going to get us some more of this?' She held up her empty glass.

'I see you're drinking red. They do a decent Cabernet here, if that's all right with you.'

As long as it contains alcohol, it's fine with me, she thought. 'Sounds perfect.'

She watched in amusement as he literally snapped his fingers at a passing waiter. 'Can we have a bottle of the house Cabernet? And the menus, please.' She was surprised he'd bothered to add the word "please".

The wine and the menus duly arrived, and he spent the next few minutes earnestly perusing the list of dishes. She spent them knocking back the bulk of another glass of wine.

'I'd recommend the smoked duck starter, then the venison. How does that sound?'

She was tempted to disagree with him just for the sake of it, but she didn't really care too much what she ate. Anything here was bound to be okay. 'Lovely.'

She waited while he ordered for both of them, then asked, 'So what do you do, Dennis? I'm guessing it's something important.' She'd long ago learnt that it was worth feeding their egos. It got you a few brownie points and, more importantly, it made them more likely to talk entertaining bollocks as they tried to live up to your assessment.

'I'm a *Director of Finance,* actually.'

'I knew it.' *Bean counter,* she thought. *Probably a jumped-up clerk.* 'That must be interesting.'

'It can be,' he said, modestly. 'A lot of responsibility, of course.'

'All that money.'

'Exactly. You can't afford to make an error. Jobs depend on it.'

'Where do you work, then?'

'You probably wouldn't know the company,' he said. 'We're not a household name ourselves. People never know who really owns shops and restaurants. It's one of those behind-the-scenes things.'

'The power behind the throne. Is that the line you're in, then? Shops and restaurants?'

'The leisure sector,' he said. 'Mainly, anyway. We have our fingers in various pies, but we've a string of hotels. Couple of gyms. That sort of thing.'

She was mildly impressed despite herself. If he really was FD of somewhere like that, he was likely to be worth a bob or two. The only question, as ever, was how much he was bullshitting. 'Sounds fascinating. Would I know any of the hotels?'

'They're country house-type places. All over the UK. Top quality.'

She noted he hadn't actually answered her question. 'Sounds wonderful. You'll have to take me there one day.' She hadn't actually fluttered her eyelashes, but she felt as if her tone had had much the same effect on him. *Men,* she thought. *They're so bloody transparent.*

'We'll have to see.'

She'd almost made him blush, she thought.

The waiter spared him further embarrassment by bringing their starters. She cut a small piece of the duck and chewed it appreciatively. 'Mm. Excellent. You've good taste.'

'I like to think so,' he said. 'I get to eat out a lot in my line of work, so you become fairly discerning. So what about you?'

'Me?'

'What do you do?'

'Oh, you know, a bit of this, a bit of that. Business stuff.' It was essentially true. She mainly earned her living looking after holiday lets around the area for their often absentee owners. She had enough clients now to make a decent income, along with some domestic cleaning in the week and a few other odds and ends. None of these were details she felt particularly inclined to share with Allsopp.

'Sounds intriguing. Ducking and diving.' It was clear that Allsopp had little interest in learning much more.

'I get by.'

'That's all we can do, isn't it? Tough times at the moment, but when isn't it?'

'Must affect a business like yours, if people have less money to spend?' She was happy to steer the conversation back onto what was clearly Allsopp's favourite subject, namely himself.

'It's swings and roundabouts, really. The drop in the pound's attracted more overseas visitors, so we're not doing too badly...'

So it went on. Allsopp clearly enjoyed listening to the sound of his own voice, and she had no strong objections to that. It meant she could concentrate on enjoying the food and wine without having to worry too much about what to say. She managed largely to tune out of his monologue, tuning back in only on the rare occasions he asked her a direct question or seemed to expect some kind of response.

By the time the main courses arrived, they'd already emptied the bottle of wine. Allsopp waved the bottle vaguely in her direction. 'Another?'

She recalled what he'd said about the traffic and wondered whether he was planning to drive home. Not that it was any of her concern. 'Fine by me,' she said.

After that, she focussed mainly on the venison, which was as good as Allsopp had promised, and ensuring she procured her share of the wine. Allsopp was clearly surprised that she managed to keep pace with him in knocking back the alcohol, but he seemed to treat it as a positive quality. *Maybe,* she thought, *because he is trying to get me drunk. Well, good luck with that.*

She was tempted to order a dessert simply to obtain maximum value from the evening, but decided she couldn't manage to eat any more. Nevertheless, she happily accepted Allsopp's offer of a coffee and brandy.

Allsopp leaned back in his chair, with the air of a man about to loosen his belt several notches. 'Pity you can't smoke in these places anymore. This is where I'd love to get out a fine cigar.' He made it sound like an innuendo.

She sipped demurely at her brandy. 'We could always think about moving on for another drink, if you wanted. Make an evening of it.' It wasn't what she wanted, but she was happy to string him along a little, at least until he'd paid the bill.

'Well, there's an offer. I could fancy spending more time with you.'

Jesus, she thought. *Don't even think about being subtle, will you?* She realised that, up to this point, she hadn't been paying much real attention to Allsopp himself. She'd had him pigeonholed from the start of the evening as just another pompous, self-obsessed man, and hadn't really looked beyond that. She hadn't been listening to most of what he'd been saying, allowing his endless verbiage to wash over her. She hadn't focussed much on the man himself, other than to register that he was the usual physical type that she tended to encounter on these dates.

Now, though, she was beginning to realise she really didn't like him. Generally, she could tolerate men like this, no matter how irritating their behaviour might be. But there was something about Allsopp that went beyond that, something that was starting to make her feel genuinely uneasy. She couldn't pinpoint what it was, but she knew she didn't want to find herself alone with him.

She was already regretting her jokey offer of a few moments before. She hadn't meant it, and had assumed that she would be able to fob him off once they'd left the restaurant. That was how it had usually gone, with her claiming that actually it was getting a bit late and she had to be up early in the morning. Then she left them with a chaste peck on the cheek and the promise of a future date both of them knew would never happen. It was a game, but both parties knew they were playing it.

But she was becoming increasingly sure that Allsopp wasn't the type to take no for an answer. She was conscious of the way he was looking at her, already appraising her as if she was his property. She knew now that the last thing she wanted was to spend any more time with him.

She wondered vaguely if she could somehow discreetly ask one of the waiters to order a taxi for her so she could slip away without alerting him. But she couldn't really see how it would be possible.

The best bet, she thought, was to get him to settle the bill so that they could get out of this place. Once they were outside, she could make it clear that was the end of the evening and get the hell away from him, up to Academy Street where she could get a cab. It was still relatively early in the evening so there should be plenty of people around if he tried to follow her.

'Are we done here, then?' she said.

He did the finger-snapping thing again to summon the bill. When it arrived, he made a semi-joke about going Dutch, but she batted that away with an airy, 'Oh, I'm an old-fashioned kind of girl, Dennis. I like to leave that sort of thing to you men.'

For a moment, she thought he might be about to argue, but then she saw him smile as if he'd struck a successful deal. She had little doubt what he imagined he was buying for the price of her dinner. He brandished what she took to be a platinum credit card with the air of a medieval knight displaying his sword. She wondered whether he was capable of doing anything without behaving like a total arse.

He helped her on with her coat in a way that enabled him to stand much too close to her. The cloying smell of his aftershave was overpowering, and she was relieved when he finally stepped away to lead her to the door.

Outside, the night was colder than she'd expected. She pulled her coat tightly around her shoulders against the sharp breeze blowing off the river. The streetlights were doubled in the choppy water, and it felt as if there might be the scent of snow in the air. She suddenly felt unexpectedly alone. She glanced around her. There were one or two people further along the street, but no one nearby.

'So,' he said as he joined her, 'where now?'

'Look, Dennis. It's been a lovely evening, but I'm more tired than I'd realised. I need to be up early in the morning, so think I'd better call it a night.'

He looked genuinely affronted. 'But you said–'

'I know I did, Dennis. And I meant it when I said it, but when I got out here I realised how tired I was.' She gave a mock playful giggle. 'To be honest I think I might have already had one drink too many.' This was bollocks, of course. She'd be more than capable of making a night of it, just not with this man.

'But I–' She could tell he wanted to say he'd paid for the meal, but even he knew that would be crass. She could also tell he was not only disappointed. He was angry.

'I'm sorry,' she said. 'Perhaps some other time.' *How about never,* she thought. *Is never good for you too?*

'You're all the same, aren't you? Your sort.'

'My–' She swallowed the words she'd been about to say. 'I've said I'm sorry. I know I'd just be lousy company now.'

'You've been lousy company all evening,' he said, brutally. 'You've shown no fucking interest in anything I've had to say. You've been leading me on all night, just to get yourself a free meal.'

So he's smarter than he looks, she thought. Not, at this moment, that that offered her any kind of reassurance. 'That's not it at all,' she said. 'It's been a lovely evening but, like I say–'

She'd moved away from the restaurant with the aim of walking back up towards the main drag. She realised now that had been a mistake. They were standing at the end of one of the narrower roads that led up to Church Street. She could see the occasional passer-by at the far end, but there was no one on the street itself.

'Bitch.' He almost spat out the word. 'Whore. No, you're not even a whore. At least you get something from a whore when you pay them.'

'Now, wait a minute...' She was already turning away from him, wanting to run but knowing her high heels would prevent it. It was no distance at all to the top of the street, she thought. Once she was there, there'd be too many people around for him to do anything.

But, before she could move at all, she felt the rough grip of his hand on her arm.

26

Fiona was still sitting at the dining table, her eyes fixed on the laptop screen, as if her gaze might change the content or meaning of what she was seeing. Chrissie was sitting next to her, holding her hand but clearly with little comfort to offer.

It's all about to get a hell of a lot worse, McKay thought.

Chrissie looked up at him quizzically and he nodded. He could lip-read the silent expletive that she mouthed in response. He nodded again, and took the seat to the other side of Fiona.

He took a breath, then began. 'Fiona. I'm afraid there's something else I need to tell you.'

She looked up at him, her expression suggesting she desperately wanted him to say nothing more. He wanted more than anything to oblige her, but he knew there was no possibility of delaying this. He had no idea what the full implications might be, but Fiona would need to begin dealing with them as soon as she could.

'I've just spoken to Kevin's employer,' he said.

'I called them,' she said. 'To tell them about Kevin.' She frowned. 'I was disappointed no one got back to me. You'd think–' She stopped, clearly reading his expression.

It was perhaps fortunate, he thought, that she hadn't managed to speak directly to Bob Chalmers' secretary. If she had, she'd have received this news much more brutally. 'I'm afraid,' McKay said slowly, 'that Kevin was no longer working there.'

'What do you mean?'

'He hadn't worked there for over a year. I was told he left suddenly.' He was already wondering about the possible circumstances of that sudden departure. Something else to look into.

'But that's not possible.' Fiona was staring at him wildly. 'It can't be true.'

'I don't know how it's possible. But it's what I was told.'

'There must be a mistake. They must have got the wrong person.'

'I spoke to the head of IT's secretary. She seemed to know exactly who I was talking about. I'm sorry.'

'I just don't see how it's possible,' Fiona insisted. 'I mean, he got the promotion. He went out to work every day.'

McKay had come across stories of men – it was always men – who'd been made redundant but couldn't face the humiliation of telling their wives or families. They maintained the facade, leaving the house promptly each day, spending the empty hours in coffee shops or wandering aimlessly through shopping centres until it was time to return home. It happened. 'I don't know where he went,' he said, 'or what he did. But he wasn't working there. Maybe he'd found another job. I don't know.'

'But why wouldn't he tell me?'

'If he'd been made redundant, maybe he was too embarrassed to tell you.'

'But that's ridiculous. We'd have dealt with something like that together. We'd have found a way through. He knew that.'

'I don't know, Fiona,' McKay said again. 'All I know at the moment is that he left working there a year ago. I don't know why or what happened. We'll have to look into all that for you.

But I needed to tell you, because this might have implications for your finances.'

'How do you mean?'

'We don't know what Kevin was doing for the last year. We don't know if he had a job. Presumably he was transferring the equivalent of his former salary into your joint account every month. But we don't know where he was getting that money from. The one thing we do know is that he'd defaulted on the car payments. But we don't know if he might have had other debts.'

He could see Fiona was struggling to process what he was saying. He didn't blame her. He was having difficulty making sense of it himself. He looked helplessly at Chrissie.

'Look, Fi,' Chrissie said. 'None of us really understands what's going on here. But we'll help you sort it all out. First thing tomorrow, we'll get onto the banks and such, and we'll find out what the situation is. Then we'll see what we need to do to sort it out.'

Fiona had started to cry, and it wasn't clear whether she was even taking in what Chrissie was saying.

Chrissie placed an arm round her sister's shoulder. 'Let's get you back to bed for a bit. You've had a stressful day, and you need more rest.' She rose and took Fiona's arm. Fiona offered no resistance, but followed meekly out of the room, her face blank and heavily stained with tears.

IT WAS a good half hour before Chrissie returned. McKay had busied himself in the meantime, first making himself a cup of tea, then searching on the internet for any reference to Kevin's employer from around the time of his departure. He was looking for anything that might shed some light on the reasons for Kevin's behaviour – a report of redundancies or changes to the workforce. The company, some kind of financial services operation, was a relatively large employer, so there were a number of references in the local press, but nothing that seemed pertinent to Kevin's departure.

'Any chance of a cup of tea?' Chrissie said on her return. 'I suppose it's too early for anything stronger.'

'Maybe not on a night like this,' McKay said. 'We may all need a wee dram or two before the night's out.'

'I don't know if she'll sleep,' Chrissie said. 'I gave her a couple of the sleeping pills, but she's obviously in a state. I just thought she needed a bit of time to herself.' She followed McKay into the kitchen and watched as he filled the kettle. 'How could that bastard do it to her?'

'Kevin?' McKay said. 'I don't know. I mean, we ought to reserve judgement till we know the full story, but even so–'

'Even so, we know he was lying to her for the past year. He may well have left her with all kinds of problems. How could someone do that?'

'I'll be glad when we know the full picture at least. Christ knows what he was up to. I didn't like the way the secretary said he left suddenly.'

'You think he left under a cloud?'

'It was the way she said it. As if it was a euphemism for what she really wanted to say. So, yes, I think it's possible.'

'Shit. If so, he'd have had a difficult time finding another job. But do you think Kevin really was the type to get himself sacked? He always seemed like the ultimate company man.'

'I'm beginning to suspect that we never really knew Kevin at all. Not even Fiona. It takes a particular type of person to lie to their spouse like that, whatever the circumstances. Kevin always came across as the silent type. I'd assumed that was mainly shyness, but maybe there was more to it.'

'You think there's more about him that we don't know?'

'I've no idea. But you wouldn't have got any inkling from his behaviour before his death that there was anything seriously amiss in his life, would you? I don't know if it was deliberate lying or some kind of weird denial, but he must have been a real stranger to the truth.'

'You think this is what Charlie Farrow's got hold of?'

'I'm guessing he must have got some of it, aye. He'll be having a grand old time.'

'Can you talk to him about it?'

'I wouldn't want to give him the satisfaction. And, to be honest, until we know what the full situation is, I wouldn't want to offer him any additional ammunition either. Whatever Kevin might have done, we don't know that any of it was criminal. It's only relevant to Farrow if it sheds some light on the likely cause of his death.'

'If Kevin was in a financial mess, it provides a motive for suicide.'

'It might. But we don't know yet what kind of a mess he was in. We shouldn't jump the gun.'

'Christ, you don't need this, do you, Alec? You've enough on.'

'I've always got enough on. Looks like we've another one today too. Body up near Dingwall.' They'd made a point of never discussing McKay's work – partly for reasons of confidentiality, but mainly because McKay preferred to keep his professional and domestic lives as separate as possible. He always let Chrissie know when he was working on a major enquiry, but he knew she wouldn't ask about any of the detail.

She nodded. 'I reckon we're going to need that dram then, don't you?'

27

She tried to pull away but his grip was too strong. He dragged her round then threw her hard against the wall, driving the breath from her body. She could smell the stench of the after-shave again, this time mixed with the sour alcohol note of his breath. His face was inches from hers, and he had a hand across her throat.

'Bitch,' he said. 'You're all the fucking same. Every one of you. You know exactly what you're doing.'

He can't really do anything, she thought. *He can't. There are people around.* She could even see them, no distance at all away, strolling past the end of the street. One of them was bound to look down here and see what was happening.

But see what? From any distance, in the darkness, it wouldn't be clear she was being attacked. Maybe they couldn't even be seen from the more brightly lit main road.

But even if no one up there saw her, someone would surely come up this road at any moment. It wasn't really late. Someone would come out of the restaurant and walk up here.

His grip tightened on her throat. She knew she ought to scream, attract the attention of the people passing by. But it was as if the sound had dried in her throat. All she could see were his two furious eyes staring directly into hers, an anger there that she'd never previously encountered.

'Christ, you're pathetic, aren't you?' he said. 'Think you're sexy and hot, when you're just an old scrubber who's long past her sell-by date. I don't know why I wasted my time and money on you. I could buy a youngster for a fraction of that.' He seemed to be talking mainly to himself now. 'You're just an old bitch. And you don't know what I do with old bitches like you. You don't know how many I've dealt with. How many I've punished until they were begging me for it.'

She could barely breathe now. She didn't know what he was intending to do, and she suspected he had no sense of anything beyond his incoherent all-consuming fury. At that moment, though, she felt that it was quite possible that he would tighten his grip to the point where she could no longer breathe.

It was quite possible he would kill her.

The realisation struck her like an electric shock. Even with his hand on her throat, she somehow hadn't really believed he was intending to harm her. Not really harm her. That didn't happen in public, in the middle of a city, in the middle of the evening.

But now she realised he was far beyond reason. This was not a man who had any control over what he was doing. This was a man who, just in this moment, was capable of anything.

She squirmed away from him, and managed to free herself from some of the pressure of his body. Scarcely knowing what she was doing herself, she managed to move a little further away from him, finding some limited room to move. She tensed, then brought her knee up into his groin as powerfully as she could. At the same moment, she jabbed a finger in his eye.

'Shit–' He stumbled backwards, clearly in pain, doubling over with one hand pressed to his eye. 'Shit, you fucking bitch–'

She was already running, oblivious now to her high heels, her eyes fixed on the relative brightness of the main street ahead of her. Not daring to look back, she stumbled forward until she finally reached the corner, almost running into a young couple strolling, hand-in-hand, past the end of the street.

'Watch where you're going,' the man said, then stopped. 'Are you okay?'

'I was attacked,' she said. She turned and pointed down the street behind her. 'That man–'

But he was already gone. As far as she could see, the street was empty, the only movement the glimmering of the river at the far end.

HELENA GRANT PULLED up in front of the house, and glanced in her rear-view mirror. Despite McKay's reassurances that Elliott was unlikely to trouble her again, she still felt nervous arriving back here late in the evening.

She'd hoped to get back earlier tonight, but as so often the work had overtaken her. After what had felt like months of mainly administration, they were back dealing with two major investigations, both of which had the potential to suck up resources.

She'd finally agreed with comms how they would conduct the media appeal for information on the unidentified body. *The first unidentified body,* she added to herself, thinking of the second find near Dingwall. From what McKay had told her, she was hopeful that the case might be more quickly resolved, at least in respect of identification.

The appeal would go out the next day, timed to catch the early evening news on both Scottish and local television. They'd have to have a team primed to take the inevitable flood of calls that would follow. As always, the vast majority would be a waste of time, some well-intentioned, some less so. They just needed one half-decent lead and they might finally start to make some progress.

She turned off the engine and took out the keys. Since her previous experience, she'd made a point of ensuring they were firmly gripped in her hand. She climbed out of the car, and was immediately hit by the rising wind from off the firth. The sky had clouded over. They'd predicted snow and sleet in the radio weather forecast. They'd had a few sprinklings before Christmas but nothing since, despite the freezing temperatures.

She looked around her. There were lights in a couple of the houses along the street, but no other sign of life. Even so, she had the uneasy sense that she was being observed. The sooner she got inside, the better, if only for her own peace of mind.

It took her a few moments to get the front door open, but then finally she was inside, locking it firmly behind her. She was already feeling more relaxed. She now realised how tense she'd been even in those few short steps from her car to the house.

She walked through the sitting room and went to close the curtains. She'd turned the light on in the hall, but hadn't yet switched on the light in the sitting room, so she could see outside quite clearly.

There was a car passing the house, moving more slowly than she might have expected. Perhaps someone looking for a particular address.

There was no reason for her to be anxious. It was a public road and people were perfectly entitled to drive up it. There wasn't usually much traffic at this time of night, but there would be some.

She drew the curtains closed, and then moved across the room to turn on the light. Her heart was beating more quickly than usual, and she could feel a prickle of anxiety.

Don't be an idiot, she told herself. *You're safe in the house, and there's no one out there. Elliott is just a pathetic old lech who's been well and truly scared off by Alec McKay. There's nothing to worry about.*

She went rapidly through the downstairs rooms, closing the curtains and blinds and double-checking all the windows and doors were locked. It was a routine she went through every night and every morning, so she had no doubts that they would be. But she still found the process reassuring.

It had been a long day, and all she wanted was a bite to eat and a glass or two of wine. Then an early night. She found some left-over pizza in the fridge and stuck that in the oven, then poured herself a large glass of red.

Her only consolation, such as it was, was that at least her evening had been better than Alec McKay's. He'd phoned her to apologise for not returning to the office, explaining what had happened when he'd returned home.

As he'd told her, it seemed likely that Charlie Farrow must have got hold of at least part of the truth about Kevin. She expected Farrow to get as much as he could out of it – he was that sort of copper – but she wasn't sure whether it would help or hinder McKay's position. On the one hand, it would allow Farrow to drag out his investigation. On the other, if it looked as if Kevin had had a possible motive to take his own life, that would at least indicate his death was unconnected with the unidentified body. She hated herself for even thinking in those terms, knowing the distress that might be caused to McKay's family, but it was the reality.

While she waited for the pizza to heat through, she returned to the sitting room with her wine. She began to flick aimlessly through the television channels, hoping to find something sufficiently mindless to suit her mood.

It was then that the doorbell rang.

The unexpected sound literally made her jump, causing her to spill wine on her sleeve. The doorbell rang again, a little more insistent this time.

Shit.

She never had visitors. At least not visitors who turned up

unexpectedly, late in the evening. She knew no one who would do that. Even if they'd just been in the area for some reason, they'd still phone her first to check that she was in and was happy for them to turn up.

So it wasn't anyone she knew. Who else could it be? Jehovah's bloody Witnesses? Not at this time of the night, surely. The same was true of every other option she could think of. Door-to-door charity collectors, or those sad types who tried to sell you overpriced tea towels. No one like that would turn up on your doorstep this late. Certainly not in Scotland. Most sane people would be heading for bed.

The ringing stopped, and then resumed for a third time.

Some neighbour needing help? But the same arguments applied. Any of her near neighbours, the ones who might conceivably look to her for assistance, would have her number and would call first.

Once or twice, she'd thought about putting a spyhole in the door, but had never got round to it, so there was no way to see who was out there without revealing her presence.

She was a copper, and, even putting aside her own current anxieties, opening a door to an unknown visitor late in the evening would not be a smart move. Indeed, if the visitor persisted, she might be wise to call 999.

The ringing stopped and there was silence for a moment. Then there was the sound of something banging hard against the door. *Someone banging with their fist,* she thought, *or maybe kicking the panels.* Whichever it had been, it felt like a vindication of her decision not to open the door.

The sudden thump was followed by a lengthy silence. She was clutching her phone tightly in her hand, poised to dial 999. Then she heard the sound of a car engine starting outside. She moved cautiously to the sitting room window and pulled back the edge of the curtain.

The car she had noticed earlier had clearly pulled in just

beyond her house, and was now doing a U-turn, presumably with the aim of heading out of the village back up to the A9. She kept as still as possible, not wanting to alert the driver to her presence, until she had seen the rear lights disappear into the darkness.

There was no real way of knowing whether her mysterious visitor really had departed, but it seemed probable. She looked at her phone, wondering whether she should still call 999.

She decided that, for the moment, there was little point. She'd do so immediately if it looked as if there was someone still out there. Otherwise, she'd report this in the morning, and it could be followed up from there.

Had it really been Elliott? Would he really have taken the risk of coming here after his meeting with Alec McKay? She realised she honestly couldn't be sure. There'd been something about Elliott – and she knew that McKay had felt it too – that had been beyond reason, beyond the behaviour of any normal person. She didn't know what he might be capable of.

She took out her now overdone pizza, returned to the sitting room and picked up her wine, her ears alert for any sound, any evidence that her visitor was still out there.

There was nothing, and eventually she took her plate and glass to the dishwasher, turned off the lights, and climbed upstairs to bed. She knew, though, that now there was very little chance of sleep.

28

'You're kidding.'

'Does it look like I'm laughing, Alec? Actually, don't answer that. I must look like death warmed up.'

'You really think it was him?'

'I don't know who else. Looks like you're losing your persuasive touch.'

'I thought I'd given him a clear enough shot across the bows. He's a piece of work, isn't he?'

Helena Grant nodded, wearily. 'The bit I really can't believe is the texts. Like he wanted to taunt me. Beautifully timed, too.'

'Bastard,' McKay commented succinctly.

'Too right. Three in the bloody morning. I just thought I might finally be about to get off to sleep, and then the phone buzzes.' She shook her head. '"I know you're in there." I mean, I was fairly confident he hadn't returned and was outside. He'd just sent it from wherever he was to scare the hell out of me. But even so.'

McKay raised an eyebrow. 'And you still didn't call 999?'

'I thought about it. But I knew there'd be no one there, and I'd just end up feeling stupid.'

'You didn't *know* there was no one there.'

'Fair play. But it's one of the problems of getting to this rank as a woman. You don't want to give any ammunition to people who think you're not up to the job.'

'It's not a question of not being up to the job. If I'd been in your position, I'd have called 999.'

She doubted that, from what she knew of McKay, but it wasn't really the point. 'Aye, but in your case, no one would have thought you were a poor wee scaredy woman.'

McKay held up his hands. 'Okay, you survived anyway. What are we going to do about Elliott?'

'Strictly speaking, it's still on Farrow's books.'

'Aye, luckily I haven't drafted my report for him yet. I'll have to take a bit less of a triumphalist tone than I was planning. Pity.'

'There's something else, though. We had this through earlier.' She slid a print-off across the desk to him.

It was a short report of a complaint made by a member of the public about an assault, with apparently sexual intent, carried out in the city centre the previous evening. McKay looked up at Grant with a quizzical expression.

'Read the description.'

McKay read through the rest of the report then nodded. 'Elliott.'

'Calling himself Dennis Allsopp. But sounds like it, doesn't it?'

'Certainly fits the pattern. Man with anger management problems.'

'Among other things. I've just had a telephone chat with the officer who took the statement. The woman involved, this Sheila O'Rourke, nearly didn't bother to report it. She thought it would probably end up being too much hassle. She sounds like a woman who can more than look after herself. But she realised she'd been genuinely scared by Elliott. Her words were, "I don't know what he might be capable of." She decided to report it before he attacked someone else.'

McKay was silent for a moment. 'We've all felt the same about him, haven't we? He's not just your run-of-the-mill middle-aged white misogynist. There's something more there. Something that doesn't recognise the usual limits.'

'That's the way I felt last night. I mean, assuming it was him, it just wasn't rational to come to my house like that. He knows we know who he is. He knows we know he followed me back that first time, and that he sent the texts. If he knows the police are onto him, why would he risk returning?'

'What time did your unwelcome visitor arrive?'

'Must have been getting on for nine thirty. I left here around eight thirty last night. Got home a little after nine, probably. I'd not been back long when the doorbell rang.'

'So that would fit in with the timing of this.' McKay gestured towards the report.

'Pretty much. She reckons they left the restaurant sometime before nine. Then the assault and the delivery of the knee to the balls. Takes you through to nine or so. By the time he's recovered, collected his car and got up to my place, it would be around nine thirty.'

'So, assuming it was him, he arrives at your place with his balls still aching – and not in a good way – and the rich scent of sexual humiliation, as he'd see it, still in his nostrils.'

'You paint a beautiful picture, Alec.'

'So since he can't take out his anger on this Sheila O'Rourke, he decides to take it out on someone who he thinks has humiliated him before.'

'Doubly humiliated him,' Grant pointed out. 'First by rejecting his sexual advances, and second by setting her copper mates on him.'

'Is that it? I mean, is that how he thinks? Or rather doesn't think.'

'That's the way it looks.'

'Christ, that's scary.'

'Look, I'm inclined to take this one on ourselves. His assault on O'Rourke was a serious attack. Okay, she wasn't seriously injured but apparently the bruising on her neck was significant. It wouldn't have taken much more pressure...' She shuddered involuntarily, recalling that this was the man who had most likely been standing outside her door the previous evening. 'It's a different level of seriousness from just getting threatening texts. And I've a bad feeling about it.'

'What about Farrow?'

'I'll present him with a fait accompli. Tell him this one's ours, and that we'll deal with my relatively minor complaint as part of it. I'll make sure I square it in advance upstairs. You know me, I don't go into battle unless my arse is well protected. Obviously, I'll need to keep my distance but you can look after it.'

'Aye, like I haven't enough on,' McKay said.

'You like to keep busy, Alec.' He'd already told her about the previous night's revelations. 'Speaking of which, and of Farrow, is there anything I can do to help on that front?'

'Not for the moment, I don't think. Chrissie's following up with the banks and suchlike this morning. Just trying to get a sense of how big the problem is. She's good at that sort of stuff. Doesn't take any shite.'

'I can imagine. Sounds a mess, though.'

'Hell of a mess,' McKay agreed. 'Christ knows what he was thinking.'

'You reckon his death wasn't accidental?'

'Who knows? We'll probably never find out for sure. He'd certainly painted himself well and truly into a corner, though. It was all going to come crashing down before very long, whatever he did.'

'Jesus. People, eh?'

'Aye, world would be a better place without them.'

She nodded, then pulled another file across the desk towards her. 'Okay, what about our late friend up in Dingwall then? You were going to give me a briefing before we got so distracted.'

McKay had already had a briefing that morning with Jock Henderson and Willy Ingram. *The three wise bloody monkeys,* he thought. Certainly, Ingram was likely to speak no evil or much else either. He and Jock, on the other hand, had probably seen more evil between them than either would want to acknowledge.

It had been a fairly productive meeting, at least in terms of summarising what they had so far. Ingram might not say much, but he ran a tight crime scene. They'd worked late the previous evening, then, having left the scene guarded overnight, they'd resumed at first light with a search of the immediate surrounding area. Henderson had left one of his men up there, with a couple of uniforms, sorting out the final evidence, such as it was.

'White male,' McKay said now to Grant, 'mid-twenties, probably. Cause of death: most likely a bloody great whack to the back of the skull with a heavy object—'

'Most likely?'

'Like I said, the only question is whether that actually did for him, or whether it needed some combination of that, drowning or hypothermia.'

'Poor bugger. He was going to cop it one way or another, wasn't he? Any ID yet?'

'Not yet, but we're hopeful. There's nothing on the body. If he had a wallet or something like that, it maybe fell out into the firth somewhere. That's one of the questions we need to think about. Whether it's worth trying to do a search at that end of the firth. I'm no expert, but I'm assuming when the tide's out it wouldn't be difficult to do at least the area around where the body was found. Might be worth seeing if we can find the wallet and maybe the murder weapon.'

'Worth a try, if you don't think it would require huge resource.'

'I'll look into it,' he said. 'But we might well identify him without the wallet. He's got a couple of distinctive tattoos, so that may help. And he's a drug user or ex-user. Track marks on his arms, though not recent.'

'That might mean he's on our system.'

'Exactly. I've got someone checking that out. The druggie thing would maybe provide a motive, too, if he owed the wrong people.'

'We could do with a quick breakthrough on this one,' Grant said. 'We're still getting nowhere on the other. I'm hoping this afternoon's appeal will help us with the ID but that would still only be the start.'

'You need Alec McKay working on the case.'

'Too right I bloody do. I'm seriously thinking about bringing you back onto it.'

'If Farrow's got his teeth into Kevin's financial problems, it's difficult to see how he's going to conclude there was any link between the two deaths.'

'That's what I'd have thought. Probably one to push for in due course, but not worth it till you've a bit more time on your hands.'

'Don't hold your breath for that.'

'You'd better not be sitting here, then,' she said. 'Haven't you got stuff to be getting on with?'

She ignored the finger he gave her as he left the office.

29

This time, they weren't even bothering to hide their panic.

'He must be somewhere,' Mr Big said. 'Have you looked upstairs properly?'

'Of course, we've looked upstairs.' The young one was shouting now. Jana had never heard him raise his voice like that before. 'We've looked in every sodding room. I thought he must be shagging one of the girls somewhere.'

Mr Big was looking at him. 'He does that, does he?'

The young one made no response, realising he'd spoken out of turn. 'I was just joking,' he said finally.

'I bloody well hope so,' Mr Big said. 'If I catch him putting his hands, or anything else, on the goods...'

Goods, Jana thought. *That's all we are. Not women. Not people. Not human beings. Goods.*

She knew the young one hadn't been joking. She knew Jitters had made advances to some of the younger women, and some of them had responded. She suspected they'd done so more in an effort to ingratiate themselves with him than from any physical or sexual attraction. If so, she could have told them not to waste their time. Jitters had no power, no influence. He was a nobody.

Just a pair of hands. Even less important than the young one. That was obvious.

Now, it seemed, he was missing.

Jana had little interest in Jitters' whereabouts, except to wonder about the apparent cause of his absence. It was the young one who'd noticed first, the previous evening. He'd been walking around the place asking if anyone had seen Jitters. He hadn't called him Jitters, of course. No one called him Jitters except Jana, and that was only in her head. The young one had called him Cal, which was his real name.

She had just gazed blankly back at the young one, as had most of the women. Some had no idea what he was asking. A few, like her, didn't want to show they understood. No one wanted to help him.

Jana had seen Jitters go out, earlier in the afternoon, though she had no intention of telling the young one. He'd been curled up on the sofa in one of the lounges, in his usual way. Then he'd suddenly sprung up, grabbed his old anorak, and headed out of the front door.

She watched him go down the path towards the road, wondering where he might be going. There was nothing else nearby, so she'd assumed he was just going out for a walk, although she knew it would be dark soon.

She'd expected Jitters to return before darkness fell, but he hadn't reappeared. An hour or two later, the young one had noted his absence. At first, he'd seemed only mildly concerned, obviously assuming that Jitters was around the house some-where. But when Jitters still hadn't appeared later in the evening, she could see the young one becoming genuinely worried.

She wondered what he might be worried about, what he thought might have happened to Jitters. She couldn't imagine herself what might have prevented him from returning, but the ways of these people remained largely a mystery to her. Whatever she might have thought, it was clear that the young one was on the edge of panic.

Jana wondered also why the young one cared. He had never shown any real signs even of getting on with Jitters. They were a similar age, but the young one seemed largely to treat Jitters with ill-disguised contempt. If he was worried, she thought, he was most likely worried about himself.

Perhaps he was worried about how Mr Big would react. Mr Big had not been there the previous evening, and Jana had no idea whether the young one had reported Jitters' absence to him immediately. He had turned up in the middle of the morning, entering the building with the air of someone taking control. But his arrival had seemed only to panic the young one still further.

It was clear to Jana that Mr Big had no more idea how to handle the situation than the young one. He had walked around, barking out orders, but, as far as Jana could tell, adding nothing new.

'You need to go and search the woods,' he'd said to the young one.

'Why would Cal be in the woods? He wouldn't have been out there all night.'

'He must be out there. He's not in here.'

It was difficult to argue with the logic at least, Jana thought.

'He's not going to be in the woods either. Anyway, I'm not going anywhere out there till we know what's happened to Cal.'

So it had gone on all morning, round and round, with nobody taking any real action. Mr Big had disappeared into his office, and Jana could hear him making call after call through the thin partition. She couldn't make out most of the words, but she heard him say 'Another one' and 'I don't know.' He said the second phrase repeatedly in one of the calls.

Eventually, he'd emerged from his office and strode to the main door, calling out that he was going and would be back in the morning. The young one had emerged from the lounge. 'You can't just go.'

'Watch me.'

The young one had raced across the large hall, grabbing Mr Big by the arm. 'You can't just leave me. Us.'

Mr Big said nothing, but pulled his arm out of the young one's grip. The young man was still trying to hold on, but Mr Big pushed him back. 'Fuck off, you deadbeat. We'll have a rethink tomorrow if he still hasn't turned up.'

Then he was gone and the young one was reduced to walking aimlessly round the downstairs as if trying somehow to conjure Jitters back into his presence.

Jana watched, knowing that, for a short while at least, no one would be interested in what she was up to. That was one of the few good things about being here. It was not difficult to make herself almost invisible to the likes of the young one.

She waited until he had continued his wandering into another room, then carefully let herself out through the front door. To her surprise, there had been a sprinkling of snow overnight. She had been so fascinated by events in the house she hadn't even thought to look out of the window.

The only footprints in the thin snow were those left by Mr Big as he'd entered and left the house. The tyre marks of his car swept in a large curve across the drive. No one else had left or approached the building since the snow had fallen.

She would leave her own footprints, of course, but she didn't suppose that really mattered. The snow would probably thaw in the course of the day, and even if the prints remained, no one was likely to notice them or care who had made them.

She walked hurriedly down the drive then turned right in the direction that she had seen Jitters go the previous afternoon. She guessed that, unwittingly, Mr Big had probably been correct. It was most likely that, for whatever reason, Jitters had gone for a walk into the woods.

She had left the building without a coat, and she was already feeling cold. The temperature seemed higher than on previous days, perhaps because of the covering of light grey cloud, but there was a brisk wind blowing. Still, she did not intend to be out for long.

She entered the canopy of trees and continued to walk in a straight line, pushing her way through the branches and twigs. After a few moments, she saw the light of the water ahead of her.

It took her just a few more minutes to reach the edge of the trees, the firth just a few metres beyond. There was only a narrow strip of land between the woods and the water, but it contained what, somehow, she had known it would.

Jitters was lying prone on the wet ground, his back covered with a fine coating of snow. She made no effort to check, but he was clearly dead.

She nodded with apparent satisfaction, as if some question, or perhaps some prayer, had been answered. Then she turned and made her way back to the hotel, the cold wind at her back.

30

McKay had spent the morning chasing up the various administration and facilities that would be needed for the Dingwall investigation. It was the kind of work he hated, and he normally made a point of trying to push it in Ginny Horton's direction, on the supposed grounds that it was better for all of them to play to their strengths.

This time, though, Horton was up to her ears in the Fort George enquiry, particularly since the appeal would be going out that afternoon. Even McKay couldn't think of any justification for trying to offload this one on her as well.

It was lunchtime before he finally received the call from Chrissie that he'd been waiting for. 'How's it going?'

'I suspect my morning's been even worse than yours,' Chrissie had said.

'That bad?'

'To be honest, not as bad as I'd feared. Not so far, anyway. There might be more to come crawling out of the woodwork. But bad enough.'

'Go on.'

'Apart from the car stuff, it looks as if Kevin had also taken out a fairly hefty loan secured against their house.'

'Bloody hell.'

'It was a business loan. God knows how he sweet-talked them into giving it to him. He had a whole spiel apparently about how he'd been made redundant and had some redundancy payment he was going to invest in setting up his dream software business. Even produced a credible business plan. Well, credible if you're a know-nothing bank relationship manager bamboozled by technical jargon, I'm guessing.'

'Had he been made redundant? Is that what happened?'

'I don't know yet,' she said, 'But this is where it gets complicated. The bank are getting onto it now, so some of this is just guesswork. I phoned Kevin's ex-employer this morning, but they were very cagey about why he left. They might be prepared to tell Fiona a bit more when she's up to it, but just told me it was all confidential. I didn't get the impression he'd left on good terms, though.'

'So no redundancy payment?'

'That's the weird thing. A sum of money did appear in the business account Kevin had set up as part of securing this loan. Best part of twenty-five grand. That was what persuaded the bank to give him the business loan, along with the business plan. They matched it with a £75,000 loan, secured against their house. There was a fair bit of equity in the house because they bought it years ago and have paid off a fair portion of the mortgage, so that part wasn't a problem.'

'But Fiona said they had a joint mortgage. If they owned the house jointly, wouldn't she have had to agree to it?'

'She would and she did. Or at least the bank believed she had.'

'Jesus.'

'Aye, he forged the signatures. Forged the signature of the witness as well. You wouldn't have thought he could have got away with it, but I suppose the bank wouldn't really have expected that a husband would be lying to his wife to secure a business loan.'

'Even so,' McKay said, 'it's a bit remiss.'

'You could say so. I suspect quite a few people are going to end up in the shite over this.'

'But the result was that Kevin ended up with the thick end of a hundred grand in the bank. But maybe he *was* setting up a business? Is it possible that's what he's been working on for the past year?'

'If so, why not tell Fi?'

'Maybe he's got other secrets. Maybe he wasn't planning to stay with her?' McKay was conscious these suggestions didn't paint Kevin in any better light, but they would at least have been more rational. More rational than embezzling money just to pour it into some dead-end fantasy that was always going to fall apart.

'I don't know what was in his head,' Chrissie said. 'But there's no evidence he ever really made any headway in setting up a business. With one exception, the sums that were taken out of the business account match exactly what was being paid monthly into their joint account. Nothing more than replicating Kevin's old salary. No significant money was taken out for any other purpose, so there's no sign of any investment in a business. There were no other payments in, so he clearly hadn't started trading. The bank was getting concerned and were pressing him for a meeting, but he'd kept fobbing them off. He'd produced a quarterly summary for them of what he was supposedly doing, which sounded plausible enough, but so far there's no evidence that anything was actually happening. The bank gave me the name and details of the accountant he'd appointed at the time of setting up the business, but he'd had no contact with Kevin since. Kevin had registered a company at Companies House, with himself and Fi as directors, but they weren't due to file accounts yet so that tells us nothing.'

'Except that again he'd involved Fiona fraudulently,' McKay pointed out. 'If he wasn't intending to stay with her, why include her as a director? Takes the wind out of my idea.'

'None of it makes much sense,' Chrissie agreed. 'I had a brief chat with the solicitor Fi's appointed, who basically advised me that the whole thing's a big fucking mess, which I think I'd worked out without legal training. The picture's not as bad as it might be. Kevin had burned through about £35,000 of the loan so there's a fair chunk left that can be repaid. Solicitor reckons they'll struggle to make the covenant on the house stand up, given that it was done without Fi's knowledge, so the house isn't at risk from that. There's the car, but the car can be repossessed and Kevin's death complicates the picture with the outstanding debt.' She paused. 'Oh, and it looks as if Kevin had life insurance.'

'Will they pay out if it's confirmed as suicide?'

'According to the solicitor, that's a bit of a myth. I don't know the details of Kevin's policy, but apparently there's often a suicide clause which says they won't pay out if the individual commits suicide within a defined time limit. That's to stop someone just taking out a policy with the sole aim of securing a payout for their next of kin. But this was something Fi and Kevin took out as part of their original mortgage loan so it dates back years. Fi had almost forgotten about it, but we've checked and it's still current. It's not a fortune but if they pay out it'll tide her over for a bit anyway.'

'It's all a bloody mess, though, isn't it? What the hell was Kevin thinking? If you're right, it was all going to come crashing down eventually.'

'I don't know,' she said. 'I can't fathom what his logic was. My guess at the moment is that, after whatever happened with his job, he had some kind of mental breakdown. That he was desperately trying to hold something together that was rapidly falling apart. Even the car looks like it was just another attempt to keep the show on the road without Fi knowing. He took out the lease on the basis of the business loan supposedly as part of setting up the business. But that meant he could sell their own car, so that gave him another few thousand he could draw on if needed. It's like he was just keeping on at it in the hope or expectation that something would turn up.'

'But what was going to turn up? Unless there was some real business there, he was going nowhere.'

'There's just one thing,' Chrissie said.

'What?'

'This is the detail that bothers me. You know I said that the withdrawals from the business account matched his former salary with one exception.'

McKay had forgotten that detail. 'Go on.'

'There was one further withdrawal. A very recent one. A transfer to another account. It was another bank so we don't know if it was to another of Kevin's accounts or to someone else. Ten grand.'

'That's a lot of money to go nowhere.'

'Exactly. The thing is, it was transferred just a couple of days before Kevin died.'

McKay was silent for a moment. 'Are you thinking it might have been linked to Kevin's death.'

'I've no idea,' she said. 'That sort of thing is rather more your department than mine. It just seems a huge bloody coincidence. Just the one unaccounted for payment, and then Kevin topples off the battlements.'

31

'Jesus, I'm glad that's over.' Helena Grant dropped herself down in the seat opposite McKay. She had just finished her interview with the local television news.

'How did it go?'

'About as well as could be expected, given I was largely running on empty. God, I'm tired. But I think it was okay. We did a couple of retakes but I didn't screw it up entirely.'

'We should all adopt that as a motto,' McKay said. 'At least we didn't screw it up entirely.'

'I'm sure you did great,' Ginny Horton said. She and McKay had been comparing notes on the two investigations. McKay was still trying to keep his distance from the Fort George killing, although he was increasingly concluding that, whatever the nature of Kevin's death, it was unlikely to have any connection with the other victim. For the moment, it was more a question of identifying available resources and how these should be allocated across the two enquiries.

'I'm not sure about that,' Grant said. 'But I managed to string a few sentences together. Now we've just got to hope we get a response.'

'We'll get a response,' McKay said, gloomily. 'Those kind of appeals always draw the attention-seekers out of the woodwork. Whether we'll get a useful response is another question.'

'We only need one. One lead as to the identity of our mysterious body. It's not a lot to ask, is it?'

'We'll get it,' Horton said. 'Someone must know him. Someone must be missing him, or have at least noticed he's gone.'

'You'd hope so, wouldn't you?' Grant shook her head wearily. 'That's one of the things I find most depressing about this job. Realising how many people out there are almost off the grid. People without family or friends. People whose work colleagues, if they have any, know and care nothing about them...'

'It's modern life,' McKay said. 'And maybe it's being up here in the back of beyond too. People move away from here to find work, then they lose touch and don't come back. Or people move up here because they want to escape something and don't want to be found.' He was thinking, as he still did too often, of his own daughter, dying alone among the London crowds. He was thinking, too, about all the lost souls they'd dealt with in his years in this job.

'I'm glad I'm keeping cheerful, anyway,' Horton said. 'You two sound as if you're on the point of throwing in the towel.'

'I'm just knackered,' Grant said. 'Bad night and a stressful day. And it's not over yet.'

'Why don't you head home?' McKay said. 'You could do with a break. Nothing's going to stop because you take an hour or two off.'

'I must have missed the meeting where you were appointed my boss, Alec.' Grant laughed. 'It's a nice thought but I want to be here when the calls start to come in. I don't think I'd get much rest if I returned home at the moment. Not after last night.'

'You'll have to go home eventually,' McKay pointed out. 'On that subject, how are things going in persuading Farrow to let us take on Elliott?'

'I've escalated it,' Grant said. 'Farrow was being his usual pig-headed self. Insisted he was on top of it. Made a point of thanking you for your contribution, Alec.'

'Aye. Right.'

'I just don't think he's going to prioritise it. And, frankly, I'd like it prioritised. Not just for my sake, though I'm not too proud to admit that's part of it. I just think Elliott's a nasty piece of work. I wonder what he's done already that we're not aware of.' She shrugged. 'Anyway, I've suggested to the powers that be that we take it on, even though we've got more than enough on our plates already.'

'If you're worried about Elliott, couldn't you get some protection?' Horton asked.

'On what grounds? A few texts that may be nothing more than bluster? Someone ringing my doorbell late in the evening? At the moment, we don't even know that it was Elliott who was involved in that assault last night. It seems likely, but we don't have the evidence. There's not enough there to justify allocating a uniform for my personal use.'

'You're more than welcome to stay with us for a few nights, if that would help,' Horton said. 'Isla would be more than happy to have you there.'

'I'd say the same,' McKay added, 'if we didn't have Fiona in the spare room. We could only offer you the sofa.'

Grant smiled. 'Thanks, both. It might come to that,' she said to Horton, 'and I really appreciate the offer. But I'd rather stick it out if I can. I don't want to be intimidated by the likes of Elliott.'

McKay was about to offer some response when he noticed the slightly plump figure of DC Josh Carlisle standing in the doorway. McKay wasn't sure how long the young officer had been standing there, but he had the sense that Carlisle might have been waiting for some minutes to interrupt his more senior colleagues. 'Josh?'

'Sorry, boss. Looks like we've got something.'

McKay waved him in. 'We're all hoping this is good news, Josh. We could all do with it.'

Carlisle was clearly slightly overwhelmed at the prospect of having to deliver his news to such a large and imposing group. 'We think we've identified the Dingwall body.'

McKay sat up. 'Go on.'

'He's on the system. Fingerprints and DNA. Gordon Tennant. Had a record. Possession. Housebreaking. Couple of other instances of petty theft. All a good few years ago, though, so he's been off the radar for a while. Last address we had for him was somewhere in Inverness, but he seems to have moved about a fair bit over the years.'

McKay nodded. 'Any evidence that he was still a user?'

'Nothing on the records,' Carlisle replied. 'Like I say, no sign that we'd had any dealings with him over the last few years. So my guess would be he'd got clean, but who knows?'

'Even if he was,' McKay said, 'that doesn't mean he still wasn't carrying some baggage from the bad old days. If he owed money to the wrong people, they wouldn't forget. At least it gives us a starting point. Well done, Josh.' McKay assumed that Carlisle hadn't actually done much other than be the bearer of the news, but Grant was always telling him he needed to motivate the younger officers. Carlisle, who always had the air of an over-eager schoolboy, seemed pleased with the recognition.

'Now all you've got to do is find out his current address, work, any known associates, and anything else you can about it. Shouldn't take you long.'

If anything, Carlisle seemed even further enthused by McKay's instruction, but after Carlisle had left the room, Grant said, 'One day he's just going to tell you to bugger off, Alec.'

'Then I'll know that my work here really is done,' McKay said. 'He's a decent lad, though. Reminds me of myself at that age.'

Grant shook her head. 'You never were that age. Right, I'm going to go and get myself the first of what will no doubt be innumerable cups of coffee while I wait for the calls to come flooding in.'

'One down, one to go,' McKay said. 'Maybe our luck's beginning to turn.'

32

The first calls were just beginning to come in. A clip from Grant's interview had been broadcast on the local radio news bulletins in the latter part of the afternoon, and a longer excerpt would be featured on the regional television news in the early evening. That was when they were expecting the real flood of calls to start coming in. For the moment, it was little more than a trickle.

As always, the majority of the calls were unpromising. They'd so far had few that were really off-the-wall, but many were little more than well-intentioned individuals who honestly believed they'd seen the figure Grant had described in various places around the city on the day of his death. They would all have to be followed up, and it was possible some leads might emerge from them. Even so, Grant wasn't hopeful that they would produce any new information.

For the first hour or so, she'd sat in on the call handlers, partly to get a feel for the types of calls that were coming in, and partly to ensure the handlers could deal with any questions or issues that might be raised by callers.

It all seemed to be going as well as she could have hoped. The real test would come after the television broadcasts but she was confident they had the resources to cope. The other elements of the investigation, such as they were, appeared to be running smoothly. It was all routine stuff – checking CCTV footage, interviewing the drivers of the buses that served the fort in case their victim had arrived by public transport, trying to track down other visitors on that Sunday. The work was painstaking and progress was almost non-existent, but it was the only way to proceed until they had some firmer leads. Ginny Horton was co-ordinating much of it, and seemed to have everything well in hand.

She made her way back upstairs and peered into McKay's office. He was ending a call so she waited discreetly in the corridor till he'd finished, then poked her head round the door. 'Sorry. Didn't mean to eavesdrop. Assume that was Chrissie?'

'Just the latest update on the Kevin Andrews' estate.'

'Anything new?' McKay had already updated her on what Chrissie had discovered about Kevin's financial affairs.

'Yes and no. Nothing really new on the financial issues. Fiona's basically just stuck all that in the hands of the solicitor to try to get what clarity she can. But she also had a shot at talking to Kevin's ex-employer to try to find out more about why he left. They refused to say anything to Chrissie, but they felt obliged to be a bit more forthcoming with Kevin's widow.'

'And?'

'Bad news. It seems as if Kevin was sacked. For embezzlement.'

'Oh, sweet Jesus. That doesn't sound good.'

'Not remotely good. This was a financial services company. Pension funds. I don't know any of the detail, but Kevin cooked up a scheme, in conjunction with one of the finance guys, to siphon off money via some smart tweaks to the IT system. Small amounts from each account, but adding up to a tidy sum of money.'

'And he was caught?'

'Sounds as if the other guy blew the whistle. Don't know if he got cold feet or if there was some falling out between him and Kevin, but Kevin was left carrying most of the can. Maybe rightly.'

'They didn't prosecute?'

'Reading between the lines, they did as much as they could to sweep it under the carpet. Difficult to know because they were very cagey with Fiona, but my impression is that, though they fired Kevin, they didn't make much of an effort to recover whatever money had been removed. It would have been small beer to them, and they'd have been far more damaged by any enquiry that exposed how lax their systems security had been.'

'So Kevin just walked away with it?'

'Who knows? They don't seem to be telling, and Kevin never will. But it would explain the money Kevin was able to invest to help secure the business loan.'

'It's always the quiet ones, isn't it?'

'I still can't quite believe we're talking about Kevin. I'd have had him down as one of the most boring, law-abiding people I've ever met. Not the master of the computer heist.' He paused. 'There's one other thing.'

'Go on.'

'Fiona was contacted by Charlie Farrow. He's asked her to come in for an interview.'

'I suppose that was always bound to happen eventually. Farrow's not exactly Mr Sensitive, but she shouldn't have anything to worry about.'

'Let's hope not. If Farrow's got the whole story, though, he might be interested in whether she was an accessory before or after the fact. Apparently, he dropped a couple of hints in that direction. Enough to make her anxious.'

'That's ridiculous, surely.'

'It doesn't make much sense, though I suppose you can argue

that Fiona unwittingly benefitted from Kevin's fraud in that he continued to transfer money to their joint account every month. But it's clear that Kevin went to great lengths to keep Fiona in the dark. She had no knowledge of the source of the money, or that it wasn't simply Kevin's salary. Her supposed signatures on the business loan agreement are quite clearly forgeries. Nothing like her real signature. I can't see how you could make a case stand up.'

'But?'

'It's just that the whole thing's so bizarre. That Kevin managed to keep her in the dark for so long. I suppose if I were in Farrow's shoes, I'd probably want to take a close look at that before I was satisfied.'

'He needs to do his job,' Grant agreed. 'Just hope he does it with a degree of sensitivity.'

'Oh, aye. It's his middle name.'

'How are you getting on with Gordon Tennant?'

'Surprisingly well, actually. Sometimes you just need the one fact and things start to open up.'

'Don't rub it in. I'm still waiting for the one fact.'

'Sorry. It's not as if we've cracked the case. But we've been able to take a few steps forward at least. Thanks to the dear old council tax, we've got Tennant's last known address. It's in Dingwall so I thought I might take a drive up there when I finish for tonight. See if I can track down anyone who can tell me more. We're also in contact with the revenue and DWP to find out if they have any useful gen on him.'

'Sounds like progress. We could do with some.'

'I'll do my level best to chivvy things along, then.'

It took McKay a few minutes to locate the address, and a few moments more to find any way of gaining entrance.

Gordon Tennant's residence had apparently been one of a small group of flats above and behind a row of shops in the High Street. Dingwall High Street always reminded McKay of a town from the 1950s, with the kind of shops that you didn't find in most places anymore – proper butchers, a master tailor. There was even a Wimpy Bar further down the street. The earlier sprinkling of snow had largely melted in the town centre and the road was slick and wet, doubling the welcoming lights of the shopfronts. Even in the darkness of a midwinter afternoon, the place looked attractive enough.

The entrance to the flat was through an archway between the shops, resulting in the gap in numbering that had initially left McKay baffled. The archway led into a short alley that ended in a small parking area. At the rear of the building, there was a common door for the flats.

The details McKay had been given did not include a flat number. There was a speakerphone device next to the row of bells, so he pressed a bell at random and waited. When there had been no response after a few moments, he moved his finger down to the next bell and tried again.

This time, the speaker buzzed and a voice said, 'Yes?'

'I'm looking for Gordon Tennant.'

'Gordie? You want flat two.'

'Oh, right, thanks.' He pressed the bell for flat two, expecting no response. His plan was then to try some of the other neighbours, including the one who had just answered, in the hope of extracting some more information about Tennant.

Unexpectedly, though, the speaker crackled to life and a female voice said, 'Yes?'

'Is this Gordon Tennant's flat?'

'Gordie?' There was something in her tone he couldn't interpret through the poor speaker. 'Who's asking?'

'Police. DI Alec McKay.'

'Police. Shit–'

The speaker went dead and, for a moment, McKay thought he might have scared the woman off. But after a few seconds the door rattled and opened on a chain. A pale face peered out at him. 'You sure you're police? Where's your uniform?'

McKay held his warrant card carefully in front of her. 'CID. DI McKay.' He glanced around, as if to remind her that neighbours might be watching. 'Can I come in?'

She released the chain and ushered him in. She was a slender young woman, with a very white complexion and dyed blonde hair. 'Aye, you'd better. Has something happened to Gordie?'

He followed her through a door on the left of the hallway into the flat. It was a small place, sparsely furnished, but tidy and apparently well maintained. 'I'm afraid so. I think you might want to sit down.'

He hadn't been expecting this. He'd assumed, for no particularly good reason, that Tennant would have lived alone. His objective in coming here had been to try to obtain some information from Tennant's neighbours, not to end up breaking the bad news to a dependent.

'Are you Mr Tennant's partner?' It was probably better that he shouldn't make any more assumptions before proceeding.

'His wife, aye. Aileen. What's happened?'

There was never any easy way to say it, and McKay was conscious that he'd have handled this differently if he'd known in advance what the visit would entail. 'I'm afraid your husband's dead, Mrs Tennant. I'm very sorry.'

She was staring at him as if she had scarcely understood what he was saying. She didn't even look surprised by the news. She just looked mildly put out, as if she'd been expecting it but perhaps not quite at this moment. 'What happened?'

'That's what we're trying to find out. When did you last see your husband?'

'I don't know.' She shook her head, as if trying to clear it. 'I mean, a couple of days ago. When he left for work.'

'You weren't expecting him back before now?'

'He does a bit of travelling for his job. Van driving, I mean. He's sometimes away for a couple of days if he's heading south.'

'I see. So you were expecting him to be away?'

'For a day or two, yes. He was a bit vague about when he'd be back. He doesn't always know for certain.'

McKay noted the present tense. It was always like that. This woman hadn't really registered yet that her husband wouldn't be coming home again. 'Where did he work?' He knew he was in danger of interrogating her, but his instincts told him that, for the moment at least, she wanted to keep talking rather than think about the implications of what he'd told her.

'He worked for a hotel.' She mentioned the name of a place some miles west which McKay vaguely recognised. 'Just doing odd jobs and stuff.'

'Including van driving?' McKay wondered what sort of hotel work would involve travelling.

'They're a chain, you see. The hotels. National. Gordie takes stuff between them when they need it, or picks up stuff from suppliers. So sometimes he has to go to places in England.' She stopped. 'But what happened?' It was as if she'd only just remembered what McKay had told her.

McKay took a breath. 'We think he was killed. Murdered.'

She looked up, startled, as if this news really had been unexpected. 'Murdered?'

'We're not certain till we know the full circumstances, but it looks that way, yes.'

She frowned, clearly not processing what he was telling her. 'But where?'

He took a breath, deciding that it was better to speak straightforwardly. 'His body was found quite close by. On the edge of the Cromarty Firth on the road back to the Ardullie roundabout.'

'I don't understand. Was he drowned?'

'We're still waiting to confirm the exact cause of death. But it looks as if he was attacked. Do you know any reason why anyone might have wanted to harm him?'

She shook her head. 'I mean, he mixed with some dodgy characters in the old days and he's still got one or two friends that are – well, you know. But everyone liked Gordie. He was just one of the lads. We were just starting to get things together. He'd got the hotel job and I work in one of the shops here. We'd found this place. It was all just beginning to be okay...' Finally, the emotion hit her and she dropped her head into her hands, sobbing.

This was where McKay wished he could start all this again. Turn up here knowing what he was going to find, ideally with another officer who could offer the kind of empathy he struggled with. 'I'm very sorry,' he said, conscious of how feeble his words sounded. 'I know it must be an awful shock.'

'I don't understand,' she said, still crying. 'Why would anyone hurt Gordie? Why would anyone do that?'

'I don't know. That's what we need to find out. The more you can tell me, the more we'll be able to help you.'

'Will I be able to see him?'

'Of course.' He didn't tell her that they'd probably need her to confirm the identity of the body. That, like everything else, would be something for later. He'd already pushed her further than he felt comfortable with. 'We'll arrange all that. Is there someone you can go to now? A friend or relative?'

'There's my friend Cathy upstairs. She's the nearest. I don't have any other relatives. Not close by, anyway.'

Shit, McKay thought. He'd been hoping there might be a sister or even a mother she could go to. 'Do you want me to go and see if Cathy's there?'

'I think she's in. I heard her moving about. But, aye, thanks.' She had regained a little of her composure, but gave the occasional sob as she spoke.

McKay left the flat door open and made his way upstairs to the door that Aileen Tennant had indicated. He knocked gently and, after a few moments, the door was opened by a woman. She was older than Aileen Tennant, probably in her mid-thirties, plump and cheerful-looking. She appeared surprised to see McKay. 'Oh, Christ, I was expecting Aileen.'

'I'm sorry to disturb you.' He held out his warrant card. 'DI Alec McKay. I'm afraid I've just had to break some bad news to Mrs Tennant.'

The woman glanced down the stairs behind him. 'Bad news? What kind of bad news?' She paused. 'Is it Gordie?' There was something in her tone that caught McKay's interest.

'I'm afraid so. He's been found dead.'

'Oh, God, you're kidding? No, I mean, of course you're not. But dead? Jesus, poor Aileen.'

'I was wondering if you'd be able to sit with her. She's in a bit of a state of shock, I think.'

'I'm not surprised. What happened to him?'

'We don't know the full circumstances yet. His body was found on the edge of the firth.'

'I saw the mention on the local news. So that was Gordie. Bloody hell. I even drove past the cars yesterday. Wondered what was going on. Never dreamed. I'd intended to mention it to Aileen. Glad I didn't now.'

She clearly had a capacity to continue talking without worrying too much about what she was saying. That might be just what was required at the moment, McKay reflected. 'Is that okay? Are you able to sit with her for a bit?'

'Aye, of course. I'll bring her up here and give her a bite to eat. No problem.'

'That's good of you.' McKay extracted one of his business cards and handed it over. 'We'll have to be back in touch with her, but we can do that when she's up to it. If she needs anything in the meantime, she can call me on this number. I'll get her contact details and yours before I go.'

'Poor Aileen,' she said again. 'And poor bloody Gordie, too.

Though I'm not entirely surprised. Aileen doesn't want to hear it, but he was a bad 'un. Always was and still is– Well, not now, I suppose. But I'm not surprised he came to a sticky end.'

McKay looked at her for a moment, wondering whether he should enquire further. But now wasn't the moment. There'd be time enough for that later.

33

Even in less than twenty-four hours, the atmosphere seemed to have changed yet again. Yesterday, there had been a sense of panic, a feeling that things were slipping out of control. Today, Jana thought, it felt almost like despair. As if they had given up and had resigned themselves to whatever the fates might have in store for them.

She knew she was probably being fanciful. She could hear little of what the men were saying – even if the little she could hear was intriguing enough – so she was drawing her conclusions only from the odd snatch of conversation and their behaviour and body language. No doubt she was reading too much into what she was seeing.

Even so, she had little doubt that things were changing.

The fat one was there, the first time she had seen him for some days. He'd turned up that morning with Mr Big, and another couple of young ones she hadn't seen before. She decided to call the first one Mouse because he reminded her of a mouse. He was small, with slicked-back dark hair, a thin not particularly flattering moustache, and large, sticking out ears. Mouse. The second one she called Stick because he was tall, skinny and ungainly. *A thin, unreliable stick of green wood,* she thought. *Stick.*

She assumed that at least one of the two young men was there to replace Jitters. He'd never seemed to do much, Jitters, but she supposed he must have had some function here. The young one cooked the breakfasts when needed, and she'd seen Jitters helping out with that, along with the women, but that was about it. They hadn't had any guests staying for the last couple of days, but presumably more would come soon. Perhaps that was why Mouse or Stick were needed.

Like Mr Big the previous day, they had turned up in the early afternoon as if bearing the solution to whatever problems might have arisen. As on the previous day, no action had followed their arrival other than endless discussions. No one had followed Jana's path down through the woods to the edge of the firth. As far as she was aware, Jitters' body would still be lying there. She assumed it would be well-preserved in these cold temperatures, but before too long the creatures of the woods would start to take an interest in it.

She wondered vaguely why no one else had gone down there. When Jitters went missing, it had been one of the obvious places to look. She had even heard Mr Big suggesting they should search down there. The young one had refused, perhaps understandably. But, when Mr Big had returned today with the others, she had assumed that the group of them might institute a more serious search. But they had not done so.

Perhaps, she concluded, they were scared.

And perhaps they were right to be. Perhaps she was the one who had been foolish, going down there by herself with the light fading. But she didn't think so. Someone had killed Jitters, but somehow she thought that whoever had done so would have no interest in her.

She continued with the usual cycle of pointless activities, working as hard as she always did with no understanding of why this was needed or what she was achieving. The men had gathered in the downstairs meeting room again, so she couldn't hear what they might be saying. But every now and then one of them would emerge to grab a coffee or use the lavatories, and she'd hear brief exchanges through the open door.

She heard one of them – she thought the fat one – say that this was now the third one and that someone was clearly out to disrupt the business. Someone was trying to scare them, he said. The young one had replied that, in that case, they were bloody succeeding.

She wasn't sure what had given her the impression of despair. It was mainly the behaviour of Mr Big, she thought. Yesterday, she'd thought he'd lost his air of authority, the apparent assurance that he'd always carried about himself like a heavy coat. Suddenly, he'd seemed unconfident, hesitant, out of his depth. It was as if he was looking for someone else to tell him what to do.

Today, that air seemed to have deepened. It was as if, even if someone had told him what to do, he wouldn't have cared. It was as if it had all slipped beyond him, and he just wanted to bring things to an end. His body language was that of a man who had given up.

Fanciful, she knew. But she still felt that it was not too far from the truth. The fat one also seemed to have changed. He'd always displayed his own kind of assurance – bumptious, pompous, arrogant. As if he was having to mix with a class of people who were beneath him. That hadn't dissipated entirely, but he seemed somehow deflated, as if he no longer fully believed in himself. Perhaps, she thought, he never really had.

She had always been wary of the fat one. She disliked all of the men in their different ways, but there was something about the fat one that really made her uncomfortable. It was partly the way he stared at her. He stared at all the women, of course, and she imagined he made the younger ones feel even more uneasy. But she sensed something else there.

Once or twice, she had seen him lose his temper, usually with one of the women. She had never seen what caused the outbursts. She suspected it was because he had made some advance that had been rejected. Perhaps the rejection had not even been conscious. Most of the women here were too scared not to at least play up to the men. But she knew herself that, if the fat one came too close to her, she found herself flinching involuntarily.

Whatever the cause, his fury had been extraordinary and utterly disproportionate. He had screamed and shouted, and on one occasion she had seen him strike one of the younger women across the face, knocking her to the ground. The young one had dragged him away on that occasion, but Jana wondered what would have happened had the fat one not been interrupted.

He scared her. All the men scared her, but with the fat one she felt as if the veneer of self-control was almost non-existent. Like most of the women, she did her best to avoid him, shuffling past in silence if she found herself encountering him unexpectedly.

Today, he seemed different, but she found him no less frightening. She felt that, whatever was going wrong here, his anxiety would quickly translate into the same kind of fury she had witnessed previously. She could almost see it in the way he moved, the way he interacted with the other men. That anger was seething just below the surface.

Someone will suffer, she thought. *Someone will pay.*

The men's meeting went on for most of the afternoon, with Jana occasionally catching glimpses of their apparently aimless coming and going. She had no idea what was happening, but she had the sense, from their demeanour and from the few further snatches of conversation she overheard, that they were making little progress with whatever they were discussing.

She had assumed at first they had gathered because Jitters had gone missing. But it seemed to be more than that. It was as if Jitters' absence was a symptom of what they were facing, rather than the issue itself. She wondered whether they knew, or at least had guessed, what had happened to Jitters. And she wondered if they knew or had guessed why it had happened and who was responsible.

Whatever was happening, she felt as if in some way things were coming to a head. *Something is going to change soon,* she thought. And, whatever the outcome, whatever it might mean for the men in there, she had no doubt that it would be worse still for her and for the other women.

Someone would suffer.

34

Helena Grant had remained in the office until after seven. The expected deluge of calls following her appearance on the television news had duly materialised, and she and Ginny Horton had spent much of the early evening reviewing the emerging information.

There were the usual sprinkling of attention-seekers and time-wasters, some obvious, others that would no doubt be exposed only when they were followed up. As earlier in the afternoon, the vast majority of the calls were well-intentioned supposed sightings of the victim across the city, most of which would turn out unprovable or unhelpful. And there were a small number which sounded more promising, including some suggesting a potential identity for the victim.

They would collate all these overnight, and then in the morning assess their relative credibility and determine a strategy for checking out this intelligence. But there was enough there for her to feel encouraged.

She'd been chain-drinking coffee for most of the afternoon to stave off her exhaustion, but recognised that any more would have her bouncing off the ceiling. 'I'm going to have to call it a night,' she said to Horton. 'Otherwise, I'll be comatose.'

'I'll stay around for a little while,' Horton said. 'Isla's in London today so we'll be eating late anyway. But I'm not sure there's much more we can do tonight.'

McKay had called her as she was driving back over the Kessock Bridge to update her on his meeting with Aileen Tennant. She could tell that he was in the car too, talking on the hands-free.

'Poor woman,' he said. 'I could have handled it better.'

'You weren't to know she'd be there.'

'I should have considered it as a possibility. I'd just got Tennant pegged as one of those wastrels, you know. Some druggie scraping by on the dole. Teach me not to make assumptions.'

'Sounds as if you're making progress, though.'

'Maybe. We'll interview Aileen Tennant as soon as she's in a fit state and see what further light she can shed. I want to talk to the neighbour again too. She seemed to have a fairly strong opinion about Tennant that didn't entirely square with what his widow told me. Might just be gossip, but worth checking out. And we'll talk to his employer tomorrow and see if they can give us anything useful. Now we've got a thread to tug on, we may be able to start unravelling what's behind this.'

'Sounds like we've both had a productive day, then. We seem to be getting some potentially useful responses to the media appeal. It's early days but I'm keeping my fingers crossed.' She signalled left to pull off into the village. 'Oh, and the super got back to me. He's okayed our taking over the Elliott case. Or at least the assault complaint that we're assuming is probably Elliott. He agreed that, as a potentially serious assault, it should sit with us, particularly as, for the moment, we've no evidence that it's linked to my texts.'

She heard McKay laugh. 'He doesn't much like Farrow either, does he?'

'Not for me to say. I'll no doubt have Farrow on the phone in the morning to bend my ear about it.'

'Give him my regards. By the way, I hope you're heading home. You were looking a bit knackered this afternoon.'

'You say the nicest things, Alec. Thanks. But, yes, I am heading home. Where I'll have something to eat, a glass of wine and an early night.'

'Glad to hear it.' There was a pause and she could almost hear his hesitation. 'Look, by all means tell me to bugger off, but I'm only just heading back from Dingwall myself. Chrissie asked me to pick up a few bits and pieces from the supermarket on my way past. If you wanted me to stop off at your place and help you check that everything's okay, I'm only a couple of minutes away.'

Normally, she would almost certainly have told him that it was a nice thought but that, yes, he should just bugger off. Tonight though, as she turned off onto the road down to the village, she realised how much she was dreading arriving home. Not being at home. She wanted that. But that moment of arrival in the winter dark, the short walk from her car to the front door, the agonising few moments when she'd fumble with the key before getting the door open. The constant sense that she was being observed, that at any moment someone could be behind her. It wasn't remotely like her, but she was genuinely rattled. No doubt, it was partly just tiredness. Maybe another part of it was just the buzz of the caffeine in her veins. But the largest part, she knew, was the unease left by her encounters with Elliott.

'If you really are only a couple of minutes away, aye, why not? I can make you a cup of tea. I'd offer you some of the wine if you weren't driving.'

'Tea's fine. I'm just pulling off the A9 now.'

'You're right behind me, then. I'll pull in outside the house and wait for you.'

'Two minutes.'

She ended the call and turned left towards her house, drawing up outside the front door as usual. As she turned off the engine, she noticed another car, maybe twenty metres up the road. It was parked on the opposite side, beside the firth, facing towards her. The car was positioned inconspicuously midway between two streetlights, with no other cars around it. She couldn't be entirely sure in the darkness, but in the light from the nearer streetlight she thought she could see a figure sitting behind the wheel.

Her first thought was that somehow McKay had managed to arrive here before her. She was on the point of leaving the car to wave to him when she saw a set of headlights coming along the road behind her. A moment later, McKay's car pulled up in front of hers.

She waited until she saw McKay leaving his car, and then climbed out to join him. Almost immediately, the car opposite started its engine. Its headlights came on and it pulled out into the street, passing them before heading back down the road, presumably back to the A9. She squinted after it, but could not read the registration plate in the darkness.

'Not our friend, surely?' McKay said, voicing her own thoughts.

'I don't know,' she said. 'People do sometimes break their journey down here if they want to make a phone call or kill a bit of time between appointments.'

'Even at night?'

'Less so at night,' she acknowledged. 'If it was him, he buggered off pretty quickly when he saw you get out of the car.'

'Must be my winning personality.' He gestured towards the house. 'Let's get you inside, shall we? It might be picturesque but it's bloody cold.'

Once inside the house, she allowed McKay to do a quick check of the rooms while she filled the kettle. She was trying to treat it as a joke, but they both knew how jittery she was feeling.

'All seems to be okay,' he said, 'though the intruders have left your bedroom in a terrible mess.'

'Ha bloody ha.'

'Seriously, all looks fine. I'm more concerned about whether it really was chummy outside. Whatever his intentions, that would be getting seriously obsessive.'

'But if it is him, why so obsessive about me? I can't be the only person who's ever spurned his advances. To be honest, I'd worry about any woman who hadn't.'

'Maybe because you also represent a form of authority? But he must know he's on dangerously thin ice. If he's always been like this, I'm surprised he's not appeared on our radar before now.'

'We don't know for sure he hasn't. We don't even know for sure that Elliott is his real name. But maybe it's just that he's now slipping from his moorings for some personal reason.'

'If we've got the go-ahead, I'm more than happy to start doing some digging. If it was Elliott who assaulted Sheila O'Rourke, we'll have him bang to rights on that, if nothing else.'

She finished making his tea and poured herself a glass of wine. 'I feel bad about asking you to come here, Alec. Apart from anything else, it's such a sexist cliché. I should be able to look after myself.'

McKay shrugged. 'But that's the trouble with slimeballs like Elliott, isn't it? It's all about intimidating someone who's physically weaker. Though, to be honest, if there was a fight between you and Elliott, I know where my money would be. He wouldn't know what hit him.'

She laughed. 'You're probably right. But he knows how to manipulate. Knows how to play on your fears. When he sent those last texts, he knew precisely when to send them – the middle of the night, when I was feeling exhausted and isolated.' She shook her head, her expression suggesting she was reliving the moment. 'Anyway, thanks for coming, Alec. Even if that wasn't him outside, it was helpful having you around.'

She knew she was leaving unspoken the other awkwardness about McKay being in her house. They'd had one other encounter, during his separation from Chrissie, which might have ended with her spending the night with him. That had been fuelled by a few drams, and in the end they'd both seen sense. But the moment had been there. 'How are things with Chrissie?' she said, not knowing if she ought to be asking.

'We're getting there. Closer than we've been for ages, really. The stuff with Fiona's been a distraction, but in some ways, weirdly, it's beneficial. We've had to team up to help her.' He laughed. 'It's an ill wind and all that.'

'I'd better let you get back,' Grant said. 'You've enough to be dealing with back there.'

'Too right. There don't seem to have been any more developments this afternoon, from what Chrissie said. So now we've just got Charlie Farrow to deal with. Looks like he wants to interview Fiona personally.'

'Always one for a hands-on approach, our Charlie.'

'Aye. Especially if it gives him a chance to screw me over, even if only by proxy.' He swallowed the last of the tea and climbed to his feet. 'I'd best be getting back. You sure you're going to be all right?'

'I'll be grand. I'll make sure everything's locked up, microwave a lasagne or something, then aim to sleep the sleep of the just. A perfect evening.'

'If anything happens, don't hesitate to call me. And don't hesitate to call 999 as well. You know that's the advice you'd be giving to any member of the public in this situation.'

'I know.' She followed him back to the front door. 'And, Alec, I really do appreciate this. Thanks.'

He grinned. 'As long as you don't forget when appraisal time comes around, eh?'

Archie Donaldson was a man of simple tastes. Simple but bloody expensive. That was what he always told people. It was his idea of a joke, though he'd never entirely understood the point of jokes. He didn't have much of a sense of humour, and he laughed mainly at the misfortunes of others.

For Donaldson, that was pretty much the purpose of life. To get one over on others before they got one over on you. That was what it was all about. That was the bloody hokey-cokey. If you didn't keep your wits about you, you were dead. It was as simple as that.

He'd always believed that. And that was what was worrying him.

It was easy to believe in the survival of the fittest, as long as you were confident you were top of the pile. It started to become harder if you thought your standing was slipping.

The truth was someone was having a laugh.

That was the real problem. Straightforward head-to-head competition he could have coped with. He knew how to deal with that. He knew how to keep his share of the market, how to drive out the opposition, how to make sure his operation was that one step ahead. You could do that if you knew what you were dealing with.

He'd thought they'd had it all sewn up around here. He wasn't greedy. He wasn't looking to be one of the biggest fish. He'd chosen territory that no one else seemed really to be bothered about, and made it his own. That had been a smart business move.

He'd carved out his own niche, and taken all the necessary steps to make the entry threshold too high for anyone else to muscle in. He knew his stuff. Some of them had ripped the piss out of him when he'd embarked on the MBA course at the uni. But he wasn't thick, and he wanted them to know that. That was what made him different. Unlike most of them, he had two brain cells to rub together.

In the end, he hadn't had the time to finish the programme. But he'd mostly enjoyed it and he'd learned a lot. It had influenced his business strategy, given him yet another means of maintaining an edge.

At the same time, he'd been careful not to tread on anyone else's toes. None of the big players, anyway. He knew his limits, and he was only too aware he lacked the resources to take on any of them. If he'd devoted real time and money to it, he could have taken on anyone. But it wasn't worth it. The risks were too great. And he wasn't a greedy man.

Just a man of simple, expensive tastes.

So he'd chosen to work with the big players down south. They were happy enough to let someone run the business up here – Christ, he imagined that none of them had ever been north of Perth, except maybe on holiday – as long as they got their cut. So he gave them their cut, and they gave him, in effect, a licence to operate. It had been a great wee arrangement.

And now it all seemed to be going tits-up. That was the trouble with dealing day in, day out with low-life scumbags.

Someone, sometime, would want to try it on. And now someone was.

He'd expected it to happen eventually. The big players wouldn't be interested, but some deadbeat would see what he'd achieved, and would want a slice of it. He'd never been particularly worried about that, assuming he was more than capable of dealing with anyone who might try.

But he'd expected a full-frontal assault, not this kind of insidious, intimidating, cowardly bollocks. This was a war of attrition. Taking out one at a time, apparently at random, until he was forced to capitulate. He didn't even know for sure what they, whoever they were, wanted him to do. Just withdraw from the business, he supposed, cut back, or even stop entirely so they could muscle in as they wanted.

Once or twice, particularly over the last couple of days, he'd felt tempted to do just that. He'd amassed a bob or two over the last few years. Maybe it was time to cash it all in, and let someone else take the flak for a change. He was sick of feeling exhausted, sick of feeling anxious, sick of always having to take the responsibility, sick of always having to decide what to do next.

He could retire. Maybe slip away overseas to somewhere warmer than this. Somewhere he could just sit in a sunlit bar by the sea, sipping fancy cocktails and counting his money.

The feeling never lasted too long. Not even today, when he'd been feeling lower than usual. As always, he ended the day thinking, *Fuck 'em. Fuck 'em all.*

He didn't mind thinking about retirement. But he'd only retire when he was good and ready, at a time of his own choosing. He wasn't going to retire just because some wee scrote was trying to frighten him out of business.

That was what today's meeting had been about. He'd needed to know exactly where things stood. What people were hearing. What the state of the finances was. How they could gear themselves up for a fightback.

It hadn't been encouraging. The business was struggling and even Elliott couldn't entirely explain why. Which made him suspicious of Elliott. Donaldson wondered now if he'd made a mistake in taking a more 'hands off' approach to the business over the last year or so. He wanted some deniability if the shit should ever really hit the proverbial, and in any case he'd had no real option other than to trust Elliott's convoluted accounting schemes. The man had come highly recommended, and Donaldson could see why. He knew his stuff, there was no question of that. The issue was whether he could be trusted, and Donaldson was beginning to have his doubts.

The three managers were something else again. Not so much wet behind the ears as still fucking embryonic. The one at the place today, Franny Hooper, looked about twelve and seemed to behave in roughly the same way. The other two weren't much better. Donaldson had asked himself why he'd appointed them in the first place, but he knew the main reason was that they'd all been willing to work for a pittance. It had seemed the right decision at the time, but now, when he needed some brains around him, it seemed a false bloody economy.

He'd left the meeting in a sense of despair. None of them seemed to realise how serious things were. They were all scared, yes, but they were scared only for their own safety. They weren't concerned with what this meant for the business. They weren't concerned that someone out there seemed to be trying to drive them out of their territory. They were just concerned that someone was trying to take them out, one by one.

They didn't even seem to get it when Elliott talked them through the finances. That was the real hit job. The fact that people out there were getting cold feet about doing business with them. That people thought they were too high-risk. Their current financial issues would become even more acute if they started losing customers.

And those people – customers and suppliers – were right. At

least up to a point. It wasn't just that someone was dicking them around, though that was bad enough. If you couldn't even look after your own staff, you were no longer top dog. And once you lost that reputation, it would be the devil's own job to claw it back.

But it was worse than that. If this continued, it would be noticed. Donaldson didn't know what had happened to any of those who had gone missing. It was possible that some of them might simply have been lured to the other side. Offered whatever inducements – not much, Donaldson guessed – it would take to persuade them to jump ship and join the competition.

Maybe that had happened. But Donaldson guessed it was more likely that they'd simply been taken out. Disposed of. Discreetly maybe, for the moment. But that discretion probably wouldn't be maintained. Soon, the disposals would become less subtle, more likely to attract attention. That in turn would begin to attract the attention of the authorities – the police, the revenue, immigration – and then they were well and truly screwed. Their suppliers and customers would melt away like the previous day's thin coating of snow, and whoever was behind this would take over.

He'd been thinking all this as he drove back from the hotel in the late afternoon, trying to work out what his next move ought to be. The despair had lifted a little and been replaced by anger. He wasn't going to let these bastards win. He needed a way of fighting back. He just needed to know who was behind this, and then he could find some means of retaliating. After all, he thought, there couldn't be too many candidates. There couldn't be too many people who were likely to have the desire and the ability to try to muscle in like this. He could make a guess at one or two of them, and if he put the word out with the right people, he could probably identify other potential contenders.

He had some local pop music station playing on the car radio, though he was scarcely paying attention to it. He was sitting at the lights at the Longman roundabout as the news bulletin came on. He idly turned it up.

The lead item was some cop talking about a body that had been discovered at Fort George. Police were apparently treating the death as suspicious but were having difficulty identifying the body. The cop had given a brief description of the individual in question, and asked anyone with any information to contact the police on a number provided.

The lights changed to green, but Donaldson sat motionless until the car behind him sounded its horn insistently. Hurriedly, he pulled away and continued over the roundabout.

Shit.

He told himself that the description had been sparse and could have applied to any number of people. It meant nothing.

But in his heart he knew. He knew who the body belonged to. And he knew that this was the beginning of it. The beginning of the end.

DONALDSON HAD CALMED SLIGHTLY by the time he reached his home. He lived on a new-build estate in Tornagrain. Nowhere flashy. Just an anonymous three-bedroomed detached.

That was deliberate. He didn't want to attract attention to himself. No ostentatious wealth. A man of simple tastes. The expensive stuff was discreet, stuff that wouldn't be noticed unless you really knew what you were looking at. It was the same with his car. A 5 series BMW. A decent car, but nothing that would look out of place belonging to a decently-paid middle manager. It was a pretty high-spec model, but you wouldn't know that unless you were sitting inside, and Donaldson was careful about who got to do that.

He was on nodding terms with his neighbours, and they no doubt took him for what he appeared to be, a fairly successful management type. If he'd ever been pressed, he had a story to tell them, about the company he worked for and what he did. Territorial manager for a company based down south. It was even sort of true in its way. He'd concocted enough detail to make it plausible, without including anything that was likely to trip him up.

The truth was, though, that no one had ever asked. The neighbours were pleasant enough, and he made a point of being pleasant back, but they had no interest in him or his work. One or two seemed mildly interested, or perhaps concerned, that he lived alone, but he'd just told them that he was divorced and that, for the moment, he was content just to be by himself. He made the story sound sufficiently boring that no one ever enquired further.

This is what I am fighting for, he thought. This cosy life, where he could have the creature comforts he wanted without attracting anyone's attention. That was what was under threat.

If he was right about the body described on the news, he would have to act quickly. He told himself that, for the moment at least, the police were in the dark. That might continue. As far as he knew, Roddy had had no relatives locally, and he'd had no close friends outside the firm. It was possible that his body would remain anonymous.

But there was always the risk that the media appeal would pull someone out of the woodwork who knew Roddy. Someone who had stayed at the hotel who recalled seeing the scrawny youth around the place, maybe, or just someone who'd come across him in the pub or a shop. Someone who might know just enough to arouse the police's interest in the hotel and who worked there.

Even if that didn't happen, the body had been found. Donaldson kept trying to tell himself that he didn't even know for sure that this was Roddy, but the coincidence seemed too great. And if this was Roddy, then presumably the others would start to turn up soon, in a similar state. Some of them, with their weird tattoos and piercings, would be far more easily identifiable than Roddy.

He had to find some way of fighting back or he was screwed. And he had to do it quickly. He probably had no more than a day or two.

The only problem was he didn't have the faintest idea what to do. Even if he managed to discover who was really behind this, he might not have the time to retaliate. Even if he found some way to fight back successfully, the police might still come sniffing round his door as a result of what had happened already.

There was no point in worrying about that, he thought. He couldn't undo what had taken place. All he could do was try to stop it getting worse, and maybe take some steps to ensure that, if the police did have reason to start looking into him, they wouldn't find too much.

Was that feasible? He'd always tried to be as careful as possible, and Elliott had files of false accounts that Donaldson hoped would stand up to scrutiny. He'd covered his tracks as well as he could.

The main problem was dealing with the physical assets. The stock, for want of a better word. You couldn't just hide them. And, if the police did come sniffing round, they wouldn't be fobbed off with fake documentation or some cock and bull explanation.

So maybe that was the only solution, he thought, as he pulled into his driveway. Perhaps the answer was a temporary pause in operations. What did they call it in the uni where he'd done the MBA stuff? A sabbatical. Maybe he should take a brief sabbatical. Temporarily close the hotels. That would be easy enough. It was midwinter in the Highlands, after all.

He only really kept the hotels open because it didn't cost him much. Anyway, he needed a place to house the stock, and he could attract a few passing guests to help cover the running costs. No one would be surprised if he closed them for a few weeks.

Half the restaurants and guest houses closed at this time of year and he could always come up with some bollocks about refurbishment.

The only question was what to do with the stock. The hard stuff was probably okay. He could shift that somewhere where it wouldn't be easily traceable. The people were more of a problem. He didn't have much doubt he could offload them easily enough. Most of them were already allocated to customers and would be moved on before the next consignment arrived. But he'd probably take a financial hit on them because the buyers would soon work out he was in a poor bargaining position. But that was probably a price worth paying if it enabled him to weave his way through all this.

It was worth a shot, he thought, and he couldn't really see an alternative. At least it might buy him some time to find out what was going on here, who was behind this. It would give him a chance to fight back.

He felt cheered even by the thought. He was an optimist by nature, though the last few days had stretched his positivity to the limits. He just wished he had a better team to rely on. That was a lesson for the future. Don't try to do it on the cheap. *Still, if this continues I'll have to replace most of the team anyway. Always look on the bright side.*

He turned off the engine and climbed out, struck by the unexpected chill of the east wind. God, it was cold. Maybe he really should think about jacking this in. Cashing in his chips and heading south.

It feels like a storm is brewing, he thought. A literal one tonight, and maybe a metaphorical one in the days to come.

He glanced down the drive behind him, suddenly feeling as if someone was watching him. The security lights had turned on as he'd entered the driveway, and he was conscious that he was caught in the glare, visible to anyone who might be observing from the surrounding darkness.

He had never felt any sense of personal threat even during the last few difficult days. He'd been confident that no one would dare try it on with him. They wouldn't do that. They wouldn't want to rock the boat too much. They might pick off the small fry to make their point, but they'd respect him. You didn't mess with the big guys. That was one of the rules, because it made all the big guys jittery and then they'd soon put you in your place. Everyone knew that. The big guys were businessmen who wanted to keep their businesses at least superficially respectable.

Except suddenly he wondered if that was true. Whoever these people were, they'd already taken three of his team. They seemed to have done it without really trying. If they didn't get what they wanted, who knew what they might be capable of. Maybe they weren't playing by the same rules he'd always assumed applied.

Maybe those rules had never really applied in the first place.

He hurried up the path towards the front door, hearing the wind building in the trees around him. He fumbled with his keys, struggling to get the door open.

Finally, he was inside and, slamming the front door behind him, he turned and double-locked the door. For all his supposed confidence, he'd always had strong security here and he felt safe now he was finally in the house.

Even so, there was a clutch of fear in his stomach, a flutter of panic in his chest. He couldn't remember the last time he'd felt like that.

Tomorrow, he thought. *Tomorrow we start to deal with this. Tomorrow we seize the initiative, and we put these people, whoever they might be, back in their fucking box.*

Tomorrow.

36

Alec McKay was having a mixed day so far. He'd arrived at work, a little later than usual, to find Helena Grant and Ginny Horton with a small team of officers already working through the results of the previous night's calls.

'What time do you call this?' Grant said.

'About half an hour before I'm officially due to be here,' McKay pointed out. 'Got a bit held up because I was coaching Fiona on how to deal with Charlie Farrow.'

'If she's taken advice from you, she'll end up serving ten years.'

'Just told her not to take any bollocks from him. Anyway, how's it looking?'

'Not bad,' Grant said. 'We weren't short of calls. There's going to be a lot of legwork going into following these up. We've got some that feel like solid leads including some claimed identifications. So fingers crossed.'

McKay left them to it, and went to check on progress with his own investigation. The confirmation of Gordon Tennant's identity had opened up a range of avenues to explore, and he'd allocated a team of officers to each of them. The key one for the moment was Tennant's employment, and that had intrigued

McKay. When Aileen Tennant had mentioned the hotel where her husband had worked, the name had rung a vague bell in McKay's head. At first, he thought he'd just come across the name in some local advertising or publicity. But overnight, waking at some point in the small hours of the morning, he'd remembered that he'd last seen the name on the Muir Hotels website, when he'd been trying to identify Gerry Elliott. It was one of their small chain of hotels, just outside Strathpeffer.

That kind of coincidence always attracted McKay's attention. He didn't quite believe the old detective's adage that there was no such thing as coincidence, but over the years he'd learned not to take it at face value. He'd been planning to head over to the hotel himself to try to talk to some of Tennant's colleagues. He could delegate that, but he somehow felt that his own unique style of interviewing might yield better results.

But now, prompted by the unexpected coincidence, he decided to postpone that till later in the day. Instead, he picked up a car and drove over to the serviced offices where he'd previously met Gerry Elliott.

The striking-looking Ruby Jewell was still there, sitting behind the desk in the lobby. She looked up as McKay entered, clearly taking a moment to place him. 'Oh, hi,' she said. 'If you're looking for Gerry, I'm afraid he's not here.'

'Sorry to hear that. I'd have liked another chat with him. Are you expecting him back?'

She shrugged. 'No idea. He wasn't around at all yesterday, and there's been no sign of him today.'

'Is that unusual?'

'Not really. He travels around the various sites so he's out a fair bit. But he usually calls in once or twice a day to pick up any messages, and to give me an idea what he's up to. I didn't hear anything from him yesterday, and he's not called today yet.'

'Must be busy.'

'I think there's something going on. Not sure what. But he

was here with Mr Donaldson the other evening and they were getting their heads together about something. There was some sort of argument. To be honest, my impression is that the business isn't doing as well as it might be. I know they're looking for new investment.'

McKay wasn't sure whether Jewell was always this open with visitors, or whether it was because she knew he was a police officer. He suspected a mixture of both. 'Was that what they were talking about?'

'Certainly got the impression they were dealing with some business crisis, arguing about who was to blame. It's been going on for a while.' She gestured to the list of companies on the wall behind her. 'I hope it's nothing serious. Between the various companies, they give us a lot of business.'

'I can see that,' McKay said. 'I'm sure they've got it all under control.' He paused, then asked, 'What do you make of him? Gerry Elliott, I mean.'

He wasn't sure whether he was pushing his luck asking a personal question, but Jewell didn't seem concerned. 'Gerry? To be honest, I don't like him much.'

McKay nodded. 'Oh, I assumed you got on well. The first name thing and all that.'

'God, no. He insists on that. Likes to think we're bosom buddies. Or he wants other people to think that. To be honest, he gives me the creeps.'

'I can see what you mean,' McKay said. 'I didn't exactly warm to him.'

She gave a mock shudder. 'He always stands a bit too close to me. That bloody aftershave. He thinks he's God's gift.' She suddenly seemed to realise that she might have said too much. 'You won't tell him what I said, will you?'

McKay tapped his nose. 'Safe with me. To be honest, I'm keen to know as much as possible about Mr Elliott.'

'Is he in trouble?'

'We just think he may have information to help us with an enquiry we're engaged in. But I'm interested in finding out more about him.'

'He used to keep trying it on with me, when he first came here. Nothing serious, but, you know, flirting, dirty jokes, putting his arm round me.'

It sounded potentially serious to McKay, particularly given everything else he knew about Elliott. 'You shouldn't have to put up with that kind of thing. Did you make a complaint?'

'I didn't think anyone would pay much attention. Trouble is, like I say, the Muir Group is a big customer of ours, so I don't think I'd be thanked for complaining.'

It is always the way, McKay thought. *Don't rock the boat. Don't do anything to offend the customers.* 'Even so.'

'It wasn't anything I couldn't deal with. If it had been anyone else, I'd have just told him to piss off.'

'Why didn't you?'

'I didn't want to get too much on the wrong side of him. I've seen him lose his temper once or twice, and it's not pretty.'

'Have you seen him be violent?'

She thought for a moment. 'Not really. Not, you know, physically violent. But I've heard him shouting, and I've seen him throw stuff across the room. It was a bit scary. You couldn't even tell where it came from. Something annoyed him, and he just suddenly lost it.'

'Not nice,' McKay agreed. 'So how did you deal with him?'

'Ach, you know, I just fobbed him off jokingly. I suppose I strung him along a bit. I never took him very seriously even when he asked me out.'

'He asked you out?'

'I couldn't believe it. Maybe I'd strung him along a bit too much. Let him think I might be interested. One night he asked me if I wanted to go for a drink after work.'

'I take it you didn't go?'

'Christ, no. I told him I was in a serious relationship and that my boyfriend didn't like me seeing other people, even as friends. He said my boyfriend didn't need to know, but I said I was always honest with him even if it meant him getting angry. I showed him a picture. Hang on–' She picked up her mobile from the desk and flicked through the photographs. 'Here.'

She showed him a picture of a muscle-bound young man dressed in gym gear. He looked to McKay like someone who might already have served a stretch for GBH. 'Is your boyfriend really that possessive?'

She giggled. 'I don't have a boyfriend. I think my girlfriend might object. The picture's just a photo of some male model I found on the internet.'

McKay shook his head, grinning. 'You could have just told him you weren't that way inclined.'

'Christ, no. He'd have seen that as a challenge. But this worked like a dream. He bought the whole thing. I wouldn't say he's not bothered me since, but he's not pestered me as much.'

'That's something,' McKay agreed. 'But you shouldn't have to tolerate that kind of harassment. If it continues, you really should report it.'

'You won't do anything, will you?' she said. 'I mean, you won't report any of this?'

'Not if you don't want me to,' McKay said. 'It's got to be your choice.'

'I don't want to risk losing this job. Apart from Gerry, I really like this job. I meet interesting people and it's not badly paid for what I do.'

'I understand.' It was a tragedy, McKay thought, that someone like this young woman should have to put up with the behaviour of a slimeball like Elliott. He wouldn't do anything to put her job in danger, but he'd do his best to make sure Elliott got what he deserved. 'What about Donaldson? Is he okay?'

For the first time, she looked slightly uneasy. 'I don't see that much of him, to be honest. He seems okay.' She smiled. 'At least, he's one of us.'

'One of us?' For a moment, McKay wondered whether this was a reference to Donaldson's sexuality.

'A local. He's from Cromarty.'

He felt there was something she wasn't saying, but decided there was no point in pushing it. 'Is that right? Look, I'll leave you to it. Thanks for your time and for everything you've told me. I promise I'll be discreet.'

'Thanks. Do you want to leave a message for Gerry?' she said. 'Or I can give you his mobile number.'

He took the mobile number but declined to leave a message, asking her not to tell Elliott about his visit. He didn't want to alert Elliott to his continuing interest and, in any case, thought that there'd been no harm in some mutual secrecy with the receptionist. Maybe it would help reassure her he'd keep his mouth shut. There was something about his conversation with her that had left him feeling slightly uneasy, though he couldn't pinpoint exactly what.

He'd already arranged for Sheila O'Rourke to be interviewed again that morning, following her initial complaint, so they could confirm that her attacker really was Gerry Elliott. McKay was conscious that, as matters stood, it might be difficult to pin any serious charge on Elliott. They had O'Rourke's account of the assault, and they'd get the bruising checked out today. But there were no other witnesses, and Elliott would no doubt deny that it had happened as O'Rourke had described. It was little more than 'he said, she said', but the more evidence they could gather, the better.

With that in mind, McKay took another detour to call in on Maggie Clennan. He was still keen to talk to her to see if she could add any further details about her own evening with Elliott. He'd tried to give her a call on the mobile number that Clennan had left with Helena Grant at the end of their evening together, but had been taken straight to voicemail. He'd left a brief message but so far had received no response. He had little expectation that she would be at home, but, as he was passing, it would be worth a shot.

As he'd anticipated, there was no response to his repeated ringing of her doorbell. As before, he had no real reason to assume there would be. She was most likely at work.

This time, no obliging neighbour emerged to provide him with any further information. He contemplated ringing some of the other bells to see if anyone could give him an idea of Clennan's whereabouts, but knew there would be little point.

He took a step back and stared up at the blank windows of the house, wondering which belonged to Clennan's flat. There was no reason for any concern but he realised that, somehow, he was feeling uneasy. Uneasy at her failure to answer the door. Uneasy at her absence.

It was Elliott, he thought. He made you feel like that. He created that unease. That sense that something was wrong.

He turned and walked back to his car, at one point stopping to look back at the house, as if he expected Clennan to be watching him from one of those sightless windows.

37

'I did warn you,' McKay said.

'Even your description didn't do the arsehole justice,' Chrissie said.

He'd been on his way up to Strathpeffer when she'd called him and he had answered on the hands-free. She and Fiona had just emerged from the interview with Charlie Farrow and one of his minions.

'He allowed you to sit in then?'

'Oh, aye. He kept saying it was just a wee informal chat and that he was more than happy for me to be there to hold Fi's hand. He actually used those words. "Hold her hand." Patronising git.'

'He probably wanted to grill you as well as Fiona.'

'I'm not a numpty. That's exactly what he did. Two for the price of one. All very chatty to start with, then it became a bit more aggressive.'

McKay wondered whether Farrow might have stepped over the line in terms of what might be acceptable in an informal interview with someone who, presumably, was at this stage no more than a witness. No doubt, knowing Farrow, he'd pushed it to the very edge. 'Anything you didn't expect?'

'Not for the most part, no. I don't know how much he's really got. A lot of it seemed to be basically fishing, waiting for us to tell him stuff.'

'I hope you told him the truth, the whole truth and nothing but the truth.'

'Absolutely. But only the stuff we knew for certain. Farrow was trying to push us on what Kevin might have been involved in, how and why he'd got himself into this mess, whether he had any associates and suchlike.'

'You reckon Farrow had the whole story. I mean, as far as you and Fiona have it.'

'The key points, anyway. He obviously knows about Kevin being fired and something about the reasons why. I don't know how much the company has been prepared to tell him. I imagine they're not keen to wash their dirty linen in public even if the police are asking. He knew about Kevin being in debt, and it was clear he knew about the business loan. That was when he started giving Fi a hard time. How could she not know what her husband was up to? How could she not be aware that he'd been sacked? On and on.'

'He had to do his job,' McKay argued, reluctantly. 'They're reasonable questions.'

'Then don't ask them like an arsehole.'

Fair point, McKay thought. Though he wasn't sure that Farrow had many other operational styles. He did most things like an arsehole. It was his default setting. 'Was Fiona okay?'

'She's a tough cookie. I could tell she was upset. She really just wanted to fire a string of expletives at him, but she could see that wouldn't improve her position. So she just answered his questions accurately and politely.'

'He wouldn't know how to deal with that,' McKay said.

'That was my impression. You asked if anything new came out of it. I think the answer might be yes. Fi and I almost missed it at the time because we were feeling so wound up by him. It was only afterwards when we were sharing what we'd thought that it struck us.'

'Go on.'

'Farrow's obviously got access to all Kevin's bank details, and he was asking us about all the payments from his private account.'

'And you told him you knew nothing about them?'

'Yes. And the only one that Fi knew about were the monthly transfers into their joint account, which she had assumed was Kevin's monthly salary payment. But the one he was really interested in was the final payment, the ten grand that went to God knows who. He wanted to find out if Fiona had any more information.'

'Which she didn't.'

'Quite. But when Farrow talked about it, he twice used the word "investment" to describe the payment. He asked if we knew what Kevin was investing in, or what return he hoped to get on his investment.'

'So Farrow thinks that Kevin was investing in – what? A business of some kind?'

'That's what it sounded like.'

'Wonder if that's just guesswork or whether he's got some evidence. With Farrow it could be either.'

'Like I say, a lot of it sounded like fishing. Seeing whether Fiona could add to his total of knowledge.'

'That's Farrow's way. Get someone to do your work for you. Interesting, though. Maybe Kevin was hoping that that investment would be what would dig him out of his hole. If he discovered it had failed, or that he'd been ripped off–' He stopped. 'Sorry. I'm worse than Farrow. That's the trouble with being a copper. How did he leave things?'

'Vague. Said he might want to talk to us again. He'd be completing his report for the procurator fiscal. Blah, blah. I couldn't tell whether there was more to come or whether he was just stringing us along.'

'Let's hope it's the latter and we can put all this to bed.'

'Too right. Apart from anything else, till they're prepared to release Kevin's body, it's difficult for Fi to get on with anything. It's all up in the air.'

'What are her plans?'

'She doesn't really have any. Her work has given her compassionate leave for as long as she needs it, which is one good thing. I've told her she can stay here as long as she wants to. But to be honest, I think she's itching to move on now. Get some sort of closure.'

'I don't blame her. She's had her life turned upside down in more ways than one. She'll struggle to come to terms with that.'

'And at the moment she can't even start. I'd better get back to her and let you get on, anyway. Where are you?'

'Strathpeffer. Long story. I'll tell you later.'

He finished the call as he entered Strathpeffer. It was an old spa town, a cluster of attractive old buildings in a leafy setting. He and Chrissie had occasionally come out here for a walk and a bite to eat, but it wasn't an area McKay knew particularly well.

The hotel was to the north of the town, up a narrow single-track road that would have been lethal in worse weather. McKay passed a battered sign with the hotel name on it, and continued up the road until he saw a further sign pointing into a car park dotted with potholes.

The hotel was in an attractive location, looking out over the valley of the River Peffery. It had obviously once been an imposing, if not overly large, country residence. McKay imagined that, with a little investment and a lick of paint, it could be a pleasant place to stay.

Nevertheless, the building before him bore little resemblance to the images on the Muir Hotels website. He couldn't tell whether the pictures were simply old or had in some way been touched up, but certainly they depicted a building in better shape than the one before him. He could imagine that any guest who had booked on the basis of the website would be severely disappointed.

He wondered what sort of guest this place would attract. In the summer the area was overrun with tourists, some visiting the surrounding area, many more on their way further north and to the west coast or the islands. He could imagine that this place might attract some of the latter, particularly the foreign tourists who would have booked online and wouldn't know what they were letting themselves in for till they arrived. In fairness, if the place was inexpensive and the rooms were clean, they probably wouldn't worry too much. The next day they'd be moving on somewhere else anyway.

He climbed out of the car and stood for a moment, looking around. The view was striking. In the distance, he could see the firths that surrounded the Black Isle on three sides and beyond that the open sea. Between were rolling hills and pastureland, with the low sun casting long shadows. It was a blustery day, clouds building in the east, and he was buffeted by a strong wind.

McKay turned and made his way into the porch marked 'Reception'. A set of double doors led him into a small lobby, with an unoccupied reception desk. The place was silent.

He looked around for a moment, taking in the worn furniture and shabby carpets. It was tidy enough and the wood looked well-polished, but he guessed that no money had been spent on the place in at least a decade. He stepped forward and rang the small brass bell on the reception desk.

There was no sign of life for several minutes, then the figure of a woman in overalls appeared from a door behind the desk. She stared at McKay for a moment as if in astonishment, then retreated back through the door. McKay was tempted to follow her, but decided to give the bell another try.

After a moment, the rear door opened again, this time to

reveal a gangling youth in jeans and a T-shirt emblazoned with the name of a heavy metal band. It was unclear whether he'd appeared in response to the bell, been summoned by the woman, or was there purely by coincidence. He stared at McKay as if to challenge his right to be there. 'Yes?'

The famous Scottish welcome, McKay thought. For a moment, he considered pretending to be a potential paying guest, just to see what would happen. But he lacked the time or the energy. Instead, he produced his warrant card and held it under the man's nose. 'Police.'

The man blinked and swallowed.

Interesting reaction, McKay thought. Closer to the kind of response he might expect to his appearance on the doorstep of some known villain, rather than in the reception of a hotel.

'What's this about?'

'Is the manager around?'

'I am the manager.'

It was McKay's turn to blink. The man in front of him was probably no more than mid-twenties, with over-long dark hair and the remnants of a severe acne problem. This place was hardly the Ritz, but the man still made an unlikely manager. 'I see. Mr...?'

'Cannon. Darell Cannon. So what's this about?'

'I'm trying to find out about a man called Gordon Tennant. Name mean anything to you?'

'Gordie?' Cannon had taken a step back and was eyeing McKay warily. McKay had the sense that Cannon would have liked to deny all knowledge of Tennant, but had already betrayed himself in his response. 'What about him?'

'I believe he works here.'

McKay could almost hear Cannon's brain working. Whatever he was going to say, it was unlikely to be anything approaching the whole truth. 'That's right. Well, he did.'

'Did?'

'We haven't seen him for a few days. We'd sort of assumed he'd buggered off.'

'I see. Does that happen often?'

'What?'

'Your employees. Just buggering off?'

'I– Well, from time to time. It's the industry, isn't it?'

'Is it?'

'Casual. I mean, it's basic stuff. Gordie was just doing bits and pieces for us. Labouring. Bit of handyman stuff. Some driving. Whatever he could turn his hand to, really.' Cannon was getting into his stride now, obviously feeling more confident in whatever half-truths he was spouting. In McKay's experience, this was usually the point at which people said too much.

'Had he been with you long?'

'Few months, I guess.'

'Where did you find him? Or did he find you?'

'I can't remember, to be honest. Maybe he knew someone. Or just came up on spec. Seemed decent enough. Hard worker.'

'But you weren't surprised when he buggered off?'

'It happens. People get a better offer, or something happens in their private life.'

'But you wouldn't expect them to call and tell you?'

'Look, what's this about, man? He worked for us for a bit. He left. That's all there is to it. What else can I tell you?'

'What sort of a man was he? Would you say he was trustworthy?'

'Trustworthy?'

'Honest.'

'I suppose so. He seemed to do what he was told. Got on with things. What else can I tell you?'

'You didn't try to contact him after he'd disappeared?'

'I had a mobile number that he'd given me. I tried it a couple of times. Left messages. He never got back. That's why I thought he'd fucked off.'

McKay nodded. 'Do you know if there was anyone who might have wanted to harm him?'

Cannon blinked again. 'Harm him?'

'Can you think of anyone?'

'I don't know. I mean, I chatted to him a bit, but we weren't exactly close.'

'No, of course. Did you get the impression he might have been worried about anything? That he might have been in trouble?'

'Trouble?' Cannon hesitated, obviously playing for time. 'What sort of trouble?'

'That's what I was hoping you might be able to tell me.'

'I don't– I mean, I don't know.'

'The thing is,' McKay went on, 'a body was discovered, just the other side of Dingwall, which we believe may well be that of Mr Tennant.'

Cannon looked as if someone had punched him hard in the gut. 'Gordie?' he said, finally. 'You're serious?'

'Deadly.'

'Shit.' Cannon leaned back against the reception desk, which creaked alarmingly under his weight. 'Bloody hell. Do you know what happened?'

'Only that we've reason to treat the death as suspicious.'

'Suspicious?'

'It's possible that Mr Tennant was murdered.'

'Oh, Christ.' Cannon's face had gone a deathly pale, and McKay wondered whether the man might be about to throw up. 'I ought to tell Mr Donaldson,' he said, finally.

'Mr Donaldson?'

'The MD. He owns the hotel. He'd want to know.'

'He'd want to know about the death of a former casual employee of the hotel who, until now, you thought had just left without notice?'

'I–' It was clear that Cannon didn't know how to respond. 'He just likes to know stuff. I mean, he likes to know what's going on.'

'I'm sure he does,' McKay said. 'A real attention to detail.' He reached out and ran his fingers through the flaking paint on the reception room wall, as if to offer an ironic commentary. 'These things matter.'

'Look, I ought to call him.' There was a note in Cannon's voice which went far beyond the anxiety of a dutiful employee faced with an issue above his pay grade. Something not too far removed from panic, McKay thought.

'You busy at the moment, son? The hotel, I mean.' He cast a sceptical eye back at the window overlooking the empty car park.

Cannon looked baffled by the unexpected question. 'It's that time of year, isn't it?'

'Surprised you don't close.'

'We get some passing trade,' Cannon said. It sounded like a pat line he'd been given. 'Even at this time of year.'

'That right, son?' McKay nodded as though absorbing this information. 'Anything else you can tell me about Gordon Tennant?'

McKay's distinctive interview technique tended to disconcert people, and Cannon's discomfort was obvious. 'I– I don't think so.'

'He was an employee, was he?'

'How do you mean?'

'I mean, on the payroll. Minimum wage. Tax. National Insurance. All that.'

'I don't– I didn't look after any of that stuff.'

'Though you were the manager here, son?'

'I am. But Mr Donaldson and Mr Elliott looked after all that stuff.'

'Mr Elliott?'

'He's our finance manager.'

'I see. So you don't know what Tennant's employment status was.'

'I–'

'What about you, son? I assume you're an employee?'

Cannon looked as if this question might be beyond him. Finally, he said, 'Yes, of course. I don't know what you mean.'

'No worries, son. Just making conversation. Is there anyone round here who might have known Tennant better? Did he have any particular friends?'

'I don't think so–'

'Any of the women, for example?' This was a long shot on McKay's part. He'd seen the women who'd emerged before Cannon's appearance and, while glancing out at the deserted car park, he'd spotted a couple of women in overalls pulling wheelie bins past the hotel.

'Women?'

'You seem to have quite a few working here. Just thought that Tennant might have got to know someone.'

'I– I don't think so.'

'Oh, well. Just trying to find out whatever we can about him.' McKay slid one of his business cards across the desk. 'If anything else occurs to you, son. Or if you think of anyone else who might be able to help. Feel free to give me a call. Thanks for your time.'

He turned and walked back out to the car park, pausing momentarily in the doorway to glance back. Cannon was already on his phone, he noted.

38

'You reckon this is worth doing?' Josh Carlisle spoke without looking up, his eyes fixed on the screen of his mobile phone.

Ginny Horton glanced across at him. 'That some game you're playing?'

He looked up at her with the measureless contempt of the young for the very slightly older. 'No, social media. I'm just looking up this Roddy Gray. Just to see if there's anything I can find out about him.'

'Ah, right. Any luck?'

'Not sure. There are several Rod Grays. Some of them seem to be around here. But there's not much information about any of them.'

'You think we might be wasting our time?'

They were heading along the A96 away from Inverness. The Moray Firth was to their left, the low sun behind them. There were dark clouds ahead of them, and it felt as if a storm was brewing.

'No idea,' Carlisle said. 'It sounds a decent lead. Just surprised you decided to come.'

The truth was that Horton had been feeling slightly stir-crazy in the office. She'd spent the morning supervising the teams going through the results of the media appeal. There was no shortage of leads, of varying quality, but this had looked to be one of the more promising. A call from a woman living some-where near Nairn who had reckoned that the young man being described sounded very like her lodger, one Roddy Gray.

Horton had listened several times to the recording of the call. 'It was the clothes you said he was wearing,' she'd said. 'That thin cream anorak. He wears it whatever the weather. I kept telling him he should get something warmer, but I don't think he's got the money...'

The call handler had pressed her, and she'd provided some descriptive details of Gray that matched what they knew but which, deliberately, had been excluded from the appeal. There was enough there for them to investigate further. Grant and Horton had decided to give the call first priority.

Grant had called the woman, a Mrs Madeline Ferris, and veri-fied the details she'd provided in the initial call. She lived in the outskirts of Nairn, just along the coast, and they set up a visit later that afternoon. *Always better to see the whites of the eyes,* Horton thought, echoing one of Alec McKay's mantras.

She could, as Carlisle had rightly indicated, have delegated the job to a couple of keen DCs. But she felt eager for a change of scene, and decided to do the job herself, taking the always enthu-siastic Carlisle as her companion.

They found the place easily enough – a small bungalow in a small estate that probably dated back to the 1970s. Neat gardens, well-maintained houses. Horton guessed that the occupants were likely to be relatively elderly, perhaps retired couples who had downsized from larger properties in the town.

Madeline Ferris more or less fitted the bill. She was probably in her early sixties, fit-looking and with a slightly mischievous glint in her eyes. At the same time, her expression on greeting them at the door was one of anxiety. 'I'm not sure whether to hope I'm not wasting your time, or to hope that I am,' she said, as she led them into a plainly-decorated living room. She gestured for them to take a seat on the small sofa. 'I mean, I hope I've not dragged you out here on a wild goose chase, but I'm also hoping nothing's happened to Roddy. Can I get you some tea?' She was talking a little too quickly, her nerves showing.

Horton exchanged a glance with Carlisle, then decided to accept. She had a sense that Ferris might be more forthcoming once she'd had a little time to grow accustomed to the idea of the two police officers in her home.

While Ferris made the tea, Horton glanced around the room. There was little revealing – a couple of anonymous pictures on the walls, a few ornaments that looked like holiday souvenirs, a photograph by the television that presumably showed Madeline Ferris and her husband at their wedding. Horton assumed that the husband was no longer around.

The room was tidy enough, but had few personal touches. It wasn't the sort of place Horton could imagine a young man being comfortable, but maybe Roddy Gray had kept himself to his own room.

After a few minutes, Ferris returned bearing a tray laden with a teapot, cups, a jug of milk and a bowl of sugar, along with a plate of biscuits. It looked as if they were being treated to the best china. Ferris poured the tea and then sat down in one of the armchairs facing them.

'Now, then, what can I tell you?'

'Please do stop us if any of this becomes distressing, Mrs Ferris. As you know, we're investigating an unexplained death. We haven't as yet succeeded in identifying the deceased, hence the television appeal last night. You said you had reason to think it might be your lodger?'

'That's right. Young Roddy. I last saw him about a week ago.'

'Were you concerned about his disappearance?'

'Not at first. He went off on the Friday evening after work, and he'd told me he was going into Inverness with a few mates. It was someone's birthday at his work or something. Anyway, he said he'd probably be staying over with someone on the Friday and Saturday nights, so I shouldn't worry. I was a bit concerned when he didn't come back on the Sunday, but I thought maybe he'd decided to stay over Sunday as well and then go straight into work.'

'And after that?'

'Then I did start to get a bit concerned. But he'd never given me a contact phone number, so I didn't know what to do. I mean, he's a grown man and can look after himself, so I couldn't just report him as missing. He'd taken a bag with him for the weekend but he'd left some things behind so I knew he hadn't just decided to leave. In the end I'd left it a few days to see if I would have heard from him and then I'd decide what to do...'

Horton could see that Ferris was close to tears. 'Have you known Mr Gray for very long?'

'Just a few months. He responded to an advertisement I'd put on one of those online sites, looking for a lodger. I've got a spare room which I've let since my husband died. Mainly for the company, though it's good to have a bit of spare money as well.' She paused. 'To be honest, Roddy wasn't the sort of lodger I'd normally take. I preferred females. Well, you feel a bit safer, don't you?'

'But you were happy to take Mr Gray?'

'I hesitated at first. But my previous lodger had had to leave rather unexpectedly because her mother fell ill, and I hadn't been having much luck finding anyone. So, in the end, I thought why not.'

'And it worked well?'

'On the whole, yes. I was a little worried at first because I thought Roddy might not be the sort of person I wanted. Not just that he was male. But also that he was young and, well, a bit of a tearaway, I thought. He came from Inverness, and I had the feeling that there'd been some sort of falling out. He never told me the details and I didn't like to ask.'

'You think he still has relatives in Inverness then?' Horton registered that they were still talking in the present tense though she had a growing certainty that Ferris's identification had been correct.

'Just a father. It was the father he'd had the row with, I think. He never talked about it much. It was just the odd comment he made.'

Another potential line of enquiry, Horton thought. 'Was he any trouble here?'

'No. I mean, that was what I was concerned about. I thought he might bring back his raucous friends or something. I'd told him I didn't mind him bringing friends back from time to time as long as he wasn't too noisy or disruptive. But actually, he's been very considerate. He's occasionally had a bit too much to drink when he gets back in the evening, but he's never caused any problems.' She gestured towards the window. 'He's been quite helpful, really. Offered to keep the garden under control, and has done bits and pieces around the house. He tells me I remind him of his nan. She passed away a few years ago, he told me, but I think she was nicer to him than his dad was.' She stopped, as if she'd only just remembered why they were there. 'Do you think it really is him?'

'I'm afraid it might well be, Mrs Ferris. I'm sorry.' Horton had a photograph of the young man's face taken in the mortuary by one of the forensic photographers but she didn't want to produce that unless she really had to. 'I don't suppose you've any kind of photograph of Mr Gray?'

'I don't think so– No, wait a minute. I do have something on my phone.' She fumbled in the handbag by her chair for her mobile phone, then flicked through its cache of photographs. 'He bought me a little cake for my birthday. It's just a few days before

Christmas so I've never really bothered much about it, but Roddy found out and surprised me with this cake. It was just a wee shop-bought thing, but, well...' Suddenly she was crying.

Horton rose and stood beside Ferris, resting a hand on her shoulder. 'Take your time, Mrs Ferris. We understand this must be very difficult for you.'

'I'm just being silly,' Ferris sniffed. 'I hardly knew Roddy, really. But he was a decent young man. There.' She handed Horton her phone. 'Since he'd gone to all that trouble, I told him we ought to have a selfie together, me cutting the cake.'

The photograph showed Madeline Ferris standing behind a small sponge cake, a single lit candle in its centre. She was holding a kitchen knife in the manner of a bride cutting a wedding cake. A young man was standing beside her, his arm stretched out to take the photograph. Horton had little doubt the face matched that of the young man currently lying in the mortuary.

'Would it be possible for you to send me this photograph? I'd like to compare it to the deceased. But I'm afraid it does look to me as if this might be the person in question.' She could feel herself slipping into the bland euphemisms that police officers tend to use when dealing with emotional issues. 'I'm very sorry.'

Ferris shook her head. 'He was a poor wee thing, really. He played tough, but I always thought he was just a little boy. He must have been mid-twenties but you wouldn't have guessed it. We never had children, Ross and I...' She gestured towards the photograph by the television. 'But some of my lodgers...'

'I understand,' Horton said.

'Would you like to see his room?'

Horton had been trying to think of a tactful way to ask this, so was grateful for the offer. 'That would be helpful, if you don't mind. Thank you.'

'What happened to him? You said it was an unexplained death. It didn't say much on the television either.'

'We don't know exactly,' Horton said. *There was no point in being too coy,* she thought. The story would be covered in full by the media before too long. 'We think he was the victim of an unlawful killing–'

'Murdered?'

'Murder or manslaughter, yes. It looks that way. He was suffocated. Do you know if there was anyone who might have wished to harm him?'

'Roddy? I can't imagine it. He could be a bit rowdy, but there was no malice in him. I can't imagine why anyone might want to hurt him.' She looked genuinely bewildered by what she was hearing.

'If this is Mr Gray, then that's what we need to find out. Can you think of anything else that might help us? Did Mr Gray seem worried about anything? Do you think he might have been in any sort of trouble?'

'Not at all. He seemed his usual self. That last Friday evening, in particular, he seemed very cheerful. I think it was the first time he'd been out with his mates from work, though he had a couple of friends he'd got to know in the pubs round here.'

'Where did he work?'

'A hotel. A mile or so out of town. He used to get the bus there, then walk the last bit, from what he told me. Not sure what he did exactly – various bits of maintenance, labouring. Just helping to keep the place up to scratch. They were part of a chain, I think, though he never told me much about them.'

Horton glanced over at Carlisle, who was dutifully taking notes, wondering if he'd picked up on the same point she had. McKay had told them that morning that it looked as if the victim in the Dingwall killing had also worked in a hotel. Part of a chain. The Muir Group. The Finance Director of the Muir Group was a Mr Gerry Elliott, the man they believed had been behind the threatening texts to Helena Grant. She had no idea what, if anything, these coincidences might mean, but they were certainly beginning to stack up.

'I don't suppose you can recall the name of the hotel, Mrs Ferris?'

'Not off the top of my head, I'm afraid. Moray something, I think.'

'We can track that down easily enough. If some of his colleagues were at the session in Inverness, then they should be able to give us a better idea of what happened over that weekend.'

'I hope so. It's an awful thing.' Ferris had managed to dry her tears, and now looked simply anxious, as if she hoped still to be able to do something for Roddy Gray. 'I'll show you his room.'

They followed Ferris down the hallway to a door at the rear of the house. 'This is his room. I always give the lodgers this bedroom because it has an en-suite bathroom. It was originally the master bedroom, but I thought it better to switch them over so the lodgers could be more self-contained.'

The door was locked but Ferris fetched the spare key and opened it. The room was less tidy than the rest of the house, but probably not too bad by the standards of young men, Horton thought. There were some items of clothing on the floor, and the bed was unmade.

It appeared that Gray had had few possessions. There were a handful of clothes in the wardrobe, although Gray had presumably taken some with him on his weekend in Inverness. That was another question: what had happened to whatever bag he had taken with him?

Other than the clothes, the only other personal possessions visible were a rather battered old laptop on the dressing table and a small stack of motorcycle magazines.

'Did he ride a motorbike?'

Ferris shook her head. 'He kept saying he wanted to get one, but he couldn't really afford it.' Her eyes were still wet with tears, perhaps more so now she was able to look again at the small evidence of Gray's time here.

Horton pulled open the drawers in the dressing table, but they were empty except for a handful of small change, a few chewed pens and what she took to be a phone charger. 'He had a mobile phone, presumably?'

Ferris nodded. 'I should have taken the number, but I never did. I suppose he must have phoned me a couple of times when he responded to the advertisement, so I might have it somewhere in my call log. I hadn't thought of that before, or I'd have tried to call him when he didn't return.' Her expression suggested that this would give her another reason for blaming herself. It would almost certainly have made no difference, Horton thought. Gray had died sometime on the Sunday after he'd left here, so it would already have been too late before she had reason to be concerned.

The real question was what had taken Gray from drinking with his mates to what had turned out to be a fatal assignation at Fort George. The fort was midway between here and Inverness. Had someone offered to give him a lift back and then made a detour there?

'If you can track down Mr Gray's number, that's likely to be helpful. We haven't found his mobile – it wasn't with him – but the number might help us track his movements over that weekend.'

'I'll go and look,' she said, disappearing back towards the living room.

Carlisle had been standing by the door, watching Horton check the room. 'Poor woman. She reminds me of my nan, too.'

'She's everyone's nan,' Horton said. 'Gray was probably lucky to find her, if only for a few months. And probably vice versa.'

'Not much in here, is there?'

'Bugger all.' Horton had picked up a pair of trousers from the floor and was gingerly checking the pockets. 'We'll take the laptop, assuming Mrs Ferris has no objections, just in case there's anything useful on there. But I'm not hopeful.' She took another look around the room. 'This is where we're supposed to find some clue that blows the case wide open, isn't it? A matchbook with the name of a bar on it and a telephone number scribbled inside. That sort of thing.' She tossed the trousers onto the bed. 'Not a grubby pair of jeans with nothing but fluff in the pockets.'

They packed up the laptop and made their way back to the sitting room, where Ferris was still scrolling through her phone's log. 'This is the one, I think. There are a couple of calls from it at about the time Roddy moved in.' She read out the number for Carlisle to note down.

'That'll be very helpful, Mrs Ferris,' Horton said. 'Are you happy for us to take Mr Gray's laptop? There may be information on there that's likely to be useful to us.'

'Yes, of course. I don't even know who it really belongs to now...'

'I suppose strictly, if Mr Gray's father is still alive or if he has another next of kin, it probably goes to them, assuming Mr Gray hadn't indicated otherwise.' She didn't imagine that Gray had been either the age or the type to have made a will. 'But I don't imagine anyone's going to care if you wanted it back once we've finished with it.'

'I don't think so, do you?' Ferris said. 'I'll pack up his other stuff and put it somewhere safe, just in case anyone should want it. I don't suppose anyone will. Poor wee thing.'

There wasn't much doubt that she was right, Horton thought. It wasn't much of an epitaph, even for such a short life. But it was unlikely that Roddy Gray would ever receive much more.

39

B ack in the car, Carlisle was once again engrossed in something on his phone. Horton made her way out of the estate and eventually found her way back to the main road. 'More social media?'

'I was just looking up the name of this hotel where Gray worked. Looks like it's Moray Towers. Just off the A96 in a couple of miles. You think it's worth calling in, as we're in the area?'

'Hang on.' Horton pulled suddenly into an unused farm entrance at the side of the road, causing the driver of the speeding car behind her to sound its horn. 'Pillock,' she said. 'Shouldn't have been driving up my backside, then, should you?'

'I think you're gradually morphing into Alec McKay,' Carlisle observed.

'Less of your lip, young man. Let's have a look at that hotel.'

Carlisle handed over the phone, which was open on the hotel's website. "An exclusive country house residence," it read. She scrolled down the screen. At the bottom of the page, as she'd expected, "Part of the Muir Hotel Corporation."

'Well, there we go,' she said.

'What?'

'Remember what Alec said to us on his way out this morning? We have two apparent murder victims. And it turns out that both of them were employees of the Muir Hotel Corporation.'

'Really?' He took the phone back and looked at the website. Then he clicked on the link to the Muir Hotel Corporation site, and then from there to the site of another of the group's hotels. 'Jeez, you're right. That's the place Alec was heading for today, wasn't it?'

'The very same. Quite the coincidence, don't you think? And the other interesting fact is that Mr Gerry Elliott, the FD of the self-same Muir Hotel Corporation, is the arsehole who's been sending these threatening texts to Helena. The guy that we think is probably behind that assault in Inverness the other night.'

Carlisle frowned, clearly trying to process these links. 'You think Elliott might be behind the killings?'

'Who knows? From what Helena and Alec have said, he sounds a nasty piece of work with real anger management problems. Whether that would translate to murder – well, it's a big step.' She pulled out her mobile and thumbed through the numbers. 'Normally, I'd agree we should stop off at the hotel and strike while the iron's hot. But I'm a bit wary of blundering into something if this is linked to Alec's enquiry. Let me check with Helena in case there've been any developments we need to be aware of.'

Grant answered on the second ring. Horton could hear voices behind Grant's that suggested she might be in some kind of meeting.

'Sorry to interrupt but I just wanted to update you and check on next steps.'

'No worries. Things going on here that I can tell you about, but how'd it go?'

'Looks like Roddy Gray is our man.' She recounted the detail of their visit to Madeline Ferris, ending with their discovery about the hotel. 'We were wondering whether we should call in while we're out here. See if we can find anyone who can tell us more about this weekend in Inverness.'

There was an unexpected silence at the other end of the line. Finally, Grant said, 'I don't think you'd better. Not just at the moment. There've been a few developments and, funnily enough, they concern the Muir Hotel Corporation. Synchronicity. Might be best if you get back here and join us, so we can bring you up to speed.'

'Sounds good. See you shortly.' Horton ended the call and glanced at Carlisle, who'd been watching her quizzically, clearly wondering what Grant had said. 'We're heading back to the ranch,' Horton announced. 'It sounds as if the world is getting even smaller.'

Horton eventually tracked Grant down to one of the small meeting rooms on the third floor. She poked her head round the door and Grant waved her in. 'Come and join the brains' trust,' Grant said.

'The only room in the building where you'll find a combined IQ in treble figures,' McKay added.

McKay was sitting next to Grant. Sitting around the table were two other men and a woman who were all unknown to Horton.

'My colleague, DS Horton, who's working with me on the Fort George case,' Grant explained. 'She's just come from an interview where, funnily enough, the name of the Muir Hotel Corporation came up yet again.' She gestured to each of the three individuals in turn. 'Tess Adams, National Crime Agency. Simon Derrick, immigration. Pete Wilson, HMRC.'

An august crew, Horton thought, *and an interesting combination.* 'What's going on?'

'Alec?' Grant prompted.

McKay took a deep breath before beginning. 'I visited one of the Muir Hotel Corporation's fine establishments this afternoon in connection with the Dingwall enquiry. Got three-fifths of bugger all out of the guy I spoke to, who was supposedly the manager. But formed a very interesting impression of the place.' He paused for a theatrical beat. 'As I've just been explaining to our colleagues here, it was a run-down old dump, nothing like the image that they try to convey on their website. I imagine they still get guests, especially in summer when the tourists are pleased with any bed they can find, but I don't imagine anyone stays there twice. A generous one star on any online review site, I'd say. So that led me to wonder how they kept the place going, especially in the winter. Why they don't just close for a few months.' He stopped again, this time to pour himself a glass of water. McKay was never one not to relish being in the centre of attention.

'They seemed to have quite a few women working there, mainly fairly young. Late teens, early twenties. As I was heading back to the car, I saw a couple of them who were coming back from dealing with the garbage. So, being a sociable sort of chap, I stopped to make conversation with them. Sadly, neither of them appeared to speak any English.'

'And you think not EU nationals?' Simon Derrick said.

'No way to be sure, just from trying to talk to them,' McKay said. 'I didn't recognise whatever language they spoke, but that doesn't prove much. They probably wouldn't have recognised what I was speaking as English, if I'm to believe what some of my colleagues tell me. The interesting thing was that both of them seemed very keen to get away from me. Again, not a particularly unusual reaction, according to my colleagues, but these two seemed genuinely scared. So, just out of curiosity, I showed them my warrant card. It was clear they understood the word 'police' clearly enough, anyway. They both went white and scurried off sharpish.

'That left me interested enough to have a bit of a nosey around before I left. I didn't stay long because I didn't want to make myself conspicuous, but I found a couple of outhouses that seemed to be full of crates. I saw a couple more young women at the rear of the building, so there's obviously a pretty substantial staff there for early January. Not at all clear to me what they can all be doing.'

The immigration man, Derrick nodded. 'I'm glad you got in touch with us. You probably won't be surprised to learn that they're already on our radar. Their name's come up in a couple of enquiries relating to illegal immigrants and people trafficking. They seem to have carved out a niche for themselves up here, almost like a holding bay or a wholesaler, if that's not too cynical a description.' Derrick had a slow Glaswegian drawl that was almost a match for McKay's Dundonian intonation. 'They've not quite risen to the top of our to-do list yet, given the resources we have, but we've been building quite a dossier on them, in conjunction with our friends here.' He gestured to the others round the table.

'Pity you didn't think to consult with us too,' McKay said. Grant shot him a look, but Horton couldn't tell whether it showed disapproval or the opposite. Not that McKay was likely to care.

'We weren't really at that stage,' Tess Adams responded. 'Just trying to pull together the evidence. The challenge we always have with these cases is making them stand up in court. When things go pear-shaped, the big players tend to disappear into the undergrowth. We're left with the small fry, which gets us nowhere.'

'And why were the NCA and the revenue involved?' Horton asked. It was probably a dumb question but no one else was going to ask it for her.

'Because these people seem to have their fingers in a number of pies,' Tess Adams said. She was a smartly dressed woman who looked as if she wouldn't suffer fools, or, probably, most other people, gladly. 'We think the hotels are vehicles for money laundering, for example.'

'We were initially a bit baffled by the set-up,' Derrick added. 'Couldn't see why they would bother with this physical infrastructure. But it's not a bad set-up for fudging the finances. Still a fair bit of cash floating around in that sector. Lots of transactions and bookings in overseas currencies. The hotels seem to run currency exchanges at decent rates for the tourists in the summer, so that gives them an opportunity to exchange dodgy cash for clean stuff. That's small scale, but it helps hide the larger swaps going on.'

'And we think they're involved in trafficking of goods as well as people. Cigarettes, alcohol, fake designer stuff. All the usual.'

'A nicely diversified business,' McKay commented. 'Spreads the risk in these difficult economic times.'

'That's pretty much it,' Adams said. 'Sound business practice, but just applied to the black economy.'

'So what were you planning as your next steps?' Grant asked.

'Before I went stomping in there in my clumsy size nines is what she means,' McKay added.

Tess Adams shrugged. 'You were just doing your job. We sometimes ask the police to back off if we've got a subject in our sights. But we wouldn't do that with a murder enquiry.'

'Well, that's something,' McKay said, earning another sharp look from Grant.

'In itself, I don't think your visit did any harm. They know why you were there, and it shouldn't have alerted them to our wider interest. The real question, or at least one of them, is why this Tennant was murdered.'

'And we now have a second killing,' Horton said, 'where the victim appears to have been an employee of Muir Hotels.'

'So Helena was just informing us,' Adams said. 'Which is more than intriguing. Either they're fighting among themselves, for some reason, or someone has a grudge against them. Both are possible. And either would make them very unstable.'

'So they're going to be very jittery,' Grant said. 'The prospect of a police investigation, even if it's not focussed on their real business, is going to make them even more so.'

'Especially given that, as your colleague here so expertly demonstrated this afternoon, whatever they're investigating, the police have a habit of uncovering all manner of unpleasantness.'

'Pleased to be of assistance,' McKay said.

'I don't really think we can afford to delay,' Derrick said. 'If they're getting nervous, they'll start trying to cover their tracks. They'll offload all the physical stuff they can, dispose of the people somewhere–'

'How do you mean?' Horton asked. 'How do they dispose of the people?'

Derrick shrugged. 'All kinds of work. There's no shortage of demand for slave labour. Sex work for the younger ones. Agricultural work. Even domestic servitude. If they can't dispose of them that way, they'll just get dumped somewhere for us to pick up. They'll know nothing about where they've been held and won't be able to tell us anything useful about who's been holding them. They'll end up in some immigration centre and, unless they're very lucky, most likely be shipped back to where they came from.'

'Shit,' Horton said before she could stop herself.

'Which, in fairness, is probably what will happen to most of them anyway, even if we can reach them in time. It's not a nice world.' It wasn't entirely clear whether or not Derrick approved of this. 'But that's what they'll do. They probably won't succeed entirely, and we'll be able to make something stick. But it won't be much and, again, it'll probably be the big boys who land on their feet.'

'Who are the big boys?' McKay asked.

'Mainly this guy Archie Donaldson,' Adams said. 'He's

certainly the brains behind it. He's got a few backers down south, but he's the main player up in this neck of the woods. He's got a guy called Elliott doing the financial stuff. We've come across Elliott before. He gives new meanings to the term "creative accounting". He's somehow avoided being sent to prison or even struck off so far, but I'm not sure how.'

McKay exchanged a look with Grant, who nodded. 'We've got Elliott in the frame for something else,' she said. 'An assault.'

'I'm not surprised,' Adams said. 'He has a reputation as a nasty piece of work. That's got him closer to being banged up than his accountancy skills. I'd ask you not to pursue that for the moment, though.'

'If he's as unpleasant as you say, doesn't that carry risks?' Horton asked. 'We're pretty sure he's assaulted one person. She was okay, but it could easily have had a much more serious outcome. If we don't take action and someone gets hurt or worse...'

'Another reason we can't delay with the bigger picture stuff,' Adams said. 'I don't want to give Elliott any more reason to think he's on our radar before we've had the chance to take action. But we need to take action quickly.'

'And when you say action...?' Grant prompted.

'I mean a raid. A co-ordinated raid. All the sites at once. Get as much as we can. People. Goods. Paperwork. Computers. The lot.'

Grant nodded. 'Okay. And when you say quickly...?'

Adams picked up the stack of papers from the desk in front of her and tapped the edges against the surface to even them up. She had the air of a chairwoman bringing the meeting to a close, even though Grant had convened it.

'I'm thinking tomorrow,' she said.

40

It was just dumb luck, of course. But he'd always been lucky when it mattered. That was one of his most valuable qualities. Sure, he had some unique skills and he had a hell of a lot of brass neck. Those had taken him a long way. But it was often luck that had got him across the line. What was it that Napoleon was supposed to have said?

Anyway, this was just luck. He'd been back at the office for a couple of hours doing what Archie had told him. It hadn't taken long, but he'd known it wouldn't.

Just dispose of the evidence, Archie had said. *Anything remotely incriminating. I want us to be clean as a whistle, at least on paper. I don't want anything left that might trip us up.* That was what he'd said.

He'd reassured Archie that he didn't need to worry about that. He'd always kept things clean. Always covered his tracks. The authorities could descend at any moment, and they'd find nothing that would stand up in court.

It wasn't quite true. There were always one or two working documents that, at any point in time, might be tricky to explain. Elliott tried to deal with most of that in his head, but it wasn't always possible if he wanted to ensure everything tied up. Whatever fictions he concocted had to be consistent, and that occasionally meant committing details to paper. But it was always just paper. There was nothing on any of the office systems or his laptop that would cause them any problems.

So this afternoon's clear-up hadn't taken very long. He'd shredded a few documents and then, just to be sure, he'd taken the shredded paper and dumped it in the bins belonging to one of the shops in the next street. Then he returned to the office and spent a couple of hours checking through the files to ensure there was nothing he had missed.

It wasn't watertight, of course. It never could be entirely. A very thorough review by a forensic accountant would eventually identify some anomalies. But he was confident it would convince even an expert eye for long enough.

He'd done his bit. He just hoped that Archie would be able to handle his side of things. Elliott had had a few doubts when he'd first got himself tied up with Archie. He was bright enough, certainly, even if he did have a tendency to spout a little too much business babble. And Elliott had seen enough of Archie's ruthlessness to know that he wasn't going to be overly squeamish.

But he still wasn't entirely comfortable about Archie's ability to perform under pressure. Elliott hadn't been reassured by what he'd seen over the last few days. When the trouble had kicked off, he'd just frozen at first. He'd carried on spouting the macho business bullshit, but Elliott had seen it in his eyes. He hadn't known what to do. There was nothing in there but blind panic.

Elliott had pulled him through it, and in fairness over the last few days Archie seemed to have at least partly got it together. They were doing the right thing, Elliott thought. Within a few days, they'd have the whole thing shut down, all the goods disposed of. It would cost them, but it would buy them a bit of time to find out what was really going on, who was behind this. Then they could continue or not.

It didn't worry Elliott much either way. He'd come up here because he'd sailed a little too close to the wind down south. He'd taken one risk too many and he needed to lie low for a while. Someone had put him in touch with Archie and he'd headed up here, which was about as far away as he could get without actually leaving the country.

But now the dust had settled and, if need be, he could head back south and take up where he'd left off. He had a few quid stashed away that would tide him over in the meantime. Maybe it was time for a change.

He'd tied up all the loose ends, and he couldn't do much more. But he'd had a sense for a while that things were beginning to go awry here. He'd felt it, even before the current troubles. For all Archie's supposed business savvy, Elliott was beginning to think they had their fingers in too many pies. He was trying to do too much too quickly. He had his suspicions about Archie, too. The business was doing less well than it should have been and Archie, for all his skills, hadn't been able to pinpoint exactly why. He'd begun to wonder if there were things Archie wasn't telling him.

Elliott was all for ambition, but you had to be realistic. This was a dangerous game and you had to be watchful all the time. You needed good people around you, and Elliott hadn't liked the way Archie tended to cut corners. Some of those tosspots he had working in the hotels could hardly string a sentence together. He wouldn't want to rely on them if the authorities ever did come knocking.

As for Archie's efforts to bring in more funding, he didn't even want to think about that. It had been so half-baked. Accepting investment from some guy he hadn't seen for thirty years with the promise of some sort of stake in the business. It would have been kind even to call the guy an amateur. He wasn't just out of his depth. He'd lost sight of land. Just some shyster. It hadn't even been clear to Elliott that he'd really had the money he claimed. Elliott had been almost able to smell the man's desperation, but Archie had never accepted it. He'd told Elliott that the guy had come highly recommended, but he wouldn't say by whom.

Still, it seemed to have gone nowhere. He was still nervous about the money they'd accepted, not knowing its provenance, but he thought he'd managed to redistribute it safely. But it had taught him something about Archie.

That was why he'd been so on edge lately. One of the reasons, anyway. He knew he had an anger problem. It had almost got him into serious trouble once or twice, and he'd thought he'd learned how to keep a lid on it. *Not that that is necessarily a good thing,* he thought. When it flared up, his anger could be incandescent. When he had it under control, it was more like a cold fury in his heart. He could feel it there, growing, intensifying, waiting for the moment to explode.

He never quite knew what might set it off. It preyed on his insecurities, he knew that. It preyed on his fears and anxieties. It preyed – and he wasn't ashamed to acknowledge this – on his sexual frustrations. He'd found ways of dealing with the last of these. Money could buy you anything. But it wasn't just sexual frustration. It was the lack of respect women tended to show him. Even the ones he paid for. Or perhaps especially the ones he paid for. He wanted women to show him respect. But if they weren't prepared to do that, he wanted them to show fear.

That was where tonight's luck came in. A chance to replay one of those recent encounters. To make it go the way he wanted, for a change.

She was on the opposite side of the street when he emerged from the office into the chilly late afternoon. It was luck that she was there, and it was luck that she'd momentarily stopped to fiddle with something on her mobile. Sending a text or a message, he thought.

Elliott didn't stop to think. If he had, he knew she'd be walking away and his opportunity would have passed.

'Hello there,' he called.

She ignored him at first, presumably thinking he was speaking to someone else. He called again and this time she looked up.

As he'd expected, she looked startled to see him. He thought at first she might just walk away. If she had, there was little he could have done about it. He didn't want the indignity of chasing after her.

But again his luck held. She stood motionless, staring at him.

'You've got a fucking nerve,' she said.

'I know. I'm really sorry. It was unforgivable.'

'Too bloody right it was. It wasn't just standing me up. It was leaving me with the fucking bill.'

He hadn't been able to recall her name at first. Maggie something. Maggie Clennan. 'I'm sorry,' he said again. 'I didn't do it on purpose. I don't know what it was. Some sort of panic attack.'

'Panic attack?'

'I knew I wasn't what you'd been expecting. It was stupid of me, putting those old pictures on the site. I thought it was just what people did. I was shocked when I saw how young you were. It wasn't what I was expecting either.' He offered her a weak smile. 'So I panicked. When you went off to the ladies, I just got overwhelmed. I'd intended to pay the bill on my way out, but I wasn't thinking clearly and I just wanted to get away before you came back...' He trailed off. 'I phoned the restaurant later to try to pay by credit card. But they said you'd already left and settled the bill.'

He wasn't sure whether she really believed any of this, but she at least seemed to be listening. 'Aye, all of it. Including all that wine you'd knocked back.'

He nodded solemnly. 'Look, I'll repay you. I kept thinking about trying to get back in touch with you, but I thought you probably wouldn't have responded if I'd contacted you through the site or if I tried to phone you. But now I've run into you, at least let me give you the money back.'

He could see she was hesitating, and he knew he'd succeeded. He'd engaged her interest. He just needed to take it step by step, and he'd reel her in.

'To be honest,' she said, 'a couple of friends helped me pay it.'

'That makes me feel even worse,' he said. 'But if I give you the money, you can pay them back. I'm so embarrassed. I've never done anything like that before.'

'Oh, shit, why not?' she said. 'I'll feel better if I can pay them back.'

'Where are you heading?' he said. 'It's just that I'll need to get the money out so I'll have to find a cash machine.'

'I'm just heading home,' she said. 'If we go up via the High Street that's sort of on my way.'

'That's great. Up here then.' He had already started to walk, leaving her to follow him. Then he looked back. 'Are you in a rush at all?'

'Not particularly. Why?'

'I just– No, it doesn't matter.'

'What?'

'It was just that I wondered if you'd let me buy you a drink. Just as a way of saying sorry. But don't worry if you can't...'

'I don't know...' she said.

He stopped and held up his hand. 'I'm not trying it on, honestly. I realised as soon as I saw you that it wasn't appropriate.' He laughed. 'I'm old enough to be your father.'

He could see she wanted to point out that he was probably old enough to be her grandfather. But that didn't matter. He'd got her on his wavelength.

'If you say so,' she said. 'Okay, just one drink. Just so you can make it up to me. Mind you, I expect more grovelling apologies.'

I bet you do, he thought. *Your kind always does.* Out loud, he said, 'I'll grovel as much as you want. And buying you a drink is the least I can do. What about in there?' He gestured towards an upmarket bar on the far side of the street, as if he'd just noticed it. As if he hadn't been deliberately steering her up there.

'Aye, why not?'

Although it was beginning to grow dark, it was still another hour or so before most people would be leaving work. The bar was almost empty, except for a young couple drinking beers in one of the corners.

'What can I get you?' he said. 'I take it you're not driving?'

'I walk home. So I can push the boat out and have a glass of wine. Rosé, if they've got it.'

He returned from the bar with a large glass of rosé and what he told her was just a tonic for himself. He'd been tempted to leave out the gin, but he knew that alcohol always made it easier.

'A large one?' she said.

He shrugged. 'I owe you a large apology.'

She took a sip of the wine. 'I really didn't like you, you know?'

'I'm not surprised,' he said. 'I behaved appallingly.'

'Not that. That just confirmed what I thought. But before then I just disliked you.'

'That's honest, I suppose.' It wasn't really what he wanted her to be saying, but at least they were making conversation.

'I'm just wondering if I was wrong. If I was being unfair to you.' She'd already finished half the glass of wine. 'I think it was because I assumed you were just out for one thing. I thought you were an old creep.'

He laughed uneasily. 'I wasn't really, you know. I mean, I can see how it would have looked like that. But I just wasn't expecting you to be so young. I don't pretend I'm not hoping to, you know, meet the right person. But I really like going on these dates just for the company. It gets me out.' He hoped he wasn't laying it on a bit too thick.

'I can see that.'

She was feeling sorry for him. It was what he'd been aiming for, but he still found it infuriating. Was that really the best he could hope for, these days? That some young bitch would feel sorry for him?

He'd noticed in the restaurant that she was more than capable of knocking back the booze. She'd already polished off the glass of wine.

'Another?' he said.

'I really shouldn't.'

But he already knew that she would.

41

Jana knew that something was happening, and she could tell in her heart that it was nothing good.

She didn't know whether the other women had recognised it yet. Probably they had, or most of them had, but like her they were keeping their heads down and hoping none of it would affect them.

She couldn't believe that. She knew that things were about to change, and she knew that, as always, they would be changing for the worse.

The men seemed almost to have lost interest in what the women were doing, anyway. Everything was happening outside, and Jana was able to stand undisturbed at the window, watching what was going on.

Mr Big was there, and all of the others. The young one, the one she called Mouse and the one she called Stick. Jitters was still down there in the woodland, as far as she knew, his body no doubt slowly being consumed by the nature surrounding him. The only other one missing was the fat one.

They had a van pulled up in the car park at the rear of the hotel. The men were slowly loading it with crates from the sheds behind the building. They had already loaded the van once, and the young one and Mouse had driven it off somewhere. They'd returned an hour or so later and begun the whole process again.

They looked to be in a hurry. Almost in a panic. As if the time to do this was rapidly running out. As if something was on their tail, she thought. A cat about to catch a rat.

Her sense was that they were trying to clear the place out. Which raised in her mind the question of what they would do with their human cargo. With her and the other women.

She wondered whether that question had entered any of the other women's minds, or whether they were just watching all this fatalistically. It was clear, anyway, that no one wanted to talk about it. Most just carried on with their work, scrubbing away as if they were doing something worthwhile.

It was late afternoon before they finally finished emptying the sheds. They loaded the final crates in the van, and Mr Big watched while the young one and Mouse once again drove away. Then he gestured to Stick to follow him into the hotel.

Jana resumed polishing the furniture in one of the lounges, watching as the two men made their way through into the room they used as a meeting space. 'We deserve a drink,' she heard Mr Big say. 'I've got some whisky in my bag.'

He seemed relieved, she thought, as if a burden had been lifted from his shoulders. Stick said something she couldn't hear, but she heard Mr Big speaking in response. 'I don't like the thought of the police sniffing about, whatever their reasons. It just confirms we're doing the right thing. And I'll see you right. Don't worry about that. You help me out with this, and I'll see you right till we're through it.'

Police.

The word had never had good connotations for Jana. Where she came from, the police were always bad news. She imagined it was different here for most people. But she was not most people. She knew she shouldn't be here. She knew she had none of the necessary documentation. If the police came, even here, it would not be good news. Not for her.

She glanced nervously over to the main doors, as if expecting that the police might already be there. She had been here before, she thought, sometimes with the police, sometimes with the soldiers. Waiting for the knock on the door, the call in the middle of the night. The early morning raid.

If the police were coming, she thought, she would no longer be here.

'YOU THINK WE CAN DO THIS?' McKay said.

'I don't think we've got much choice,' Grant replied. 'I've spoken to the Assistant Chief Constable and he'd already been got at by some bigwig in the NCA. We've been told to jump, and we don't even get the chance to ask how high.'

'Funny how they can find the resources when they want to.'

'Funny how they can make us find the resources when they want to.'

'Aye, that's what I meant, obviously. So how are we set up?'

They were sitting in Grant's office, trying to finish co-ordinating the raid that was planned for the following morning.

'We've got the staffing more or less sorted,' Grant said. 'A lot of people will no doubt be very pleased with the overtime. Immigration are providing us with some additional officers, one for each site–'

'Big deal.'

'HMRC, likewise. That's mainly to make sure we collect the right stuff.'

'Because they don't trust us to get it right ourselves.'

'And the NCA are supplying – well, they're supplying their expertise.'

'Which means?'

'Tess Adams is going to give the benefit of her wisdom.'

'Well, that and a fiver will get me a meal deal,' McKay said. 'They're not supplying any resources?'

'Well, we're all the way up here and their resources are already stretched to the limit…'

'Unlike ours, you mean?'

'Alec, I assumed you'd realised by now that our job is to do their dirty work.'

'I've realised all right. Doesn't mean I have to like it.'

'Welcome to my world. Anyway, that's the way it's been set up. I've being doing all the risk assessments. The advice from immigration is that it should be relatively straightforward. There are only a handful of people involved, and most of them are real small fry. They'll probably just bottle it as soon as we appear. The staffing at each site is pretty minimal, so there shouldn't be any resistance.'

'What if immigration are wrong? What if one of them decides to take a potshot at us?'

'We'll be wearing suitable protection just in case–'

'I'm not sure that a condom's really going to make much difference.'

'I've not asked for any armed police, but I've made sure backup will be readily available on the off-chance we need it. All the warrants and documentation are sorted and signed off. So we're pretty much there.'

'Apart from actually doing it, you mean? What about their HQ?'

'That's on the list. It's just a serviced office in town. We can't really just go bursting in there in the wee hours of the morning, so we're going to station a couple of uniforms there till their receptionist opens up at eight. Then we'll go in and seize everything.'

'The wee hours? What time are we doing this again?' McKay already knew, but he wanted to make her say it.

'We go in at five. That way the on-site staffing should be at its lowest, and we shouldn't get any real trouble. We've got home addresses for Donaldson and Elliott so we'll pick them up at the same time. We can round up any other key players later.'

'I hope this is going to produce the evidence that Adams and the others think,' McKay said. 'Otherwise we could end up looking like a right bunch of numpties.'

'I don't suppose Adams cares. If it goes well, she'll take the credit. If it goes badly, it'll magically become our operation. You know that.'

'With our arses on the line. Aye.'

'But I've done everything I can to cover them. All up to the ACC and all in writing.'

'Like that'll make any difference. But, I know, it's how it is.'

'You're finally getting the hang of this, Alec.' She sighed. 'There are times when I love this job, and times when I really fucking hate it. Guess which category this falls into. Right, let's go and get this briefing kicked off, and then we can all get off for an early night. We're going to bloody well need it.'

42

He had to admit he was quite impressed by how she could put it away. They had been in the bar for less than an hour, but she'd already knocked back two large glasses of rosé and was contemplating the option of a third. She was beginning to demonstrate the effects very satisfactorily.

'Are you trying to get me drunk?' she asked him for the second time.

'Not at all. I just want you to think a little better of me. To persuade you that I'm not the total bastard you probably assumed after the other night.' Elliott had already picked up her glass, prior to heading for the bar.

'Anyone who's prepared to buy me wine is all right in my books.' She was giggling in a way that, in other circumstances, he might have found quite attractive. Now, it just confirmed to him what he was dealing with. And this woman had had the nerve to treat him with contempt.

He was a little longer at the bar this time. The place was beginning to fill up with people who'd presumably finished work at the neighbouring shops and offices. He glanced repeatedly over his shoulder to make sure she was still there. He didn't want to risk losing her now.

But she showed no sign of wanting to move. When he glanced back, she even gave him a brief wave in a manner he assumed was intended to be playful. This was going better than he could have imagined. It was amazing, he thought, what a few glasses of wine could do. It probably helped that it was still only early evening and she, presumably, hadn't eaten anything recently.

He'd partly been telling the truth about the panic attack, though not about the reasons. He'd been disappointed, partly because he'd thought the evening was going okay. He hadn't particularly expected it to. It was always harder work with the younger women. You could feel their distaste as soon as they realised you weren't the young stud your profile had suggested. But he liked younger women – the younger the better within reason – and it was always worth a shot. Sometimes they were sufficiently flattered by his attentions, or at least his willingness to spend money, to respond positively.

But that night he thought it was all going pretty well. She wasn't exactly throwing herself at him, but she'd seemed interested in what he had to say. She'd seemed impressed by his relative wealth, and by the supposed importance of his job. He was beginning to think that there might be at least half a chance of buying his way into her knickers for not much more than the price of a few more after-dinner drinks.

But it hadn't worked out that way. She'd gone off to the ladies, and that was when he'd spotted that bloody policewoman. He'd eyeballed her first a couple of minutes before that, sitting in the far corner with some woman friend. At first, he'd assumed that was just a coincidence. After all, there weren't that many decent restaurants in the city. If she liked eating out, it wasn't that surprising she'd be in here. He wasn't sure whether or not she'd spotted him.

But then he'd seen the way that, as soon as Maggie Clennan

had entered the lavatories, the policewoman had jumped up and followed her. That couldn't be coincidence. He knew at the time he'd been stupid to follow her and send those texts after their disastrous evening. It had been one of those times when he'd just let his anger get the better of him. The last thing he needed was to attract the attention of the police, especially for something as stupid as that. That was why he'd clammed up when she'd first told him what he did. But then he'd tried to behave normally and had ended up taking that stupid lunge at her.

Even so, there was no reason for her to treat him with that much contempt. That was why he'd been so angry. He just couldn't help himself. But he knew it wouldn't have been difficult for her to guess who was responsible. At least, he'd been smart enough to use one of the burner phones he kept for business, and he'd got rid of that straight afterwards. He hoped that, even if she assumed he'd been behind the texts, she'd realise she couldn't prove it and would just write him off as an arsehole.

But then he'd seen her follow Clennan, and he'd wondered whether, after all, he might actually be under some sort of observation. It would be ironic, he thought, if he was brought down by something as stupid as that, given everything he was involved in. Like bloody Al Capone being done for tax evasion.

At the very least, he'd known the policewoman would warn Clennan off, so that was the evening at an end. He hadn't exactly panicked, but he had been overcome by an irrational fear that both women might emerge to confront him. If he'd been thinking more clearly, he'd probably have settled the bill before leaving, if only to avoid giving the policewoman any further reason for interest in him.

But he hadn't been thinking clearly. His brain had been scrambled by a cocktail of booze, anxiety, humiliation and, yes, that familiar anger. He'd stormed into the night and driven home, not caring how much he'd drunk. Back at home, in his comfortable villa near the river, he'd cracked open a bottle of single malt and knocked back another few drams, fuelling his fury at how he'd been treated.

He just couldn't help himself. He'd eventually fallen asleep in his chair, and had woken the next morning, aching and still fully dressed, the cold fury still burning in him. That was when he'd sent her the second set of texts. He'd regretted it almost immediately. But in the moment it had felt cathartic.

His regret had proved justified, when that bloody smart-arse detective had turned up in his offices. He'd left Elliott in little doubt they knew he'd been behind the texts. The only positive was that it was equally clear to Elliott that they had nothing definite they could pin on him. He hadn't handled it well, but he'd conceded enough to undermine any case they might try to make. But he'd known he'd put himself in their sights unnecessarily.

He paid for the drinks and took them back over to the table where Maggie Clennan was waiting for him. It was beginning to look as if his instincts on that first evening had been correct. It wasn't exactly that she liked him. But she was prepared to tolerate him for a few drinks and maybe the prospect of a decent meal later.

He wondered momentarily if he should do that. Take her out for a meal. Get her even more in his debt, make her feel she owed him something. But bugger that, he thought. He didn't need to spend that kind of money to get what he wanted. Especially since what he wanted now really was just to put this bitch in her place. Teach her, teach all of them, that he wasn't someone to be screwed around with.

He realised that, over the course of the last hour or so, he'd come to a decision. He hadn't been conscious of even thinking about it. But he knew now that this was it. He'd been weighing up whether to continue up here, stick with Archie and try to make a go of it once they'd sorted out their current problems.

There were attractions to that. They'd carved out a neat little niche, and had been doing pretty well. But, when it came to it, he didn't have as much faith in Archie as he'd have liked. If the police were beginning to sniff around, it was all getting too risky.

It would be better for Elliott to cash in his chips and head back south. It wouldn't be difficult. He had always made a point of travelling light. His house up here was rented. He'd have to forego a couple of months' rent if he moved out now, but nothing he couldn't afford. He had enough liquid assets to keep him going while he decided what to do next. He could just disappear.

If he was going to do that, he might as well make the most of it.

He smiled at Maggie Clennan, who seemed to have already drunk most of her third glass. 'Do you fancy moving on somewhere else after this one?' he asked.

43

The young one and Mouse had returned after an hour or so, and had joined Stick and Mr Big in what Jana now thought of as the meeting room. They'd left the door half open as if they no longer cared about being overheard.

She knew what was happening now, or she thought she did.

They were moving on. She'd seen it before, though she'd assumed that wasn't how things worked here. Things seemed more permanent here. Things might change, but she'd expected them to change slowly.

But now she could almost taste the urge to move on, as potent as if this was some nomadic tribe off to seek new pastures. That was why they had cleared out all the goods in the shed. This place would just be an empty shell, perhaps retaining only the furnishings to recall its former life.

The only question was what they were going to do with the women. Were they planning to take them? If so, to where and to what fate?

Or were they planning just to leave them here? She had heard the word "police" earlier, and she had felt her stomach tighten with fear. She had no right to be here. If the police were to come, they would take her to – what? Imprisonment? Deportation? A return to the place she had come from, or, more likely, somewhere even worse?

She couldn't face any of that. She had looked around at the other women, and even tried to talk to one or two of them, but as ever they had rebuffed her attempts. They didn't want to know. They wanted to pretend nothing was happening. They probably smelt it in the air as strongly as she did, but they would never admit it to themselves. There was nothing they could do anyway. All they could do was wait. Wait, accept and suffer. That had been their lives for as long as most of them could remember.

A few of the younger ones might have hope of something better. But Jana knew their youth simply meant there were more ways for them to suffer. They had always been destined for something worse than this, she thought. It had always been only a matter of time.

Jana knew that she could face no more. She wasn't old, not really. But she felt as if she had already lived for ever and had seen far too much. She needed no more.

Most of the other women had hidden themselves away in the kitchen. They knew as well as Jana did that the men no longer cared what they were doing. They had never really cared. It had all been a matter of control. Keeping them under their thumb. Keeping them too exhausted to think of anything else.

Jana stayed in the lounge, within earshot of the meeting room. She wanted to know how much time they had. She wasn't even sure why she cared anymore, now that she had made up her mind.

This is partly about control too, she thought. She had always resented their control over her. She had always resented that they could use her as they liked, and that she had no means of retaliating. Her only tiny victory had been to conceal her ability to speak their language. They had never realised she could understand what they were saying, and that she could guess at least part of what they were thinking.

It had never really helped her, of course, but it had at least meant that there was a part of her mind that they couldn't fully control. Something she could keep for her own. Something she had over them.

She could hear Mr Big saying, 'We've got to get it all done tomorrow. Tomorrow morning, if possible. Do you think we can get all of them in the van?'

'All of them?' the young one responded. 'All together. Jesus. That'll be tight.'

'We can live with tight,' Mr Big said. 'Well, they can. They won't have a choice. I'd just rather they all arrived still breathing. I'm losing enough on this deal already. I can't afford any stiffs.'

'It's not that far,' the young one said. 'Just down to the borders. Six, seven hours? Most of them will have experienced a lot worse than that.'

That was true enough, Jana thought. She recalled how she'd got here. Hours and hours in the darkness, never knowing when it would end. Never knowing whether she would survive. Knowing that no one, not even those she had paid handsomely supposedly to look after her, cared either way.

'I just hope those bastards turn up,' Mr Big said. 'I don't want us to find ourselves stuck in the middle of nowhere with that lot.'

'If they don't show,' the one she'd called Mouse said, 'we should just leave them to fend for themselves. They don't know anything about us. They'll either get picked up or they won't.'

'And I'll have lost the little money I stood to make on this deal,' Mr Big pointed out. 'But it might come to that.'

Not for me it won't, Jana thought. *Whatever happens, it won't come to that.*

She had already decided. If they were shipping them out tomorrow, whatever their destination, then she would leave tonight. At least that way, finally, she would be in control.

I n the end, they'd stayed for one more drink. She'd seemed up for it, and he'd decided that the more she'd had, the easier it would be. He'd not had a lot to say, but she'd talked enough for both of them, blethering on about her dead-end call centre job as if telling him something he might want to hear.

He'd been happy enough just to let her talk, occasionally nodding politely or responding if she asked him something. Normally, he preferred to impose himself on the conversation, let them know who they were dealing with. But that didn't matter now. He knew how tonight was going to pan out, and he no longer really had to make an effort.

In any case, it didn't take long for her to finish the fourth glass. That was more than a full bottle she'd consumed, and she was showing the effects. She wasn't drunk, exactly. She clearly knew how to hold her drink. But she was getting increasingly giggly and flirty, and she was beginning to stumble over her words. *Perfect,* he thought.

'Do you fancy moving on somewhere else, then?' he said.

'What have you got in mind?' she said. 'As if I didn't know...' She collapsed into another fit of giggles.

It was definitely time to get them out of there, he thought. If she had any more, she'd start drawing attention to herself. And that would mean drawing attention to him.

'Maybe a bite to eat?' He was assuming that, by now, she'd probably forgotten about his promise to repay her for the previous meal. If she remembered when they got outside, he could still withdraw the money and hand it over to her, just to keep her sweet. He shouldn't have any difficulty retrieving it later.

'Aye, why not?' She leaned forward and peered at his face, as if trying to recall who he was. 'Long as you don't leave me to bloody pay again.'

'I won't. And I'll give you the money for the last time.' So she hadn't forgotten, though whether she'd remember to ask him for the money was another matter.

He stood up and helped her to her feet, conscious she was swaying slightly. He assisted her with her coat, and then encouraged her to hold onto his arm as they left the bar.

'Where do you want to go then?' she asked once they were outside. She seemed slightly sobered by the chill air, although her gait was still unsteady. The weather had begun to close in, and the first flakes of fresh snow were falling.

'I was thinking,' he said, his tone suggesting that the idea had just come to him. 'There's a little place I know just outside the centre. It's a bit upmarket but I feel I owe you something decent after last time.'

'Sounds good. Is it far?'

He glanced up at the sky. 'Not that far. But my car's parked nearby, and given this weather...'

He wasn't sure whether she'd resist coming in the car, but she was obviously at least partly aware of her own drunkenness so seemed relieved by the suggestion. 'That's good. Don't want to have to walk too far in these heels.'

His car was parked in an allocated space at the rear of his

office. She even seemed impressed by that. 'Blimey. You've got your own parking place here. Mr Big Shot.'

'I'm an important man,' he said, going along with the joke.

He helped her into the passenger seat of the car. Her brief moment of sobriety seemed to have passed, and now she appeared more drunk than ever.

He climbed into the driver's seat and started the engine.

'Nice car,' she said.

It wasn't all that nice, he thought. It was like all his possessions, bought for convenience and ease of disposal rather than for its intrinsic qualities. The car was a prestige make, moderately large and new enough to impress those with limited knowledge. He'd bought it for cash and it was registered under the name of Elliott.

The truth was, of course, that Elliott wasn't his real name. It was probably the most well-developed of his fake identities, with sufficient history and pedigree to ensure that it would pass muster even under most official scrutiny. But he could slough it off tomorrow and either return to his real identity or take up one of the other aliases he had prepared. It would be a pity, given how well established Elliott's history now was, but he would have no hesitation in doing it. The car would be sold on, and someone new would purchase its replacement.

'It gets me from A to B,' he responded to Maggie Clennan.

'I bet it does,' she said, in a tone that implied some kind of innuendo.

He pulled back out into the street, then headed out of town back onto the A82 heading south. After a short distance he turned left, and then wound his way among the network of residential streets.

His house was a sizeable Edwardian detached villa, set back from the road. It was really too large for him, but the rental price had been very reasonable. The owners were a youngish couple with two children, who'd been taken overseas for a year by the husband's work. They'd discovered that there wasn't currently much of a letting market in the city for properties of this size and quality, so Elliott had been able to drive a relatively hard bargain. The place suited him perfectly. It was comfortable and convenient for his travel to the office and the other sites. Most of all, tucked away in this quiet backstreet with its own gardens and parking area, it was discreet. He had a gardener and a cleaner who each came in once a week to help keep the place tidy, but otherwise he was undisturbed. The neighbouring houses had largely been converted into either guest houses or flats.

He'd almost thought that Maggie Clennan had dozed off in the seat beside him, but as they turned into the driveway she stirred and sat up. 'Is this the place? It doesn't look much like a restaurant.'

'It isn't exactly.'

She frowned and looked around her. 'So what is it?'

'It's where I live.'

She looked at him. 'Oh, you're a bad man, aren't you?' He'd expected her to be angry, but instead she giggled. 'So, you going to cook me dinner here?'

He shrugged, happy to continue the game. 'I told you it was upmarket.'

'Can you cook then?'

'You'd be surprised.'

She giggled again. 'A man of many talents.'

'Are you prepared to come in, then? I can fix you a drink while I cook something.'

She looked as if she was about to refuse, then grinned at him. 'Aye, why not? Always happy to accept free booze. Just don't go thinking you can try it on, eh?'

He held up his hands in mock horror. 'I wouldn't dream of it. A few drinks, a decent meal. Then I'll drive you home.'

'Fair enough. And don't forget you still owe me for that last meal.'

Drunk as she was, she clearly wasn't going to forget, he thought. Not that it mattered now. It was all proving much easier than he'd expected. But maybe, with a few glasses inside her, that was just the kind of girl she was.

He helped her out of the car and then across the gravelled drive to the house. It was snowing harder now, the thickening flakes swirling around them. She looked up. 'Jesus, it's fucking cold,' she said.

'Let's get inside.'

She was pressing herself against him, seeking shelter from the biting wind. He had no objection to that, though frankly it didn't matter much anymore. It would be better if she was willing, but he didn't really care. He certainly wasn't prepared to waste any more time and energy wining and dining her. Once they were inside and he'd got the front door shut firmly behind them, he could do what he wanted.

The only question was how far he was prepared to go. In some ways, now, there was no point in half measures. If he let her go, she'd presumably head to the police. But then again, he supposed she might decide against reporting it, particularly if he scared her sufficiently.

But that was all a risk. If he went further, if he left her in a state where she couldn't report him, then he'd have time to deal with things in comparative leisure. He'd have to dispose of her, but there were plenty of places he could do that. But he'd give himself the time he needed to cover his tracks and vanish.

That was part of his thinking. A large part. But not the whole of it. There was something more.

If he did that, if he went all the way with her, he might finally satisfy his anger. He might finally put a woman in her place. He might finally give a woman what she really deserved. He might finally quench that cold fire of fury that had always burned inside him.

She stumbled against him and he pulled her impatiently

towards his front door. It took him a moment to find his keys and get the door open, and then finally they were inside and he was able to slam it shut behind them.

She moved away from him, and looked around at the spacious hallway. 'Nice place. You must have a bob or two. So where do we go now?'

'Upstairs,' he said.

She blinked. 'What?'

'Upstairs. My bedroom.'

She took a step back. 'If you think–'

'God, you're a stupid little bitch, aren't you? You really bought all that crap about drinks and dinner.'

'I don't–'

Her face was ashen. He could see that she was trying to work out whether she could somehow get past him, get back out into the open air, where she'd no doubt scream her lungs out.

He walked forward and grabbed her by the arm. 'Come on. I'm not prepared to waste any more time on you.'

She tried to struggle, but he knew she would be too weak. He'd thought she might try to shout but she was clearly too terrified even to do that. It didn't matter either way. This was a solidly built old place. None of the neighbours would hear anything no matter how much noise she made.

He dragged her forcibly up the stairs. Maybe he should have just kept it simple and dealt with her downstairs. It would have been quicker and easier, but he wanted to do this properly. He didn't want it quick or easy, certainly not for her. He wanted to do it properly, in the proper place. She owed him that. They all owed him that.

In any case, he had little difficulty handling her. She kept trying to kick out at him but he found it easy to avoid her flailing feet. His only worry was that she might send them both tumbling down the stairs, but in a moment they were on the upper landing and he was thrusting her into his bedroom.

He was a tidy man and the bed was neatly made, the white duvet cover stretched pristine across the mattress. It was a pity she would make such a mess of it, he thought, one way or another. But that couldn't be helped.

She was trying to reach for his face, clawing at his eyes, but he had no difficulty fending her off. He grasped her by the shoulders and, lifting her from the ground, he threw her bodily onto the bed.

She was wearing a smart black skirt with a pale cream blouse. He hadn't particularly registered her clothing earlier in the evening, and it struck him now that it was an unexpectedly demure look. Presumably, it was what she was expected to wear at the call centre, though he couldn't imagine why it would matter.

She looked gratifyingly terrified, he thought. The way it ought to be.

He began to fumble with his trousers, preparing for the moment when he would throw himself on top of her. The moment when he would finally give her what he needed, and what she deserved.

A moment later he was on her, his hand at her throat, his face inches from hers.

He was about to start tearing at her clothing when he suddenly realised that her expression had changed. The terror that had been etched into her features only moments before had been replaced by something that looked almost like amusement.

At the same moment, he felt something cold and sharp pressing against the side of his stomach, through his shirt.

Before he knew what was happening, she had wriggled out from beneath him and had moved the pocket knife up so that its point was resting against his Adam's apple. She grabbed his shoulder and thrust him firmly onto the bed, so that he was lying on his back. She was kneeling beside him, and the sharp blade of the knife was resting across his throat, pressing so hard that he thought it must have already drawn blood. There was a knowing smile playing across her face, and her previous drunkenness had evaporated.

'Now,' she said, 'that's really not appropriate behaviour, is it? Not at any time or in any circumstances.' She paused and the smile broadened. 'But especially not when your boss's daughter's involved.'

He had only a moment to register bafflement and then the first glimmer of understanding before her hand pressed firmly down on the knife.

45

McKay was beginning to wish he'd pulled rank and stayed back in the office. The offer had been there from Helena Grant – nobody really expected a DI to be on the front line in an operation like this – and for a few moments he'd been sorely tempted.

After all, it was five in the fucking morning in the middle of a Highland winter. Nobody in their right mind would be out at a time like this unless they really needed to be. He had every right to take his due place in the command structure. That place being somewhere warm and dry, preferably with a cup of coffee by his side.

Nevertheless, although McKay knew he probably wasn't much cop as a manager, there were a few principles he tried to apply consistently. Perhaps the most important one was that you didn't ask your team to do anything you weren't prepared to do yourself. So if you wanted your team to be out in a blizzard at sparrow fart, you had to be prepared to do it too.

That was why he was here. In fairness, he knew that in other circumstances Helena Grant would be doing the same. As it was, she was back at the office with Tess Adams playing silver command to the other woman's gold. Adams had assumed the role of multi-agency commander without, as far as McKay was aware, bothering to consult with anyone. Grant had had no real objections. She supposed it marginally increased the chances that Adams would end up carrying the can if anything went wrong or, more likely, if this proved to be a monumental waste of time and resource.

Grant was co-ordinating the police resources which, as they all knew, were what really counted here, with McKay, Horton and a couple of other experienced officers acting as bronze commanders at each hotel, all supported by a small team of uniforms. Every team included a couple of immigration officers who would handle any formalities on that side of the business. McKay's and Horton's teams included a representative from the revenue who would supposedly advise on the value of any documentation found in the course of searching Donaldson's and Elliott's houses. In practice, McKay assumed that they would simply seize anything that wasn't nailed down, along, no doubt, with a few items that were.

No one was expecting a particularly challenging operation, but McKay knew it was never smart to be complacent on a job like this. You could pretty much guarantee that anything that could go wrong would. He was already beginning to form an opinion about the experience of his non-police colleagues in this kind of environment.

He'd been allocated Archie Donaldson's house on the basis that Donaldson was the biggest fish in this particular fetid swamp. It didn't matter if they lost a few of the small fry, but they couldn't afford not to pick up Donaldson if they were going to make anything stick. Otherwise, it would just be a few more illegals to be shipped off to some hellhole of an immigration centre. McKay wished there was some way of avoiding that outcome, but he couldn't pretend that it would help anyone if they didn't take action against the likes of Donaldson.

Horton had been allocated Elliott's house on the same basis. In some ways, Elliott might be even more critical to their case than Donaldson. Donaldson was the big player, but McKay suspected that Elliott was likely to be the brains.

The rest of the team were then spread across the various hotel sites. The assumption was that the staffing at the sites was likely to be minimal overnight, so the primary objective was to pick up any illegals that might be working there along with the night staff, and then mop up the other small fry subsequently. If some of those slipped away into the undergrowth in the meantime, no one would care too much.

McKay had been up here the previous evening to reconnoitre the location. As far as he was concerned, this was all being done much more hurriedly than he would have liked. He'd been caught out before on this kind of operation by a failure to take account of some local geographical or other idiosyncrasy – a gate that wouldn't open, a path that unexpectedly led into a quagmire, a road blockage that wasn't shown on the map. Last night, he'd checked out the lay of the land, and made sure there was an area for them to park that was sufficiently distant from Donaldson's house not to attract his or his neighbours' attention. He'd found a spot of rough ground just off one of the adjacent roads that he thought would fit the bill. It wasn't perfect – it was a little nearer and more exposed to Donaldson's house than he'd have preferred – but he hoped they would be there only for a few minutes to gather their resources and double-check everything was in place.

As it was, events didn't go entirely to plan. For a start, the weather had deteriorated overnight, and they'd found themselves conducting the operation in the middle of a moderately heavy snow shower, with a strong wind blasting in from the coast. Luckily, even the backroads were still easily passable, but it meant their progress was slower and more cautious than expected.

McKay had hoped that, once off the main road, they could

switch down to sidelights and perhaps even turn off their car lights entirely for the final few hundred metres. But visibility was poor, and he decided that the risk was too great. That of course increased the possibility that they might be spotted by Donaldson or some busybody neighbour, but he hoped that the thickening snow would help conceal their presence.

They met, as planned, shortly before five, and McKay gathered the team around him to check that everyone knew and understood their allocated role. Two of the uniforms would be deployed to the rear of Donaldson's house in case he should try to abscond through his garden, which had vehicle access to an adjoining road. The two uniforms would set off first to ensure they were in place before McKay and the others approached from the front, and would park their car to block the rear access. There was a risk that the sound of the car engine might alert Donaldson, but by that point McKay's team would already be approaching from the front. The revenue officer would hold back until told it was safe for him to approach. It wasn't entirely foolproof, but McKay was hoping it wouldn't need to be.

The two uniforms set off and McKay waited till he received the signal that they were in place at the rear of the house. Then he pulled out, and turned into Donaldson's driveway. The third car followed behind him and stopped to ensure that the exit was blocked.

It was at that point that McKay had the first inkling that something was wrong. Donaldson's car, which the previous evening had been parked in front of the house, was no longer there. McKay radioed to the two uniforms, 'Is Donaldson's car at the back?'

'Nothing here, boss.'

'Shit.' He couldn't believe they'd been this unlucky. That today of all days Donaldson would have decided, for whatever reason, either to be away overnight or to leave in the small hours. This was why McKay hated carrying out this kind of operation without due preparation. Normally, they'd have had surveillance on Donaldson for some time beforehand, checked out his typical movements and patterns of behaviour.

'You reckon he's not here?' the uniform sitting next to him said.

'Looks to me like there's every possibility.' McKay radioed back to Grant and updated her on the situation. 'You think we should go in anyway?'

He heard Grant consulting with Tess Adams before she responded to his question. 'I don't think we've much option. You don't know for sure he's not still in the house. And we've got a warrant so we can search and seize whatever's there.'

'That's what I assumed,' McKay said. 'But after this he'll know we're onto him. It'll be that much harder to track him down.'

'Not much we can do about that,' Grant said, in a tone that suggested she'd also had doubts about the wisdom of handling the operation this way. 'We've just got to get what we can out of this.'

'Here we go then,' McKay said.

He heard the sound as he climbed out of the car. It was barely audible against the rushing of the wind in the surrounding trees, but he had no doubt. The noise of a car engine starting somewhere to the rear of the house. At the same moment, his radio crackled into life. One of the uniforms at the rear. 'Boss, he was parked out on the road somewhere...'

McKay gestured frantically for the uniforms in the rear car to get in pursuit. It was most likely, he thought, that Donaldson would take the single-track road to the west, with the aim of rejoining the A96 further back along the coast. The uniforms did a rapid U-turn and then set out, blue lights flashing, but they'd already lost precious minutes. He called back in to Grant to update her.

'Christ,' she said. 'Okay, I'll get whatever resources we can throw at it. You reckon he's most likely heading back towards Inverness?'

'He didn't come back this way, so that seems most likely.' He paused. 'Oh, there's one other thing. The car pursuing him also has our revenue chum on board. Just thought you'd want to know.'

'You always know how to make the worst of a bad situation, Alec, you know that?'

'I do my best.'

He ended the call and turned to the uniform sitting beside him. 'Not going so well, this, is it, son? Oh, well. Let's at least see if we can find anything inside to help cheer us up.'

46

Ginny Horton had received the update from Grant just as she'd been about to kick off the raid at Elliott's house.

They'd followed the same routine here, initially gathering in a public car park a few hundred metres from the house in order to carry out their final preparations. Implementing the operation in an urban environment, as opposed to Donaldson's rural location, had both benefits and drawbacks. On the positive side, their presence here was much less conspicuous. If any passer-by saw a cluster of marked police cars in a city car park at this time of the morning, they were more likely to make themselves scarce than to nosily enquire what was going on.

The downside was that they had to be that much more cautious about how their actions might impact on those in the immediate vicinity. Even at this time on a snowy winter's morning, there was some traffic on the roads, and even the odd pedestrian heading into the city centre. They couldn't afford to take any undue risks if things didn't go to plan.

But it sounded as if the need to apprehend Elliott was greater than ever. If there was a chance that Donaldson might slip through the net, Elliott was the only big player they had.

The plan was pretty much the same as that for Donaldson. They'd checked out Elliott's house and there was no easy rear exit, other than to scramble over a high stone wall into a neighbouring garden in the parallel street. Even so, they were intending to position a couple of uniforms to the rear, and Horton and the rest would enter from the front, with their cars blocking the drive. This time, given that the rear was enclosed, they would all arrive together.

The bad news was evident as soon as Horton turned into the drive. 'Shit.'

'What is it?' the uniform behind her asked.

'There's no car.'

'Should there be?'

'We know Elliott's got a car. So where is it?'

'Maybe he left it at the office. That's in the centre, isn't it? So he could have walked back from there.'

'Why would be do that?'

The uniform shrugged. 'Maybe he'd had one drink too many. We've all been there.'

From what Horton had heard about Elliott, that didn't sound a particularly probable explanation, but she supposed it was possible. Even so, after McKay's experience, she was beginning to have a bad feeling about this. 'Okay, then. Let's give this a go.'

She climbed out into the snow-filled air, and gestured for the two designated uniforms to take up their positions at the rear of the house. Then she walked forward, the other officers close behind her, and pressed the doorbell.

She hadn't really expected a response. She'd already noticed that there were a couple of decent quality CCTV cameras sited above the front door, covering the door itself and the wider driveway.

In any case, Elliott wasn't likely to answer the door at this time in the morning without being sure who was waiting outside. Even so, she leaned forward and pressed it again, this time leaving her finger there so it rang insistently for several minutes. She could hear the shrill tone from inside the house. No one was going to sleep through that.

Eventually, she released the bell and took a step back. 'Okay, let's get in there, shall we?'

She'd expected that the door might be fortified, and that gaining entry would be a challenge. In fact, there seemed to be little more than standard domestic security. One of the uniforms had produced a crowbar which he jammed between the door and the frame. As he leaned on the bar, the frame creaked, groaned and splintered, and the door burst open. 'Easy,' he grinned.

Horton took a step forward into the hallway. It was a spacious place, elegantly decorated. Not what she'd have associated with Elliott, somehow. 'Police!'

The house remained silent. She took another few cautious steps forward to allow the uniforms in behind her. 'You check the rooms down here,' she said. 'I'll check upstairs. Keep someone by the door in case he somehow slips past us.' Even as she spoke, though, she was becoming increasingly convinced that the house was deserted. Not a living soul, she thought.

There was something else too. Some half-familiar trace of a scent that she couldn't recognise, and behind that a deeper, stronger smell.

She took the stairs two at a time, by now sure what she was going to find. She stopped on the landing and looked around at the array of doors. Only one, to her left, was open.

By now, the smell was unmistakeable.

She pushed the door fully open and stopped on the threshold, staring into the room.

She'd been expecting it, but it was still worse than she could ever have envisaged. The upper half of the white-covered bed was stained a deep red. The body was on its back, and the slashed throat gaped like a second mouth. Inside the room, the stench of blood was overwhelming.

'Christ.' One of the uniforms had followed her up the stairs and was standing behind her, peering into the room.

'Quite.'

'Is that him?'

Horton had taken a couple of steps forward to check. 'Looks like it. I don't think we need to worry too much about him absconding. Can you check the other rooms up here? Just make sure no one's hiding in there. Then we need to get this place sealed off as a murder scene.'

She made her way downstairs and told the others what she'd found. 'So, change of plan,' she said. 'We touch nothing in here till the examiners have dealt with it. We'd better get back outside, and I'll get onto our colleagues back at the ranch to break the good news.'

'But who the hell would have done that to him?' one of the uniforms asked.

Horton had stopped in the hallway and was sniffing softly at the air. The other scent she'd detected on her way in. It was definitely there, not yet overwhelmed by the smell of blood.

It was a perfume, she thought, and one she recognised. Nothing particularly special or distinctive, just a well-known brand that her partner Isla used from time to time. It was unexpectedly strong at that end of the hallway. As if, Horton thought, someone might have used a quick spray of it to help rid their nostrils of the richer aroma from above.

The other question, of course, was how Elliott had allowed himself to be killed like that in his own bedroom. She imagined he'd been a cautious man, given his line of business, and she couldn't believe he'd willingly have allowed an intruder that far into the house. Unless he was being threatened. *Or perhaps,* she thought, *seduced.*

'I don't know who did it,' she said to the uniform. 'But I'm suspecting it was the last person he expected.'

47

Donaldson had been sleeping badly for days, and tonight had been the worst of all. Up to now, it had largely just been the stress, the knowledge that things were going awry and his uncertainty about how to respond.

He'd got into a habit of knocking back a few drams before bed, and that at least seemed to help him get off to sleep. But then he'd wake at three or four, countless anxieties racing through his head, and find himself unable to sleep again. In the end, he'd get up, have a shower, make himself a black coffee, and sit watching some mindless television until it was time for him to face the world. He felt as if he ought to have used that time more productively, made some plans to start dealing with all this. But he'd usually felt too groggy to think properly. It was only in the last day or so that he'd finally begun to get himself together.

Tonight had been even tougher, though. Now, it wasn't just the stress. It was also the sense of personal fear that had first struck him a couple of nights before, standing outside his front door. He'd suddenly felt vulnerable here, even in this place which he'd always thought of as his own personal fortress. Since then, he'd felt uneasy in the night, always having the sense that someone was watching him, watching the house. Tracing his movements. Wishing him harm.

He hadn't been able to sleep at all. Even the whisky hadn't done the trick, but seemed to have left him more wakeful than ever. He'd tossed and turned in bed for a while, then, around two, he'd finally given up and headed downstairs for his familiar routine of coffee and television.

He supposed it was also anxiety about tomorrow. Today had gone as well as he'd hoped, and they'd got all the hard goods cleared out quickly enough. Some of them had just gone into what he hoped was untraceable storage. The rest he'd passed on. He'd taken a loss on the deal, of course, but not as bad as he'd initially feared.

Tomorrow would be more of a challenge. The soft goods were always more tricky, not just because of their human unpredictability but because he was never confident that the buyers would uphold their end of the deal. The hard goods weren't, for the most part, perishable, and they needed no looking after, other than somewhere to store them. Buyers were prepared to take them on and, if they could afford it, sit on them till they could maximise their investment.

The soft goods were a different matter again. They were expensive to maintain and they had a shelf life. Sometimes buyers' needs changed or they got cold feet, leaving you in the lurch with an expensive problem. The buyer tomorrow would be getting a bargain, but that didn't guarantee they'd be reliable.

There was nothing much he could do about that, though. Maybe the others were right. If it came to it, they could just dump the soft goods. Abandon them somewhere. They'd either be found and picked up, or they wouldn't. Either way, there'd be nothing to connect them to him, and he'd be free of the problem. He'd lose out financially, of course, but if it came to it, he might just have to accept that.

He'd sat in front of the television till about four, not really taking in what it was showing, then he'd decided he might as well shower and dress, get himself ready for the day. They'd got a fairly early start planned, anyway, and it might be worth leaving even earlier if the snow continued to fall. The last thing he wanted was to end up stranded in the middle of the Cairngorms with that cargo if the A9 became impassable.

It was as he was standing in the bedroom, having just finished dressing, that he spotted them. It was just luck. He'd turned off the lights for a moment so he could look out of the window to check the state of the weather. Otherwise, he'd never had seen them.

It was just a flickering of headlights through the trees a few hundred metres from the house. Not one vehicle, though, but several.

He froze for a moment, staring out into the darkness. He didn't know whether it was whoever had been behind the last few weeks' troubles or the police embarking on a raid. But he had little doubt they were coming for him. Why else would they be gathering here on a bleak morning like this?

He'd made some half-hearted attempts to prepare for this moment, without ever quite taking it as seriously as he now realised he should have done. He took a breath, trying to control his mounting panic.

He grabbed his coat and the case he'd kept packed with a couple of changes of clothing and the few possessions he didn't want to leave behind. It was only now, though, that it really struck him that this might actually be it. He might actually be leaving this place for good. He hadn't really planned for that. He'd laid down too many roots here. His ownership of this house and of the hotels was through a complicated network of businesses, and he'd struggle to disentangle that from a distance. He'd kept much of his own wealth separate, siphoning it offshore, so he could look after himself without difficulty. But he'd never envisaged leaving like this.

Maybe it still wouldn't come to that. He was still optimistic that, if he could keep himself safe, buy himself some time, he'd be able to resolve matters. But at the moment, even the first of those looked to be a challenge.

He'd taken a few steps to prepare, though, and at least his glimpse of the vehicles outside had bought him a few extra minutes. The house had decent security – there was CCTV on the front and rear boundaries, and the downstairs was pretty much impregnable without some serious equipment – but that was designed to deter visitors less committed than these were likely to be. The only real option was to get out of here before it was too late.

For the last couple of nights, he'd left his car parked in the road to the rear of the house, to give himself an opportunity to slip away if the police or anyone else tried to blockade the house. He hurried downstairs, clutching the case, and opened the back door. Somewhere in the night he could hear the sound of car engines growing closer. Head down against the billowing snow, he scurried across the rear lawn to the narrow driveway leading to the road. His car was parked just along the roadside, concealed in a patch of woodland.

He reached the car only just in time. As he slipped between the trees, he saw the glare of headlights back near the house, the sound of a car turning into his rear drive.

He fumbled with his keys in the darkness, his fingers wet and cold, and finally managed to get the car unlocked. He threw his case into the footwell in front of the passenger seat and then climbed in, preparing to start the engine.

As he inserted the key in the ignition, he heard the rear door of the car open behind him. Before he could turn in his seat, he felt a hand reaching over his shoulder. Something cold and sharp was pressed against his throat.

'Morning, dad. Shall we get moving?'

48

It had taken them some time to force their way into Donaldson's house, but they'd eventually succeeded. Their initial search hadn't taken long and had produced scant reward. As McKay had expected, there was little business documentation in the house and nothing that was likely to aid their investigation. The only item of value had been Donaldson himself, and they'd managed to let him slip away.

Shortly after they'd begun, Grant had been in touch to break the news about Gerry Elliott.

'Christ, this is turning into the mother of all balls-ups, isn't it?' McKay said.

'You might say that. Not sure what we could have done differently, but Tess Adams is definitely not a happy woman.'

'We might have been better not to have embarked on an operation like this with less than eighteen hours' notice and minimal preparation,' McKay said. 'But I don't imagine Adams is ever going to acknowledge that.'

'I doubt it. The only good news so far is that the operations at the hotels are going well. We've rounded up a number of individuals, all women, who appear to be immigrants without documentation, along with what we're assuming to be four members of Donaldson's staff.'

'So a bunch of poor sods who'll be whisked off to an immigration centre and then deported to Christ knows where. And a bunch of nobodies who'll deny all knowledge of anything. Great. That's really made my morning. What about Donaldson?' The car that had initially set off in pursuit of Donaldson had already returned, having lost Donaldson somewhere on the backroads. McKay had been tempted to bollock the driver, but he'd known it would be unfair. Donaldson had had a good few minutes' head start and had been going like shit off a shovel, so the attempt to catch him had always been a long shot. McKay imagined that the driver would also have been constrained by the presence of the revenue officer in the rear of the car. It wouldn't have gone down well if they ended up in some multi-agency collision.

'Nothing yet. We deployed what vehicles we could get mustered to try to apprehend him, but it looks as if he got across the Kessock Bridge heading north. We've got vehicles looking out for him on the A9 but there's no telling where he might turn off.'

'It's amazing how much can go tits up before it's even six-thirty in the morning,' McKay commented. 'I wonder what the rest of the day has in store for us.'

'A long and patronising lecture from Tess Adams, in my case,' Grant said. 'She's already given me the preamble.'

'Maybe she'd be better devoting her attention to the question of who killed Gerry Elliott. You reckon this is part of a pattern of killings, along with the Dingwall and Fort George ones?'

'Someone gradually picking off members of Donaldson's team, you mean?'

'Something like that. Some competitor looking to up their market share, for example.'

'It's possible. Maybe that's why Donaldson was so eager to leave this morning. Perhaps it wasn't us he was worried about.'

'It doesn't quite feel right, though, does it? I mean, I've seen this kind of inter-gang warfare before, and the intimidation doesn't usually go this far.'

'Something more personal, you think?'

'I don't know. It's just a hunch. And Ginny has another hunch about Elliott's killer.'

'Go on.'

'She thinks it might have been a woman. There was a strong smell of perfume in the hallway. Something Ginny recognised because Isla uses it. And then there's the question of why Elliott would have let the killer into his bedroom. Other than the killing itself, there doesn't seem to have been any kind of struggle.'

'Not much to go on, but it's plausible enough,' McKay said. 'It's not difficult to imagine Elliott being flattered into letting his guard down. But even if Ginny's right, it doesn't get us any closer to finding out who the woman is.'

'It doesn't,' Grant agreed. 'But I'm beginning to think we need to find out a bit more about Elliott and Donaldson.'

'Is there much on the system about them?'

'Elliott doesn't have a record. Donaldson does, but it's relatively trivial stuff from years ago. Fraud and embezzlement. He spent a couple of years inside when he was younger. My guess is he started obeying the eleventh commandment.'

'Don't get caught. Aye. Sounds like it.'

'They've both been on Adams's radar for a while, but they've never been able to build enough of a case to make it stick. That's why she was putting so much weight on this.'

'Maybe shouldn't have been quite so gung-ho about it, then.'

'Donaldson's a local lad, from the look of it, though he's spent a lot of time down south. Looks like he was from Cromarty originally.'

'Like Kevin,' McKay said. He wasn't sure why he'd made the connection, except that his life outside work had been largely dominated by Kevin and his fate over the previous days. 'You say Donaldson's record was for fraud and embezzlement?'

'Apparently. He was working in some clerical job. Found a way of diverting money to his own accounts. I've got this from Adams so I don't know the detail, but it was smart stuff, apparently. He got away with it at first, and probably could have remained undetected except that he got greedy. You're not suggesting some link between Donaldson and your brother-in-law?'

'Seems unlikely, doesn't it? But it's another coincidence. They always make me uncomfortable.' He paused, thinking. 'This is probably a stupid question, but I wonder whether Charlie Farrow's made any progress with checking out that final payment that Kevin made. Ten grand to an unknown account. I'm assuming Farrow's getting it checked out?'

'I can email him and ask him to get in touch when he comes in. He'll probably be more receptive if it comes from me.'

'Unless he's got some bad news for me he wants to gloat about.'

'Like there's some link between your brother-in-law and Donaldson?'

'Aye,' McKay said grimly. 'Exactly like that.'

49

G inny Horton stood on the doorstep and took a breath. There wasn't much more she could do here. She'd ensured that the scene was secured and then waited until the designated crime scene manager had arrived. She was relieved that Willy Ingram tended to be the preferred manager for this type of complex scene. This was partly because she knew he was effective at the job, but it was mainly because he was likely to complain less than most at being dragged from his bed at this time in the morning. As far as she knew, he lived alone and he seemed happier at work than anywhere else. Which, she acknowledged, wasn't saying much.

Once they'd secured the scene, she'd told all but a couple of the uniforms to return to the station. There wasn't a lot they could do here until the scene examination had been completed, and there was no point in tying up resources unnecessarily. Any search of the rest of the house, in line with their original objectives, would have to wait.

There'd been one exception. She'd spotted, in Elliott's living room, the wireless control and recording unit which linked to the CCTV cameras at the front and rear of the house. If the killer had been careless, there was a possibility that their arrival might have been caught by the cameras.

Given that the killer was still on the loose, she'd made an executive decision to remove the CCTV unit and get the footage checked out. She'd sent one of the uniforms on ahead with it, asking him to check in with Helena Grant when he arrived.

It was still not yet five-thirty when Ingram turned up. The snow had lessened for the moment, leaving only a thin coating of white on the drive and surrounding undergrowth. Ingram nodded to her as she approached. 'Sounds like a nasty one,' he said.

'Very.' She briefly filled him in on the background, preparing him for what he would find in the house. He seemed unfazed. 'I'll take it from here, then. Examiners are on their way. Presumably you'll kick things off back at the office.' He seemed to speak only in these staccato, factual sentences.

She nodded. 'I'll speak to Helena and get the wheels in motion.' She gestured up at the CCTV camera. 'I took the liberty of seizing the footage and getting it sent back to the office.'

'Long as I know. Okay, I'll take it from here.'

WHEN HORTON finally arrived back at the office, it took her a while to track down Helena Grant. She eventually found her in one of the meeting rooms, sitting with Tess Adams in front of a laptop.

Adams looked up as she knocked and entered. 'You did well,' she said.

There was a patronising edge to the comment, but it was the first time Horton had heard Adams say anything complimentary, so she decided to accept it in good grace. 'Did I?'

'Shockingly so,' Grant said. 'With the emphasis on the word shock.'

Horton pulled up a chair and sat herself down next to Helena Grant. She could see now that they were looking at the footage from Elliott's CCTV.

'Watch,' Grant said.

The split screen showed the footage from two cameras: one pointed at Elliott's front doorstep, the other at the driveway. The camera had been triggered by the movement of a car pulling onto the drive, the beam of its headlights visible on both screens. The car pulled to a halt and, after a second, Horton saw Elliott emerge from the driver's side.

'This is from last night?' Horton asked.

Grant nodded. 'Fairly early in the evening according to the timer. About eight.'

Elliott made his way round the car and opened the passenger door. They watched as a young woman, dressed in a heavy-looking coat, stumbled out, steadying herself against the side of the car.

'Pretty drunk,' Horton commented.

'You'd think,' Adams said.

The woman staggered again and Elliott slipped his arm under hers to support her as they made their way towards the house. They reached the doorway, and Elliott fumbled with his key in the lock, the young woman still hanging unsteadily onto his arm.

Up to this point, Horton had been unable to see the woman's face. As she and Elliott had approached the door, the woman had kept her head bowed down, apparently sheltering herself from the falling snow.

Now, suddenly, the woman looked up above the door, staring directly into the camera. She was smiling and then, unexpectedly, she winked. A moment later, Elliott had the door open and he and the woman disappeared into the house.

'I'd say she knew exactly what she was doing,' Adams said. 'She spotted the camera and played to it.'

'And we think this is our killer?' Horton said.

'Looks likely,' Grant said. 'The cameras are motion activated. This footage was triggered by the arrival of Elliott's car. They get triggered again about twenty minutes later by the woman leaving. She drives off in Elliott's car, presumably having helped herself to his keys. After that, the cameras are undisturbed for the rest of the night.'

'If she was in and out in twenty minutes and then stole his car, that smacks of something pretty premeditated,' Horton said. 'If that's the case, then why reveal her face to the camera? As you say, that didn't look accidental.'

'I don't think it was,' Grant said. 'I think she wanted to be recognised.'

'Why would she want that?'

'Because she doesn't care what happens to her once she's done what she wants to, maybe. Or because she wants us to discover who's responsible for this.'

'So why not just hand herself in? By the time we discover who she is from that footage, we're likely to have caught up with her by other means, especially as we know she's taken Elliott's car.'

'My guess,' Grant said, 'is that she's not handed herself in yet because the job's not yet finished. This isn't just about Elliott. We've also got the bodies found at Fort George and up in Dingwall. Like Elliott, all employees of the Muir Group.'

'You think she might have been responsible for all of them?'

'The way she dealt with Elliott suggests a pretty ruthless, not to say psychopathic, operation,' Adams commented. 'So it seems probable.'

'This doesn't sound like it's just some inter-gang face off,' Horton said.

'I wouldn't have said so,' Adams replied. 'Not the way Elliott was murdered. This feels like something more personal.'

Horton frowned. 'So when you say the job's not yet finished...?'

'Now she's killed Elliott, there's only one person left.'

'Donaldson. But we're likely to catch up with him before she does.'

'Maybe. Except that we've just had a bit of news from Alec. They've been finishing up at Donaldson's house and Alec sent one of the uniforms out to check the spot at the rear of the house where Donaldson had concealed his car. They found a second car left there, almost hidden further into the trees. We've just checked out the registration.'

Horton was ahead of her. 'Elliott's?'

'So our friend may already have caught up with him.'

'So why not kill him then and there?'

'That was our first thought. That maybe she'd killed him there, and then taken his car to buy herself a bit of extra time. But Alec had the team out there search the area around the car and there's no sign of Donaldson's body. Alec reckons she'd only have had a few minutes so she wouldn't have had the chance to conceal the body except in some very limited way. It's difficult to be absolutely certain in the dark, but I think we have to assume that either she's killed Donaldson and taken the body with her, or that he's still alive and they're together.'

'Maybe they're working together,' Horton suggested. 'Maybe this was a way for Donaldson to burn his bridges before we caught up with him?'

'Anything's possible,' Adams said. 'But then why would the woman deliberately allow herself to be recognised? If they were planning to disappear, even if they had some motive for the killings, wouldn't they want to keep as anonymous as possible? And why go to the lengths of stealing Elliott's car? If they'd got this set up, why wouldn't Donaldson just be waiting for her? They could have just headed off last night, and they'd be hours ahead of us.'

Horton shrugged. 'I suppose. But we've still got the problem of actually identifying her. All we've got is a few seconds' footage of her face on CCTV.'

Grant leaned forward and wound back the footage to the shot in question. 'That's the final bit of the jigsaw we haven't shared with you yet. We don't need to identify her. I know who she is.'

50

'I haven't been here with you in a while,' the voice said.

Donaldson could still feel the blade of the knife pressed against his throat. He had little doubt about its sharpness and, at some points as they'd driven up here, he'd been terrified that, if the car had hit an unexpected pothole, she might slit his throat accidentally. He suspected she wouldn't much care.

At first, he'd been too scared even to speak. She'd told him just to drive, and he'd done that without really thinking at all about what he was doing. Somewhere in the distance behind them he could occasionally see the flicker of headlights from what he took to be a pursuing car.

What if he just stopped? What if he allowed whoever it was to catch up with him?

Then she'd simply kill him, he concluded. If it was the police back there, as he now assumed, they'd arrive too late. She wouldn't care.

Somehow, he had little doubt about her ruthlessness. She'd told him what she'd done to Elliott, and how much satisfaction she'd derived from it. And she'd told him what she'd done to the others, and how easy it had been. He had little doubt what she was intending to do to him.

The truth was, he wasn't surprised. He'd known what she was like, even as a child. That strange mix of burning righteousness and utter relentlessness in pursuing what she wanted. Her mother, his late wife, has been able to control her at least to some extent. But on his own he'd never stood a chance.

His own solution had been to match her anger with his own. He'd known even at the time that that was just a vicious circle, that he was stoking up her anger rather than quelling it, but he had no other solutions. In some ways, they were too alike. The cold-heartedness, the lack of concern for consequences – those qualities were all his, even if the obsessive righteousness was her own addition.

So he'd not challenged the decision for her to be taken into care. Not that he'd had a choice. He knew he was heading for prison and there was no one else to take care of her. She'd told them he'd been violent towards her, and no one was much interested in his claims that the abuse had been only in response to hers.

When he came out, the authorities had already made it clear he was considered unfit for her to be returned to his custody. He hadn't objected. She'd stayed in care, eventually been fostered, and finally had been adopted by a couple up in Tain. He could only feel sorry for the poor bastards.

He hadn't seen her for more than fifteen years. She'd been a child then, however much she might have been capable of. Tonight he hadn't even recognised her voice at first, even in the brief moment before the cold blade against his throat had removed any doubt.

Once, on their way up here, he'd said to her, 'What if I just drive off the road? Kill us both.'

'Then we're both dead. Whereas you don't know that I'm going to kill you.'

He did, though. He was sure of it. His only hope was that, once they reached her intended destination, he might find an opportunity to prevent her. She was still only a young woman, he told himself, while he was a relatively fit, well-built man. She'd be no match for him.

Except that, again, he knew she would be.

She had instructed him to drive up the A9 over the Kessock Bridge and on to the Black Isle. He assumed that the police would by now be in pursuit, and he wondered whether some attempt might be made to stop them. But, for whatever reason, they reached the Tore roundabout unhindered. She directed him to take the A835 towards Conon Bridge, and then a while later told him to take a right.

He had little doubt now where they were going, and he understood why they were going there. It was quite possible, he thought, that the police might be waiting for them. If that had been the police raiding his house this morning, then they would surely have arranged similar raids on the various sites. An hour ago, he thought, that would have mattered to him.

She was right about not having been here for a while, he thought. She'd made the comment as they had turned into the road that led to the hotel. He thought he could recall the first time he'd driven her along this route. She'd been about ten, sitting in her booster seat in the back. Her mother had been in the passenger seat, excited to view the house they were considering buying. It had been when he'd first started making money. That brief period when it had seemed that life might turn out okay. The brief period before it had all fallen apart.

They'd gone ahead and bought the place, selling their anonymous detached house in Inverness. It had been his first real experience of money laundering, he thought, on a very small scale. Plunging some of those ill-gotten gains in the deposit.

He'd bought the place as a home, not to use as a hotel. It was big and grand, but not too large for the kind of family they'd had planned. It needed a bit of work, which he'd duly carried out, and they'd moved in later that year.

'I always hated the fucking place, you know?' the voice from behind him said, as if reading his thoughts.

That was no surprise. She'd made her displeasure evident right from the start. He couldn't even entirely blame her. They'd taken her away from her friends and school in Inverness, and brought her up here to the back of beyond. She hadn't fitted in at the local academy, and quickly gained a reputation as a trouble-maker and tearaway. Donaldson had just thought she was an ungrateful little cow who didn't appreciate what he did for her and the family.

In any case, the dream had evaporated quickly enough. It was only a few months later that his wife had been diagnosed with cancer, and less than a year before she died. It wasn't very long after that that the police had come knocking at the door.

He'd allowed his mind to follow this train of thought as he'd been driving, trying to distract himself from the awareness of the blade against his skin. It had worked in that at least he'd managed to retain his sanity. It was only now, as they were approaching the hotel, that the reality of his situation began again to hit home.

'Stop here,' she said, suddenly. 'Pull off the road.'

They were just a few hundred metres from the hotel. It was still dark, and somewhere up ahead he could see the recurrent flash of blue lights. The police had raided the hotel, as he'd expected. He followed her instructions and turned off the road onto a vacant patch of land, trees looming to their left. It had stopped snowing, but the land was white around them.

'I want you to get slowly out of the car,' she said. 'Don't try to get away. I'll be on you in a moment, and I'm not worried about using the knife.'

Despite her words, he wondered whether this was the moment to try. He might not have another opportunity, and he had little doubt that she intended ultimately to kill him in any case.

He felt her move the knife away from his throat, and he pulled open the car door, hearing the rear door open behind him. He'd intended to seize the moment and run, but realised immediately that he'd already left it too late. She was out of the car, standing immediately behind him, and he could feel the sharp point of the knife digging through his coat into the skin of his back.

'Like I say,' she continued, 'I always hated the fucking place. You thought you were building a home for us, but it was always just a fucking prison. Just as it has been for those poor fucking bastards you've got in there at the moment.'

'I've treated them okay,' he said. 'Better than where they've come from.'

'But that's because you're just a holding pen, aren't you? You get your pound of flesh from them while they're here. You use them in whatever ways you want, and then you sell them on to some even bigger bastard who'll abuse them, exploit them and finally just dispose of them.'

'It's all over anyway,' he said. 'The police are there.'

'The police are only there because of me,' she pointed out. 'Because I started dealing properly with you bastards. They'd have got you eventually, sure, because you're not the fucking criminal genius you think you are, but then you'd just have got yourself a few years in prison. I wanted you *eradicated*.' There was a venom in the last word that left him almost breathless. He felt the knife press harder into his skin.

'I was intending to take you back to the hotel,' she said. 'But the police were a little more efficient than I'd expected. But out here seems fitting, given it was the only place I could get away from you in the old days. I used to sit out here, imagining what I was going to do to you.' She paused, and when she next spoke he could hear the smile in her voice. 'And now I'm going to do it.'

51

It took Horton a few moments to place the name. 'Maggie Clennan,' she said finally. 'The woman you met in the restaurant?'

'One and the same,' Grant said. 'The woman who was being wined and dined by Elliott that night.'

'I've had some bad dates,' Horton commented, 'but this seems like an overreaction.'

'Too right. I'm thinking I got her wrong that night,' Grant said. 'And in more ways than one.'

'How do you mean?'

'I thought she was scared of Elliott. That's what I read in her expression. But maybe that wasn't it. Maybe she was just preparing herself to do what she finally ended up doing last night. Maybe psyching herself up for it – though she doesn't strike me as someone who needs much of that – or maybe just getting her head straight to do it.'

'You're saying you interrupted her?'

'I'm wondering that now. I told her I was a police officer, I told her my rank, and I told her I'd had dealings with Elliott before. Maybe she decided to change her plans. Maybe it struck her that she could sow the seeds for what she did last night. Made sure she'd be recognised on Elliott's CCTV. I don't know. But it's hard to imagine she was scared of Elliott in the way she was claiming.'

'So who is she? Why has she done all this?'

'The thing is,' Adams said, 'she seems to have been hiding in plain sight. I've just had someone doing a bit of digging around for me this morning.' She spoke as if it was usual for people to be working on her behalf at six in the morning. 'I'd assumed that Clennan would be some sort of fake identity. But it seems not. She really is Margaret Susan Clennan, and she has a record. Relatively minor stuff, but telling. A couple of breaches of the peace for supposed assaults on men who she claims were trying to grope her. A more serious assault on an ex-boyfriend who she said had tried to rape her–'

'Maybe he had,' Grant said.

Adams shrugged. 'I'd say it was more than possible. Her claims were investigated but it came down to her word against his, whereas his injuries were pretty undeniable. But I suspect there might have been some sympathy for her claims of mitigation because she walked away with a relatively small fine. Then there are a couple of odd ones. An apparently unprovoked attack on some neighbour who'd been accused of child neglect. She was part of some vigilante type group who attacked a supposed paedophile. She ended up inside for those. Three months for the first, and then six for the second. More recently we've reports of her on various protests, most recently outside an immigration centre where there'd been allegations of child abuse by staff.'

'Seems to be a pattern, then?' Grant said.

'Looks like it. Though nothing like this.'

'Was she from Inverness?' Horton asked.

'We're not sure. She's definitely local. She was brought up in a care home and adopted in her teens. Reading between the lines, it sounds like she was trouble even then. Had already been in trouble a few times, but had avoided prosecution. Eventually walked out on her adoptive parents – I'm suspecting partly to their relief – and lived in Glasgow for a while. Moved back up here just a few months back. The stuff you told me about working in a call centre sounds like it was bollocks. The truth seems to be that her adoptive parents died and left her a few quid and she's been living on that. Looks as if that might be what prompted her to move back.'

'So what's the connection with Donaldson or the Muir businesses?'

'That's the tricky bit. We don't know about her birth parents. But prior to adoption she'd been in care in Inverness. And the timing of her being taken into care ties in almost exactly with Donaldson first being sent down.'

'You think she might be Donaldson's daughter?'

'I'm fishing in the dark,' Adams admitted. 'But it feels like a possibility. Like I said before, this seems personal to me.'

Grant nodded, thoughtfully. 'So the question now is where the hell have she and Donaldson gone?'

JOSH CARLISLE WAS FEELING pleased with himself. He'd been feeling decidedly anxious about being designated bronze commander for this particular leg of the operation. His anxiety hadn't lessened when he'd realised that several of the uniforms under his command seemed to be significantly older and more experienced than he was.

He hadn't really wanted to take on the job, but Horton had encouraged him, telling him it would be good experience. He knew the operation here was expected to be relatively straightforward, but he also knew how easily this kind of job could go awry.

In the end, though, it had pretty much all gone to plan. They'd announced their presence and been greeted at the door by a bleary-eyed, confused-looking young man who'd clearly been disturbed from sleep. They arrested him and then proceeded through the rest of the building, ultimately finding more than a dozen women, of varying ages, who were sleeping on the upper floors. They were all accommodated in a single cramped dormitory, furnished only by two rows of very basic camp beds and some small lockers where the women had kept their few personal possessions. The walls were damp and peeling, and there appeared to be just one lavatory and shower room for all the women.

As the women were led downstairs by one of the uniforms, Carlisle had stood with the immigration official and stared round the room. 'Is this typical?' Carlisle asked.

'It varies. This is better than some.'

They'd rapidly searched the rest of the building and found nothing more. They'd found some financial documents in the offices downstairs which would be collated and bagged, but Carlisle suspected that they related only to the legitimate business of the hotel.

He made his way back downstairs. The immigration official was in one of the rooms dealing with the women one by one. It was clear that they were all immigrants and it was equally clear that none of them had any documentation. Only one or two of them spoke any English, and the immigration official was trying to work out what types of interpreter would be required once they were taken into custody.

As Carlisle poked his head into the room, the immigration official rose and walked over to him. 'A real tower of Babel,' he said. 'By the way, they reckon one of them is missing.'

'Missing?'

'It's hard to be sure because none of them admits to speaking more than a few words of English, but they reckon there was another woman here, a bit older. She was there last night, but isn't there now.'

'You think she somehow evaded us?' Carlisle was hoping this wouldn't be a black mark against his leadership here.

'I don't see how. Unless by sheer dumb luck she happened to exit the building just before we came in.'

'All the external doors were supposedly locked overnight,' Carlisle said. 'We checked that with our friend there.' He gestured towards the far end of the lounge where the young man was being carefully watched by one of the uniforms.

'Maybe I'm misunderstanding what they're telling me. Like I say, English definitely not spoken here.'

Carlisle left him to it and decided to have a check around outside with a couple of the uniforms. If the missing woman had slipped out before they arrived, she might be cowering somewhere nearby. Carlisle had some reservations about handing the women over to immigration, but it was probably still preferable to being left outside in the middle of a Highland winter.

He sent the two uniforms off in different directions to check out the garden at the rear of the hotel and the surrounding woodland. Carlisle himself set off in a third direction, down towards the firth.

The rough terrain of the woodland made for difficult going, particularly after the fall of snow. Carlisle forced his way through the undergrowth, flashing his powerful torch cautiously around him.

He had nearly reached the edge of the firth when he saw it. He almost missed it at first under the newly fallen snow, but something about the incongruous shape had caught his eye. He moved the beam of his torch back and peered more closely.

He took a few steps closer to be sure, but he already had little doubt. It was a body, lying on its side, just a few metres from the edge of the water.

Carlisle moved closer and crouched down to brush a little of the snow from the head. He'd expected initially that this would be the missing woman. If she'd not been out here for too long, he thought, there was a chance life had not yet departed.

But it wasn't her. The face in front of him was that of a young white male. The body had been preserved by the low winter temperatures, but he suspected that it had been here for longer than a few hours.

Not wishing to disturb the scene any further, Carlisle pushed himself to his feet. He looked around him in the darkness, suddenly feeling nervous. There was a strong wind blowing off the sea, and the trees swayed noisily around him, as if an unseen crowd was whispering in his ears. He kept catching sight of what looked like something or someone moving among the trees, but when he shone his torch it was nothing but the endless shifting of the branches.

As he made his way back up to the hotel, he radioed back to HQ to update Helena Grant about his discovery.

'Jesus, it never stops, this one,' she said in response. 'If it's a young male, it could be another of Donaldson's employees. Which means she'd picked off three of them before she got to Elliott. Okay,' she added wearily, 'can you get the scene sealed off up there? I'll see if I can get all the admin wheels in motion here. I think Alec's more or less finishing up so I'll see if he's in a position to join you.'

'That would be good,' Carlisle said. He hadn't been looking forward to trying to co-ordinate the beginning of a murder enquiry by himself. 'It's turning into quite a morning.'

52

J ana had let herself out of the rear door of the hotel around three in the morning. She'd tried to leave the dormitory as quietly as possible, though she knew some of the other women would have been aware of her departure. They'd probably just assume she was heading for the lavatory, but they probably didn't care much what she was doing.

The building was silent as she made her way down the stairs. As far as she knew, only one of the men was on duty here tonight. That had been the case most nights since Jitters' disappearance. The building was always locked up at this time of night, but she'd noted where the main keys were kept behind the reception desk. The men had never been particularly careful about that sort of thing, mainly because, as ever, they underestimated the intelligence and acuity of the women.

By the time she'd reached the ground floor, her eyes had grown accustomed to the darkness and she proceeded more easily. She found the keys and opened the main door, carefully replacing the keys before she left the building.

It had been snowing earlier, but now the sky had cleared and the night felt colder than ever. She had nothing to protect her other than her thin overcoat, but that no longer mattered.

She made her way across the car park into the woodland. She would join Jitters, she thought. That somehow seemed fitting. She didn't know what had happened to him or who was responsible, but he'd had no say in the matter. She was doing this voluntarily. It was the one time since she had arrived here when she could exercise more freedom than the men. She could derive a grim satisfaction from that, at least.

The body had been covered by a thin coat of snow, and it took her a few moments to find it in the darkness. It was a little nearer the waterline than she recalled. Perhaps some animal had attempted to move it.

She sat herself down on the hard, snow-covered ground, and stared out across the firth, watching the flickering lights of the town on the far shore. She had sometimes wondered if she would ever visit that town, or leave this place ever again. Now she knew she never would.

She lay back, closed her eyes and waited for the darkness to close over her.

DONALDSON STUMBLED several times as she forced him forward towards the shoreline. He had wondered whether the darkness and the rough ground might provide him with an opportunity to overpower her, but she seemed to move with an almost preternatural ease through the undergrowth, the knife unerringly pressed against his back.

'There,' she said.

His eyes had grown accustomed to the dark but he could still see almost nothing but the tossing of the trees in the wind. Then, just ahead, he saw the glimmer of water, a shimmer of distant lights.

He felt the point of the knife jabbing into his skin, urging him forward. The trees fell away, and he found himself on the shoreline, the water lapping roughly just ahead of him.

'Sit there,' she said.

It was bitterly cold. He hadn't expected to be outside for so long and his coat was too thin for this weather. The clear sky to the south had begun to lighten, but it was still at least a couple of hours till sunrise. Even so, he obeyed her instruction and lowered himself to the ground.

He finally looked back and saw her standing behind him. He couldn't see her face in the darkness and he wasn't sure he would have recognised it anyway.

He ought to be able to escape, he knew. However ruthless she might be, she was still only a slender young woman, much smaller than he was. He could overpower her, take the knife. Perhaps even kill her before she could kill him.

But something stopped him trying. Partly it was because he had no doubt that, if it came to it, she would have no hesitation in using the knife. He didn't even know why he was so certain of that. It was the way she'd spoken in the car. It was the way she'd held the knife so steadily to his throat. There was a ruthlessness to her he couldn't match.

That was only part of it, though. He felt as if she had some power over him, as if she was somehow keeping him in thrall. As if, until she said the word, there was nothing he could do.

He looked along the shore. Just a few feet away there was a snow-covered mound which he knew immediately to be a human body. That was what had happened to Cal, then. He was hardly surprised. He'd assumed Cal had gone the same way as the others. If he was honest, the reason he hadn't come looking for Cal was because he didn't want that confirmed. He wanted to think that Cal had just decided to bugger off of his own free will. But he'd known all along that this was more likely.

She had sat herself down just behind him, and he could still feel the point of the knife pressing against his back. He suspected she had already drawn blood, and he knew it would take only a small additional pressure to drive the blade into his body.

'She used to come and sit here, you know. That child.' There was no emotion, no real inflection in her voice. She was speaking in the third person, he realised, as if to distance herself from the girl she'd once been. 'After her mum died. After she realised you didn't want her. When you hit her or screamed at her, she used to run outside and head down here and just stare at the water. She used to wonder if she had the courage just to step into it and keep walking. Just to get away from you.'

'I'm sorry if I got angry,' he said, knowing that it was years too late to offer any kind of apology. 'Everything was falling apart.'

'She didn't understand that then,' she said. 'And now I don't care. I just know you let her mother die, then you abused her. Then you went away and you let them take her so she could be abused even more. Much more. You never cared about her. You never cared about anyone.'

'I cared about you.' He knew, even as he said the words, that he was lying. 'I cared about your mum,' he added, recognising this was closer to the truth.

'You let her go away.'

'She *died*. Do you think I wanted that to happen?'

'I don't think you cared. I don't think you care about anything.' She was silent for a moment. 'Look at what you're doing here. Those women. How can you treat people like that? How can you even allow that to happen?'

He had no answer to that. The simple truth was he'd never allowed himself even to think about it. He could do this only by pretending the women were less than human, that this was no more than the equivalent of dealing with livestock. He had never articulated it in those words, not even in his own head. But he knew he'd closed a part of his mind to stop him even thinking about the implications of what he did.

'What about you?' he said, before he could prevent himself. 'You're simply a killer. Poor Cal over there had a life, too. He was a person.'

'He knew what he was involved in, just as you do. But, you're right. I don't care. I'm like you. I don't care about people. Not people like you, anyway. I just want to put things right. Repair some of the damage.'

'And how do you think that's going to work?' he said. 'What do you think's going to happen to these woman once you've done your noble thing? They'll be sent to some dump of an immigration centre where they'll be treated even worse than they would be by us. And then they'll be deported. Probably not even to the hellholes they came from, but just to somewhere else where they can be exploited and abused.'

'It's a hell of a world,' she said.

The knife was unexpectedly withdrawn from his back. Before he could move, her arm was back over his shoulder, just as it had been in the car, and he felt the cold of the blade back against his throat. This time, she pressed a little harder and he felt the agonising incision as the blade pierced his flesh.

It took him a terrified moment to realise she had inflicted only a flesh wound. Before he could react further, she was pulling his head back so that he was lying on his back.

For the first time, he saw her face clearly. He had expected she would have changed utterly from the child he remembered. But somehow, he thought, the image of that child was still visible in her features. He felt now that, if he had not known her identity, he would still have recognised her instantly.

As his head had fallen back, she had withdrawn the blade from his neck, and he could feel the warm blood dripping down his skin. For a second he thought that, after all, she was intending to show him mercy. Perhaps, when the moment had finally come, she could not bring herself to kill her own flesh and blood.

But he knew he was deluding himself. As he watched her face

looming over his, transfixed by the ghost of the child he'd once known, he saw that her arm was raised to plunge the knife into his chest.

53

It was still dark as McKay headed over the Kessock Bridge across to the Black Isle, though there was a growing haze in the south-eastern sky and he could see the first gleam of daylight on the waters of the Moray Firth.

He'd left the uniformed team to finish the search of Donaldson's house, but he wasn't hopeful much would be found. They'd discovered some business documentation but nothing that had aroused much interest from the revenue representative. McKay guessed anything interesting would be in the office premises, and even then he wondered how effective Donaldson and Elliott would have been at covering their tracks. Elliott hadn't been the type to leave many dangling ends. McKay could imagine teams of forensic accountants trailing over this stuff for months, if not years, to come.

Assuming, he added to himself, *they ever catch up with Archie Donaldson.*

That wasn't even the most urgent issue now. The more desperate need was to track down this Maggie Clennan. If her actions really were the result of some personal grudge against Donaldson, as that smart-arse Tess Adams seemed to think, she'd presumably want to finish the job. Fair enough, McKay thought, but the real question was what she might be capable of doing to achieve that.

In that context, the discovery of another body was not comforting. From what Grant had told McKay, the dead man wasn't Donaldson, but another younger man – presumably a third missing member of Donaldson's team. Whether he'd gone missing at the same time as the others or whether the death was more recent remained to be discovered. But, assuming this was another of Clennan's victims, it suggested a psychopathic ruthlessness. It would probably be better for Donaldson if the police found him before Clennan did.

His phone buzzed on the seat beside him, and he answered it on the hands-free. Helena Grant.

'How are you doing?'

'Nearly there. Take it Josh has everything well and truly under control?'

'He's pretty reliable is Josh. But he was sounding a bit over-whelmed.'

'Kids today, eh?'

'I was actually calling about something else, Alec.'

'Oh, aye, because we've not got enough on our plates with four corpses, a multiple killer, an absconded people trafficker, and three groups of illegal immigrants? Go on, make my morning. What else?'

'Just had a call from Charlie Farrow in response to my email.'

'Charlie started working mornings, then? I wouldn't usually expect to find him in at this time.'

'You never give up, do you? Actually, he was calling from home–'

'Of course he was.'

'He'd picked up my email,' Grant said, 'and thought he ought to give me a quick response in case it was relevant to our investigation.'

'And presumably because he would have realised that, if there was some link between Kevin and Donaldson, it would potentially cause me some embarrassment.'

'I'm sure Farrow would never be that small-minded. But, actually, you're not far from the truth.'

'Oh, shit. Go on.'

'Farrow's team managed to obtain the details of the bank your brother-in-law's money was transferred to. It turns out to be a business account belonging to a company called Muir Holdings.'

'You're kidding.'

'Aye, Alec. I'm having a laugh. What do you think?'

'And this is definitely one of Donaldson's companies?'

'It looks like it. I've just done a check on Companies House and the named directors are Donaldson and Elliott.' She paused. 'You had a hunch about this, Alec. Any reason?'

'Nothing I could put my finger on, other than the Cromarty connection. And what that wee lass in Donaldson's office said about the business being in trouble and looking for new investment.' McKay was silent for a moment, thinking. He'd felt an odd unease about that conversation even at the time, and the latest news had done nothing to allay it.

'You still there, Alec?'

'Aye, I was just thinking. It's a struggle doing that and driving at the same time. Don't be expecting me to talk as well.'

'You're only a man, Alec. I never expect too much.'

'That's for the best. I'm just coming up to the Tore roundabout so I'll be there in a few minutes. Will keep you posted.'

'I'll wait to hear.'

5 4

J osh Carlisle had finished explaining to the uniforms what he'd found down by the waterside. As a group, they'd seemed mildly gratified by the news, as if it had somehow made their early start more worthwhile. Carlisle supposed it would improve their bragging rights.

He commandeered a couple of them to come back out with him to secure the scene. He presumed this was largely a formality, as it was unlikely many passing sightseers would disturb the scene at this time on a midwinter morning. On the other hand, he also knew that, if that stray visitor were to materialise and compromise the scene, McKay would make the rest of his career an unremitting misery. The freezing cold of a January dawn was a far more enticing prospect.

On top of that, they still hadn't tracked down the missing woman, assuming she even existed. She could still be out there somewhere. If so, judging from the sparse wardrobes of the other women here, she was unlikely to survive long.

Once outside, they retraced their steps through the woodland. The sky was clear of clouds now, lightening in the south-east.

The white of the fallen snow glimmered eerily between the tangled branches.

It took them only a few minutes to find their way to the waterline and the body. Carlisle gestured for the others to keep back, directing them where to seal off the scene. He paused for a moment, shining the beam of his torch on the face of the prone figure.

He had a feeling it had been disturbed since their previous visit. He recalled brushing some of the snow from the face but he thought now that the snow had been disturbed more than he recalled.

Perhaps he'd removed more snow than he thought. Or perhaps, with the arrival of morning, the temperature was gradually rising and the snow beginning to thaw. But as before he had the sense of another presence, someone else watching them.

He straightened and shone his torch into the trees, but there was nothing. He took a few steps towards the edge of the firth, and looked along the shoreline.

It was only then that he saw them. They were almost beyond the reach of his flashlight beam and, even a short while earlier when the darkness had been more complete, they might not have been visible. Now, though, the tableau was unmistakeable even though he had no idea what it might mean.

There was a figure sitting awkwardly on the ground, and a second figure couched behind with its arm round the neck of the first. As Carlisle peered into the darkness, he saw the second figure suddenly pull back the head of the first, forcing it back to the ground.

He was still staring, trying to work out what was happening, when the first figure raised its arm. Carlisle took a few steps closer and for a brief second something caught the light of his torch, glinting in the darkness.

It took his brain a moment to process the significance of what he was seeing. Then he was running towards the two figures, shouting, trying desperately to prevent what he knew was about to happen.

55

Donaldson watched, paralysed, as she slowly raised her arm above his head. He had no doubt now about what she intended to do and no doubt about her willingness to do it.

In that brief moment when he had looked into her face he had been unable to read the emotions in her eyes. Not hatred, he thought. Nothing as positive as that. Just indifference. Just the blind disinterest of someone who saw him only as an inconvenience to be eradicated from her life.

He wanted simply to close his eyes and wait for the moment to come but couldn't bring himself to do so. All he could do was watch in horror as she tensed her body, preparing herself, her arm poised to plunge the knife.

And then he had no idea what was happening.

There was a sudden shouting from somewhere to their left along the shore. At the same moment, she was pulled away from him, her arm grabbed unexpectedly from behind. He heard a thump from behind him and, as if released from a spell, Donaldson realised he was able to move. He rolled away, pulling himself round so he could see what was going on.

There were two figures struggling together on the ground

behind him. In the dim light, it took him a moment to work out that his daughter was being held by another woman. Despite the initial surprise his daughter was beginning to gain the upper hand, forcing the knife increasingly close to the other woman's chest.

Donaldson dragged himself to his feet and stumbled towards them, reaching out to grab his daughter's arm. She twisted away from him, but that allowed her opponent a brief opportunity to retaliate and reach for the knife.

But the woman was too slow. Donaldson watched in horror as his daughter plunged the knife hard into the woman's chest. She pulled it out again almost immediately, but the blood was already seeping onto the woman's thin pale anorak.

As his daughter withdrew the knife, Donaldson reached for her wrist, trying to force her to drop it. Her attention turned back to him, and she raised the blade again, slashing it savagely against his face and then down against his chest. She thrust hard and he felt the tip of the blade penetrate his skin, gouging into him. He pushed her back, seizing hold of her arm.

He told the police later he'd only intended to disarm her, though he had no idea whether that was really true. Struggling to escape his grip, she pulled against him and he tumbled forward, his weight unintentionally forcing the blade of the knife back towards her.

Donaldson tried desperately to regain his footing, but it was already too late. Both of them fell and, as they did so, the knife blade sliced into her neck, cutting deep into her throat. She fell to her knees, blood gushing from the wound onto the snow. He reached out, wanting to staunch the bleeding, but she dragged herself away and crawled out of his reach. Then her strength finally gave out and she slumped to the ground, blood pooling deeply beside her.

Donaldson turned to see a figure looming out of the darkness towards him, the light of a torch bouncing as it ran. He raised his arms to ward off a further attack, but the figure stopped, allowing the torch beam to play first across Donaldson's face then across the rest of the scene.

'My God...' The torch beam moved hesitantly back to Donaldson's face. 'What did you want to do that for?'

56

MⅽKay had arrived just as Josh Carlisle and one of the uniforms were escorting Archie Donaldson back into the hotel.

'Christ, Josh. I didn't know you had it in you. We've got half of bloody Police Scotland chasing this guy and you just walk in with him. How the hell do you do it?' McKay was standing by the main door to the hotel gazing at the scene in what seemed like genuine amazement.

Carlisle looked just as bewildered. 'I don't even know who he is,' he admitted. 'It's a long story.' He gestured vaguely in the direction of the firth. 'We have three more deceased down there. Two women. I think one of them's one of the women from here. I don't know who the other is.'

'I'm guessing it's Maggie Clennan,' McKay said. 'You sure she's actually dead?'

'Her throat was slashed,' Carlisle said. 'So I'm pretty sure.'

McKay looked sceptical. 'So what happened?'

'I'm not entirely certain.' He described to McKay what he'd witnessed outside.

'So you think she was preparing to kill Donaldson?'

'I hadn't realised that's who he was. But, yes, that's the way it looked. I was some way away and it was still pretty dark, but that was how it struck me. That was why I started running.'

'Then this other woman intervened?'

'I think so.'

McKay shook his head. 'So as her last act she saved the life of the man who's been holding her captive?'

'Stockholm Syndrome?'

'Maybe, son. Or maybe just humanity. When it comes to it, some people are better than scum like Donaldson. It's one of the things that just about keeps me going. Shall we go and have a chat with him?'

McKay led the way into the hotel lounge, where Donaldson was sitting on one of the sofas, a uniformed officer sitting awkwardly beside him.

McKay pulled up a high-backed chair from the side of the room and sat down facing Donaldson. 'Quite a morning.'

Donaldson looked up at him, as if having no idea where he was or why he was there. 'What's going on?'

'I was hoping you might be able to shed some light on that, Mr Donaldson.' McKay waved his warrant card. 'DI Alec McKay. My colleagues here have had a warrant to enter and search these premises, along with two other sites you own in Dingwall and Nairn. We've also gained a similar warrant to search your office premises and houses occupied by you and your colleague, Mr Gerald Elliott.'

Donaldson offered no response other than a shrug. It wasn't clear whether he was genuinely beyond caring or simply waiting for McKay to show his hand.

'We found Mr Elliott dead. We've reason to believe he was murdered. Do you know anything about that?'

'I presume she did it.'

'She?'

Donaldson gave a jerk of his thumb towards the external wall. 'Her. Out there. My daughter, allegedly. She did the others.'

'Others?'

Donaldson shook his head. 'The guys who worked for me. The ones who went missing. It was her.' He laughed mirthlessly. 'I thought it was someone trying to muscle in on my business. And all the time it was my own fucking daughter.'

'And it's your daughter who's out there now, is it?'

'That's her. She tried to kill me.' Donaldson gestured towards Carlisle. 'He saw it. She was going to stab me, then…' He trailed off.

'Who was the woman who intervened?'

Donaldson hesitated, for the first time looking as if he was weighing up what to say. 'I don't know.'

McKay had little doubt the man was lying. 'You don't know?'

'I didn't recognise her.'

'She wasn't one of the women who worked here?'

'I've no idea. I suppose she might have been.'

'I see. You don't know the people who work for you? With respect, it's not a large business, Mr Donaldson.'

'I–I've been very arm's length from the business in recent years. I left all the management to Gerry. I kept an eye on the finances, but I've really been semi-retired. Gerry would have been able to help you with the detail.'

McKay could see the way this was heading. Donaldson was going to claim he knew nothing of what was going on in his businesses. If they really were engaged in human trafficking or money laundering or slave labour, that was all Elliott's responsibility. Donaldson would no doubt be clutching his pearls in horror at what they'd uncovered, and most likely all the formal documentation would back him up.

It might not save him in the long run – as a director, he still carried legal responsibility – but it would make the process of securing a conviction that much harder and more laborious.

'I assume you can provide documentation to confirm that all your employees here are in the UK legally, have the right to work here, and are employed in line with relevant employment legislation?'

'All our employees?' Donaldson gave the impression of looking bewildered. 'I assume so. I mean, again, Gerry…'

McKay realised he'd made a mistake in revealing that Elliott was dead. Donaldson would no doubt have taken this line in any case, and Elliott would probably have tried to delegate responsibilities to the poor wee buggers charged with actually managing each site. But if Donaldson had thought that Elliott was alive, he might have at least scapegoated him with less confidence.

'I see, Mr Donaldson. You know nothing.'

'As I say–'

'What about your daughter, Mr Donaldson? Why did she try to kill you? Why did she kill your employees?'

'To get at me. To destroy my businesses. To scare the hell out of me. And then finally to kill me.'

McKay raised an eyebrow. 'That's quite a list for a loving daughter. What did you do to deserve all that?'

'It's a long story. When she was young, we lived in this place. Me, her and her mother. My late wife. My wife died young and unexpectedly, leaving me to look after Maggie. I was pretty crap at it, to be honest. And I wasn't in a good state. I was devastated by my wife's death. She was the person who kept me stable. I'd been doing all right, workwise. Then all that went to shite as well. I presume you know I was inside?'

'Fraud, I believe?'

'I can't blame anyone but myself, but I was treated harshly. I couldn't believe they gave me a custodial sentence. And a lengthy one.'

McKay saw no point in challenging this assessment. 'And your daughter?'

'We tried to find another option. But she was taken into care.

She was a difficult child. In the end, I gave up all rights to her. I never saw her again.'

McKay suspected that, whatever the full circumstances, this man had been only too keen to offload the burden presented by his daughter. Maybe that was understandable, but it didn't feel excusable. He wondered what might have happened to the young girl in the subsequent years. Enough to create such violent hatred of the man who'd placed her in that position, presumably. But something still nagged at McKay's brain.

'And you're sure the woman out there's your daughter?'

Donaldson looked surprised by the question. 'Of course–' He stopped. 'I saw her in there. My little girl. I could see her in that woman's face. Like a ghost...'

Like a ghost.

There was something in the way Donaldson was talking that seemed to reinforce the barely-rational belief that had slowly been developing in McKay's mind. It was as if even Donaldson didn't really believe what he was saying. It was as if it was just something he wanted to be true.

'Did she say anything that confirmed her identity? Anything personal that your daughter would have known?' It was a crass question, but McKay could think of no other way to ask it.

Donaldson nodded slowly. 'She talked about her childhood. About life here.' He looked up and stared bewilderedly at McKay. 'She spoke as if she was talking about someone else. As if she wanted to separate herself from the person she'd been then.'

'How do you mean?'

Donaldson shook his head as if struggling to explain. 'She talked about "her", as if she was talking about another person.'

The fanciful notion slowly germinating in McKay's head suddenly felt much more material. He gestured to Josh Carlisle. 'Can you keep an eye on him? I need to make a call.'

He made his way back out into the lobby, thumbing Helena

Grant's number into his phone as he did so. He glanced at his watch. Coming up to 8am.

Grant answered the call almost immediately. 'Alec? How's it going up there? Any more bodies?'

'You think you're being funny,' McKay said. 'We've got Donaldson. And, aye, two more bodies. One who claimed to be his daughter, and one who we think is one of the women working here.'

'That's some morning's work.'

'Thank Josh. But that's not why I'm calling. The search of Donaldson's offices. That must be due to start about now?'

'When the offices open at eight, yes. We didn't see any point in being heavy-handed.'

'Can you humour me? Can you get them to detain the receptionist there? She goes by the name of Ruby Jewell.'

'Ruby Jewell?'

'Aye, I know. Not her real name, obviously.'

'You think she's involved in this?'

McKay took a breath. 'I may well be losing the few marbles I have. But I think she's Donaldson's daughter. Not the woman known as Maggie Clennan. And I think she's behind everything that's been happening to Donaldson's business.'

'I'm not sure I've the foggiest idea what you're talking about,' Grant said, 'but when has it ever been a mistake to listen to you? Oh, yes, apart from all those countless times. Okay, I'll get onto the officers there and make sure she's held. On what grounds?'

'Suspicion of fraud, embezzlement – oh, and accessory to murder.'

'As long as it's nothing controversial. Leave it with me, Alec. I'll get back to you as soon as I've some news.'

McKay ended the call and, instead of rejoining Donaldson, took a moment to step back out of the main door of the hotel into the morning air. The sun was still not risen, but the light was spreading from the south-east, turning the sky a pale mauve.

Beyond the trees, across the firth, he could see the vast snow-covered bulk of Ben Wyvis.

They'd been played, he thought. All of them. Donaldson. Elliott. The police. Those poor wee bastards that had been killed. Perhaps even Kevin. That last one would need disentangling.

But now McKay had little doubt it was true. She'd almost told him to his face when he'd spoken to her in Donaldson's office. If he'd thought to put the pieces together and listen to what she was telling him.

She played them all, every step of the way.

57

'She'd been there,' Grant said. 'Turned up about 7.45. Once she was shown the warrant, she happily opened up Donaldson's offices for us. Then, while our people got down to work, she walked out of the building and didn't come back.'

'Of course she did,' McKay said wearily. They were in Grant's office, a couple of days after Donaldson's arrest. It had been a hectic period, and McKay had spent most of it frustratedly trying to deal with the consequences of several dozen illegal immigrants. It was work he hated because there was nothing he could do about what would happen to them, either in the immediate or the longer term. All he could do was ensure they were treated as well as possible while in police custody, and that the paperwork was complete and accurate. This was the first real opportunity he'd had to catch up with Grant about the rest of the investigation.

'By the time they got my call just before eight, she'd long gone.'

'And she left that?' McKay gestured to the object in the evidence bag on Grant's desk.

'The keys to Donaldson's office were on it,' Grant said. The object in question was a key ring in the form of a red plastic jewel. A fake ruby. It was also a data stick.

'She'd hacked into all their systems. Elliott's security wasn't as smart as he thought it was, apparently. And he wasn't as clever at covering his tracks as he'd thought, either. The forensic accounts people have had a quick first look at it, and reckon they could probably have dug out enough at least to convict Elliott.' She gestured to the data stick. 'But what's on there will make it much easier to make it stick to Donaldson as well, despite his attempts to distance himself.'

'What sort of stuff?'

'The really damning stuff is all on paper rather than the systems. It looks as if Jewell managed to infiltrate their offices and take pictures of stuff they subsequently destroyed. We'll have to work hard to confirm the provenance and credibility of the documents, but there's a lot of stuff so I think we'll get there.'

McKay shook his head. 'It's really very impressive. She was about as garish an individual as you can imagine. Which rendered her pretty much invisible to the likes of Donaldson.'

'You really think she was his daughter?'

'I think it's probable. That was how she knew so much about him. She virtually told me when I was chatting to her in the office. She said he was "one of us" and was from Cromarty. Yet she'd said previously she didn't see much of him and didn't really talk to him. So how did she know that detail?'

'Maybe Elliott told her. He seems to have talked to her plenty.'

'That was why I didn't think much of it at the time. She also seemed to know stuff about the state of the business that I don't imagine either Elliott or Donaldson would have wanted making public. Again, I thought maybe she just kept her ears open. Now we know she'd hacked into their system and was actually responsible for those troubles. She was toying with me. Letting slip bits of information with the confidence I wouldn't pick them up.'

'But you did.'

'Too late. And it wasn't much more than a feeling. I wouldn't have been surprised to have been proved wrong.' He shrugged. 'She's a piece of work.'

'She's that, all right. Before she disappeared, she managed to clean out the Muir business accounts. Looks as if she'd been siphoning money out of them for months. Enough to affect profitability badly, which is why Donaldson was getting so concerned about the business, but cleverly dispersed across a range of accounts and transactions, so Donaldson and Elliott couldn't identify the cause and were beginning to blame each other. Which just helped undermine the business still further, as well as ensuring that Donaldson was forced to get closer to the business than he'd ideally have liked.'

'Smart.'

'She seems a smart woman. I wouldn't be surprised if she's taken more than just money over the past few months. Donaldson's business contacts, clients. You name it. She seems to have known exactly what she was doing.'

'What do you think are the chances of catching up with her?'

'Who knows? We've put out a national alert, but we don't even know her real name. The serviced office people had just taken her at face value. Job didn't pay much and they weren't bothered about checking documentation. And, from what you've said, she could quickly and easily change her appearance.'

McKay nodded. 'I've no idea even if the dyed hair is permanent. Change that, change into more anonymous clothing, get rid of the jewellery, and no one would recognise her. And she's probably got the skills to set up a new identity without too much difficulty.' He paused. 'She'll be back, though.'

'You reckon?'

'She's not done this just for fun. And not just to get back at her father, if she really is his daughter. That was one of the ways she played us. She wanted us to think this was personal. But I think it was mainly business. Donaldson was right. Someone was trying to muscle in on his business. And she was right under his nose.'

'You were right about Maggie Clennan, though. Whether or not Jewell was his daughter, it looks like Clennan definitely wasn't. Adams has had her people doing some digging. She's been calling herself Maggie Clennan for a while, but they think they've managed to link her to a woman who was in care at the same time and in the same location as Donaldson's daughter. Which would explain why the timings fitted. She had a reputation even then. Adams has tracked down a couple of disciplinary cases where she'd attacked other residents or staff in the care home. Nothing seems to have come of them – partly, Adams reckons, because of the mitigation she offered which included accusations of physical and sexual abuse. It was maybe easier to brush her violence under the carpet than deal with the endemic issues. After that she seems to have learnt to control her anger, but maybe it was replaced by something altogether more cold-blooded.' She paused. 'Looks as if she and Jewell were partners. A pretty formidable pairing, I imagine. They'd been together, off and on, since their days in the care home. Clennan provided the psychosis, Jewell provided the brains.'

'And they'd been working up to this.' There was a touch of admiration in McKay's tone.

'Looks like it. Jewell knew what Clennan was capable of and pointed her in the right direction. My guess is that when they cooked up this scheme they effectively switched identities. Partly to help deflect any attention from herself. But I'm guessing mainly because she wanted Donaldson to believe, right to the end, that he'd raised a psychopath who would kill her own father without compunction. A sick form of revenge for what she'd been through.'

'Although that's exactly what he had raised,' McKay pointed out. 'Only she did her killing by proxy.' He was silent for a moment. 'The sad thing is that Donaldson was only too happy to believe Clennan was his daughter. He convinced himself he'd recognised her. As if he wanted it to be true. As if he wanted to be punished for what he'd done.'

'There's always more to you than meets the eye, isn't there, Alec?'

'I do my best. Christ, though. Clennan might have been the violent one, but Jewell's even more of a psychopath, isn't she? She knew what Clennan was capable of and cold-bloodedly used that to achieve what she wanted. And she presumably had no qualms about what might happen to Clennan.'

'Probably just a partnership of convenience as far as Jewell was concerned. But you're right. It scares me she's still out there.'

'Trust me,' McKay said, 'she'll be back.'

'I know.' Grant rose from her chair and walked over to the window, as if hoping to spot Ruby Jewell somewhere in the city landscape. 'And that scares me even more.'

58

It was another fine chilly winter's afternoon. It was exactly a month since Kevin's death, and Fiona had made them all attend church that morning. McKay was no church-goer, and the whole paraphernalia of the service made him feel deeply uncomfortable. But he'd gone along with it for Chrissie's sake, baulking only at taking communion.

Afterwards, they'd had a forgettable Sunday roast at some pub on a retail park, and then come out here to Fort George. Fiona had wanted to pay whatever respects she thought Kevin was still due. He'd been a liar and a cheat, she'd said, but he'd been her husband for a long time and she'd loved him.

She'd said no more than that, and neither McKay nor Chrissie had felt able to probe further. But they'd been happy to bring her here. They'd walked through the site in silence, each of them no doubt conscious of their individual memories. When they reached the far end, Fiona had walked up onto the battlements with a bunch of flowers. McKay and Chrissie had left her staring out across the Moray Firth in the low mid-afternoon sunshine.

'She's not planning to top herself, is she?' McKay asked.

'Sensitive as ever. No, she isn't. She just wants to throw the flowers out to sea in his memory.'

'It's probably more than he deserves.'

Chrissie was clearly looking to change the subject, if not very far. 'Have you lot worked out what happened on that Sunday yet?'

McKay shrugged. 'Charlie Farrow's done his usual thorough job. So, no, we haven't. I think Farrow just got bored with it and decided to conclude it was accidental.'

'And what do you think?'

'We know a lot more now Donaldson's started to co-operate. There was a lot going on here that Sunday, though we'd never have known it. Kevin had set up a meeting here with Donaldson to discuss further investment. Looks like he'd been trying to see Donaldson all the time he was up here because he was getting jittery, but he wanted to do it without arousing Fiona's suspicion. That was why he suggested coming here. His plan was to shake us off – that was why he was doing all that loitering by the exhibits – and meet Donaldson at an arranged location. If any of us spotted them, he'd have claimed Donaldson was an old acquaintance he'd bumped into. That wasn't even a lie. The two of them grew up together in Cromarty. Bosom buddies at one stage according to Donaldson. Looks like it might have been our Kevin who introduced Donaldson to the fine art of IT embezzlement.'

'You're joking. You mean Kev had been at it for that long?'

'According to Donaldson. Anyway, they were due to meet but, also according to Donaldson, Kevin never turned up. He might be lying about that, but there's no obvious reason why he would.'

'So what happened?'

'What happened is the woman known as Maggie Clennan.'

'Your psycho?'

'As you so rightly say. Jewell had known about the intended meeting with Kevin, because she seems to have known every bloody thing about Donaldson. So she arranged for Clennan to bring young Roddy Gray here. They'd already planned Gray's killing, but Jewell wanted Clennan to do it publicly here so it would happen under Donaldson's nose while he was meeting his supposed source of new investment. I think it was them we saw apparently messing about on the battlements. She'd intended to push Gray and disappear while everyone was distracted by what had happened. But our angry ticket-man interrupted that and she had to change her plans. I reckon she lured Gray into the old barracks as some sort of sexual dare.'

Chrissie blinked, as though contemplating that scene. 'So what about Kevin?'

'We can only guess,' McKay said. 'But I think Clennan tracked him down up on the battlements and told him Donaldson had sent her.'

'And?'

McKay had been dreading this question, partly because he didn't really have an answer for it. And partly because any answers he might have were likely to be uncomfortable. 'There are various possibilities. She wouldn't have known how much funding Kevin really had at his disposal, so she might have been concerned he'd come in as a white knight. That last thing she wanted was for Donaldson to salvage the business and bring in a new business partner. That would have complicated everything. So maybe she made it clear to Kevin that his investment was being wasted. Or maybe she told Kevin the full truth about what Donaldson was involved in. My guess is that Donaldson wouldn't have told Kevin everything.'

'Given the mess that Kevin was in, either of those might have been enough to push him over the edge.' Chrissie stopped as she realised what she'd said.

McKay smiled. 'Exactly. But equally, from what I saw of Kevin, either might have been enough to distract him so he went over the edge accidentally.' He paused. 'And, of course, there's a third possibility.'

'That she killed him?'

'We know what she was capable of. If she wanted him out of the picture...'

'There's no point in raking any of this up, is there?'

'I don't see what would be gained. Kevin's dead. Clennan's dead. We don't know where Jewell is.'

'You'll find her, surely?'

'We'll keep looking. But I suspect she'll be found only when she wants to be.' He shrugged. 'Though I've a hunch that might happen quite soon.'

'And in the meantime?'

'In the meantime, I suggest we just go with Charlie Farrow's considered judgement. The Fiscal will accept that, so there's no point in rocking the boat. The body will finally be released and Fiona can get on with her life–' He stopped as he saw Fiona descending the stone ramp from the ramparts towards them.

'How was it?' Chrissie asked.

Fiona shrugged. 'I threw the flowers. The wind caught them and tossed them out across the water. I watched them for a few minutes as they drifted away. That was it.' She gave a weak smile. 'And I was thinking. About the last time we were here. About how your life can change in just a few minutes. The way everything you think you know can just evaporate.'

McKay nodded. 'Aye, that's true enough. In my job, you see it too often. But maybe it's better to face the dirty truth than live a scrubbed-up lie.' He exchanged a glance with Chrissie. 'That's what I try to tell myself, at least.'

THE END

ACKNOWLEDGMENTS

My first thanks this time should go to Janet Adams, who was good enough to supply the names of two significant characters in the book, Tess Adams and Ruby Jewell. Janet won the opportunity to provide character names for the book as the result of a prize draw in aid of the excellent Culbokie Community Trust, a group looking to improve facilities in our local village (which has also provided various settings for scenes in the Alec McKay books). You can find out more about them at www.culbokiect.org

I'd initially assumed the named characters would have only walk-on parts in the book, but the name Ruby Jewell in particular intrigued me and ultimately inspired a wonderfully memorable character. I suspect she may well reappear in future books. Thanks to Janet for the inspiration. I should perhaps add that the two names are actually the names of her dogs – in Janet's words, 'a neurotic collie and a calm springer'. But, of course, there are no similarities between my characters and any real canines.

Thanks as ever to all those who helped me with the book, including Betsy, Tara, Sumaira, Clare and all the other good people at Bloodhound Books – a delight to work with as always.

And, again as ever, thanks above all to Helen, my first and best reader and advisor.

Printed in Great Britain
by Amazon